CHILDLESS

Childless is the third volume of a trilogy by Brian J. Gail
Volume 1: Fatherless
Volume 2: Motherless

CHILDLESS

THE CRITICALLY ACCLAIMED NOVEL BY
BRIAN J. GAIL

EMMAUS
ROAD
PUBLISHING

Steubenville, Ohio

Emmaus Road Publishing
827 North Fourth Street
Steubenville, Ohio 43952
www.emmausroad.org

ISBN: 978-1-937155-31-5

Cover design by
Devin Schadt

Layout by
Theresa Westling

For John F. Gail (2000+) and Mary E. Gail (2004+).
Thank you Dad and Mom for everything,
especially Barry, Kevin and Eileen.

Feast of All Souls
November 2, 2011

PROLOGUE

It was a day like any other; it was a day unlike any other.

John Sweeney knelt alone on a small mercifully thick Persian carpet at the foot of the altar. He was bent in excruciating pain, a gift from a pair of knees that seemed to be on fire. Behind him, also on aging knees, were the graying faithful of Narbrook. The sound of their voices, ebbing and flowing in that unique rhythm that is the prayer of the Rosary, filled St. Martha's and spilled out onto the street where many hundreds more also knelt in prayer.

It was 3:00 p.m. eastern standard time. It was the hour of Divine Mercy.

The consensus of the earth's best scientific minds appeared to be that "the twins"—two relatively small comets—would strike earth sometime within this hour. The first and smaller of the two was believed to be headed toward the South Pacific and due to splash down somewhere between Australia and New Zealand; the other was scheduled to hit land roughly twenty minutes later somewhere in North America. Best estimates placed the exact location between Manitoba and Montana.

Caveats—any changes in their trajectory or any changes in the earth's projected barometric and atmospheric pressures—abounded. Predictably, fear also abounded. Since their surprise sighting by NASA officials at the Ames Research Center in California over a year ago, "the twins" had recently dislodged prime time reality shows as the leading topic of discussion around the nation's water coolers.

The initial reports indicated that there was only a relatively small chance of an actual collision, or two. But scientists in Israel, then Japan, and finally Germany and England, began to suggest these calculations were indeed flawed. And so it began. The estimates of impending disaster filled the air waves and clogged the arteries of the wired world.

Scientists at MIT calculated that the second and larger of the twins would dissipate the energy equivalent of one trillion tons of TNT. They predicted over two hundred million tons of the earth's crust would be thrust into the atmosphere creating an unprecedented and unimaginable level of pollution. The strike would create a hole in the earth at point of impact roughly twenty miles in diameter and almost ten miles deep. This would, they concluded, "result in shock waves, pressure changes, and thermal disturbances that would cause massive earthquakes, hurricanes, and heat waves of incalculable magnitude throughout North America and beyond."

This drew the attention of the radical Muslim world, who immediately cranked their uranium enrichment program into overdrive in anticipation of a welcoming celebration for the return of the Twelfth Imam.

Meanwhile Chinese and Indian scientists released a joint statement suggesting the first strike in the South Pacific would instantly create a tsunami that would engulf New Zealand, inundate Australia, and threaten Southern China. They predicted the tsunami would release the equivalent of one million megatons of TNT, move at speeds of five hundred miles an hour, and strike land with a two hundred-foot wall of water. If it hit New Zealand, they added, there would no longer be a New Zealand.

A noted American geologist went on network television and suggested these "events" occur roughly every ten thousand or so years. The planet, he concluded, was therefore "overdue."

In one subsequent network, on-line poll, some 72 percent of viewers did not find this consoling.

The G–10 leaders convened in Zurich to develop "a massive and coordinated plan" to divert the trajectory of the twins. They departed without one. The Americans proposed a scenario right out of Hollywood. They offered to save the world by nuking the twins the moment they entered the earth's atmosphere. The Russians and the Chinese immediately made it clear they did not trust the Americans. As one of the Chinese UN Security Council representatives was reported to have said: "How can we be sure the Americans don't regard Russia and China as the twins they wish to obliterate?"

Discussions on how to integrate an attack with all G–10 member countries launching one nuke a piece went nowhere.

As the day Christian evangelicals referred to as a "day of reckoning" approached, civil society teetered on the brink of incivility. There was a mass exodus of peoples away from the predicted points of impact. Banks and food stores and pharmacies were overrun in nearly all developed nations, and municipal governments in twenty-six American cities—the majority of which were located on the east coast—imposed curfews and called up their contingents of the National Guard. Opening Day for Major League baseball was postponed in Boston, New York, Philadelphia, Baltimore, Washington D.C., and Miami.

The strangest phenomenon of all was not the run on the banks but the run on the churches. Pastors had no choice but to leave them open for the solace of their flocks who came and went all hours of the day and night. In Catholic churches the weekday morning Mass attendance came to resemble the Sunday Mass attendance.

Over the past three months, in addition to his 7:00 and 8:00 weekday morning Masses, Father John Sweeney added Masses at

9:00 a.m., 12:00 noon, and 7:00 in the evening. All were filled, increasingly by non Catholics and even un-believers.

He remained confused. The broad outlines were clear. At the end of this age there would be an apostasy that would bring with it schism within the Church. The "smaller, holier Church" would face persecution. This would occasion the rise of the son of perdition, which would in turn occasion the return of the Messiah and the mass conversion of the Jews who had begged in existential fear for his arrival.

And as John Sweeney would tell his confreres: "Oh, and somewhere along the line, everyone seemed to agree, 'fire will fall from the skies.'"

Sweeney couldn't read the times. There were simply too many "event gaps" in the present moment and he refused to fill them with private revelation, which he did not trust—though he did tend to accept the private revelation the Church granted approbation, like the apparitions of the Blessed Virgin Mary in Fatima, Portugal in 1917.

Some scholars went to great lengths to differentiate between the "end of the age" and the "end of the world." The former was to be followed by "an era of peace"; the latter by a "new heaven and a new earth." It was simply all too conjectural in Sweeney's opinion, and so he counseled his flock to live in the present moment and put their trust in God, not man.

As he began the fifth and final sorrowful mystery—the crucifixion and death of the Messiah for the sins of mankind—an intense blast of luminescent whiteness suddenly and noiselessly penetrated and filled the church. Sweeney immediately turned around so he was half facing the faithful in an attempt to locate its source. What he saw momentarily paralyzed him. He struggled to his feet. All bodies in the pews and beyond were immobilized, eyes transfixed in horror. His first thought was they were dead and, somehow, he had miraculously been spared. Then it occurred to him that perhaps he was dead and in the midst of an out of body experience.

Suddenly he saw movement. Then came sound. A sound he

instantly knew would accompany him to the grave. It was the sound of a great wailing—a searing cacophony of lamentation bathed in terror and self recrimination. He was filled with a sense of helplessness that rose from an unknowable depth within him. His lips began to move but he heard no sound.

Then it happened. The great light that now consumed the church and all who were in and outside it suddenly penetrated his being; he fell to his knees and pitched face forward in sheer fright. His forehead struck the marble floor but he did not black out. He attempted to roll onto his back to rid himself of the interior vision that was now running on a giant screen in high definition.

He saw the face of a child in his mother's womb. It was the face of someone he knew. Then he saw the face of the child's mother. He recognized her. She was a woman he knew far too intimately many years ago when he was a young man in college. Then he saw the face of the child's father. It was his face. Then the face disappeared. He cried aloud at the top of his lungs. Suddenly he saw himself before the throne of Divine Justice. He heard himself rendering an accounting of his life. He saw everything as clearly as though he were reliving it in real time. The life scan seemed to slow after his ordination. He saw the compromises he had made with truth. He saw the pain these compromises had created in the lives of those within his spiritual care. He felt but did not see their presence behind him. The preternatural kindness in the eyes of the luminous figure on the throne was unsettling. He felt acute pain, a sense of irredeemable unworthiness, at being in His presence.

He saw himself fall to his knees and beg forgiveness for his transgressions. He felt himself lifted to his feet by the all consuming warmth and power of unconditional love, and he heard its voice. It said to him, simply: "Repent and sin no more." The voice entered through his heart and penetrated every pore and fiber of his being before returning to its point of entry where it quietly lodged in permanent residence. It was a voice John Sweeney would hear, and converse with continually, right up to the dramatic moment of his final breath of life on this earth.

He struggled to his knees and felt his forehead. There was a small knot about three inches above his right eye. *Just a battle scar. There'll be no icing down this one.* In great pain, he lifted himself to his feet and turned to face his flock. All eyes were now fixed on him. He felt instant embarrassment and wondered how much of what he'd just experienced they had observed. Immediately he chastised himself. *If they saw it, good. I am who I am before God. Nothing more. Just as they now know they are only who they are before God. Nothing more.*

He felt a need to say something but he was still greatly unsettled and did not know what to say. He immediately bowed his head and prayed: *"Immaculate Mother, please summon the full power of your Spouse. Ask Him to fill the hearts of the faithful in this church. Please do not let my sins be in any way a barrier to their rightful need for hope and consolation. Ask Him to speak to them, Mother, just as you asked Him to speak to the Apostles and your Son's disciples in the Upper Room. We will listen. I promise you, Mother. We will listen."*

Father John Sweeney lifted his head and looked out at the people of God. He felt the full weight of the expectation that now filled his church. He walked to the pulpit, climbed the two steps, and adjusted the microphone so he could also be heard outside where thousands had gathered. He bowed his head briefly. *"I entrust and trust O Immaculate Mother."*

Then, he began. "My brothers and sisters in Christ . . . We can *now* indeed be certain we live in an age of Divine Mercy." He paused, waiting for some acknowledgement. In that instant he heard several souls involuntarily give voice to anguished pain. He avoided looking in their direction. "If you just experienced what I just experienced . . ." He paused to beat back a wave of emotion that suddenly threatened to engulf him. *Please Mother! Not here! Not now!* "There are no words . . . and certainly none that are necessary." Tears filled his eyes and began to run down his cheeks. He refused to wipe them off and resolved that his voice would hold.

"I don't know what we will find out there," he continued, as he spread wide his arms to embrace the world outside the church, "but each of us now knows what we found in here." He tapped his heart. "We have been given the gift of gifts. We now know all we need to know for safe passage through the rest of our journey in this vale of tears." He paused and added: "We know what is real and what is not. We know what is of love and what is not. We know what is worthy of us and each other, and what is not."

He looked down and was surprised to see his hands shaking. He asked the Immaculate to still them. He immediately felt awash in peace. He looked up and saw his people in a way he had never seen them. He recalled the verse in Sacred Scripture when Christ peered deeply into the hearts of the people who had followed Him to the Mount: "He looked at them, and his heart was moved with pity." Father John Sweeney, an *alter Christus*, now felt what his Divine Master felt in that instant, and his heart was flooded with an intensely inexpressible joy.

He felt a sudden stirring within. He waited patiently for it to form thoughts, then words. "I am moved to say this to you as your shepherd. Let us remember 9-11. This church was filled for nearly two weeks after that tragedy. Many of you complained to me that you couldn't get inside to hear Mass unless you left your homes a half hour earlier." He smiled the smile of a benevolent prince. "Do you remember what I said to you then?"

Heads slowly began to nod and a smattering of smiles appeared throughout the church. "I told you," he paused, "Come early and stay late, and surprise God. He's used to you coming late and leaving early." Laughter erupted, rolling through the congregation like a wave from the back of the church to the front. It lapped the altar and receded.

"Then," he shook his head sadly, "nothing." He heard pain given reflexive voice from pockets within the congregation. He paused and lifted his chin. "My brothers and sisters in Christ, the time for business as usual has come and gone. It is no more." He paused and allowed his eyes to sweep the congregation. His vision was blurred by tears. "We have just entered a new moment in our relationship with Christ. He will expect us ... *all* ... particularly me

. . . to make the most of the relatively few moments that remain in our brief time here on earth."

He paused, gathered himself and thundered in conclusion. "My friends, we have just tasted Divine Mercy. Let us not tempt Divine Justice." He turned and descended the steps, strode across the altar, passed through the sacristy without stopping, and headed to the crosswalk that connected the church and rectory. In less than a minute he was alone in his room. He immediately knelt by his bed and wept like a child.

He was awakened two hours later by the voice of his house-keeper, Carmella Francone, who told him over the intercom that the networks were reporting the twin comets had collided several hundred miles above their earth's atmosphere. There were no earth-quakes, no tsunamis, no hurricanes, no tornados, no thermal distur-bances, no environmental pollution, no riots and civil disturbances, and reportedly, no injuries or fatalities.

Instead, network field correspondents in Los Angeles, Auckland, Melbourne, London, Jerusalem, Moscow, Beijing, New Delhi, Rio de Janeiro, and Cairo were reporting an inexplicable, preternatural calm among the earth's nearly seven billion inhabitants.

Slowly, cautiously, elites emerged from their apocalyptic underground bunkers quite astonished to discover civilization intact and themselves objects of ridicule.

NASA officials immediately announced a very public inves-tigation into what they referred to as "the twelfth hour anomalies" in the twin comets' trajectories.

It was closed, quietly, six months later.

1

Father John Sweeney sat in the confessional reading his breviary in silence.

Outside St. Martha's Church, a surprisingly strong, late autumn sun bathed the little borough of Narbrook in a soft golden hue.

The priest looked at his watch. It was 4:30 p.m. He'd been sitting in the box for precisely one hour. *Penitents complain about priestless Sundays; priests need to complain about penitentless Saturdays.*

He heard sound and assumed it was the Delgados. They came every week, usually just as he was ready to close up and prepare for the 5:00 p.m. Saturday evening liturgy.

The door opened. Both mother and daughter entered. The daughter, an attractive divorcee in her late thirties, offered an explanation: "Sorry, Father. We couldn't remember where we left mother's leather hand bag," she said as she rolled her eyes in mild exasperation.

Her mother protested immediately. "I knew exactly where I left it. You just refused to look there."

"Thank you, Terry," John Sweeney said, nodding gently. "Fran, come sit. It is always good to see you."

Fran Delgado, with his assistance, sat in a cushioned wooden arm chair opposite him. The confessional door closed. John smiled as he surveyed the wreckage. Though her face gave evidence of having been treated cosmetically, her eyes revealed deep pain and, John thought, a hint of fear. She was growing old without a husband. She had a daughter with two preteen boys living with her. And her friends had moved south with their husbands.

Life had been unfair as John Sweeney was about to be reminded, yet again.

"That daughter of mine is driving me out of my mind, Father," she began without prayer. "She . . ."

"Fran . . . let's begin with a prayer," he interrupted soothingly. He recited the brief introductory prayer, read briefly from Sacred Scripture, and concluded by inviting his penitent to confess her sins confident in her divine Lord's mercy.

"Well, Father," she began with some difficulty. "I suppose I could be kinder to Terry and the boys." She stopped and looked at him and shook her head. "But they are driving me crazy." Without pausing, she launched into the weekly rant. He listened in silence. When she finished, he inquired ever so solicitously: "Fran, is there anything else you did this past week for which you'd like to ask our merciful Lord's forgiveness?"

She began to cry. "Father, I am so angry at Joe for leaving me alone."

He made no attempt to interrupt the tears; nor did she make any attempt to dry them. Her mascara began to run and her face took on the unfortunate appearance of an aging diva. "Fran, I know our dear Lord understands how much you miss Joe."

"I never got to say goodbye, Father," she replied as the tear ducts opened again. "We were so in love. I don't know why he did what he did."

John knew otherwise. Her husband had also been one of his penitents. John revered Joe Delgado's memory. He died a hero, speaking truth to power, at the cost of his own blood. He cleared his throat and replied: "It is one of life's cruelest ironies that the better a marriage, the greater the pain of separation." He thought of offering her his own copy of C.S. Lewis' classic *A Grief Observed* but decided against doing so.

Fran Delgado looked at him in desperation. "Father, why did God take my husband? Doesn't He care about me?"

John Sweeney peered into the face of his own generation's singular narcissism. He feared Fran Delgado would die a bitter woman. It was his responsibility, he'd decided after her husband's death, to insure she died in the sacraments. "Fran, God knows your pain. It's why He's surrounded you with love. Terry and those grandsons are His gift to you. Think of what your life would be like if she was still living with her husband in London." He paused as she crinkled her nose, and said in a hushed voice: "Fran, despite the little frustrations of daily living, you must recognize God's goodness, and praise and thank Him for it." He smiled. "Like the poor creatures He created in His own image, He likes to hear thank you."

Fran Delgado gathered herself with some difficulty. She looked at John Sweeney and said a bit tersely: "Thank you, Father."

John Sweeney understood. "Fran, for a penance just say one Hail Mary, and do something kind this week for Terry." She stared unblinking. He asked her to say an act of contrition. She complied. He raised his hand and said the prayer of absolution over her. She stood and without another word, she left.

Her daughter entered behind her. "Thank you, Father," she said as she sat down in the chair briefly warmed by her mother.

"For what, Terry?" he asked with a smile.

"For just being you," she said blushing slightly. "You are so good to her.""So are you, and God will bless you for it."

The young mother looked like she was about to cry but she did not cry. Instead she bowed her head in invitation for her pastor to initiate the rite of reconciliation between her and her God.

When he finished, Terry Halverson looked up and confessed that she often "grew angry" with her mother and said unchristian and uncharitable things to her in the heat of that anger.

John Sweeney listened in silence. These were sins he seldom heard after the Great Illumination some years ago. Then, ever so slowly, they began to resurface. In recent years they disappeared again only because the penitents themselves had disappeared.

Gently, he led her in a self-examination of the particular circumstances in which she failed charity. He went through each circumstance with her, helping her to understand that hidden in those difficult moments was the very holiness she sought. He shared his own secret of reflexively begging the Immaculate, in similar moments of temptation, to redirect his way any and all unwanted graces at her disposal. He quietly told her how much he had grown to depend on the Mother of God and how she had become a very real mother to him well before he lost his own mother.

Tears welled up in Terry Halverson's soft brown eyes. "Father, I beg God's forgiveness. He has been so good to me and I have disappointed Him in so many ways."

John Sweeney smiled. Joe Delgado would never be dead as long as his oldest daughter was alive. "Terry, you've just made an act of perfect contrition. I have no intention of asking you now to make an act of imperfect contrition." He paused. "For your penance, just say one Hail Mary, and do something kind this week for your mother." He raised his arm, bowed his head, and prayed the prayer of absolution.

"Yes, Father, I will. Thank you, Father," she replied quickly. She stood and reached for his hands. He extended them to her. She clutched them and said: "Thank you, Father, for your vocation. It has meant so much to so many of us."

"Thank you, Terry," he replied simply. She smiled and departed, leaving the door ajar.

He sat until he was certain the women had left the church. Then he struggled to his feet and opened the door to leave. Out of the corner of his eye he saw a young man enter the church.

He looked at his watch. It was 4:45 p.m. People would soon be arriving for the 5:00 p.m. Mass. As the man approached the confessional, he recognized him. It was Patrick Burns, one of Michael's twin sons. He was dressed in his construction clothes and approached his pastor tentatively. "Father," he said apologetically, "I know I'm too late. Maybe you could hear my confession another time?"

John Sweeney was very fond of the Burns' twins. He clapped Patrick solidly on the shoulder and pointed to the confessional: "In . . ." he said with a large grin.

The young man quickly entered and settled himself. John had not removed the stole from around his neck, so he simply sat, closed his eyes, blessed himself, prayed, and read the required prayers. When he finished, he opened his eyes and nodded to Patrick Burns to begin.

"Bless me, Father, for I have sinned. It's been . . . uh . . . about six months or so since my last confession, and these are my sins . . ."

He confessed to sins of pride and anger and lust and appeared sufficiently out of sorts for John Sweeney to probe his state of mind. "Patrick, you've made a good confession and our divine Lord is very pleased with you. Now tell me how you're doing."

The young man looked at his hands, which immediately drew John Sweeney's attention. They were the hands of a man who worked with his hands—strong, calloused, slightly gnarled. *How different this one is from his father. Actually, both boys favor the mother. I hope they realize how blessed they are!*

"Okay, Father."

"Just okay?"

The young man was quiet by nature. His father boasted that he had a genius for conserving words. John liked to remind the father he, too, had a genius for words—their needless proliferation.

"I get angry a lot."

"Why?"

"I don't know."

"You still live with your brother, Michael?"

"Yes, Father."

"Are you getting along?"

Patrick Burns nodded and smiled: "Yes, Father. He works the night shift. I never see him."

The brother was a township policeman. He once stopped John and threatened to give him a ticket for "excessive penance."

"Any young ladies in your life?"

His head fell to his chest. "No, Father."

John thought of Terry Delgado Halverson who was, perhaps, three or four years older. "How about work? How are things going there, Patrick?"

Patrick Burns' head stayed on his chest. *We have found the source of the anguish.* John looked at his watch. It was 4:50 p.m. He didn't have time, and yet this young man was crying out in his own way for help. "Patrick, how's your construction firm doing?"

"Not good, Father," he replied after a painful and prolonged silence.

"What's the problem?"

"All the work is drying up."

"Is it drying up for just your firm or are other construction companies having the same problem?"

The young man shook his head. "No, we're all going through it."

"What's the problem, Patrick?"

"No money, Father. The banks aren't lending so developers aren't building."

"Why aren't the banks lending, Patrick?"

He shrugged. "I guess they think they won't get paid back."

John Sweeney understood. "And this is making you . . . and I'm sure the other men in your business . . . very anxious."

"Yes, Father."

"And the anxiety is causing . . . anger . . . in other areas of your life."

He nodded. "I guess that's it, Father."

There was a protracted silence. "Patrick, why does this upset you so deeply?"

Patrick Burns looked up, and when he did John Sweeney saw fire in his eyes. "Because I have to take work from men who have families."

John Sweeney audibly exhaled. "I understand, Patrick," he said soothingly. "That would upset me too."

"They're good men, Father. They work hard. I don't know what's going to happen to them."

"And you feel responsible for them?"

The young man looked surprised. "I *am* responsible for them, Father. I hired them."

John Sweeney heard noises in the church. He looked at his watch. He had a little over five minutes to get into the sacristy and vest for Mass. "Patrick, I understand. More importantly, God understands. You are a very special young man, and He has an important plan for your life." He paused briefly and reflected on how best to send him on his way in authentic hope. "For your penance say one Our Father and ask our divine Lord to guide you through this difficult period in your life. Ask the Blessed Mother to teach you how to channel your anger in productive ways that benefit others. If you ask, she will. That I promise you. Then put your trust in her Son. He will not disappoint you, Patrick. He is a generous and merciful Lord." He paused and nodded. "Now say your act of contrition and I'll grant you absolution in His holy name."

The young man said his prayer, thanked his pastor, and departed.

John Sweeney was already in motion. By the time he reached the sacristy he'd decided what he was going to do to better understand the cause of this relentless anxiety in the best of his young people.

2

Carmella Francone answered the rectory door bell on the fourth ring. The rings, with their signature impatience, announced Father Sweeney's visitor.

Only two weeks removed from her seventieth birthday, the housekeeper resented anything, or anyone, that set her heart to pounding. She caught her breath and opened the door. "Why . . . Michael Burns. What a surprise."

"Good evening, Carmella. I was beginning to think I had the wrong night."

"Well Michael, I've added short sprints to my aerobic work-outs. My trainer says you should see some improvement within two weeks."

Burns grimaced. He did not like being on the receiving end of sarcasm. "What's on the menu tonight?" he asked as he stepped inside.

"Oh, I haven't given it much thought yet," she replied matter-of-factly.

He quickly searched her eyes. There would be no clues from this one he decided.

"I could tell Father John you're here . . ." she said cordially ". . . but that would mean a delay in fetching your Guinness."

Burns bit. "Ah . . . maybe the Guinness first."

Carmella Francone smiled. "I'm sure Father will understand."

"And, no doubt approve," Michael Burns parried as he headed into the parlor just off the small foyer. He went to the room's only window and pulled a billowing sheer curtain back to gaze at a small, well tended grotto. It was an exquisite summer evening in August. The days were beginning to shorten, and the breeze that fed the room hinted at cooler nights to come.

Michael turned from the window and surveyed the room. Its character and contents remained largely unchanged since he first encountered John Sweeney in its midst over thirty-five years ago. He did a quick sort and pulled mental clips from his private conversations file with his pastor. There were moments of great career dilemmas, acute family crises, terrifying times of spiritual darkness. The room had played host to all of them. It was a place, he told himself, where hope came to be resuscitated.

He heard footsteps. He hoped it was the housekeeper with his Guinness.

"Michael, me boyo!" John Sweeney exclaimed as he entered.

Burns hid his momentary disappointment and quickly closed the distance between them. "Father . . ." he whispered affectionately as he clasped his friend's hand and leaned forward in a gentle shoulder bump.

John Sweeney put his arm around Burns' round shoulders and said in a hushed voice: "Michael, how is Carole?"

"She's a tough determined woman, Father."

"I know she is that . . . and more. The proof is she managed to survive forty-five years with you . . ."

Michael smiled and nodded. "The neurologist and cardiologist tell me all the tests are clean. If we can keep her off the cigarettes, she's no more at risk for another heart attack and stroke than you and me."

"I dare say she's *less* at risk than you," the priest said laughing.

Carmella Francone entered with a small silver tray that held two tall, cold Guinness' standing at attention. Michael quickly deserted the priest. "I intend to have a word with your trainer," he said to the housekeeper with a feigned hint of irritation at the modest delay.

"Well you best be quick about it," she replied with a thin smile. "Next time you see me it'll be from behind."

Noting his pastor's presence, Michael decided to leave that one alone.

John Sweeney pointed to a small couch next to the window and said: "Sit."

Michael complied.

Sweeney took a seat in a high backed wing chair opposite the couch. "Thanks for coming, Michael."

Burns shrugged. "Anytime, Father. Anything *at* anytime. You know that."

The pastor nodded. "I do indeed."

"I was intrigued by your editorial this morning . . ."

This caught Michael by surprise. In the years he'd been publishing the *Thorn*, a niche daily newspaper with pockets of distribution up and down the East Coast, his pastor had never acknowledged any of his editorials much less summoned him to discuss one.

"What *intrigued* you, Father . . .?"

"The quote from the Federal Reserve Chairman," the priest replied. He took a long slow chug on his Guinness and eyed Michael warily.

Michael did a mental search and came up empty. "Father, forgive me. I'm having a senior moment."

John Sweeney laughed. "At your age, you're forgiven."

"As I recall, you are *much* older than I am," Burns replied quickly, feigning offense.

"Yes, yes . . ." Sweeney added with a grin. "But, hey . . . who's counting?"

John Sweeney studied his friend. He had once said publicly that Michael Burns' life was filled with the highest highs and lowest lows of any life with which he was familiar. He was proud of his friend. He had risen, fallen, risen, fallen, and, improbably, managed to rise yet again. He was the Phoenix of Philadelphia. He often found himself worrying about what unfortunate event would occasion the next fall. He thought it likely it would be something he wrote.

"Actually, I'm referring to Fed Chairman Graham Forrester's quote that he intends to "monetize the U.S. debt . . ." he shrugged.

Michael nodded, waiting for a question.

"Do you remember what you wrote immediately after that . . .?"

Michael nodded grimly. "Yes."

"Do you really believe we're headed in the near future to a period of social instability . . . like Germany in the 1920s?"

"I do."

The priest set his beer on the cherry wood coffee table that served both the couch and wing chair. He directed his gaze to his guest's dark pupils. "Michael, what will that look like?"

Burns shrugged. "It will not be pretty, Father."

"Michael, what are we talking about . . .?"

Burns sat back in the couch. "For all practical purposes, the U.S. will lose its primary medium of exchange. The dollar will lose its status as a global reserve currency and, indeed, much of its present value. This will lead to panic. There could be a run on the banks, food shortages, riots in the street, mandatory curfews, martial law, organized popular resistance, even, I suspect, some States moving to secede." He paused. "In other words, the U.S. government could end up at war with its own people. The world would then no longer recognize America as America. This, of course, could set off a chain reaction abroad. The developed world would, under this scenario, remain in economic and social confusion until the monetary vacuum is filled—perhaps by a gold-backed currency issued by the International Monetary Fund, the IMF." He paused and shrugged. "Other than that . . ."

Sweeney sat back in his chair. "Is it inevitable?"

"Yes, given the hubris of our elected and appointed leaders, I'm afraid it is."

"Why?"

Burns smiled. "It's the old saw about God *always* forgiving, man *sometimes* forgiving, nature *never* forgiving." He paused and added: "We seem to have fatally wounded nature's economic order."

"How?"

"One four letter word, Father: debt."

Michael shifted uneasily. "We, our generation, have amassed much more debt than our children, or grandchildren, or even great grandchildren, could ever pay back."

John Sweeney winced. "Michael, isn't there *some* way for smart people to come together and . . . fix it?"

"Well, Father . . . there are only two possible fixes when a family or a corporation or, in this case, a nation is what the bankers call too highly leveraged . . ."

The priest nodded in anticipation.

"You can *restructure* debt . . . the holder of the debt agrees to spread it over a longer period of time with terms—a payment schedule to include interest. The debtor can then manage out of cash flow . . ."

John Sweeney leaned forward. "Or . . .?"

Burns shrugged. "Or . . . the debtor can *default* . . ."

The priest recoiled. "What happens then . . .?"

"In the case of a family or a corporation, you declare bankruptcy and the people who loaned you money take it in the shorts." He paused. "Now . . . in the case of a global leader like the U.S., an outright default is out of the question, of course."

He smiled. "Instead, our monetary authorities will just attempt to inflate the debt away by printing money."

"Haven't we been doing that?"

Michael Burns nodded: "Yes, but nowhere near the order of magnitude we're talking about in the years to come."

"So what happens next?"

"We end up with too many dollars chasing too few goods. It drives the price of everything into the stratosphere in a fortnight."

John Sweeney's eyes widened in horror: "Weimer Republic?"

"Close enough."

"Well . . . our leaders won't do that."

"Oh, but they will," Michael Burns replied quickly. "That's exactly what Forrester said yesterday in his press conference at the National Press Club in Washington that he intends to do."

"Why don't they just do the first thing you mentioned . . .?"

"Restructure the debt?"

"Yes."

Michael suddenly felt the rise of a great field of love beside him. It was the unconditional love of a shepherd for his flock. "Father, there's simply too much of it. It would cause too much pain. No politician could get elected on a platform of austerity in the Age of Entitlement. Half our people don't even pay income taxes." He shook his head. "No, no . . . the pain of repaying our debt, under any scenario, will be considered quite unacceptable. We are truly in unchartered waters."

The priest appeared to be overwhelmed. Suddenly Michael understood. *He's thinking of all the seniors in the parish . . . and the young families with mouths to feed. He knows most of them will show up at his door.*

"Michael, I'm not naïve. But, please, how could we have let it get to this point?"

Michael thought of two possible answers and chose the more prosaic. "Father, the U.S. has about a fifteen trillion-dollar economy. That's the value of all the goods and services we produce in a year." He paused. "We voted in politicians who ran up about twenty trillion dollars in debt to satisfy our demands for ease and comfort and security in all its modern forms."

He paused and leveled his gaze at his pastor. "Father, in the real world that debt ultimately *must* be serviced—paid back *with* interest. The financial world has its own 'laws,' so to speak, and those laws are a series of ratios. Some of these ratios help lenders distinguish good investments from bad investments and, in the extreme, solvency from insolvency. There is something called the "debt ratio"—that's a nation's debt as a percentage of its GDP—Gross Domestic Product. In other words, what it *owes* in comparison to what it *makes*." He paused again. "Anything over 50 percent is considered unsustainable." He paused. "Father, the U.S. debt ratio is currently running about 135 percent."

John Sweeney blanched. "We're broke."

"Yes, Father. Unfortunately, that's the least of it."

The priest's eyebrows arched.

"We've taken on commitments for another one hundred trillion dollars over the next forty years. That's Social Security, Medicare, government pensions, and the like. These are promises, Father. They are the foundation for the social contract between generations." He shook his head. "If . . . *when* . . . those promises are broken there will be breakdown of civil order."

The priest buried his head in his hands, and fell silent. "We did this to ourselves, didn't we?"

Burns smiled. "Who else?"

A silence filled the room.

Michael Burns broke it. "It's like you say, Father, the most frightening thing on earth is man unable to say 'no' to self."

John Sweeney looked away and said; "Michael, how long will it take for all this to play itself out . . .?"

Burns hesitated before answering. He knew from long experience the fragility of hope. "It depends, Father. When Forrester uses terms like "monetizing the debt" and "quantitative easing," he is signaling, in my opinion, that our elected leaders are in a state of panic. They've decided they'd rather live with *in*flation than *de*flation."

He paused to backtrack in explanation. "Father, we're now in a period of deflation because the banks chose not to lend in a time of great economic uncertainty. They've basically taken all that taxpayer stimulus money the government has given them and exchanged it for Treasury notes. They're just pocketing the interest and including it on their balance sheets to make them look stronger. In doing this they've contracted the money supply. The people who are paying taxes have financed this charade. This deflation thing is what's driving our 20 percent unemployment and, if unaddressed, could idle as much as a third of the American work force." He paused and added: "Think Great Depression."

The priest's mouth opened and immediately shut. He appeared to run dry of words.

Burns was now on the edge of his seat. "So . . . when Forrester says he's going to 'monetize' the U.S. debt, what he means is he's going to open the presses and order the U.S. Treasury to start cranking out new bonds. He'll print as many trillions of those bonds as he needs to maintain civil order. Then, as the debt monster continues to rear more and more of its ugly head in the out years, he'll continue to print whatever he needs to feed that beast . . ." he paused and shrugged ". . . until the world finally realizes the dollar has lost its value. Then . . ."

John Sweeney sat up. "Then . . . what . . .?"

"Then . . . chaos."

Beads of sweat glistened on John Sweeney's forehead. His graying temples pulsated, and his hands clenched and unclenched in anxiety. "Michael," he said finally. "How do I prepare our people?"

Michael Burns dropped his head on his chest. Knowing what he knew, he couldn't look his pastor in the eye. With a voice muffled and rasping, he replied: "I don't know, Father." He shook his head. "I mean . . . I just don't know."

A dark silence filled the room. Into its midst walked Carmella Francone with a smile on her broad handsome face. She announced dinner was ready.

She quickly read the chill in the room and quietly took her leave. John Sweeney stood first, and awkwardly waved Michael to lead the way into the dining room.

Michael hesitated. "Father, would you mind if I passed on dinner tonight? I'm just not very hungry."

John grimaced and nodded. "Certainly, Michael. I understand."

The pastor led his guest to the door and hugged him before he departed. "Michael, may I ask for a few of your prayers, and maybe a small part of Carole's suffering?"

Michael Burns smiled. "Father, you've been on our prayer list for over thirty-five years. Dead weight though you are, it's too late to take you off."

The priest's eyes moistened, and he half saluted a goodbye. He entered his office next to the parlor and removed the key to the church from the top drawer of his desk. He clutched it in the palm of his right hand and headed for the door.

He had reason to talk to a dear friend about a serious problem.

3

Maggie Gillespie hung up the phone and called upstairs to her husband, Jim: "You were right. They caved."

The next sound she heard was that of her husband's thundering footsteps cascading down the steps. "That's huge," he exclaimed as he hit the landing with a thud.

Jim Gillespie followed his wife and the familiar early morning aroma of coffee into the kitchen. He hovered beside her as she poured him a homemade version of a Starbucks Black Eye. He quickly grabbed the cup, sans saucer, and found his way to the breakfast nook just off the kitchen. He eased into a small booth and let some of the steam evaporate before he took a small, tentative sip.

Maggie, cup and saucer in hand, joined him on the other side of the booth. "How can they just . . . just . . . do that . . .?"

"Given their prior decisions, they couldn't *not* do it."

It was seven years since Maggie and Jim Gillespie walked out of Philadelphia's Regina Hospital as its CEO and Head of Oncology. They departed on principle. The Regina Order, which owned and operated the two hundred-bed hospital for over one hundred years, decided to reject their recommendation to terminate the hospital's Ob/Gyn department and replace it with a Natural Family Planning clinic. It was a decision the Gillespie's thought perhaps the Archbishop of Philadelphia might want to review, since Regina's Ob/Gyn docs were dispensing abortifacient contraceptives, referring patients to a fertility clinic next door, and accepting fees from the clinic for the online advertising of its IVF (in vitro fertilization) services.

They were wrong.

Former colleagues called from time to time to keep them abreast of the Order's other defiant decisions. They were calls the Gillespie's generally did their best to discourage. This morning's call was different. The caller, a senior nurse with over twenty-five years of service, provided advance warning of a startling development—the Order had just released an internal memo announcing Regina Hospital would comply with the Federal Government's new universal coverage mandate " . . . to provide abortion services to any and all who seek this provision—regardless of ability to pay . . ."

Jim Gillespie had seen this capitulation coming. His wife believed the Order would draw the line at surgical abortions, having beaten a hasty and unseemly retreat on septic abortions. After all, she reasoned, surgical abortions were still quite toxic within the Catholic Church even though its bishops and priests generally preferred to ignore the far more prevalent septic abortions induced by abortifacient contraceptives.

"Jim . . . this is just too in-your-face," Maggie suggested. "The cardinal will be forced to act. What do you think he will do?"

"Nothing," Jim said evenly.

"Oh, Jim . . . he's got to do *something*! He can't just let a Catholic hospital publicly defy him like that . . ."

Jim Gillespie smiled, reached across the narrow table, tenderly lifted a strand of his wife's dark hair, tucked it behind her ear, and cupped her face with his left hand. She was the very center of his existence. "I'm afraid he can . . . and will . . . sweetheart."

Very few things surprised Maggie Gillespie at this point in her life. She had survived the loss of a bipolar child, a disfiguring stroke from the use of an oral contraceptive, the abandonment and then the death of a philandering husband, the herculean struggle to raise five children as a single mother, and the humiliating public loss of a high profile executive position. But the Catholic Church in America's reluctance to exercise her divinely granted authority to "bind and loose" never ceased to genuinely astonish her.

"How can he, Jim? What would stop other Catholic hospitals from doing the same thing?"

"Nothing. I'm sure some of them will."

"Good Lord! Won't the bishops wear that into eternity?"

"I'm sure they will, sweetheart. But I imagine they're convinced they are exercising what they refer to as 'prudential wisdom.'"

Maggie shook her head vigorously as though trying to rid herself of an existential absurdity. "Jim, just where, in the name of God, is the *prudence* in looking the other way while Catholic hospitals—under your authority—are killing babies!?"

Jim shrugged and said: "I'm sure they regard it as the lesser of two evils."

Maggie put her cup down and stared straight through her husband. "And what may I ask is the *greater* of the two evils?"

"Schism."

"*Schism!?*"

Jim nodded. "They've convinced themselves that the Church here in the States will rupture along doctrinal fault lines if they draw a line in the sand on any of these Life issues—even this new universal abortion mandate. They're also petrified that when the Feds see the Catholic Church divided and impotent, they will move quickly to rescind her tax exempt status . . . which, they fear, will throw her into a death spiral."

"So what!" Maggie exclaimed. "Did I miss the memo!? Is there no longer a Final Judgment!?"

Jim laughed. "They must think they'll make out better if they presided over a de facto schism rather than an *actual* schism."

"Holy Mother of God! I can't believe what I'm hearing. They can't honestly think that. Tell me you're wrong, Jim. Please. Tell me you're wrong."

"I'm wrong," her husband replied with a smile.

Maggie sat smoldering. "Christ didn't seem all that concerned about schism. After the Bread of Life discourse, when most of his followers left him, he turned to the apostles and said: 'Are you going to leave me too?' That doesn't sound to me like he was prepared to rethink the foundational doctrine of His Church."

Jim nodded uneasily. He believed what his wife believed. He always held his breath, however, when she spoke these truths in public. Like the Church's Founder, they *were* polarizing—perhaps, he thought, intentionally so. There was, he'd come to believe, something divinely unique about the power of objective moral truth to lay hearts bare. "I think they're waiting until they have more . . . ah . . . faithful bishops in their ranks," he said. "Then they think they will be able to make their stand and trust that a majority of Catholics will stand with them."

"That's the absolute dumbest thing I've ever heard," Maggie replied. "You don't make these so called prudential judgments on human calculations. People won't follow an uncertain trumpet. You look to what Christ did, or His apostles, or even what the early Church fathers did under similar circumstances. Then you trust in the power of the Holy Spirit." She paused and added: "Why do they think they wear red!?"

"Uh . . . because it sets off the gold in their miters and crosiers?"

Maggie ignored him.

The phone rang. Jim picked up a cordless receiver on the kitchen counter. It was Maggie's daughter, Grace Seltzer. She was calling from the Natural Family Planning clinic that she opened after leaving Regina Hospital. The clinic was now in its tenth year of operations. It had delivered over one thousand babies, each a miracle of grace to their parents who'd thought themselves infertile.

"No, Grace, I did not hear that?" Jim said into the receiver.

Maggie instantly knew from the tone of her husband's voice that something was wrong. She stood and moved closer, motioning him to put Grace on speaker.

"I don't know if it's true, Jim . . ." Grace intoned. Her voice reverberated throughout the small kitchen. "I'm just passing on what I've heard from a pretty good source."

Maggie's heart leapt at the sound of a child distressed. "Grace, honey, it's Mom. What's the matter . . .?"

There was a momentary silence on the other end of the line. Then: "Oh, hi Mom. I didn't want to worry you. I was just telling Jim I got a call from John Richardson. He said the fine print in the new government mandate specifically includes Natural Family Planning clinics."

Maggie bowed her head. Something in her died in that instant. She saw this evil coming with an intuition all but unique to the feminine genius. She didn't know when, or in what form, it would arrive. She just knew it would someday knock on her door and present itself. A singing telegram from the devil himself. Her mind began to race. This was the end of their dream. The end of hope for all young fertile women convinced they were barren. The clinic, and the hundreds of others like it throughout the country, would have to be closed down. She would not compromise with evil. She knew the other men and women who ran these clinics would not compromise either.

"Who's your source, honey?"

"John, mother. John Richardson." Pause. "Our congressman."

John Richardson had been a staunch pro-life advocate in the U.S. Congress since he'd been elected to his first term in 2010. He was one of their own. "Same heartbeat" . . . as Maggie often said of him. "Did John say when this directive would be made public, Grace?"

Jim Gillespie put his arm around his wife's shoulders and pulled her to his chest. She put her left arm around his waist and held the phone up so they could both hear.

"He said it would be released tomorrow, Friday, some-time late in the day, to allow the weekend to mute some of the response."

"Oh my . . ." Maggie replied softly. She immediately thought of Grace and her husband, Scott, and their six children. Her pay-check from the clinic was essential in keeping the family afloat. Maggie didn't know what they would do. She started to pray.

"Grace . . ." Jim interjected. "Are you certain he said privately owned Natural Family Planning clinics were *specifically* included in the mandate?"

"Yes, Jim. I am."

Jim Gillespie was incredulous. "But even if we wanted to comply, they have to know we don't have access to abortionists. There's not a single one in America who would be caught dead working for a Natural Family Planning clinic."

"I know, Jim. I know."

"Did John say how they would . . . ah . . . moni-tor . . . uh . . . enforce . . . this mandate?"

"He did."

Jim waited for an explanation. None was forthcoming. "Grace . . .?"

He heard what he thought was a sniffle. "Grace . . .?"

The young wife and mother cleared her throat. "He said the federal government will create a special department within the department of Health and Human Services to monitor it. He said they are promising a prompt investigation of any and all noncompliance."

"Noncompliance . . .?"

"I suppose they mean complaints from people who present themselves for abortions and are turned away," Grace replied. "John says they have threatened 'strong and immediate measures.'"

"What's that supposed to mean . . .!?"

"John thinks it probably means the immediate closing of noncompliant Catholic hospitals and NFP clinics."

"That's an outrage!" Jim yelled into the phone. "They damn well know we *couldn't* comply even if we wanted to comply. This is a hideous farce."

Silence on the other end.

Maggie interrupted it. "That's exactly what they want. They want to shut all of us down. Our clinics will be targeted and flooded with the indigent who will demand abortions. We will all refuse and be closed down." She paused and choked back a sob. "Our closure will be the tribute tolerance pays to evil."

For several long moments nothing was said. Then, a clinic phone could be heard ringing in the background. "Mom, Jim . . . I gotta go. I'm so sorry to upset you with this news."

"We love you, Grace," Maggie said quietly. "It is time for trust. Remember, honey, we are called to be a people of trust."

"I know, Mom, I know. We'll get through this. All of us. Gotta run. Love you."

Jim placed the wireless phone in its charger on the counter. He wrapped both arms around his wife and squeezed tenderly. Then he took his cup of lukewarm coffee and emptied its remaining contents in the sink.

He now had all the stimulant he needed to begin his day.

4

---

anley Siliezar entered the dining room at the St. James hotel in London a little after 8:00 p.m. The room, even on a wintry weekday evening in late January, was nearly full, which surprised him. He searched the room and settled his gaze on a large man sitting alone at a table in a corner.

The man's eyes met his, and he nodded imperceptibly. Siliezar slipped the maitre d' a rolled up note of British currency roughly equal to one hundred dollars, and made his way over to the table.

"Vladimir Piranchenko?" he said, extending his hand as he approached.

The Russian nodded and, without rising, took the proffered hand and shook it firmly. "You are your photograph," he said in thickly accented English.

Siliezar sat down in a seat opposite the Russian. A waiter immediately appeared and took a drink order. "I thank you for coming to London and making time to see me. I know you are a very busy man."

The Russian smiled and shrugged: "*You* are the busy man, Siliezar. Anyway . . . I happened to be in London on other business."

Siliezar had been advised to avoid making penetrating eye contact with Piranchenko. The oligarch had cornered his country's deregulated oil industry in his thirties, and then turned to making serious money with a network of global hedge funds. He was reputed to be among the world's richest men and, perhaps, its most singularly amoral.

"I want to thank you for your financial support of our project," he said coming quickly to the point. "We have made strong progress and I want to share some of our achievements with you."

The Russian nodded wordlessly.

Siliezar's drink arrived. He immediately lofted it and said: "To man's promise fulfilled."

The Russian briefly hesitated. Then, with measured deliberation, picked up his vodka tonic and replied: "I hear a request for more money in your toast."

Siliezar laughed nervously. "You are much too clever for me, Vlad."

Piranchenko's eyebrows rose at the uninvited informality but he said nothing.

"I have just returned from Tel Aviv," he began slowly. "Dr. Moskowitz has developed a prototype of the chip. He has tested it. It exceeds our expectations. He tells me it will be ready for mass production by summer." He smiled and added ominously: "I tend to believe him. He has much riding on its delivery."

"How much?" Piranchenko inquired. He had more than a passing acquaintance in performance incentives.

Siliezar leveled his gaze. "Oh . . . his career." He paused and smiled: "And of course his family. We are holding his two children hostage."

The Russian nodded approvingly. He assumed Siliezar meant what he said. "And when will I see this chip . . .?"

"Tonight."

At this the Russian's eyes widened. "You have this with you?"

"No," Siliezar replied quickly. "Not with me. I have it in my room. I will show it to you after dinner."

The Russian processed this slowly and said. "Tell me about the tests."

Siliezar nodded. "We had it implanted . . ."

"*How . . . who* did this . . .?" Piranchenko interrupted, his detachment suddenly and summarily lifted.

"Geoff Benton's folks at Vennitti Inc. managed all the procedural aspects of the project. He flew a team of technicians in from their therapeutic division in the U.S. They've been in the country since fall. Over two hundred Israeli families volunteered. About eight hundred fifty chips were implanted . . ."

"Where . . .?"

"Behind the wrist . . . under the watch, Vladimir . . ." Siliezar replied revealing a hint of impatience.

The Russian peered intently to see if he'd stoked a bit of pique. It was hard to know, he told himself. South Americans are so volatile. The men are like women. In fact, he decided, Russian women had more testosterone than South American men. "And . . .?"

Siliezar regrouped. "And . . . as I say . . . the results exceeded even our own high expectations . . ." He paused for effect. "In fact, the Israelis came up with many new applications on their own, as we hoped they would. Some are quite ingenious . . ."

Piranchenko smiled. "Tell me about Israeli ingenuity . . ."

"Our 101 applications platform was quite simple," Siliezar said expansively. "We're focused on travel and trade, on a chip that will allow people to move freely, both within and beyond their own borders, and to transact, both retail and online." He smiled. "The Israelis suggested we add a monitoring capability for children and seniors." He smiled even more broadly. "*And . . .* a health alert monitor for people on medication . . ." He broke into a wide grin. "*And* . . . a financial health monitor that would alert them to sudden shifts in their assets."

The Russian's face revealed a measure of confusion. Siliezar made a mental note of it. It was easy, he reminded himself, to steal money in your homeland. It was much harder to create wealth from nothing. And much harder still to create a future worthy of man.

"How would such a thing work . . .?"

Siliezar was careful to appear patient but not patronizing. "I will show you upstairs. And I will share with you the plans for the launch of this extraordinary innovation."

The Russian nodded, satisfied.

The waiter arrived and took dinner orders. Piranchenko waited until he departed, looked at Siliezar and said: "Is it true what they say of you?"

"And just *what* is being said of me, Vladimir?" he inquired, clearly displeased.

"That you are creating an alternative to the UN, and are lobbying to run it?"

Hanley Siliezar had long ago mastered the art of knowing when not to dissemble. "Yes. It is true," he replied evenly.

"Why?"

"The United Nations has accumulated far too much baggage. It has become synonymous with dysfunction." Siliezar paused and added obliquely. "We have entered a dark time, would you not agree?"

The Russian was unmoved. He simply spread his palms out awaiting further explanation.

Siliezar moved quickly to assuage. "We will recycle many of its apparatchiks. But we will re-mission it, re-brand it, re-populate its committees, and . . . yes . . . replace its leadership."

Piranchenko was not satisfied. "Why you . . .?"

Siliezar wasn't sure he was reading his guest correctly. "Do you have an interest in such a position, Vladimir?"

"No," he spat in disdain. "I have no time for such games."

No, you just want to be in full control of whoever does rule. "We would never burden you with such an imposition, my friend. It would mean six months a year in Switzerland and most of the rest of the year traveling the continents," Siliezar explained with great deference. "There will be much stakeholdering, as the Americans like to say."

The Russian's eyebrows arched. "You are going to headquarter this new organization in Europe?"

Siliezar winced visibly. He had built his career by avoiding just such indiscretions. "I share that with you and no one else, Vladimir." He saw his delicate recovery had its intended effect. The Russian smiled.

"Why Europe?"

Siliezar hesitated. He sorted several possible explanations in nanoseconds. He chose the one he knew his guest would most want to hear. "We do not believe the United States will be a . . . a stable location . . . in the coming years—particularly for an organization doing the kind of important work we will need to do."

The Russian smiled and nodded. "The United States is no longer so united. For them . . . it is over." He paused and added. "I believe even their own people know that."

Siliezar nodded quickly. "Yes, and their leaders have known it for some time."

This interested Piranchenko. "That would explain their decisions. We in Russia believe these men are merely enriching themselves before all the public wealth is exhausted."

As you yourselves did in Russia. "Empires rise and fall. It is an immutable law of nature," Siliezar shrugged philosophically. He did not wish to comment further on those inexplicable decisions. He'd had a hand in far too many of them.

They fell into a brief silence, during which their sea food appetizers arrived. "So, you are going to ask me for more money, yes?" the Russian said, mouth all but full of lobster and wild rice.

"Of course," Siliezar countered quickly. "Why would I *not*

include you in the most significant development in the entire project?"

Piranchenko momentarily set his fork down and put his elbows on the table. "Speak," he said.

Siliezar did not want to engage this conversation in a public dining room. It was precisely why he had stocked the bar in the penthouse suite at the St. James. This man was upsetting his rhythm, which Hanley Siliezar did not like. "There will be more than sufficient time to discuss all of this later, Vladimir. As the Americans say, 'No wine before its time.'"

The Russian scoffed. "The Americans have drunk too much of their own wine. They are bloated and corrupt." He picked up his fork and pointed it across the table at Siliezar's chest. His eyes narrowed. "You tell me *now*. The details we will leave till later."

Siliezar fought off a visceral reaction. There were other men of obscene wealth. He had chosen Piranchenko for this request because he believed he would receive it as an honor, and ask the fewest questions. He was not accustomed to being wrong. Further, he did not like being reminded that his net worth, which was in the low hundreds of millions, was not considered serious by men like Piranchenko, whose net worth was estimated to run into the tens of billions.

"Alright Vladimir, as you wish," Siliezar replied uncomfortably. "Only the headlines, as the Americans like to say." He laid his fork down next to his plate and reached for his goblet. He took a measured swallow of his Cabernet. Carefully, he set the glass down in its original position. "Our friends at Vennitti Inc. need a little help. They do not want to go to the capital markets for the capstone project in our work . . . for obvious reasons. They have authorized me to approach a small handful of very influential men for some additional seed money. I am prepared to negotiate equity terms. The payout in both psychic and financial terms will, I dare say, exceed anything in your experience."

The Russian leaned across the table. This afforded Siliezar his first real glimpse of his guest's actual size. "Tell me. How is it you

profess to know what I have experienced in my business affairs?"
he said behind a small, cold smile.

Siliezar found himself prepared to yield ground yet again. An
interior voice with which he was long familiar, again counseled
patience. *It is his money we need, not his companionship. Do not deed
over control.* "My friend, I am merely suggesting we are now dis-
cussing a development that, when completed, will represent the
pinnacle of human achievement."

The Russian eased back into position. He resumed eating.
"Tell me . . ." he said as he paused, fork in midair.

"Homo Evolutus," Siliezar said in a hushed whisper. He
waited for his guest's features to contort.

"Speak plainly. I am an investor, not a scholar."

"We are speaking of the second generation of man." He
paused to let the sheer scope and mystery of his disclosure settle.
Slowly, methodically, he began to unpack it for his guest. "A new
creation—equal parts biological intuition and reason, and artificial
intelligence and cognitive capability."

The Russian nodded. "Yes, I have heard of this."

This did not surprise Siliezar. He knew the Israelis were
incapable of keeping even state secrets. Men like Piranchenko,
who moved in and out of world capitals at will, were often the
first to hear of new political and technological developments. It
was, Siliezar well understood, their business to keep abreast of such
developments. Indeed few people had more to gain or lose from
such developments.

The waiter arrived with their entrees and departed quickly.
Siliezar furtively scanned nearby tables for indications that others
might be eavesdropping. His sensors picked up no such signal.
"We are getting closer to making this dream a reality," he added
in a voice carefully modulated. "I'm sure I don't have to tell you
what this will mean for the future of mankind."

The Russian was now seriously engaged in an attack on a
lightly crusted Chilean sea bass. Siliezar did not want to test his

attention span with technological details. "This will mark the end of poverty, disease, illiteracy, and, most importantly, war."

The Russian smiled but did not look up. "An infamous Russian once said: 'the whole of man's history can be reduced to two words—who, whom?'" He paused and glanced at his host. "And in this he was not incorrect." He twirled his fork in a circular motion. "So please, do not insult me with such propaganda. You and I both know these new technologies represent only new ways to wage war."

Siliezar fought back the urge to instruct a man he considered only marginally civilized. *You are not here to educate him; you are here to sell him. Do not allow yourself to be defeated by a dead fish.* "Well, perhaps you are right." He conceded reluctantly. "There may well continue to be tribal warfare in developing countries. We will certainly do what we can to deter insurrection. But," he shrugged, "as we know, people do not always act in their own self interest."

This drew another smile from his guest. "So, how much is it you want?"

Siliezar leveled his gaze and replied. "We are looking for two hundred million dollars; I have in hand commitments for half of that amount."

The Russian did not blink. "And you wish from me the other half, yes?"

"It would make things easier," Siliezar conceded.

"This half that you have, is it conditional on your raising the other half?"

"Yes."

The Russian smiled. "I'm sure the bar in your suite is stocked with Smirnoff, yes?"

Siliezar smiled. "Yes."

"Very good, then," Piranchenko nodded and returned his attention to his plate. "We will finish dinner. Then we will go to your suite, and you will show me what you have to show me."

Siliezar smiled. *Not easy, but progress nonetheless.* "Vladimir, I am eager to show you the future."

The Russian grunted. He did not trust men of passion. He and his countrymen had learned that such men only bring with them great pain.

Hanley Siliezar waved the waiter over and ordered another drink. It promised to be a long night.

5

Father John Sweeney looked at his friend and winced. "I'm not your guy, Joe."

His friend and former seminary classmate, Joe McManus, sat across from him at a small table in an open air café outside Union Station in Washington, D.C. "You *are* my guy, John," McManus replied. "The only question is whether I'm *your* guy."

"Don't make it a loyalty test, Joe. That's unfair."

McManus smiled and nodded. "Okay, I grant you, that was a bit desperate; but then again, I *am* desperate."

Several hours earlier McManus had been notified by the papal nuncio, Angelo Montini, that he was on the short list to replace Philadelphia Archbishop John Cardinal O'Hallaran. For McManus, currently archbishop of Cincinnati, the assignment would represent a homecoming. He had been born in the archdiocese, educated in its schools, ordained from its seminary, and initiated into his priestly ministry in several of its parishes.

"Did he say how many were on the short list?" John asked.

McManus nodded. "Yeah, he basically laughed when I asked him, and said, 'one'!"

"Did you ask, 'Why me?'"

McManus laughed. "I did. He said: 'Who else?'"

John shook his head. "Well, at least he was clear."

A waiter arrived to take a lunch order. He took note of McManus' pectoral cross and asked: "Excuse me sir, are you a Catholic bishop?"

McManus smiled diffidently. "Guilty as charged."

The man looked to be in his late twenties and of Middle Eastern descent. "Your religion is false. That is why it is dying. Our religion is true. That is why it is growing." He paused as he reached into a front pocket for a pen. "Now, I will take your order."

Joe McManus was aghast. John Sweeney doubled over in laughter. The waiter, offended, turned and left.

"Hey, wait," Sweeney called after him. "I'll have the Jihad Special."

Heads turned and both priests saw fear in the eyes of patrons. McManus said: "John, let's go inside. There are any number of other restaurants."

Sweeney laughed. "Yeah, but do they provide entertainment?"

As they walked inside they felt the attention of onlookers. Neither said anything until they were safely seated at an indoor version of the outdoor café, on the main floor of Union Station. They sat on the perimeter with their backs to the main entrance. Immediately a young Hispanic waitress approached with menus. "Hello, Fathers. Can I get you something to drink?"

"Is it too early for a car bomb?" Sweeney inquired, referring to a popular drink among the young—a glass of beer with a shot glass filled with alcohol submerged within it.

The waitress checked her watch and laughed. "Father, if you want a car bomb, I will bring you a car bomb."

McManus's eyes widened in alarm. "Actually, Miss, *I'll* have an iced tea." He paused and looked at John. "And I'm sure *Father* Sweeney will order a soft drink of some sort. Am I right, Father?"

Sweeney smiled at the young woman and said: "See how we young priests look to our elders for guidance?"

The woman was young and petite and quite animated. "Diet Coke, Father?"

John cupped his hand to shield his mouth from his classmate and stage whispered: "Make that a regular Coke, but don't tell the boss."

The woman laughed and left.

John immediately turned to his classmate and said with a broad smile: "So, you were about to tell me why I'd make a perfect auxiliary bishop."

Joe McManus shivered in mock fright. "Okay, John, you made your point."

They sat in silence and watched the business class arrive and depart in great haste. John decided that if indeed it was true that time had somehow accelerated in the present age, it was these men and women who were among its primary victims. They seemed perpetually in mad pursuit of ever scarcer profits. *No wonder so many cannot find time for the Creator of matter itself from which they hope to draw their sustenance.*

"Our Muslim friends have grown extremely bold," Joe McManus said, breaking the silence. "It is no doubt a sign of their confidence."

John was momentarily puzzled, but as he turned and looked at his friend he immediately understood. "They have the Church on the run, Joe. They know it; and they know we know they know it."

McManus nodded. "The loss of Europe was catastrophic. Our bishops in the developing world believe they have lost their spiritual patrimony. One told me: 'We have been orphaned.'"

John winced. He had long wondered what the Church in the southern hemisphere thought of its sister to the north. "Well, yes, that's certainly the bad news; but," he smiled "it did get them a pope."

McManus nodded: "And thanks be to God, he is a holy man, John."

"He seems to be that indeed—joy filled, plain spoken, a man of deep prayer. It is a momentous development, Joe, for the Universal Church to have an African in the Chair."

"What do you make of his name?"

John smiled and replied enigmatically: "Perfect symmetry."

The waitress returned with their beverages and took a lunch order. When she had departed, Joe McManus turned to John and said softly: "I will have the solemn duty to propose auxiliary candidates to the apostolic nuncio and the North American Bishops Congress prior to their recommendations to the Holy Father." He paused. "Are you absolutely certain, John, you won't put a shoulder under this cross with me?"

John looked away for a moment to collect his thoughts. Then he turned and said: "Joe, I'm not cut out to be a bishop, even an auxiliary. We both know that. I am far too outspoken on the 'hard sayings.' And, frankly, I wouldn't change that even if I could . . . and I assure you at my age, I can't." He smiled and looked at his friend with affection and added: "The best way I can help you is by being a good foot soldier in the trenches."

Joe McManus looked away in pain. "I really don't know if I'm up to this challenge, John. I'm seventy years old, too. I don't know how much ministry I have left . . ."

John did not attempt to fill the silence. The cacophonous sounds of the great hall intruded on the thoughts of both men. After several minutes, McManus looked at his friend and said: "Should I refuse?"

John studied his friend's heart from his words. "Joe, if you're asking me to talk you into it, you summoned the wrong guy."

The archbishop of Cincinnati took umbrage. "John, I didn't summon you," he replied evenly. "I asked you to come down so I could share the news with you in person . . . and maybe get a little counsel, that's all."

John immediately felt a sharp pang of guilt. "Sorry, Joe. That didn't come out as I intended."

Another brief silence ensued. Presently, McManus looked at his classmate and said: "John, what am I inheriting?"

It was John Sweeney's turn to look away. *A Potemkin village.* "A shell of what was," he replied softly. "I thought we had turned a corner after the Illumination. I was wrong. The spirit of the age has returned with a vengeance. He seems hell bent on making up the lost time."

"This is not just true of Philadelphia, John," the archbishop said quietly.

"I know," John replied, "but we are the Church of Revelation 3. We were given a charism of fidelity." He shook his head. "We seem to have exhausted it."

"What is the Sunday Mass attendance?"

"It's fallen below 20 percent again."

McManus nodded. "We're a little above 30 percent in Cincinnati." He folded and unfolded his hands nervously. "It spiked into the 60s after the Illumination and held for . . . I don't know . . . maybe three and a half years. Then . . ." his voice trailed off.

"Yes, yes, we spiked too," John replied.

"How about vocations?"

"The seminary had over 245 men six years ago from about 30 dioceses. Now we're down to 155, about where we were 7 years ago. We'll ordain 6 men for the archdiocese this year. Next year, 4."

McManus bristled. "My word! What has he been doing!?"

John immediately prayed for grace. Receiving it, he determined silence was the most charitable response.

McManus looked at his classmate and said: "How about our brother priests, how are they? How is morale?"

John just shrugged.

McManus asked: "How about the remnant—the pro-life groups, the Marian groups, the daily communicants?"

John laughed. "I believe you're talking about the same people."

McManus smiled. "How about the debt?" He paused. "Any idea?"

"None," John replied. He then added: "I will say the cardinal has worked very hard to raise money."

McManus merely grunted in response.

The waitress arrived with lunch. Corn chowder soup for the bishop and a Philly Cheese Steak for the pastor.

When she departed, McManus looked at his friend and said: "Tell me again. Why do I want this assignment?"

John quickly shook his head: "I love you, Joe, but this is between you and the Lord." He studied his friend. He knew well his character—part Hamlet, part overly cautious administrator. He did *not* think Joe McManus was the right man for the moment; then again, he reminded himself, John Paul II had already come and gone.

"We are entering interesting times, my friend," McManus said, breaking the momentary silence. "I don't have a feel for where this is all headed."

John did. "I believe the next archbishop of Philadelphia will die in prison; I believe his successor will die before a firing squad."

McManus' spoon fell from his hand. It splashed down in his soup and rebounded onto his lap. Nearby, heads turned. A waiter appeared with a new spoon and wet linen. The archbishop thanked him behind an embarrassed smile. He turned to John and said in mock disdain: "No wonder you don't get invited to more archdiocesan events, Sweeney!" He paused and added: "If I thought you were serious, I'd make you pay for lunch."

John Sweeney laughed. He had no alternative. He didn't own a credit card and he hadn't brought enough cash.

6

David Ben Ami bounded into the grand lobby of the King David Hotel in Jerusalem like the mayor of the city. He mugged and hugged his way to the sitting area in a ritual that took nearly ten minutes.

Michael Burns stood and sat down twice before deciding he would wait for his bureau chief to come to stop, before standing again to greet him. "You didn't tell me you were running for election," Michael teased, when the energizer sabra came to a stop.

Ben Ami stood 5'4" tall, and possessed a ruddy complexion and charcoal lasers for eyes. Very little happened in Israel with which he was unfamiliar. He was notoriously fearless, and known to publish opinions about anything and everything that managed to find its way onto his radar screen in Michael's popular daily, the *Thorn*. "You didn't tell me I couldn't," he replied, with a smile.

Michael first met Ben Ami in New York, when he was getting started in the advertising business, and Ben Ami was a stringer for the Associated Press. They were seated together at the Waldorf one winter night at a black tie event honoring Pope John Paul II in absentia. "Finally, you have a pope who can really pope," Ben Ami had declared with a broad smile, and added: "And finally, we Jews get a pope too."

They had stayed in touch over the years, and when their careers took unexpected turns—Michael, being fired from his own firm by its new owner, Henley Siliezar, and Ben Ami, fired from the Jerusalem desk of the *New York Times* under pressure from Henley Siliezar—they agreed to meet in the Palace Courtyard on Fifth Avenue in Manhattan one mild spring evening for a drink. Michael shared his plans for a regional daily tabloid that would aggressively track the Life Sciences Revolution agenda, and the plans and activities of its primary architects, including Henley Siliezar. They had a handshake correspondent agreement in principal by the time they departed.

"Let's go somewhere quiet," Michael suggested.

"Okay, I know just the place," Ben Ami replied as he leapt to his feet. Michael followed him to the hotel's large outdoor pool, one floor below the lobby. He watched as his little bureau chief's feet scampered over the wide flagstone terrace surrounding the pool. He smiled to himself. *This is Zacchaeus reincarnated . . . with the guile of Nathaniel.* Ben Ami stopped at a brightly colored cabana at the south end of the pool. It was a little past noon and the pool was empty. "This is a good spot," he suggested. "You can see everyone who comes and goes."

A waiter immediately appeared. He was young and lithe and handsome. "What you men like to drink?" he asked through a thick Israeli accent.

"I'll have whatever you're drinking," Michael replied with a smile.

"And I'll have what *he's* drinking," Ben Ami added as he winked and nodded toward Michael.

"It is okay then. I bring you my own drink which I invent. Veddy good for you," the young man proposed, all business, focused on his aging customers' midsections. "You will much like," he added, and departed as though an air raid siren had just been sounded.

Michael immediately reclined in the lounger and looked at his bureau chief and said: "Okay, David, give me the headlines."

"The country is abuzz. We believe we're living in an existential moment," he replied. He paused and smiled. "Of course, we've been living an existential moment for . . . oh . . . almost seventy-five years now."

Michael nodded. "What are the manifestations?"

"Over 80 percent of our Jewish citizens now self-identify in religious terms—about 25 percent Orthodox and maybe 55 percent traditional," Ben Ami replied.

This surprised Michael Burns. "What's the base?"

Ben Ami shrugged. "I don't know, maybe 40 percent in 2000, maybe 65 percent in 2010."

Michael smiled. "What about the other 20 percent?"

"Oh, they're our capitalists," Ben Ami retorted with a grunt. "I call it the American influence," he needled.

"What's driving it?"

"Existential threats, of course," Ben Ami answered, with a nod to his publisher.

"Tehran?"

"No, Washington!"

"*You* don't believe that, I'm sure."

"As one of your own humorists said, Michael, there are only two certainties in this life."

Michael turned in his chair. "Do you honestly believe that America is as dead set on the destruction of Israel as Iran?"

"No," Ben Ami replied. "I simply believe that America would sell us out in a heartbeat when it's clear our interests are no longer aligned." He paused and added: "And I believe we have now reached that point."

Michael waved his right hand dismissively. "You're drunk, my friend; perhaps the health shake was a good idea."

"You do not think like an Israeli," Ben Ami replied defensively.

"No," Michael said with a thin smile. "We Americans are not paranoid."

"Maybe it's time you were."

The waiter appeared in a dead sprint. He lifted two clear thermoses with amber lids off a tray, shook them vigorously, and handed one to each man. "You think you die and go to heaven," he said with a proud smile.

Michael took his, removed the lid, and sipped cautiously. "Good," he announced allowing a measure of surprise. "I am impressed. No, what's in this thing?"

The waiter reached into his shirt pocket for a business card and handed it to Michael. "State secret," he smiled. "But," he looked at Ben Ami and then back to Michael "we work out deal for American distribution rights. Then I tell you."

Michael looked at Ben Ami and deadpanned: "One of the 20 percent?"

Ben Ami took his drink, placed it on the table, and nodded to the waiter who departed, unhappily. They sat in silence, as the lunch crowd from the hotel began to arrive and fill the cabanas. Michael was surprised at the number of small children among the guests. He carefully observed how they interacted with their parents, particularly their fathers, who did not hesitate to discipline them. It did not appear that the children found this in any way unwelcome.

"So," Michael said, breaking the silence. "When do the Israelis think the Messiah will arrive?"

"Soon," Ben Ami replied quickly.

"How soon?" Michael asked, surprised.

"Well, not this week, but maybe the week after," Ben Ami replied coyly.

"They believe His return . . . uh . . . His arrival is imminent?"

"*Imminent*?" Ben Ami repeated thoughtfully. "Yes, I would say we believe the great event is . . . *imminent*."

"Your lifetime?"

Ben Ami laughed. "I am an old man, Michael Burns. Almost as old as you."

Michael did not laugh. "So maybe *not* the week after next?"

Ben Ami smiled and said: "We are a young country, Michael. Our institutions are young. Our families are young." He waved his hands in the direction of the pool "And our dreams are young."

"In their lifetimes," Michael suggested.

Ben Ami nodded. "Yes, most certainly in *their* lifetimes."

"And what will occasion this arrival?"

"Why Mr. Burns, the existential threat of which you speak."

"From America," Michael said with an edge of incredulity.

"Yes, there is a Christian force in Macedonia, a European force, poised to strike on behalf of a Palestinian state."

Michael shook his head. He was suddenly embarrassed that he was the only man in the world willing to publish the ruminations of his friend.

"Israelis believe Tehran has sufficient uranium to make nuclear weapons?" Michael asked.

"Many times over."

"Then why hasn't Bibbi attacked their generators?"

Ben Ami smiled at his friend's use of the Prime Minister's nickname. "He believes the next Muslim attack on America has now entered the implementation phase. All the leg work, all the planning, all the procurement of materials, all the instructions, everything has been completed."

"He told you this?"

Ben Ami looked around to make sure no one was eavesdropping. "Yes," he replied tersely.

"Has he shared this with the American President?"

"No."

"Why?"

"He believes she will dismiss it out of hand."

Michael nodded glumly.

"The Muslim world wants Big Satan, not Little Satan," Ben Ami said. "Of course, once they have taken down Big Satan . . ."

Michael did not find this plausible. He believed Tehran would draw America into its war with Israel through a direct attack on the Israeli people. In fact, he believed he was sitting at Ground Zero. When the Great Satan came to the aid of Little Satan, he was of the opinion Tehran would call in its commitments from Moscow and Beijing. It was this development, most of the believing world had come to believe, that would usher in Armageddon.

"It is about honor for the Muslims," Ben Ami said. "Vengeance is part of their culture. The Wahhabi faction wants revenge for your support of the Shah, for your occupation of Iraq, for your troops' presence near their holy sites."

Michael fell silent. Then he gently asked: "What will happen, David, when they come for the Jews?"

David Ben Ami looked at his friend and said philosophically: "They have already come, Michael. They've been coming for over seventy years." He sat upright and waved his hand over the setting. "You will note, we are still here."

Michael nodded and smiled. "And not going anywhere, are you?"

Ben Ami shook his head. "Their obsession with terminating our existence has just brought us closer to our God. I think it is having the same effect in the Christian West. Your media simply will not report it."

"Maybe this is part of what they call God's 'permitting will.'"

"What is this . . . 'permitting will'?"

"We Christians are taught God *ordains* good but *permits* evil . . . if only to bring a greater good from it."

Ben Ami shook his head. "Well, He certainly has permitted a lot of evil done in His name. Much of it directed at His chosen people. I must confess, we Jews don't see much good in any of it."

Michael raised his arms to symbolically encompass the whole of Jerusalem. "That's a rather strange statement to make on behalf of a sovereign people in possession of their homeland for the first time in nearly two thousand years."

"Western guilt," Ben Ami said dismissively.

"Nonetheless, you are now here. And for a very long time, you were not here."

Ben Ami nodded. "Yes, we are here. And we intend to stay here. We have no intention of letting one and a half billion Muslims either incinerate us or put us to flight. And we will not, under any circumstances, permit the Western world to take in fear what they granted in guilt."

Michael thought the time had come for a change of venue. "How about we move to a secure location and talk about The Project?"

David Ben Ami was on his feet immediately. "Come," he said. "We will go to my home. Though my wife still bugs me, I haven't found any wires." He laughed at his own witticism and set his feet in motion. In moments they were back in the grand lobby of the hotel, heading toward its front door.

They exited through attended double doors just as a small party was entering. Michael took note of a very tall man with two significantly shorter men. He looked at the closer of the two smaller men and stopped abruptly. Their eyes met. The other man nodded imperceptibly and smiled thinly. It was Hanley Siliezar. The other man glanced at Michael without apparent recognition. It was Vennitti Inc. Chairman and CEO, Geoff Benton.

Michael's heart began to race. It was the first time he had seen the two men since they had arranged the murder of his closest friend, Joe Delgado, twelve years ago. He immediately made a mental note to have Ben Ami research the much taller man.

He wondered what the three of them were doing in Israel. He wouldn't have long to wait for an answer.

7

It was a little after 9:00 a.m. when Maggie Gillespie entered the small reception area of the NFP St. Gianna Molla Clinic in Narbrook. What she saw almost caused her to drop her coffee. A living, breathing miracle lay fast asleep in her mother's arms. The mother, Genevieve Thompson, stood talking to Maggie's daughter Grace. "Oh, Mom, look at Elijah!" Grace exclaimed, as she turned to her mother.

"Genevieve!" Maggie whispered, rushing toward mother and child. "He's perfect!" Maggie reached for the child, and his mother carefully made the transfer without disturbing the infant. Maggie clutched the sleeping child to her bosom and immediately opened her heart. "Lord Jesus, we just give you praise and thanks. You are so very good. You heard our prayers and you have answered them. Who are we, Lord, that the God who created and redeemed us listens to *our* prayers . . . and *answers* them?" Then, quietly, "Lord, please bless, guide, and protect this child and his family through all that is to come. They have put their trust in you, O Lord. Let them continue to see that *you* are the only one worthy of our trust."

She wiped tears from her eyes with the palm of her right hand, turned to her daughter, and said: "Grace, if this clinic had only assisted in delivering this one child, it would have served its intended purpose. Truly, our little Elijah is a great work of the Lord."

As the child began to stir, Grace took him from her mother and held him close to her face. "Mom, look at his eyes! Look at how much light there is and how the light is set off by the depth of the blue." She looked up and said to the child's mother: "I do believe they are the eyes of a prophet."

Genevieve Thompson laughed and replied: "Well, let's pray that God shuts the eyes of his little prophet after midnight. He's killing me!"

Maggie opened the door to her office and asked both women to join her inside. The clinic was housed in a building that the Gillespie's had converted from what was formerly St. Martha's original grammar school. The first floor was home to the clinic's administrative team and its four physicians. The second floor was used for educational programs, and the basement for social and cultural events intended to promote the work of the clinic in the community.

Despite repeated requests for the archbishop to come and bless the clinic and its staff, Cardinal O'Hallaran had steadfastly refused. The Gillespies were aware that the Pope had recently accepted his resignation and were hopeful that his successor might find time to pay them a visit. They did not know who O'Hallaran's successor would be, but they had a strong sense their friend and pastor, Father John Sweeney, *did* know.

Father Sweeney, however, was not talking.

Maggie opened the blinds to let a beautiful spring morning flood the office with light and warmth. She flipped a latch and opened the window several inches, and then turned nervously to her former patient: "Oh Genevieve, will this be too much for Elijah?"

"I'll let you know if it is, Mrs. Gillespie," she replied with a reassuring smile.

"Please, come sit. I want to hear all about it," Maggie gushed, as she dragged a wooden arm chair from a corner to the center of the office and sat in it.

Mother and child sat carefully in a wing chair across from Maggie and away from the window. Grace returned to the reception desk to answer a phone.

"Well, where do you want me to begin, when my water burst?" Genevieve asked with a laugh.

Maggie nodded excitedly: "Yes, yes. Perfect!"

Genevieve Thompson recounted the harrowing delivery of their miracle child, omitting nothing. Her water had burst a little after 3:00 a.m. on a weekday morning several weeks ago. Her husband, dazed and confused, had trouble locating the keys to the car. When he did find them where he had left them—in the ignition—he had trouble starting the car. By the time they were finally underway, Elijah himself was underway. He arrived within ten minutes, requiring roadside assistance. Fortunately, a nurse returning from a night shift saw father and mother struggling, and immediately understood what was transpiring. She endangered herself and at least one other motorist with a dramatic U turn on a two-lane back road. She arrived in time to catch a falling star and attend his hysterical mother.

The mini motorcade proceeded to the hospital with the nurse driving Thompson's car, and mother and child crying hysterically from the safety of the back seat. The husband and father followed in the nurse's car, actually stopping once for a red light that the lead car had safely ignored.

The nurse had called ahead, and the attendants were waiting outside the hospital's emergency room entrance with a wheelchair for the mother and her infant. The father parked and went in the main entrance and sat waiting for the receptionist to arrive. About twenty minutes later he was finally summoned by an on-call physician in the nursery.

Genevieve Thompson stopped twice to wipe tears of laughter

from her eyes. The infant, who again had fallen asleep, stirred once, decided nothing of interest was going on, and went back to sleep.

At that moment Grace re-entered the room with a patient. "Mom, Genevieve, meet Mary Clare Langdon. She's due in October."

The expectant mother was ineluctably drawn to the new mother and her child. "Oh, my word, he's perfect!" she said upon closer inspection.

As Genevieve beamed wordlessly, Grace pulled another matching arm chair for her new patient and positioned it so the four ladies were now in a small circle. "I'm headed to the kitchen," Grace said before taking her seat. "Who wants coffee?"

Genevieve Thompson was the only taker. "Black," she instructed. "The nights are long, the days even longer."

Maggie turned her attention to Mary Clare Langdon. "How are you feeling?" she inquired.

"I'm tired and, truth be told, Anthony and I are nervous." She replied. "This is our second try."

Noting the concern in the young woman's eyes, Maggie said: "Well, you look fine, Mary Clare. I know God will give you the strength."

The young mother looked at her, shook her head and said: "I just worry that I don't trust enough."

Maggie immediately moved her chair closer and put her arm around the young woman. She leaned close to her and said with quiet conviction: "You will be given grace, and the grace you are given you will convert into trust, which is the medium of exchange in the mystical world."

Mary Clare Langdon's eyes filled. She sat quietly looking at her slightly swollen stomach. "We've been trying for almost three years, and we lost our first little one after twelve weeks last fall." It appeared to Maggie she was about to cry. She tightened her hold around the young woman's slender shoulders. "I am just so afraid," she said in a quivering voice. "It just devastated Anthony."

"We are *not* going to lose this little treasure," Maggie reassured her. "We're going to start praying to St. Gianna today, and *she's* going to make sure your little one arrives just as safely as our little Elijah did."

Genevieve Thompson started to speak, but at that moment Grace re-entered the room with her coffee. "Here, Vieve. This ought to keep you awake until at least noon," she needled gently. Grace pulled her chair closer into the circle. "Mary Clare, before you and I start our work this morning, I thought you might want to hear Elijah's story," she said, nodding toward his mother.

Mary Clare Langdon turned toward Genevieve Thompson, eyes wide in wordless expectation. The mother of Elijah paused to sip her coffee. She sat erect and squared her slender shoulders: "Bob and I had been trying to have a child for seven years. We couldn't conceive. We consulted virtually anyone and everyone who was recommended to us." She shrugged. "Nothing."

She sipped her coffee again. "I thought it was Bob's fault; he thought it was mine. It was a really dark time in our marriage." She paused momentarily. "Finally, we looked into adoption." She blinked back tears. "But we just couldn't summon the will to do it. We desperately wanted our own child, and adopting seemed like waiving a white flag in surrender." She looked down in embarrassment.

"We hear that a lot," Grace interrupted gently. "I think it's the Holy Spirit whispering in a married couple's ear to try another way."

Genevieve Thompson smiled and replied: "Maybe. But I have to tell you; at that point I had lost my faith in God."

Mary Clare Langdon nodded in sympathy.

"Finally, in our eighth year of marriage, with both of our families praying Eucharistic and Rosary novenas night and day, we conceived," she continued. Slowly, her eyes began to fill. "We lost that child in the eleventh week." She stopped abruptly. Grace opened her handbag, withdrew a small packet of tissues and handed it to her. Genevieve accepted it with a small smile. "That loss devastated our families," she said. "My father grew very angry with God. He fell to his knees in our kitchen one night and yelled to the heavens: 'Why are you playing games with these children. If you are not going to grant them the gift of life . . . leave them the hell alone.'" Her pain turned into a smile at the memory, gradually even giving way to a laugh. "That's the way my dad is," she said with a mixture of pride and embarrassment.

She paused to recollect herself. "Within ten weeks we conceived again," she said, looking past her child to her feet. "At the news, our families came over and prayed a Rosary together in thanksgiving. My dad even said a prayer in front of everyone apologizing to God for doubting Him." She stopped. Grace and Maggie were momentarily unsure if she would continue. "We lost *that* child in the sixth week," she added. Her small body started to shake. Grace leapt off the chair and stood over her and put her arms around her. Mary Clare Langdon burst into tears and cried: "Oh my God!" Maggie moved to comfort *her*.

It took several minutes for the room to settle. Finally, Genevieve signaled she was okay to continue. "I do promise you," laughing through tears at Mary Clare, "this story *does* have a happy ending."

This simple assurance served to break the tension. Laughter filled the room and awakened the sleeping child who began to cry. "There's the proof!" Genevieve added, nodding toward the child.

Grace picked up the narrative while the mother of Elijah regrouped. "We met Genevieve at a black tie event downtown," she said to Mary Clare. "The Commodore Barry Club was honoring one of our pro-life leaders. Bob and Gen ended up sitting next to Scott and me at a table in the back of the room."

"Fate!" Mary Clare Langdon cried out triumphantly.

"Well, something like that," Grace smiled. "She asked me about our family. I asked about hers. It was immediately apparent I had leapt feet first into an open wound."

"Actually, it was head first," Genevieve corrected with a laugh. "I quickly discovered Grace is very much her mother's daughter."

At the sound of Grace's name, Maggie instantly returned to a dark night in the distant past. She, Grace, and an exorcist were kneeling in prayer outside her daughter Moia's room. Grace's prayer of unconditional love that night for her sister drew tears from her mother and the exorcist. In that moment Maggie was given a vision for Grace's life. She saw her bathed in a surreal light surrounded by a sea of infants—mother to thousands of children who would never otherwise know life.

"I came to see her, literally, the next day," Genevieve said recapturing her narrative. "It was a Saturday." She smiled at Mary Clare. "She immediately put me in her car and drove me to a lab for blood work. Monday morning she called and said they had located the problem. My *progesterone* was low."

"How low?" Mary Clare interrupted.

"Abysmally low," Genevieve replied, looking to Grace for assistance.

"Impossible-to-sustain-a-pregnancy low," Grace interjected.

"What were the levels, Grace, do you remember?" Genevieve asked.

Grace thought for several moments, then jumped up abruptly and said: "Why guess? Let me go get your chart."

Mary Clare waited until Grace left the room, then turned to Genevieve Thompson and whispered: "I think that's my problem too." She shrugged. "At least that's what my Mom thinks."

Grace returned with Genevieve's chart. She sat and peered carefully at several long columns of hand written numbers. "The first blood tests showed she was about half the normal range for women at the same point in their pregnancies," she said. "But, unfortunately, that was the good news," she added ominously.

Mary Clare Langdon leaned forward in her chair. "What happened?" she asked.

"We went backwards," Grace replied. "At the twelfth week mark, Genevieve's progesterone level had fallen in half, to a little over six. Normal is thirty-five at twelve weeks."

Mary Clare gasped. "What did you do!?"

"We prayed," Grace replied. "And we started Genevieve on a supplemental prescription of progesterone tablets; and we began bringing her in every day, literally every day, to measure her progesterone level and administer shots if she needed them, which she almost always did."

Genevieve laughed. "I looked like a pin cushion."

Mary Clare's jaw dropped and her eyes widened. "Gen, I can't believe what you went through."

The mother looked down at her child for a lingering moment, lifted her head and said: "I'd do it again in a heartbeat."

Grace said: "Vieve made it until the thirty-fourth week. She went caesarean. Her progesterone level at time of delivery registered 132." She paused. "Normal is 135."

A deep silence descended upon the room.

Mary Clare broke it with a question addressed to no one in particular: "Why do so many of our Catholic Ob/Gyn's miss this?"

It was a question that went unanswered.

The return to silence was interrupted by the sound of the door buzzer. Maggie looked at Grace and said: "Are you expecting anyone?"

"No," she replied leaping to her feet. "Let me see who it is."

She returned with her step father, Dr. Jim Gillespie, following her. The look on his face signaled Maggie it was time to end their impromptu meeting.

"Jim, look at our little miracle, Elijah Thompson," she said, reaching for his hand and squeezing it.

Jim made a fuss over mother and child. It required a not insignificant struggle. Maggie quickly introduced him to Mary Clare Langdon, even as she was giving Grace an eye signal to escort her courteously out of the office.

When the ladies had gone, Maggie quickly closed the door and pulled a chair over to where Jim had chosen to sit. "Honey, what is it?" she asked quietly.

"I just returned from a little chat with Paul Nicolosi," he replied sullenly. He looked up and gazed into his wife's eyes. "Sweetheart, it doesn't look good."

"How . . . why . . . what did he say?"

"He said, as an attorney he'd rather have the government's case."

"Oh that rascal!" Maggie said with mild annoyance. "Was he just being Paul?" she asked hopefully.

"No . . . at least I don't think so," Jim replied. "He laid out their case, then ours. It was clear he thinks they will prevail."

"Jim," Maggie put her head on her husband's chest, "what did he say?"

She heard her husband's stomach growl in protest. "He said the government will claim that because it has an ownership stake in the nation's approved insurance carriers, it will assert a legal right to demand equitable treatment of its citizens under the law."

Maggie jerked her head from his chest. "What's that supposed to mean?"

Jim Gillespie turned to avoid her glare. "It means we have a *choice.*" He smiled thinly at the irony. "We can either accept patients who want abortion on demand as the price we pay for government reimbursement of our NFP patients, or . . ."

"Or . . . what!?" Maggie demanded.

"Or we can ask our NFP patients to forgo reimbursement from their insurance carriers and watch our business go down in flames."

"Then that's what we'll do," Maggie said defiantly. "We'll explain to our families what's at stake. They'll stay with us, Jim. I know they will."

Jim cupped his wife's face in his hands. She was still the loveliest woman he had ever laid eyes on, even in the seventy-second year of her eventful life. "Please God, they will, sweetheart," he said soothingly. "Please God they will."

Jim Gillespie, however, knew otherwise. He had already advised their attorney to prepare for the worst. The St. Gianna Molla Clinic and its owners would not, he assured him, go down without a fight.

8

D avid Moskowitz was well accustomed to leading prospective investors on private tours of the Ben Gurion laboratory outside Tel Aviv. He was *not* accustomed to having to crane his neck to make his presentation or answer questions.

Vladimir Piranchenko stood 6'8" tall, a good foot taller than Moskowitz, and held himself with regal bearing as befitting a multibillionaire. He moved slowly and deliberately from station to station in the fastidiously clean laboratory where there were no walls and no other floors. Occasionally, he would stop to survey the clumps and clusters of scientists working on the floor, but only to ensure his presence among them was still the central preoccupation of the moment. Trailing closely behind was the much shorter but considerably more powerful Hanley Siliezar.

"How many work here?" the Russian abruptly inquired of the Lab's executive director.

"Almost all," Moskowitz retorted quickly, nervously eying Siliezar.

The Russian emitted a grunt intended to serve as a laugh. "So, what is this?" he asked, stopping at a large station with over a dozen scientists and technicians huddled behind two very large computer screens.

Moskowitz smiled. "This is today," he replied. "This team has reverse engineered the regions of the brain. They are developing a capability to upload neural implants to patients with Alzheimer's and other neurological disorders."

Siliezar eyed Piranchenko carefully. "Vlad, this is the bridge to the future I spoke to you about in London."

The Russian nodded in a perfunctory manner, which only served to increase Siliezar's concern about his level of attention, and retention. Siliezar nodded to Moskowitz to repeat the station's main talking points.

"The mapping of the brain has opened the door to the future that Hanley is talking about," Moskowitz continued. "This has permitted us to begin work on non-biological systems with even greater complexity than we humans possess."

The Russian's eyes grew cloudy. Siliezar immediately ventured: "When a scientist like David speaks of 'complexity' in this context, he means emotional intelligence, Vladimir."

"What are you saying? Speak plainly," Piranchenko demanded with a bit of pique.

Moskowitz and Siliezar exchanged nervous glances. "What we are saying is this," Siliezar replied. "Once we have perfected nanobots and entered them into a person's blood stream to combat aging and disease, we will be *inside!*" He paused. "And, Vlad, once we are *inside* we can begin to *program*; to upload various patterns of actual human experience—things many men have always wanted to experience but couldn't afford—like virtual sex with all its attendant pleasures. Sex on demand with anyone you want. You will be able to afford your own sensorium. *You* will choose and design your own partner and the unique experiences that will fulfill your desires in that particular moment."

Siliezar watched the Russian's interest awaken. "Vlad, think of all of this as software and think of the human body as hardware." He grew excited and his voice started to rise, which immediately drew suspicion from his potential investor. "By fusing non-biological and biological intelligence, we will greatly increase the capacity of man to think and do virtually anything and everything in our time. Man's powers will increase exponentially and continue to expand in limitless ways."

Piranchenko nodded in partial understanding. "So, man will think like machine?"

"No! Just the opposite," Moskowitz dared to correct. "Machine will think like man!"

The Russian looked to Siliezar for clarification. "Think of yourself as you are right now," Siliezar explained patiently. "You are who you are—your intelligence, your consciousness, your memories, your habits, your capabilities—all of it. Now, fast forward five to ten years. That's how close we are. *Now*, Vlad, to the you that is you, add the raw power of a computer mainframe for exponentially greater cognitive functionality. *Now,* again think of this as software and add whatever new patterns—new experiences, new capacities, new levels of consciousness—that you desire. *Now,*" he paused briefly for effect "add the final piece, the capability to live indefinitely, because all of your software—your mind— and all of your hardware—your body—will be both upgradeable and replaceable in real time."

Siliezar paused to assess the Russian's level of comprehension. He determined that he was unable to do so. He continued, "Vlad, before you are fifty, you will become the next generation you. Your mind and body will have undreamt of powers." He paused expectantly. "This, my friend, is simply evolution by another name."

Vladimir Piranchenko grunted and said, "Let's keep moving."

They came to a station where a single scientist was seated at a small computer with a network of intricate patterns on a large screen. "What is this?" Piranchenko asked.

The scientist turned around and answered in Russian. This brought an immediate smile to Piranchenko's angular face. Moskowitz, who spoke Russian, monitored the ensuing conversation with an occasional nod of reassurance to Hanley Siliezar, who did not speak Russian, although he was quite conversant in its medium of exchange—the ruble.

When the conversation ended, Siliezar asked the Russian what he had been told. "He said technology is creating its own evolution," Piranchenko said with obvious interest. "He said in ten years, maybe less, the full processing power of the entire planet's human intelligence will cost less than one thousand euros to duplicate." The Russian laughed and added, "He said that this figure assumes just the people still using only biological neurons."

Siliezar smiled, satisfied. He motioned to Moskowitz to keep the large Russian moving through the laboratory. As they moved from station to station, the Russian seemed to grow increasingly comfortable, and began interacting directly with the scientists and technicians. He appeared to enjoy the give and take, a portion of which was devoted to recent developments in their motherland.

They arrived at a final station, where at least two dozen scientists and technicians were working in small clusters around a series of computer screens with color coded decision trees. The Russian turned to Moskowitz and arched his eyebrows in curiosity. Moskowitz stole a glance at Siliezar and said: "We know that our patrons expect, no *demand*, a handsome return on their investment. This group is mapping the intersection of the three great revolutions now underway and forecasting their commercialization."

Piranchenko looked to Siliezar in exasperation. Siliezar nodded to Moskowitz that he would handle the explanation, and suggested they move to a quieter spot on the floor. They headed to an unoccupied cove near floor-to-ceiling windows, which provided an unfettered view of a small forest of large white cedars. As they took seats around a small, unadorned table, Hanley Siliezar signaled to Moskowitz to get coffee and a chigger of Smirnoff.

Siliezar waited until the Russian was settled before attempting an explanation. "Vlad, this laboratory *is* for all practical purposes the *epicenter* of the revolutions in genetics, nanotechnology, and robotics." He watched carefully for telltale clues whether or not the Russian was tuning him out. Not detecting any, he continued slowly. "I want you to think of the universe . . . and all of the life within it . . . as simply an information system." The Russian nodded impatiently. Siliezar repressed the desire to rebuke him. "An elaborate, highly complex, yet still largely undecoded information system" he said. "But, an information system nonetheless."

The Russian simply stared unblinking. Siliezar continued, "The revolution in molecular biology has allowed us to understand the information processes that form the foundations for life. We are now very close to eliminating disease and illness and, as you discovered earlier, exponentially increasing man's capacity to think, to experience, and to create."

Siliezar paused and continued, "Now, Vladimir, this *second* revolution, the nanotechnology revolution, has allowed man to redesign and rebuild, molecule by molecule, not merely our brains and our bodies, but the very world in which we live. Man will no longer have to live a short, brutish existence as the philosophers say. He can live as he wants for as long as he wants."

Moskowitz returned with the Smirnoff, and Piranchenko reached for it a little too quickly for Siliezar's taste. He removed the cap, poured an astonishingly large amount into a white porcelain coffee cup, and drained it. His face immediately radiated happiness. *I am a fool*, Siliezar thought. *I should have just sat with him at the bar of the King David Hotel, let him drink himself into a stupor, secured his signature on an open-ended agreement, and mailed him a copy.*

"Now this *third* revolution, Vladimir." Siliezar continued as he attempted to re-group. "We are talking about the revolution in robotics. This is the most important of all. This revolution has allowed us to begin to integrate far more powerful forms of intelligence with our own. I am speaking of non-biological intelligence." He paused for effect and added, "This is the foundation for Homo

Evolutis—the fulfillment of the Darwinian promise—man transforms technology that in turn transforms man. The result is the
creation of a "transhuman" being who is new and exciting, and
forever transcendent."

The Russian belched, and smiled.

David Moskowitz suppressed a laugh. Hanley Siliezar suppressed a curse.

Siliezar jumped to his feet and said: "Vladimir, you are correct.
It is high time we open the bar." He signaled Moskowitz to alert
their driver they were on their way out. As the large Russian made
his way through the intricate maze of stations, he was hailed by a
number of its scientists who were Russian émigrés. Several temporar-
ily stopped their work to approach him and shake his hand. Others
shouted farewells while seated behind computer screens.

The Russian made no effort to conceal his joy at the adulation. He didn't understand it, to be sure, but he basked in it
nonetheless. By the time they arrived at the entrance to the Ben
Gurion laboratory, their driver was waiting for them. He was a
large, thick Israeli with an enormous neck and back. Piranchenko
thought him a Judo champion and nodded deferentially. He was
grateful his host had recognized his need for security, even in a
country where such abductions were exceedingly rare.

It was dusk in late spring. The sun, which had made only
a brief appearance earlier in the afternoon, was carefully tucked
behind dark, heavy clouds that seemed to approach with a palpable
suddenness. Siliezar waited until Piranchenko was safely seated in
the back seat of the black limousine before he entered the car from
the other side, and took his seat. In moments they were moving at
high speeds on an unmarked, two lane back road heading toward
Tel Aviv for dinner.

It took them less than twenty minutes to arrive at a seaside
restaurant about a mile outside town. The Russian catnapped during the ride, while Siliezar read reports from his key operative at
the International Monetary Fund. The restaurant was a nondescript
former Kibbutz that had been converted by an Israeli government

official, who in an earlier life had been a Mossad agent. The clientele included the affluent and the influential—and those who protected them.

At the wooded entrance to the property, the driver turned onto a gravel road and headed toward the sea. At a clearing, he swung the car toward a flat-roofed one-story building and deposited his two guests just steps from the front door. Siliezar's door was immediately opened by an attendant dressed in black wearing dark sunglasses. "Good evening, Mr. Siliezar," he said in heavily accented English. "It is good to have you with us again."

Siliezar nodded and turned to watch Piranchenko exit the limousine from the other side. He seemed to extricate himself in stages, until he stood erect and surveyed his surrounding in the manner of a giant crane. Stooping slightly he stuffed several notes of European currency into the hands of his attendant, which immediately drew a smile and a wink to his friend on the other side of the car who had been stiffed by Siliezar.

The owner and proprietor emerged from the restaurant and promptly proceeded to fawn over his guests in a most un-Israeli manner. He was a short man with a stocky build and something of an affected continental aura about him. His restaurant was a popular spot for Tel Aviv entrepreneurs and scientists from the laboratory, and he wanted his gratitude to the two men who could keep them productively employed to be manifestly evident.

Once inside, the owner ducked behind a large mahogany bar, grabbed two bottles of acclaimed Italian wine, and led the men to a small table in the rear of the restaurant. It was shortly before 7:00 p.m., early by the standards of Israeli business dining protocol. Siliezar well understood most of the restaurant's clientele were winding down their work schedules in office buildings up the coast. It was his intention to get in and out before most of them arrived. He was on mission, and not anxious to feed native speculation.

When Siliezar and Piranchenko were seated, the owner opened the first of the two bottles of wine and poured a small amount in Siliezar's Waterford goblet for inspection. Siliezar nodded imperiously, sniffed and sipped, and silently signaled his approval. The owner half filled each goblet. The Russian immediately spurned his and asked for Smirnoff vodka. The Israeli did his best to hide his disappointment, communicating his embarrassment to Siliezar through heavy lidded eyes.

Siliezar was himself embarrassed by the Russian's boorish behavior. He grew quiet and glanced at his watch. He resolved to have this deal wrapped up and the Russian bear deposited at the airport for his scheduled bacchanalian rendezvous in Barcelona within ninety minutes.

The owner decided to lick his wounds in private, and sent the bottle of Smirnoff to the table in the hands of a comely young Israeli woman in her late twenties. The Russian quickly sized her up and smiled. "This I like," he said to Siliezar, who quietly muttered an oath under his breath. The woman half curtsied seductively and placed the bottle submissively in the Russian's large paws. He quickly removed the top, grabbed a wine glass from an adjoining table, and poured. He handed the glass to the waitress and said, "It is good. You drink first, then me." He smiled. "Then, together."

The woman declined demurely, careful not to give offense. "But I am working, Sir. I must wait until I am off duty," she said, with a nod to a handsome Swiss clock on a cedar mantle atop a white marble fireplace. The Russian grunted in reply and waved his free hand dismissively.

Observing this carefully, Siliezar was rethinking the all-in price of his guest's investment. *How do we hide him after we get his money?* He decided to start the close. "Vladimir, what did you think of the work being done at the Ben Gurion Lab?"

"I like," he said evenly, as he nodded his head, then emptied and refilled his glass.

"Did you have any . . . ah . . . questions that I might be able to answer for you?"

The Russian swallowed deliberately, placed the glass in its

original position within the place setting, stared into the back of Siliezar's eyes, and said, "Yes. You will tell me how all this is to work."

Siliezar reached for the opened bottle of wine and poured himself another glass. He smiled at his guest and said: "But of course. That is why we are here."

Siliezar launched into a carefully scripted monologue on the geopolitical sweep of the Life Sciences Revolution. He spoke of its agenda, milestones and timetable. He discoursed on the state of the accelerated development of a global governance infrastructure to facilitate its great commercial possibilities for men like Piranchenko. He talked in headlines only, not wishing to confuse his guest. When he finished, as he expected, he was still at some distance from closing the sale.

A tuxedoed waiter arrived, sized up each man, offered off-menu suggestions, succeeded in securing two dinner orders and, perhaps on the counsel of his owner, departed quickly. When he was safely out of ear shot, Siliezar looked at Piranchenko and said, "What we are offering you, my friend, is *not* simply more billions in return for your investment." He shook his head amidst a wave of cognitive dissonance. "No, what we offer *you*, Vladimir Piranchenko, is this: a once in a lifetime opportunity to convert enormous wealth into even more enormous *power* in the new age of man."

The Russian smiled coyly. "Tell me of this power."

Siliezar fought off a ferocious temptation to tell his guest that he would be kept as far from the levers of actual power as the pope. "*You* will decide how much power you want," he replied cagily.

"And if I say, I want total power, what would you say to me?"

Siliezar's rise to power had proceeded in stages. He was born in Brazil of a Jewish mother and father of uncertain mid-Eastern origin sometime in or about 1952. Some had later claimed that his parents had changed their name and had been forced to leave the country of their origin, Germany, to evade Jewish bounty hunters.

It was said that as a child he experienced first-hand the scourge of anti-semitism, which forced his family to move seven times in the first eighteen years of his life. He told friends that he blamed the Catholic Church for inciting the pogroms that afflicted the small communities in which his family lived. Reportedly, his mother died under rather tragic circumstances. In the midst of the family's final flight to Argentina, she contracted malaria and was apparently unable to access medical assistance. He and his father buried her by the side of a road. Hanley Siliezar was eight years old.

He startled the advertising world in his early thirties by nimbly scaling the jungle that is Madison Avenue from an outpost in South America. Once in New York, he artfully leveraged the global power and reach of Free Masonry to become the most influential business-man in the world. Ultimately, he managed to transcend his business platform to become the architect and catalyst, and unrivaled global leader, of the Life Sciences Revolution. This Fourth Revolution was now being universally heralded as man's capstone revolution built on the achievements of the Industrial, Cultural, and Technological revolutions of the nineteenth and twentieth centuries.

Hanley Siliezar had no peer in the art of manipulation. He seemed to be born with extraordinary powers of intuition, and he had developed them assiduously in his business career, which spanned four decades and five continents. It was said he was able to discern a man's deepest yearnings within minutes of meeting him. Once known, he fed, nurtured, and cultivated clients with the artistry of a renowned maestro. Indeed, he regarded, as his singular triumph, his ability to attract otherwise powerful men, who had never quite gotten over feeling like outsiders in their youth, and convincing them they were now insiders in the greatest power game in the history of man.

"I would say to you that no single individual will be granted absolute power," he parried deftly, holding the other man's gaze. "The future of man is beyond the capability of a single man, *any* single man."

The Russian smiled. "And that would include Hanley Siliezar?"

"That would *absolutely* include Hanley Siliezar," Hanley Siliezar responded instantly.

The Russian nodded and attacked his plate. Siliezar picked at his squid. After several moments of silence the Russian looked up and said to Siliezar behind a cynical smile: "So, what is it Hanley Siliezar wants from this revolution he leads?"

Siliezar nodded. He hadn't expected this question from this man. "I want to extend the boundaries of man. This Revolution will do that. Man has been living in a self-imposed Dark Age from our beginnings. It has caused endless wars, disease, and human suffering on a scale that continues to grow in direct proportion to man's fertility."

He paused to briefly assess his guest's comprehension level. "The cause of this darkness is the 'Myth.' I speak of the belief that there is a benevolent Creator, somewhere, who rewards and punishes man to the degree he follows or ignores laws written into his own heart." He shook his head with vehemence. "This criminal creed must be exposed for what it is—a radical means of controlling the earth's population by a tiny minority who seek only wealth and power at the expense of the rest of us."

The Russian laughed mischievously and waved his fork at Siliezar "But *we . . . we* do not seek wealth and power?"

Siliezar stared hard and spoke softly. "No," he replied firmly. "We seek man's *liberation* from this . . . *incarceration.*"

He folded his hands and looked at his plate momentarily. When he raised his eyes he focused them on the Russian's dark pupils. He modulated his voice so it assumed an ethereal dimension that accentuated its natural rhythms and power. "I will speak to you businessman to businessman," he said evenly. The Russian's eyes widened. He understood he was about to hear what had brought him to this god-forsaken desert and to this table with this enigmatic man. He stopped eating. "Think of this Revolution, Vladimir, as our business model," he stopped and waited for an acknowledgement. It came immediately. "Think of our global governance infrastructure as our operating model." The Russian nodded imperceptibly. "Think of the alternative creed, the New Age creed, as our mission statement and guiding principles." Another slight nod from Piranchenko. "And think of our product, Vladimir," he paused for effect, "as Homo Evolutis."

Siliezar leaned across the table and whispered, "For me, Vladimir, it is *not* about wealth and power. It is about legacy." He sat back, and waited for the Russian to respond.

The Russian drank without taking his eyes off Siliezar. He poured himself another full glass of vodka. It would be his final glass before he boarded his private jet for the flight to Barcelona. He lifted the glass and motioned Siliezar to do the same. When Siliezar had lifted his glass, the Russian opened his mouth and said: "I salute you, Hanley Siliezar. You are a bold man." The Russian quickly drained his glass. Then he smiled and said, "Now about this power I am to have . . ."

They left, together. Forty minutes later, Hanley Siliezar had a commitment for one hundred million in U.S. currency with half due within ninety days; Vladimir Piranchenko had a 10 percent equity position in a patent code identified simply as H.E.

The Russian also departed with a seat on the new Global Governance Council. His portfolio would include the oversight of the integration of the Americas into an international consortium of regional governments under the auspices of the United Nations, the International Monetary Fund, and the World Court.

9

Bill Fregosi handed his boss a Guinness and quietly took a seat beside him in a rocking chair on the rectory porch. It was half past nine on a warm summer evening; a soft breeze carried a hint of rain. The two men rocked silently, attended only by a chorus of screeching cicadas serenading them from atop large oak trees. The trees arced toward the stars from a small parcel of land that adjoined the rectory, forming a lush green canopy for the Blessed Virgin's grotto some forty feet below.

Each man was alone with his thoughts. It had been four years since Fr. William Fregosi arrived as the new assistant pastor at St. Martha's in Narbrook. His was commonly referred to as a late vocation. He'd been an electrical engineer for a large chemical manufacturer in Delaware until he turned thirty. He felt a gentle tug one night in a small Catholic church about ten miles west of Philadelphia. A holy, powerfully built man was in the pulpit preaching the first night of a Triduum. Two months later he went to see this man about the tug that became a call. After a year of discernment, he entered St. John Chrysostom Seminary. He was

76 / BRIAN J. GAIL

ordained four years later. His first assignment returned him to his vocation's point of origin, working for the mentor who had become his superior.

"How are you doing, Bill?" John Sweeney asked after a protracted silence. His Guinness sat cupped in his hands, untouched.

"Can't wait for Saturday, John."

"What time you leaving?"

"Early," he smiled, "if my boss lets me."

John grunted. He didn't mind saying the 8:00 a.m. Mass on Saturday morning, *and* the 5:00 p.m. Mass on Saturday evening. His young associate needed the break. His mental and physical health had become an ongoing source of concern. "Just don't wake me on the way out, Billy Boy. Our 8:00 a.m. crowd would never forgive you."

Bill Fregosi laughed. It was a sound reminiscent of five and dime firecrackers going off and it delighted John Sweeney. "Wally picking you up?" Wally was Fr. John Wallingford, another late vocation John had mentored.

"Yep, at 6:00 a.m."

"How long a drive?"

"We ought to be out on the Vineyard in time for lunch," Bill replied, lifting his bottle in a small salute to spirit liberated.

John calculated driving time to Woods Hole, the destination of the ferry to Martha's Vineyard, the forty-five minute trip to the Island itself, and said: "It'll be a late lunch."

"John, we won't be bringing our watches."

"No, I don't suppose you will," John said as he sought his first taste of Mother Ireland. He envied his young associate. He loved the Vineyard, and had for many years made a pilgrimage of sorts in early autumn, when the grandeur of its foliage rendered a man mute in stunned homage. He hadn't traveled much in recent years. He joked with friends it was simply a matter of conserving what little energy he had left; but in truth his own spirit of adventure had taken flight some years back and had not returned. In his seventh decade of life and fifth decade of priestly ministry, his spirit both sought and found its refuge in the little community of his birth.

"How about you, John?" Bill Fregosi asked. "You planning anything?"

John Sweeney shook his head in the dark. "No," he said softly. "Not this year, Bill."

An awkward silence ensued. Bill Fregosi tiptoed into it with a simple, pregnant question. "What's going to happen, John?"

John Sweeney made a clumsy attempt to evade the question. "You're going to leave me alone with 875 families. You and Wallingford are going to have a wonderful time out on the Vineyard. Eventually you will run out of money and have to come home. Then I will own you and work you like a slave."

Fregosi laughed, "So who'd know the difference?" He grew serious again and half turned in his chair toward his superior and said, "You don't know where we go from here either, do you?"

John shook his head. "No, I do not," he said flatly. He reflected silently, and added: "Mankind appears to be in uncharted waters."

Fregosi exhaled loudly. "I thought we had actually turned a corner some years back." He had been in the seminary at the time of the Illumination and had watched with his classmates in astonishment as its aftershocks swelled their ranks.

John chose to reply indirectly. "I find myself thinking more and more of what Christ once said to the apostles—'When the Son of Man returns, will He find any faith left upon the earth?'"

Bill Fregosi nodded in silence before replying, "I worry about our families, John. I don't think they are prepared for a sudden downturn."

John had watched his young associate expend enormous energy and considerable personal capital building trust among the parish's young families. He was particularly proud that Bill Fregosi had accomplished this without compromising the uncompromising nature of the Gospel itself. "No, I am sure you are right, Bill," he replied quietly. "None of us is prepared for what it is to come."

"I see fear in the eyes of our young men, John."

"I believe that is because they see fear in the eyes of our old men," John replied matter-of-factly. "Your generation knows my generation sold them out long ago."

Fregosi intended to stay focused. "Our plumbers and electricians and carpenters tell me not only is their work drying up, they're having an increasingly hard time getting paid for the work they are doing."

"What's that about?" John asked pointedly.

"I don't know," Fregosi shrugged. "They say people will give them half, and promise to pay them the rest over time. Then they don't pay. The men think people are hoarding cash."

"That's not right!" John erupted. "'A workman is worth his wage.' Christ himself said that."

Fregosi was more interested in direction and less interested in dudgeon. "Our young white collar professionals see the bigger picture and they think they're road kill."

"What are they telling you?"

"They say even the tech sector is struggling. And, according to them, if the technology companies are off-shoring jobs, nobody is safe."

The inner workings of capitalism always befuddled John. He was driving a truck for his uncle when he felt a stirring in his heart to minister to men in His Master's name. He worked for an hourly wage, and he identified with men who did the same. His associate's experience was entirely different. Bill Fregosi had an undergraduate degree in electrical engineering from Lehigh University and an MBA from Wharton. He understood the laws of a market economy. If Fregosi was concerned, John told himself, then he ought to be concerned. "Do they say why our companies keep sending jobs overseas?" he probed.

"Yes," Fregosi responded quickly. "They say the emerging economies in Asia have started harvesting the investments they made years ago in their children's education, particularly in math and science. Their young people coming out of college are just as skilled as ours, maybe even more so, and they're willing to work for a lot less money."

"What kind of jobs are they taking from our kids?"

"High-end stuff," Fregosi replied. "We're not talking call centers anymore. There used to be this concept of a global hierarchy of technology work. All the serious value-added work—the research and development, the product innovation and design— that was all supposed to stay in the U.S. Everything else was supposed to be shipped out where it could be done by people in the developing countries at far less cost. But that's all changed now. Much of the best innovation is now coming from these emerging economies." He paused reflectively: "I think our schools have let our children down. The Guerra's and Gaudini's were forced to move out of the parish this spring because, in both cases, the men's jobs were shipped overseas. Rob Guerra was a software engineer and Frank Gaudini was a systems analyst."

John Sweeney groaned into a light mist that had just begun falling. "How can we help our families, Bill?"

Bill Fregosi took a moment to reply. "I just don't know what we can do, John. Most of our young families are trapped in credit card debt they can't repay with jobs that are disappearing in the night. The older families tell me they can't afford to get sick and they fear their IRAs will turn out to be worthless." He shrugged. "It just seems like we're kind of trapped."

"We have to prepare them," John replied with quiet resolve.

"I know, I know."

"Maybe when you get back we could plan something for after Labor Day."

Bill Fregosi made no attempt to hide his caution. "What are you thinking, John?"

"I don't know," John replied. "I really don't. But I know we just can't stand by and let our families go under."

"We're priests, John. Not financial planners," Bill pointed out discreetly.

"I know that, Bill," John retorted, slightly irritated. "But we must *do* something. Our people have to be prepared to give witness to the hope within." He reflected, and added: "And it is our job to help them do that." Suddenly, he rose on uncertain knees, looked at his assistant with affection and said: "And Bill, I believe our world will very shortly be in desperate need of their witness."

John Sweeney then turned and headed for his darkened church.

10

"Goombah."

"Shamrock."

"I want to sell."

"Don't *want* if you don't *need*, Michael. Not in this market."

Michael Burns nodded into the phone. Once he charted a course of action, he brooked neither dissent nor delay. "Joe, put it up." Brief pause for effect, then, "Today."

Joseph Donato wanted to reach through the phone and strangle his boyhood friend. His recklessness scared him in their youth, and the advance of years had not in any material way tempered it. "Okay, Michael," he replied sullenly. "We're going to reverse the numbers. You paid $5.2 million 10 years ago. We'll go out at $2.5 million and hope for the best."

Michael Burns felt the pain of a rusted out samurai sword pierce his heart. His palatial home on the most private lagoon in Ocean City, New Jersey, had been his refuge from the growing pressures of the newspaper business. It was also his family's summer retreat. His five children came and went all summer long. The three girls who were married brought grandchildren, five in total, whom Michael treasured—principally because he regarded their obstreperous natures as his revenge on their mothers.

Selling the home would be difficult enough, and it was sure to cause him no end of trouble within the family. The girls planned summers around their coordinated trips down to the shore, once school let out. His sons came down, when their work schedules permitted, to fish and surf and, mostly, drink beer on the dock and watch an orange sun slip slowly from a magenta sky into the bay. Worst of all, when he told his wife she simply registered acute pain, and said nothing.

Selling any asset, much less a home, at a significant loss caused *him* acute pain. The considerable success he had enjoyed in his business career was attributable, in his judgment, to a good sense of timing. He had a knack for seeing things develop before most other men. When he moved, he moved quickly, decisively, impatiently. And, ever confident, he was not afraid to bet on his ability to exploit opportunities he chose to believe were uniquely his to exploit. Occasionally, those bets were indeed quite large. But, always, they had paid out, returning profits in equally large multiples.

This would be the first that did not. He knew immediately he couldn't rationalize $2.7 million in lost value away. The terrible reality of his loss began to work its way through his volatile system, absorbing a good measure of his clarity and buoyancy. "$2.5, Joe,?" he repeated quietly.

"Still want to do it, Michael?"

Painful pause, then, "I've got to do it, Joe."

"Why, whyyougottadoit, Shamrock?" Joe Donato repeated, staccato, in first generation dialect.

"Because I do," Michael replied evenly. "I just do."

A painful, protracted silence filled the small black cable lines between Philadelphia and South Jersey. Michael was keenly embarrassed to reveal his motivation, fearing ridicule. His friend understood. You didn't retain a sixty-year friendship with a man like Michael Burns without mastering the art of indirection.

"Hey, Shamrock," he bellowed into the silence. "Did I tell you about my Big Cat?"

Michael immediately welcomed the diversion. "You been bottom feeding again, Giuseppe?"

"Yep."

"What little toy have you stolen now . . . and from whom?"

Joe Donato laughed easily. "I think he's onto me, Franny" he yelled to his wife. Michael immediately understood Franny Donato may or may not be within hearing distance of her husband.

"How big?" Michael inquired.

"Thirty-seven feet, with a twenty-foot beam."

"How old?"

"Seventeen, but the engine's only got fifteen hundred hours on her."

"How much?"

"Little over half a million."

"Ouch! Okay," Michael said with a theatrical sigh. "Tell me about her."

"She's a Lagoon Catamaran. Three staterooms, a nine kilowatt generator, a tricked-up galley, two heads, three showers, state of the art GPS with an auto pilot."

"That'll come in handy," Michael needled, "when Franny decides she's had just about enough of you and heads for home."

Donato laughed. "That could happen the day we pick her up."

"Where is this big kitten now?"

"Puerto Rico."

"Puerto Rico!?" Michael half yelled. "What the hell are you doing stealing from a Puerto Rican?"

"Who said I was buying from a Puerto Rican?" Joe Donato replied a bit defensively.

Michael backtracked awkwardly. "I did, and I was kidding, Goombah." He paused to let the moment slip into the ether. "How you gonna get down there to get her?"

"Uh . . . there be airplanes, Burns," Donato replied in a semi-theatrical dumb down. "I thought it best to fly down, take possession of my boat, then sail it away." He paused. "You know, rather than do it the Irish way."

Michael Burns laughed and immediately felt some of his tension evaporate. "So, where you gonna sail to, Fiji?"

"St. John in the U.S. Virgin Islands," Joe answered matter-of-factly.

"Oh!" Michael replied, surprised: "Why St. John?"

"We're gonna moor her in Great Cruise Bay on the leeward side of the island."

"Beautiful spot," Michael said with more than a hint of envy.

"We'll provision up in St. Thomas and just explore the islands one by one," Joe offered.

"How long you gonna be down there," Michael inquired.

There was an awkward silence. "They're gonna bury us at sea, Michael," Joe Donato replied quietly.

The full import of what he was hearing settled slowly in Michael Burns' distracted mind. "Are you saying you're not coming back, Joe?" he asked, incredulous.

"I am indeed saying that, Michael."

Michael was sorely tempted to get in his car and drive the fifty minutes from his office to his friend's home across the lagoon and implore him to reconsider. Instead, he got up, closed the door to his office, and returned to the sitting area with its large bay of windows overlooking the city of Philadelphia. "Joe, Joe . . . you still there?"

"Shamrock, would I leave before you dismissed me?"

Michael laughed despite himself. "Joe, talk to me," he whispered into the phone. "What's going on?"

"Michael, the boys are settled in Florida and New Zealand," he replied. "The real estate business everywhere, especially the second home market, is in the crapper." He paused ever so slightly and added, "Just where the country is headed."

Michael's heart began to pound. "What are you seeing, Goombah?"

Joe Donato laughed. "Hey, I'm a reader of the *Thorn!*"

Michael sobered quickly. *My God, people are acting on what I'm writing in this newspaper! Am I responsible for what happens to them?* "Joe, are you leaving the country because . . ." his voice trailed off.

"Yes," Joe Donato replied. "We're leaving the country because Franny and I don't want to be here when the you-know-what hits the fan. And it's coming, Michael. Quickly. Everyone with eyes to see knows that."

Michael fell uneasily into silent shock. After several moments he stood, walked to the windows, and looked at the lunch crowd flowing out of the city's tall buildings and onto its narrow streets. He tried to imagine what chaos would look like. He was unable to do so. "Joe, so you're selling too?"

"Already did," he replied cheerfully.

"Really, what did you get?"

"1.8 million."

Silence. "Joe, how could you let that place go for that!?"

"Time to get out of Dodge, Shamrock."

"When you pulling out?"

"Thanksgiving."

"My God that's only . . . what . . . six weeks away!"

"Seven, but who's counting," Joe replied with a laugh.

Michael fell silent again. Then, "Joe, I'm selling for the same reason. I want to set up on the Chesapeake."

"Figured as much."

"My God, am I *that* transparent!?"

Joe Donato laughed. "Well, we do go back a ways, don't we?"

Silence. "Joe, what am I gonna walk away from the table with?" Michael asked softly.

"My friend, you do not want to hear what I must tell you."

Michael Burns gritted his teeth. "Speak."

"Okay, brace yourself," Joe replied. "I'll get you between $2 million and $2.2 million; after paying me, the municipality, and the state, you will be very happy to leave the island with a check in your hand for close to $2 million."

Michael Burns cursed and rolled into a profane rant that stripped at least one coat of paint off the walls of his office. Joe Donato placed the phone on his desk, hit mute, and went back to his computer. Right on cue, ninety seconds later, he hit the mute button again, and heard silence. Vesuvius was at rest.

"Welcome to the *new* United States of America, Michael," he offered cheerfully. "You are not alone, my friend. That's why Franny and I are prepared to spend the rest of our lives on a boat ducking hurricanes. In the new America, there is no more economic value, or stability, left for people like us . . . or our children."

Michael was now sweating profusely. He had anticipated taking a haircut. He did not count on having his head shaved. He had zeroed in on a twelve hundred–acre farm on the Eastern Shore of the Chesapeake, somewhere below the Sassafras River. The spread was worth five million dollars but it was said the owner would take three million in cash in a quick, no-strings-attached transaction. Michael had assumed, incorrectly it was now clear, that he would be able to just roll the lagoon transaction over and have it secure what he viewed as a family escape hatch on the Chesapeake.

Apparently, unimaginably, he needed a Plan B. That meant putting his main home on Philadelphia's storied Main Line on the market too. It amounted to little more than a fire sale of his most treasured assets. Very suddenly, Michael Burns was not a happy man.

"Joe, just sell it," he said tersely. "The sooner, the better."

"Furniture, Michael?"

"Comes with the house," he instructed. "I don't want any of it."

"Okay," Joe Donato replied. He paused and said, "You okay, Shamrock?"

"No, Joe. I'm *not* okay," Michael answered. "I am outraged at what my generation has done to this country. We have ruined it. We are the most arrogant, delusional, narcissistic generation in American history. And we have left our children and grandchildren to fend for themselves in the ruins of an empire that didn't have to fall."

This was greeted by a silence well familiar for its post rant awkwardness. Into it, from a safe distance, tiptoed Joe Donato: "Yeah, but Woodstock was a blast, wasn't it?"

Michael Burns started to sputter. It was Joe Donato's cue to exit. "Gotta go, Shamrock," he said brightly. "Just got a premiere listing. Call you when I've got something for you. Best to Carole." Click.

Michael looked at the dead phone in his hand. Then he turned and threw it across the room. It hit a family portrait hanging on the opposite wall, denting it and knocking it askew, before falling, broken, to the floor.

His secretary, Marie Esposito, rushed in breathless. "Michael, are you okay?" In the silence, she saw and understood.

"How can I help, Michael?" she asked gently.

"Get me Carole. Get me Prudential Fox Roach. And get me Patrick, in that order," he replied grimly. He looked at the woman who had aged in office with him during his advertising and publishing careers, and his mood changed. She had him and no one else. He hadn't given a moment's thought to her well-being. Suddenly ashamed, he averted her eyes and said, "And thank you, Marie."

"Anything I can help with?" she probed quietly.

He shook his head. "No, not now," he replied. "I've got to figure a few things out, and when I do I'll cut you in." He looked up and forced a smile. The look on Marie Esposito's face signaled him that he had only succeeded in increasing her level of concern. "Promise," he added. She too forced a smile and departed.

When she arrived at her desk she reached for the phone. The first call was to Michael's wife who, she knew from long experience, would want a heads up. The final call was to his son, who would also ask of her to what did he owe the pleasure of a call from his fabled father.

The sound of a phone ringing caused Marie Esposito to shift uncomfortably in her chair. She felt an unfamiliar awkwardness, even embarrassment. On this call, she was simply not in a position to offer either mother or son advance notice of the patriarch's agenda.

11

The sudden sound of the front door buzzing startled Maggie Gillespie and her daughter Grace Seltzer.

"You expecting someone, honey?" Maggie said turning to her daughter.

"No, Mom." Grace replied. "Let me go see who it is."

The St. Gianna Clinic in Narbrook operated by appointment. Most appointments were scheduled in the afternoon and early evening. It was a little after 9:00 a.m. on a wintry morning and none of the doctors or clinicians had arrived yet.

Grace opened the door to what once had been St. Martha's elementary school, but now was the only Natural Family Planning clinic on Philadelphia's Main Line. She was surprised to see a young African American girl of perhaps eighteen standing alone in the rain, her hair matted and her clothes damp.

"Honey, please come in! You'll catch your death of cold standing out there like that," Grace pleaded.

The young girl entered without saying a word. Once inside she blew on her hands and trembled. She looked at Grace, eyes wide and vacant. Grace immediately left to get a blanket, returned, and draped it around the girl's slender shoulders. She hugged her and said: "Honey, what's your name?"

The girl replied "Tamika," without looking up.

"Well, Tamika, come inside and sit by the radiator, and let me see if I can get you some dry clothes."

The girl seemed reluctant to follow. Grace reached for her hand. Slowly, cautiously, the girl took it and allowed herself to be led into an unoccupied office. Grace flicked the lights on and directed the girl to a wooden chair adjacent to a hissing radiator. She encouraged the girl to sit, and when she did, awkwardly, Grace smiled and said: "Now, I can either bring you a cup of coffee or a cup of tea. Which would you prefer?"

The girl looked up and said: "Do you have a coke?"

Grace laughed and replied: "And let me guess, you want plenty of ice, right?"

The girl did not respond.

Grace went to the kitchen and returned with a can of coke, a cup of ice, a cherry Danish . . . and her mother. Maggie Gillespie held a dry change of clothes over her left arm and handed them to the young girl without waiting for an introduction. "Hello, Tamika. I'm Maggie," she said.

"Tamika, this is my mom," Grace said. "We're going to get you out of those clothes. Follow me."

She led the girl to a small changing room at the end of the first floor hallway. She entered, went to the window, and drew the curtain and drapery. She turned to Tamika and said, "Honey, just leave your wet clothes here. We'll get them washed and dried before you leave. When you're ready, just come back and see us, okay?"

The girl nodded and immediately started undressing. Her innocence surprised Grace who averted her eyes reflexively before taking her leave.

In a matter of minutes, the girl found her way back to the office where Maggie and Grace sat awaiting her return. She stood self-consciously in the doorway, anticipating direction. "Come,"

Maggie said, arising from her seat to greet her and extending an arm around the girl's narrow waist. "Are you sure you wouldn't like something warm to drink on this nasty morning?" she asked.

The girl shook her head and took a seat opposite the two older women. She dropped her eyes and stared at the floor. Grace moved the table upon which sat the small tray of food closer to the girl. Haltingly, the girl reached for the can of coke and opened it and drank from it. She eyed the Danish pastry as though it were something exotic. She reached with her right forefinger and thumb to extract a small sample. Inspecting it closely she then opened her mouth and quickly swallowed it. Her eyes cast light for the first time. She reached for the rest of the Danish, lifting it off the plate with her fingers and consumed its entirety in three bites. She quickly reached for the can of coke and consumed its remains. Looking up for the first time, she smiled at Grace and Maggie.

"Tamika, how long has it been since you've eaten?" Maggie asked.

The girl looked down at her feet and shrugged.

"Tamika, where do you live?" Grace asked.

The girl looked out the window and said: "West Philly."

"Where in West Philly?" Grace inquired.

"44th and Springfield," she answered warily.

"Do you live with your family, Tamika?" Maggie asked gently.

"Yeah."

"Brothers and sisters?" Grace asked.

The girl shrugged and nodded. "Yeah, I got four brothers and . . . um . . . two . . . no, three sisters."

Maggie and Grace exchanged glances. "Well, Tamika, we are so happy to meet you," Maggie said. "Thank you for coming to see us. How can my daughter and I help you?"

The girl pulled a crumpled piece of newspaper from her pocket and opened it. "It says here y'all help people with fertility problems."

Grace reached for the moist clump and opened it methodically so as not to tear it. She inspected it, nodded, looked at her mother, and said: "It's one of our Main Line *Times* ads, Mom."

Maggie decided not to ask the girl how the Main Line's only weekly newspaper, which carried one of their infrequent advertisements, had made its way to 44th and Springfield. "Do you have a fertility problem, Tamika?" she asked instead, matter-of-factly.

"Yeah," she replied. "I get pregnant too much."

Silence.

Grace probed. "Are you pregnant now, Tamika?"

"Yeah."

"How many other children do you have, Tamika?" Maggie inquired.

The girl looked at her with suspicion. "None," she replied.

In the ensuing silence Maggie and Grace would later discover they were thinking similar thoughts. It was clear to both women that information from the thin girl on the chair in front of them would have to be extracted in the manner of diseased molars.

Maggie sat erect in the manner of a mother preparing to address a troublesome child. "Now, Tamika, please tell us why you came to see us this morning. How can my daughter and I be of help to you?"

The girl looked at the ground and pawed it in small circles with her right foot. Without looking up, she said, "Y'all carry that abortion pill?"

Maggie tensed. *She's asking for mifepristone.* She looked at Grace who shook her head involuntarily. "No," Maggie replied tersely.

"How come?" the girl asked, curiosity suddenly piqued.

"Because we are a clinic that is committed to life, not death" Grace interjected. "The little life you carry, Tamika, is a gift from God. We help women like you carry their children to term . . . and find good homes for them . . . not discard them."

"But I can't go home with this thing," the girl replied as her eyes filled. "My momma will throw me out."

"Did she tell you that, Tamika?" Maggie asked.

"Yeah," the girl answered. "She told me, 'no mo.'"

Grace decided against asking how many other children the girl had aborted. *Not relevant*, she admonished herself. "Tamika, we know people who will allow you to live with them until you deliver your child; and even *after* you've delivered," Grace said softly. "There are other girls living there too. Some have small children, and others are expecting mothers like you."

She paused to assess the girl's reaction. She couldn't read it. "And when you deliver your child, if you decide you're just not able to provide an adequate home, even with the help they will provide, they will help you find a good family for your little one."

The girl's eyes widened. "Who would do that?"

"There are a lot of very generous people in this world, Tamika," Maggie replied. "Some are young couples who desperately want to have children, and can't."

"White people?"

"White and black, Tamika," Grace answered. "If you want to place your child with a black couple, there are many who would be very grateful to even be considered."

The girl responded to this information with surprise. "Where is this home?" she asked.

"In Darby," Grace replied. "How 'bout I take you down there so you can meet Mrs. Quinn. You will love her, won't she Mom?"

Maggie did not reply. She was studying the young girl in front of her intently. The girl felt the weight of the silent appraisal, looked at Maggie and said, "You don't like me, do you?"

"No, I don't *like* you" Maggie replied with the hint of a smile. "I *love* you!" She got up and walked over to the girl and hugged her. "Don't destroy the little child, Tamika. God gave you this precious gift for a reason."

The girl started to cry. In an instant her tiny body was convulsing. "I don't want to go home," she wailed. "My momma's boyfriend will beat me if they finds out I'm pregnant again."

Grace looked at her Mother. "Tamika, you can stay with us," she said softly. "We have plenty of room, don't we Mother?"

The girl stopped crying with an abruptness that surprised both women. She looked at Grace and said: "Can't y'all just give me that pill? That's the onliest thing gonna work for me."

Maggie cast a resolute look at the girl. "We don't carry those pills, Tamika," she said evenly. "It's not who we are and what we do." She studied the girl intently. "I'm sure there are places that *do* carry them, but we don't know where they are." She paused and added. "And to be completely honest, even if we did know, we could not in good conscience tell you where to go to get them. That would make *us* complicit in the killing of your child." She leaned closer to the girl. "And, honey, there is no one on the face of this earth that could encourage us, or force us, to do that."

The girl, now dry eyed, looked at Maggie and said, "Then you won't help me?"

"Yes," Maggie replied emphatically. "We will not only help *you*, we will also help your child."

The girl looked from mother to daughter and back. Then she got up and without another word, walked out of the office and out of the clinic.

Grace, stunned, looked at her mother and said: "What was *that*?"

Maggie narrowed her eyes and said, "I don't know, honey. I really don't know."

12

Vennitti Inc. Chairman and CEO Geoff Benton was nervous. It was an unfamiliar feeling for an iconic businessman reported to be worth almost a billion dollars. The problem at the moment was currency devaluation. A net personal worth of nearly one billion U.S. dollars was no longer sufficient to make the current Forbes 400 list of the World's Richest Men. This left him and his wife disconsolate during Saturday evening's Spring Cotillion at the Greenwich Country Club in Connecticut. They'd counted no less than twelve club members who had made this year's list, up from ten a year ago. Benton's wife, his third—this one twenty years his junior—confessed to feelings of "inadequacy."

Geoff Benton was nervous, because the men who could vault him to the pinnacle of that list for a very long time were now seated before him. It was a balmy day in Zurich, Switzerland, and the men in the drawing room of the Four Seasons Hotel penthouse suite had arrived the evening before on private planes. Over a late dinner they'd talked a good deal about the kind of personal wealth that was beyond the reach of many small countries. Benton felt their subtle disdain when he tried to redirect the conversation to either himself or other men he knew on the list. As one suggested with a hint of impatience: "We're talking here about men whose actual wealth, as opposed to reported wealth, *transcends* lists."

Benton was invited to the Global Governance Council Summit, the GGCS, as a fully vested business leader. As such, he was there ostensibly to provide counsel. In his mind, however, he was there primarily to make a sale. His patron and largest individual stockholder, Hanley Siliezar, had convened the meeting and, as a fig leaf for both of them, cast it with a broader agenda. It was officially a "Milestones" agenda—a kind of high level progress report on the Life Science Revolution's key deliverables.

In the room with Benton and Siliezar was Nicholas Kubosvak of Poland, who ran the International Monetary Fund, better known as simply the IMF. Dag Schoenbrun of Austria, who headed up the World Court, was present, as was Kimbe Motumbo, the Secretary General of the United Nations. There were three other gentlemen Geoff Benton only knew by reputation. One was a very tall Russian oligarch by the name of Vladimir Piranchenko; another was a very round Saudi sheik by the name of Musa Bin Alamin; the third was a Chinese gentleman, Lu Xiaoping, who was said to run a private hedge fund for Beijing's elite. Benton noted there were no interpreters in the meeting.

Siliezar was at the podium. He was introducing the new players with a mixture of gravity and wit that gave his de facto summit the feeling of a corporate retreat. It was early, 7:06 a.m. Swiss time, which, Benton noted, probably indicated it was in fact 7:06 p.m.

His mental acuity was heightened by the sound of his name on Hanley Siliezar's golden tongue. "Let me now introduce the famous Geoff Benton of Vennitti Inc. He has some very important work that he wishes to share with us this morning. Geoffrey." Siliezar spread his arms wide as though to envelope Benton upon his arrival at the podium, but by the time he arrived at the podium Siliezar was already seated in a wide, well cushioned captain's chair in the front row next to the sheik. Siliezar's smile would charm a bowl of milk from a kitten, Benton thought as he watched Siliezar take his seat . . . and, as he privately assured himself, knowing Siliezar as he did, he had no doubt that somewhere along the line he had done precisely that.

Benton turned the small light on at the podium and was surprised by its strength. He recoiled imperceptibly. He immediately looked up to see if his ever so subtle retreat was observed by the men seated in front of him. He was chagrined to note that it had been ever so keenly observed. The Russian smiled and said, "You are the man who sells light bulbs to the world, yet you are surprised when they work! What have you come to sell *us* today?" The sound of spontaneous laughter enveloped him and threatened to dampen his mood from the outset. He vowed in that instant that he would channel his irritation to productive ends and close the sale he had come to make within that very hour.

He waited for the laughter to die out, and looked at the Russian and said evenly, "Vladimir, I have not come to sell anyone, anything. I am here to show you a prototype of an innovation that will permit this council to usher in The New Age of Man. You can always reject this work, or purchase the patent outright and choose another corporation to take it to market." The Russian said nothing. Benton glanced quickly at Siliezar who was grimacing. He felt a flash of regret. *So much for international diplomacy. Since when does the head of a U.S. multinational have to cater to a ranking member of the old Soviet Kleptocracy?*

"I must be candid," he said in an attempt to recover his footing. "I would not be here if I wasn't excited about this." He held an all but invisible ring between his thumb and forefinger. Its circumference was no more than half the circumference of his pinkie. He reached into his left coat pocket and removed a small compartmentalized case the size of glass case. In it were twelve small vaginal rings made of latex. He removed seven of them, one at a time, handed one to each of the men in the room, and continued his explanation. "This is a vaginal ring. Any woman, of any age, can insert this ring herself in the privacy of her own room or bathroom without difficulty. The ring releases a sufficient supply of hormones that will prohibit conception." He noted their surprise and wondered if Siliezar had done the off-line stakeholdering he had requested. "Where we tested it, the men were unaware of its existence. We are prepared to distribute one billion of these to women of child rearing age in the *un*developed world within 90 days. We estimate 70 percent to 80 percent compliance within one year."

"What about the developed world?" asked Bin Alamin with a hint of distemper.

Geoff Benton reached into his other coat pocket and withdrew another case. He opened it, extracted another small ring, held it up, and smiled. "This is what we have for the *developed* world, Musa." He began circulating them among the men, handing each one a slightly larger ring. "This ring contains a microscopic pair of rods that will release the exact same quantity of hormones as the other ring," he said staring down Bin Alamin. "We are prepared to distribute up to one billion of those to women of child rearing age in the developed world within six months. And we will expect 100 percent compliance within three years."

"Total compliance! How is such a thing possible?" asked Kimbe Motumbo.

"It will be required," came a voice from the front. It belonged to Hanley Siliezar.

"And who is it who has the power to punish those who feel no such requirement in the West?" asked Vladimir Piranchenko.

Siliezar stood and moved slowly to the front of the room. He stopped next to Benton. "It is not a matter of punishment, Vladimir," he said quietly. "It is a matter of inducement." He held the two small rings up for all to see. "You will note these two devices give every appearance of being the same." He smiled. "They are not." He paused and walked closer to the chairs. "Both prevent the conception of costly and burdensome children that our world can no longer afford. But only one, this one," he held the larger ring devised for women in the developed world above his head "this one will permit women to do everything the Lock will permit men to do." He smiled coyly. "In the West the woman thinks she is man. She must have what the man has. So we will give her what we give her man."

"And what is it we are giving her?" asked Dag Schoenbrun.

"Everything," replied Siliezar, his eyes dark and animated. He put the two small rings in his left hand, reached into his left vest pocket with his right hand, and withdrew a small wafer thin chip the size of a man's thumbnail. He held it up and said, "This chip, our Golden Lock, will permit men in the developed world to access their medical records, to transact on the internet and in retail stores, and of course travel across international borders." He looked at Schoenbrun directly. The vaginal ring for women in the West will contain thirty-two molecular nanobots that will permit them to do the very same thing—everything—the men will be able to do."

Siliezar turned to the Russian. "These . . . privileges . . . are something men in the developed world will queue in long lines to secure, Vladimir. And believe me when I say this," he paused to change his intonation, ducking his chin as he did so. "This chip will greatly exceed the demand for the iPhone and every other form of retail technology known to man."

Standing next to Siliezar, Benton began to fidget. This was *his* presentation. He was not accustomed to being interrupted. Nevertheless, Siliezar was a master pitchman, and he did very much need to leave this room with a multibillion dollar sale that would, in effect, create a profit annuity for him as Vennitti's CEO. The patent on these innovations alone was worth tens of billions, he calculated. The contract to distribute both vaginal rings and the chip promised to keep him in that chair as long as he wished. And Geoffrey Benton, at sixty-six years old, currently had no plans for retirement.

"Now, let me point out the obvious," Benton interrupted in an attempt to retrieve the floor. He offered a gracious but nonetheless dismissive nod to Siliezar, who offered a courtly nod in return and went to his seat. "When you are producing a billion units of anything, you have rather significant economies of scale." He paused and smiled. "So while *one* of these vaginal rings would cost over one thousand U.S. dollars to manufacture, the cost for *one billion* is less than a single U.S. dollar per unit."

Vladimir Piranchenko applauded reflexively. The others simply looked at him without comment.

"Will the chip for men carry contraceptive chemicals?" Bin Alamin asked.

"No," Benton replied quickly. "We see no reason to build in unnecessary cost. The vaginal rings will be 100 percent effective in preventing pregnancy."

There was a brief silence. "Aren't we feeding into discredited twentieth century stereotypes?" Schoenbrun asked.

"How so?" Benton replied, clearly puzzled.

"The woman must submit herself to this . . . indignity, to which the man is not subjected?" Schoenbrun replied.

Benton felt the hair on the nape of his neck rise. With difficulty he suppressed his natural inclination to respond caustically to impertinence. "Mr. Secretary," he said patiently, "this will *not* be a procedure that causes either pain or shame to women. Women will welcome it. They are used to invasive procedures that quite often do *not* work. This is hardly invasive. They themselves will administer it in the privacy of their own homes and it actually *will* work . . . without, I might add, carcinogenic and environmentally disastrous side effects."

Benton stood erect. Even well into his sixties he was still a formidable presence in every room he entered. "My friends and colleagues, I would not come here and ask you to approve anything that has not been thoroughly tested. I make my living in the most regulated industry, in the most regulated country in the world. Allow me, please, to show you what we have learned from women in *both* the developed and developing nations about the use of these vaginal rings."

Geoffrey Benton turned and clicked his remote in the direction of a wall behind him. A large screen descended from the ceiling. He clicked again and the lights in the room dimmed. He loosened his tie unselfconsciously and began. Some twenty-two minutes later, he finished. His presentation offered a brief history of the development of the nanotechnology of the vaginal rings, a graphic illustration of a woman inserting the ring in rural India, and another woman inserting the alternate ring in metropolitan London. This was followed by an extended sequence of women from rural India, China, metropolitan Europe, and America appearing on camera to talk about their experiences.

The men in the room heard what they needed to hear. Both rings, the faces on camera told them, were easy to insert and uniquely effective. The women in the developing world explained that they could no longer bear the cost of children. The women in the developed world explained that they could no longer bear the disruption of their lives and careers that children occasioned. Each group of women reported that the facts that the ring could be painlessly inserted in a matter of seconds, that its unit cost was less than a U.S. dollar, that it would be effective for up to one year, were all compelling reasons to embrace it as a safety net for unrestricted sex.

The men in Zurich also took note that the women in the developed world were particularly delighted to learn that the nanotechnology in their vaginal ring would permit them to have all the "privileges" men would have, without having to submit to an invasive procedure in a doctor's office. They particularly welcomed the nanobots within the ring that would allow them to simply access a touch pad to travel and transact, suggesting this alone was cause for great joy in their intergenerational fight for gender equality.

The presentation reached its conclusion with a final slide that proposed an aggressive timeline for the technology's introduction throughout the world. Benton pushed a button on the podium that caused the screen to ascend, and another that caused the lights in the room to come back up, and paused. "Any questions?"

"Yes," replied the cryptic Russian. "What do you need from us?"

It was precisely the buying signal Geoffrey Benton was waiting for. "I need a loan," he smiled. "Two billion U.S. from the IMF," he said nodding toward Kubosvak.

"Suppose I want to buy the patent?" the Russian inquired.

Benton felt his knees buckle. He was suddenly limp. He found it difficult to hide the degree of sheer excitement now quickening his pulse and heart. Before he could open his mouth to reply, he heard another voice. "We, too, would like to bid for this patent." It was Xiaoping. Benton turned to the voice and saw a level of resolve in the Chinese gentlemen's eyes that he had never before encountered. *My God, a freakin' auction! I'm a freakin' genius. Wait till the Board hears this.* He turned to Kubosvak and said: "Ah, forget the loan, Nicky." He immediately heard a guffaw and recognized its source, Hanley Siliezar.

Shamelessly, Benton turned to the sheik and said, "You want in on this too, Musa?"

"Perhaps," Bin Alamin replied, unsmiling.

Hanley Siliezar jumped to his feet and strode to the front of the room and said, "You have made your sale, Geoffrey. Let's table the patent transaction for now and get back to our agenda."

Benton smiled graciously and took his seat in the second row of large chairs. Within forty-five seconds, he received two notes. One note was handed to him by the man directly in front of him, Lu Xiaoping. There were no words on the paper, only a number. The number was fifty billion dollars. The other was from the sheik. It, too, contained a number. The number was seventy-five billion. Benton made a few calculations in his head. He computed his personal take from a patent sale, given his corporate compensation structure. He then added that number to what he knew would be his personal take from the manufacture and distribution of the technology approved in this meeting. He looked at his watch. It was not yet 8:00 a.m. Zurich time. He had been on his feet a little over forty minutes. When he stood, he was not among the Forbes

400 richest men in the world. By the time he had taken his seat, he was now assured of being among the wealthiest of them.

He kicked back in his chair and slipped his shoes off, undetected. He further loosened his tie and rolled up his shirt sleeves. He set his nimble mind on auto pilot. He would catnap, eyes half closed, through the rest of the agenda. It was a skill he had developed while sitting through the interminable presentations of "staff" executives whose presentations generally followed the "line" executives. Like all CEOs, he paid careful attention to what the line executives had to say. They represented his profit centers.

The sound of a door opening caught the attention of most of the men. They turned to find a handsome young Four Seasons executive of Middle Eastern descent entering the room. He sought out Hanley Siliezar and handed him a note. Siliezar's eyes widened in seeming disbelief as he read the note. When he finished, he closed his eyes and appeared to be praying. The room was perfectly still. Siliezar opened his eyes and said with uncharacteristic fervor, "There is a God." He smiled and reported: "Northern California experienced an 8.8 mega quake one hour ago. Preliminary reports indicate San Francisco is gone." He paused and intoned, "That would mean Silicon Valley is also gone." He smiled and glanced again at the note in his hands. "The San Andreas Fault Line appears to have been sundered, all but dividing the state in two."

There was a sudden and eerie silence. It was followed by a small roar of approval that Benton found startling in both its fervor and its decibel level. The young hotel executive was now staring directly at him awaiting a reaction. Benton was numb. He had a son from his first marriage who ran a small technology hedge fund in San Francisco. That son and his wife of twelve years lived in Marin County and had two sons, ages ten and eight.

Siliezar looked directly at Bin Alamin and said, "America has lost its entire innovation community. She is no longer America." He paused and added, "Now we need to take out its capital structure. Are you prepared to take action?"

Bin Alamin stood and turned to the others in the room. He

was perhaps 5'8" tall and very nearly three hundred pounds. His face was dark and menacing even in repose. "We are prepared. We will proceed. New York will go the way of California within forty days." He sat down abruptly.

Benton jumped to his feet. "Forty days! We can't move that fast."

Siliezar eyed him coolly. "Geoffrey, we've been pressing you for contingency plans for over three years. You have resisted us. We will wait no longer. We need you to get your key people, your patent archives, and your corporate databases transferred to London within thirty days." He paused and looked through Benton and said with manifest disdain, "And I know I don't have to remind you that Vennitti Inc. stands to gain from this business too. It was you, was it not Geoffrey, who personally approved the sale of special inverters the Pakistani's required to drive ultracentrifuges in their uranium enrichment plant?" He paused and added with impatience, "We don't need to go there, do we?"

"I need ninety days," Benton bluffed, sullenly. "Our families . . . the dislocation . . . it takes time. We will require more time."

Siliezar canvassed the room without saying a word. It was a skill unique to him. He could tell what other men were thinking simply by reading their eyes. "Alright, you have sixty days," he said tersely. He looked at Bin Alamin, who nodded in silent assent. "Now, Musa," he said forcefully, to reassert his authority, "tell me about the dry run."

Bin Alamin made no attempt to stand this time. He simply looked at Siliezar and said matter-of-factly, "We have had two dry runs in the past two months. We are confident. I will say nothing more."

Benton was surprised and a bit ashamed to find his mind was now focused, not on getting over two hundred people and assorted digital archives and databases moved to London within sixty days, but instead ruminating about the precipitous decline in the value of the U.S. dollar in the wake of the carnage, actual and planned, on both coasts. Within moments he realized there was no way to calculate the likely impact on his personal wealth. He would simply have to move all his personal assets to Zurich and hope for the best.

"Will Bin Alamin's men strike the American capital?" asked Dag Schoenbrun of no one in particular. All heads turned to Bin Alamin. It was immediately clear that the Sheik had spoken his last.

"No," Siliezar replied abruptly. "It will not be necessary." He paused and said, "Men, are there any other questions?"

The room was silent.

"Good," Siliezar concluded. "Then I suggest we adjourn immediately and fly back to our respective countries." Heads began to nod.

Siliezar smiled and scanned the room. "If we delay, people may accuse us of having the power to create natural disasters." The men laughed, and started to chirp like birds that had discovered a previously undetected food source.

"Who knew there really is a God," declared Hanley Siliezar to another spasm of laughter, as the men quickly gathered their things and filed out of the room.

13

The congregation filed slowly into the small church on Narbrook Avenue like disemboweled zombies. To their pastor, watching from the sacristy, the tableau presented a palpable sense of the surreal. It was a moment that somehow seemed to exist outside time.

John Sweeney was acutely aware that a number of his parishioners had family or friends among the estimated 1,817,000 men, women, and children reported dead or missing along the San Andreas Fault, which had previously formed the tectonic boundary between the Pacific Plate to the west and the North American Plate to the east.

The epicenter was reportedly somewhere between Mussel Rock, in the Pacific, and Bolinas Lagoon, several miles north of Stinson in Marin County. The quake apparently set off a series of smaller but quite destructive quakes among "sister faults" in and around San Francisco Bay. Significant damage was being reported as far west as Yuma, Arizona, and as far south as Tijuana, Mexico. Palm Springs, San Bernardino, and parts of Los Angeles were said to be decimated. The state of California, it was being reported, had lost over 7 percent of its land mass to the Pacific Ocean. Fires raged and toxic gasses spread quickly over roughly a third of what remained. The state's infrastructure—its municipalities, highways, and hospitals—had collapsed. Over ten million of its residents were suffering from food and medical shortages.

America was numb, suffering through history's greatest natural disaster as a large fractious family suddenly united in grief. Watching its federal government struggle, and fail, to provide anything more than marginal help to its suffering citizens, triggered a national tsunami of disillusionment.

Within hours of the news, John Sweeney scheduled a special memorial Mass to help assuage the collective grief that hung over the small community of Narbrook like a dark and deadly funnel. Several hours ago he lay prostrate before the tabernacle asking for a Gospel of healing and hope for his people. As he stood now on balky knees observing the trauma on the faces of his parishioners, he questioned the wisdom of scheduling the Mass.

He simply had no words of consolation for them. He felt a stark absence of peace in his own soul. His heart skipped when he saw Maggie Gillespie walk into church on the arm of her husband, Jim. Her son-in-law, Tom Gorman, was a professor at Stanford University Business School in Palo Alto, and was reported among the missing. Her daughter was distraught, unable to provide answers to the existential questions their four children were now asking.

John saw Michael and Carole Burns arrive moments after the Gillespies. They, too, had a daughter living in the San Francisco area. She was single and living just outside the city. She had called immediately to tell her parents she was alive, but had lost everything. The devastation in the city, she told her parents, was like something out of an apocalyptic Hollywood movie. Michael told her to get to Portland where he would wire her a plane ticket to come home.

John felt a tug on his sleeve. It was Carlos Davila, his twelve-year-old altar boy. "Father, I think it is time," he said with all the seriousness of the moment. John nodded and said, "It is indeed time, Carlos." He motioned the boy to lead the way, and he followed, head down. He bowed rather than genuflected at the foot of the altar, and ascended slowly, painfully, on arthritic knees. He led the congregation in the opening prayer, and took his seat as Terry Delgado Halverson stepped to the lectern for the first reading. John bowed his head, deep in prayer. *Please Mother. Do not abandon these people. They look to you for consolation. They are your children. I know I am a useless instrument in your hands, but you know my heart, and it is ever in search of a closer union with your Immaculate Heart. Please allow the Holy Spirit to unite their hearts to yours, now, in this moment. And in your Immaculate Heart, Mother, please allow these good and faithful people to find both the consolation and the hope they seek.*

He lifted his head and opened his eyes to see the congregation rising to its feet to await his reading of the Gospel. He stood and descended the altar steps with the aid of a newly installed iron railing, crossed the foot of the altar, and climbed the two steps up to the ambo. He bowed his head and prayed the Gospel acclimation aloud, marking the sign of the cross on his forehead, lips, and heart, and asking his divine Lord to seal the Good News deeply within him.

He read the Gospel of The Unknown Day and Hour, from Matthew 24:36. "Jesus said to his disciples. But of that day and hour no one knows, neither the angels of heaven nor the Son, but the Father alone. As it was in the days of Noah, so it will be at the coming of the Son of Man. In those days before the flood, they were eating and drinking, marrying and giving in marriage, up to the day that Noah entered the ark. They did not know until the flood came and carried them all away. So it will be also at the coming of the Son of Man. Two men will be out in the field; one will be taken, and one will be left. Two women will be grinding at the mill; one will be taken, and one will be left. Therefore, stay awake. For you do not know on which day your Lord will come. You must be prepared, for at an hour you do not expect, the Son of Man will come."

Father John Sweeney paused and looked at his congregation. He held the lectionary high over his head and said: "The Gospel of the Lord."

The congregation seated itself noisily. John waited for them to settle. All eyes were on him. He felt the enormous weight of their expectations. They were so palpably heavy that his knees momentarily buckled. He immediately envisioned himself throwing a large gray anchor with its endless steel chains off the bow of a large fishing boat. He watched in his mind's eye as it splashed heavily into the ocean. He felt a sudden wave of peace wash over him. He straightened himself and silently scanned the congregation. They were ready. He was ready.

"My dear brothers and sisters in Christ, we are already hearing that what happened to the people in San Francisco, indeed all of California, is a punishment from God." He paused three beats. "If that is true, *we* are next. *All* of us. For we are *all* sinners, great and small. And in this faithless age, far too many of us are *great* sinners."

He paused again. "But I do not believe it *is* true. I do *not* believe God punishes in this world." Another slight pause. "I do believe, however, that God *does* let nature take its course. And, unlike God who *always* forgives, unfortunately, nature *never* forgives."

He paused and let his eyes survey the congregation. "My brothers and sisters, nature is *rebelling* in our time. It is speaking to us. It *has* been speaking to us. For the better part of the last forty years it has been trying to get our attention with a degree of urgency unprecedented in humankind."

"And what is it, precisely, that nature is saying to us?" He shrugged, spread his arms, and said somewhat enigmatically. "Perhaps it is reminding us that, together, we, man and matter, share a common source who is our most uncommon Creator."

He straightened and lifted his voice: "Who among us would deny the *possibility* that the Triune God may well have woven His *own* fundamental unity into, and throughout, nature itself in the beginning?"

He shifted his weight. "Who among us would deny the possibility that the Triune God, *being a unity of Divine Persons Himself,* created *all* things as both a unified reflection, and extension, of His own transcendent power and glory? Is it possible, in other words, that in the beginning, *all of it*—God and man and the rest of creation—was as we like to say, *all of a piece?"*

He paused and narrowed his eyes and lowered his voice. "But the God who creates out of pure love gave man the power to change all of that, *and man did*! And in so doing, he severed this extraordinary and original unity.

"So, today, we Americans must ask ourselves in the shadow of this cataclysmic loss: In severing *original unity* through *original sin*, did man actually gain, or lose, custody over nature?

"Said in a different way, has God's creation, in a certain sense, become *fallen man's steward,* rather than the reverse, as a consequence of his sin?"

He paused to slowly and deliberately scan the entire congregation. "Is it possible that God in the beginning imbedded a series of warnings in creation that man only discovers when he violates nature's laws . . . what in every other age was referred to as *Natural Law*?" He paused and added: "And let me add parenthetically that the reality of a Natural Law is only clear to an age that accepts that objective moral truth exists, outside of man's attempts in any particular age to subjectivize it for his own expediency."

He paused and spread his arms wide in apparent frustration to allow that pin prick to settle among the congregation, knowing it would find resistance among some. He continued, "Is it possible that these warnings are nothing more, nothing less, than *imbedded* merciful pleas within nature itself from an all loving and all forgiving God to his own children? Each plea something of a recovered dead sea scroll warning us that this wide and smooth thoroughfare, this boulevard of Moral Relativism, upon which our age traverses, is leading us ever closer to a looming precipice and, ultimately, into a bottomless abyss?"

He paused and placed his palms flat against the two sides of the ambo. "If indeed these ever escalating eruptions are just *that* . . . a series of merciful pleas from a Loving Father . . . then what is the message of San Francisco?"

John Sweeney paused, and briefly scanned the lectionary lying open on the surface of the ambo. He lifted his head, and said quietly, "Tonight, I submit to you, that Matthew provides a clear answer to that question. It is an answer that is as ageless as the Mystical Body of Christ itself. He quotes our merciful Savior as saying, 'My dear children, you do *not* know on which day your Lord will come. You, too, *must* be prepared, for at an hour you do not expect, the Son of Man *will* come.'"

John Sweeney wanted to sit down and relieve the pressure on his knees. He felt, however, the Holy Spirit had more to say. He closed his eyes ever so briefly, then opened them, and thundered. "He is coming!" The congregation appeared to sit up *en masse* in response. He looked at them with great affection. Tears suddenly filled his eyes and trickled down his cheeks. The Gerstendfeld family, in the first pew, confirmed later to those who asked that, yes, those were in fact tears running down Fr. John's face.

"He is coming and we are *not* ready!" His voice quivered momentarily. "He is trying to tell us, 'I'm coming. Please prepare yourselves. Please let me find you awake when I return *in Spirit* at the end of this age.'"

The congregation stirred, unsettled. John Sweeney then did something that no one could ever remember him doing. He climbed down from the pulpit and walked with difficulty to the center aisle of the church. He lifted his chin and spoke with a fervor and conviction that caught his flock off guard: "My brothers and sisters, we do not *have* to know the hour! We only *have* to know that He is coming, and coming soon! Some of you in this church tonight will live to see His coming in Spirit among us! This is the New Springtime our beloved John Paul spoke of with such joy. My friends, it is now visible on the horizon! It is rushing toward us. It bears a new spirit, and a new age, upon its wings. *All* will be made new. *All* things will be transformed. Man himself will be transformed. Evil will be purged from our midst. Satan will be slain by the breath from our divine Lord's lips. Sacred Scripture *promises* us the devil will be chained for one thousand years, and the Lord will reclaim the remnant of His people. The remnant from *both* the Old and the New Covenant."

He began to walk about, excitedly. "My brothers and sisters, *you* are part of that remnant!"

He stopped, abruptly, half way up the center aisle, turned, and walked back to the foot of the altar. Some said, later, they thought he was finished. Others claimed they knew he was not. At the foot of the altar, he turned and faced them. His face seemed cast in an ethereal glow. What he said next, he half whispered. "If you've never heard anything I have said to you, please hear this." He looked down as though contemplating whether he should say what he was about to say. He then lifted his eyes slowly, and said, "This . . . purification . . . is about to become more intense, far, far more intense. We must *not* lose faith! We must *not* lose hope. We must *not* lose our love for God and for each other."

The pain in his knees reached a level of intensity that was now unbearable. He immediately offered it to the Immaculate for his people. "In the days to come we must witness to others! God will expect this of us. The world is about to become dark, very, very dark. Dark in a way man has never seen. But this darkness will last but a little while. Mere hours. Then . . . Then the light will return brighter than ever before in human history. It will be the light of a promised new age of man. An age that will come to be defined as the age of the two hearts—the Sacred Heart of Jesus and the Immaculate Heart of Mary. An age of triumph. The triumph of good over evil. The triumph of truth over deception. The triumph of Christ over the anti-Christ."

John Sweeney slowly started up the center aisle again in an attempt to unlock his knees. "My brothers and sisters in Christ, can you *feel* Christ calling you now, here, in this very moment? Can you *hear* Him asking *us, we sinners,* to keep His light within us from flickering out?" He turned again and paced back down the aisle. "My friends, *we* must bear witness to the hope within us, for the sake of our brothers and sisters. And to be faithful to this task, we who are weak *know* we must plead for the grace to place, dare I say, a kind of blind trust in our divine Lord." He smiled: "To paraphrase the great St. Ignatius of Loyola, 'If you don't believe, pray like you do.'"

John Sweeney stopped pacing, and planted his feet. "This is the work we have been given to do as the people of God. This is the reason each and every one of us was created and set down by divine Providence in this very moment in time. We have been drawn together and called to unity, an imperfect unity, to be sure, but a unity nonetheless. A unity exists among ourselves in, through, and with Christ. This unity reflects at the end of time a semblance of the unity that existed at the beginning of time, a unity man severed through original sin.

"Let us cling to Christ, and to one another. Let us remain a light to this world, no matter how dark it becomes. Let us set our gaze not on the darkness which is descending, but on the Christ who will descend into the midst of this darkness and transform it— and us—into a glorious light never before seen in any age of man.

"My brothers and sisters, our moment has arrived. Let us be men and women of courage and of faith."

He paused, and thundered, "Let us be Christians worthy of the Name!"

A great hush fell upon the congregation. A sudden warmth filled the church and settled about the people assembled there. There was a mysterious scent of roses in the air. A light fog, something not unlike incense, now covered the altar. Through it walked John Sweeney. He climbed the steps to the altar and reclaimed his seat. He bowed his head and prayed.

Several minutes later, he opened his eyes, stood, and led his people in prayer.

14

————

Michael Burns sat back in his chair, kicked off his Italian loafers, rested his feet on the desk, and proceeded to read his favorite newspaper.

It was early Saturday afternoon in late spring, and he held in his hands the Sunday edition of the *Thorn*. He turned to an editorial by the publisher entitled, "The Nuclear Clock is Ticking." It was an editorial for which he had taken great pains and the better part of a month to write, such was the difficulty in getting several of its speculative disclosures directionally confirmed by sources inside the Pentagon.

He folded the paper in quarters, adjusted his bifocals, and began to read.

This past winter, the world took what may be its final step toward a *nuclear* winter. The International Association of Scientists (IAS) moved the minute hand of the Doomsday Clock in London up one minute to 11:59 p.m. IAS Nobel Laureate, Spenser MacAdams, was quoted in the *London Telegraph* as suggesting, "We are living in the last minute of civilization."

MacAdams explained the decision was reached by the IAS Board after consultation with its twenty-one Nobel Laureates and a "galaxy of other luminaries." He made reference to the Clock's origin almost seventy-five years ago in 1947 at the dawn of the Cold War. The minute hand, he pointed out, was set at seven minutes to midnight at that time to reflect the danger the scientific community believed was inherent in living in a nuclear age. In the intervening decades, the minute hand of the clock has been moved forward and backward in response to the official pronouncements and activities of nuclear countries, as well as those who aspire to take a place among their number.

So, we might ask ourselves, to what do we owe the honor of being the generation that has now officially inched a ticking time bomb one click away from Doomsday? The IAS itself provides the answer to our question. In short, we have been negligent. We have been so busy piling up debt that we have quite simply ignored what has been going on in the rest of the world. Let's let IAS Executive Director Richard Hansborough explain. What follows is an excerpt from his most recent statement to the world press: "We can no longer pretend the Islamic world does not have a nuclear capability. There are now clear indications the Pakistanis have successfully exported both the plans and the materials to include the prized isotope U-235 to Iran, Egypt, Libya, Syria, and Saudi Arabia. It will not be long, if indeed it has not already transpired, that the transfer of this technology will make its way into the skilled hands of the highly trained engineers who occupy sleeper cells in the West."

Perhaps this is why the Department of Homeland Security recently elevated the risk level to its highest in twenty years, and confirmed what it has termed "an unusually high level of chatter" within the online Islamic communities it monitors.

I don't know about you, but this does not make me sleep any better. What are we supposed to do with the news that we might well be incinerated in the next moment? Better yet, what is our government actually doing to ensure that this does not happen?

Other questions suggest themselves. In what form might this attack arrive? In what city, or cities? In what ways might we citizens help the government identify threats, protect our cities, and our fellow citizens?

We can't answer those questions because the government isn't talking. This is the same government that is only too happy to tell us how many children we can have, who our doctor must be, what healthcare services we may avail ourselves of, what portion of our incomes we may keep, and how the rest will be spent. It dictates how we are to heat and cool our homes and what temperatures we may maintain, what kind of car we can drive, and what kind of curriculum our children will be taught in our schools.

Yet, we cannot get them on the record about the greatest existential threat in the history of man. The international scientific community now considers this threat not only inevitable, but imminent.

Smuggling a nuclear device into a country, we are told, is not all that difficult. Over two hundred million freight containers move in and out of the world's ports every year. There are some five million moving in and out of New York alone every year. A ten-kiloton nuke is about the size of a big screen television, weighs about three hundred pounds, and could be delivered in the back of a delivery van. Oh, and its destructive power exceeds what was dropped on Hiroshima.

Our intelligence officials believe there is roughly an eight in ten chance that one of these devices will be detonated somewhere in the United States within the next two years! Privately, many of them are astonished it hasn't happened already.

In other words, we are living on borrowed time.

I do hope we are making the most of it.

Michael Burns gently tossed the newspaper on his large antique desk and removed his feet from its surface. He swiveled one hundred-eighty degrees in his executive chair and looked out the large windows of his thirty-eighth floor office. His view faced north. It was an exceptionally clear day, and he could see beyond the Delaware River to the east and well beyond the Benjamin Franklin and Tacony Palmyra bridges to the north. He understood for the first time that if such a device were indeed detonated in Manhattan, he would not only feel the tremors ninety miles to the south but perhaps also see the formation of the mushroom cloud rising in search of winds to transport its menace. Winds, he well understood, may lift the cloud to the heavens and turn it in the direction of his city and family.

Beads of perspiration formed on his forehead. He felt moisture under his arms. He got up to check the thermometer. It read seventy-four degrees, the government standard in warm weather for Class A buildings in large metropolitan areas. He felt warm. He flipped his cell phone open and speed dialed his son. The phone rang, and Patrick answered.

"Hey, it's Dad."

"Hey, what's up?"

"Got a business proposition for you."

Silence.

"Business?"

"Yes," Michael replied. "How long will it take you to get down here?"

Patrick Burns paused, and said "I can be there in an hour."

Michael looked at his watch. "Okay, meet me at the Sports Bar in the Lobby at 2:00 p.m."

"Okay," click.

Michael held the phone at some distance, staring at it. The economy of words that was the hallmark of his sons, and much of their generation, never ceased to surprise him. On the whole he favored a generation that placed a premium on what it *did*, rather than on what it said.

He buzzed his managing editor. Erin McCormick was a Columbia J-School graduate in her late thirties. She was the fourth such editor Michael Burns had employed in the *Thorn's* first decade. He liked this one, he told people. "She tells me I'm wrong, and when she does, she's usually right" he typically offered by way of explanation. The real reason his current managing editor was still in her job after three years was because she anticipated her boss's moods, and had developed the art of simply avoiding him when the pendulum was plummeting.

The door opened and in walked Erin McCormick. "Hey, where you been?" her boss inquired.

"I just got in from Phoenix," she reminded him. "Came right to work, on a Saturday, just like you trained us," she added pointedly.

"Oh, yeah," he nodded. "LAX still out of commission?"

"The whole state is out of commission, Michael." She replied. "It is much worse than is being reported in the major dailies and the networks."

"How so?"

"First of all, you can't get near the epicenter. The National Guard has it cordoned off one hundred miles to the north, south, and east. You can't get near LA either. The city is in chaos. Its infrastructure has collapsed. Its communications systems are fried, and its emergency teams are overwhelmed." She paused and looked at her boss with undisguised fear. "It is apocalyptic, Michael. I thought I had wandered into the middle of a post-game analysis of Armageddon."

They were both silent for a while. Then Erin said, "God help us if we ever do face a nuclear Armageddon."

Michael silently handed her his editorial. She took the newspaper and speed read it. Within twenty seconds she looked up in horror. "Oh my God!"

"We're close. Very close." Michael Burns replied gravely.

"Aren't you concerned this will create a panic here in Philadelphia?"

"My concern is that it will *not* create a panic here in Philadelphia," he answered.

"But what are we to do? What *can* we do?" she asked plaintively.

Michael turned, and looked out the window again. "I don't know," he replied softly. "But we can't just sit idly by and watch a nation of people perish."

The silence that followed was as protracted as it was uneasy. Michael intruded upon it with a question. "What's happening on the border?"

"With Arizona?"

"No," he replied quickly "with Mexico."

"That is the worst of the problems," she gasped. "Mexico sees its opportunity. They are shipping money and weapons to LaRasa, who is gearing up to seize control of whatever governmental structures remain. The people I talked to in Arizona believe they will be at war with Mexico within a year."

Michael nodded as though he was unsurprised. "Did Texas come up at all?"

Erin smiled at her boss' prescience. For all his weaknesses, and they were mostly personal, she was forced to concede he was one shrewd man. At times it seemed he had figured out some sort of geopolitical end game, and knew how events would play themselves out. This both fascinated and troubled her. "Yes," she nodded. "The people in Arizona say Texas will secede. They think it could happen quickly." She paused and added, "I didn't know the U.S. government granted Texas the right to secede when they became a state, and actually allowed them to enshrine the right in their state constitution, did you?"

Michael simply nodded. "Any word about other Southern states?"

"Yes," she replied, nodding her head. "People are saying most, if not all of them, will secede if Texas does." She paused and added, "They say Texas doesn't trust the federal government to defend them against Mexico. They think they'll sell them out."

Michael nodded wordlessly.

"Oh my God." As if it struck her for the first time, Erin McCormick exclaimed, "This is the end of the United States of America!"

"No," Michael replied calmly. "It is the beginning of the Disunited States of America."

"What does that mean?" she asked, clearly frightened.

He answered enigmatically. "It means," he said "that if Dred Scott caused a Civil War, we might well have expected that Roe v. Wade would cause an Uncivil War."

Erin McCormick just stared, wordless and wide eyed.

Michael looked at his watch. "Gotta run," he said as he jumped to his feet. He made his way to the door, turned, and said, "Welcome back."

He headed to the elevators and descended gently to the ground floor. He waved hello to a group of Philadelphia lawyers, who were suing the Saudis for bankrolling the 9/11 attack on America. *May have some more business for you fellas soon.* He slowed to wave to a former employee who was now chief of staff for the Mayor of Philadelphia. "How's he treating you, Rosemary?"

"Better than *you* ever did," she replied with a smile.

"He has to. He's not paying you as much."

"Funny," she needled. "Seems like more."

Michael shook his head in mock offense and kept his feet moving. Several onlookers shouted out editorial suggestions and complaints. He nodded and waved, not unlike a politician anxious to avoid the media.

"Mr. Burns, what are you doing in on a Saturday?" inquired Suzy McGlone, the hostess at the Sports Bar.

"Just trying to do my part to help your boss keep the lights on," Michael replied. "How is the old crank?"

"Good," she said smiling. "He'll be in later tonight. I'll tell him you were asking for him."

"Tell him I bolted the bill," Michael instructed, "and that I dared you to catch me."

She laughed. "Just you today, Mr. Burns?"

"No," he replied softly. "Today I have a very important guest."

"Well, we'll take good care of him, Mr. Burns," she said with a reassuring smile. "How will we know it's him?"

Michael laughed. "You'll know."

He followed her to a small table on a terrace overlooking City Hall. He took his seat, flipped open his cell phone, and speed dialed his wife. She answered on the second ring. "That you, honey?

"'Tis," Michael replied. "I'm having lunch with Patrick in a few minutes. What do I say if he hands me his laundry?"

The lyrical sound of laughter on the other end delighted him. They'd been married for fifty-two years and there had never been another for either of them. She was, he often told others, the greatest gift God had ever given him. They chatted for several minutes, and Carole Burns signed off as she usually did with an admonition. "Now don't spoil your dinner, honey. Remember, we're meeting the Gormans for dinner at the club at 7:00."

"*Now* you tell me," he teased. "I just ordered a big cheese steak with fries." At the sound of her laughter he flipped the phone closed, and saw his image and likeness approaching with a large grin on his face. "Hey, Dad," Patrick Burns said, as he stooped to hug his father.

Michael Burns considered himself the most unfairly blessed man in the world. One of the main reasons was now sitting opposite him in an outdoor cafe on a perfect spring afternoon.

"How's life?" Michael asked, waving a waitress over to their table.

"Good," Patrick replied, dropping his eyes.

Michael immediately understood. If you wanted to know Patrick Burns, you had to read him, because you certainly weren't going to hear him. "That bad, huh?"

Patrick's eyes remained fixed on the ground. A waitress arrived and, behind her, the hostess. "You were right, Mr. Burns. One look and I knew," she said smiling.

Michael smiled and said, "Patrick, say hello to Donna. She runs the joint."

Patrick Burns looked up and forced a smile. The hostess blushed a surprisingly deep shade of red. She lingered a moment, hoping for a word or two from the quiet, handsome young man seated in front of her. When it was not forthcoming, she turned slowly and a bit awkwardly, and left.

Michael turned to the waitress and said, "What do you have on tap?"

"Coors, Yeungling, and Samuel Adams," she replied.

"Okay," Michael smiled. "How about bringing each of us a pint of Guinness?"

The waitress nodded, smiled at Patrick unashamedly, and departed.

"So, you were starting to tell me just how well things are going," Michael said to his son.

The young man laughed and said, "Yeah, right."

Both men fell into a fitful silence. The father did not want to probe. The son did not want to whine.

"Well, it doesn't matter," the father said. "I've got a big job for you and I want you to start immediately."

The son brightened. "Where!?" His eyes betrayed a level of desperation that tore at his father's heart.

"Down on the Eastern Shore. About a quarter mile below Georgetown."

The son nodded. "What do you want done?"

"I want ten ranchers built, three thousand square feet each."

Patrick Burns' eyes popped. "Ten!?"

Michael nodded.

"Do you have the designs?"

Michael shook his head. "No, we'll do that together." He smiled and added: "Tomorrow."

"How much land is there?"

"Over one thousand acres," Michael replied matter-of-factly.

"Wow! That's some spread. What is it, a farm?"

Michael nodded.

The son fell silent. "Dad, has the county signed off on this . . . uh, project?"

Michael shook his head. "No, not yet." He smiled and added, "But, they will."

The son smiled. "Dad, Cecil County is tough. Especially if you're not one of their own."

The father smiled. "Oh, but we are."

Patrick Burns looked at his father in astonishment. His father didn't know the first thing about farming, didn't know anything about architecture and construction, and near as he could remember, didn't know *anyone* in Cecil County, Maryland. None of it mattered. They were mere incidentals to his father.

"Dad, who's going to sell the homes after we build them?"

"We're not going to sell the homes, Patrick."

The son's jaw dropped. "What are we going to do with them?"

"We're going to live in them, son."

Slowly the puzzle began to assemble itself. Patrick Burns looked at his father with a look of astonishment. "Dad, are you and Mom selling the other homes?"

The father nodded.

"You're moving to the Eastern Shore?"

The father nodded.

"Who's going to live in the other homes?"

"Our children."

The son recoiled in shock, and fell silent. He did a quick

calculation. "That still leaves four or five other homes."

The father smiled. "I know," he nodded. "I'm not much for multiplication and division, but I'm okay with addition and subtraction."

Patrick Burns laughed. The waitress returned with two pints of Guinness. He smiled at her, grabbed the first one off the tray, and handed it to his father. He returned for the second and quickly removed its head. He fell silent. Then he looked at his father and said, "Dad, are we running from something?"

The father took a long, slow draw on his pint. He wiped his mouth with the back of his hand. His son winced imperceptibly. "No, Patrick," he replied pointedly. "We are running *to* something."

The son nodded and lifted his glass and extended it across the table. The father lifted his glass in response. The son smiled at the father and said, "To our new venture, Dad."

The glasses clinked a bit noisily. The father eyed his son and said, "To our new future, son."

15

Maggie Gillespie was on her feet and moving. She closed the distance quickly between her and her guest, and offered him a welcoming hug just inside the doorway to her office. "Thanks for coming immediately, Paul," she said in greeting.

"Sounded serious," Paul Nicolosi replied tersely. He nodded in surprise to another visitor sitting on a small couch by the only window in the office. "Hello Father," he said. "This doesn't have anything to do with my not using the envelopes for the Sunday collections, does it?"

John Sweeney laughed and replied, "As a matter of fact . . ."

Jim Gillespie stood to greet his attorney. "Thanks, Paul. It *is* serious," he said behind a mask of concern.

"Coffee?" Maggie asked the attorney.

"No," Nicolosi responded after surveying the faces in the room. "Gin."

Jim Gillespie laughed despite himself and headed to the

kitchen for coffee. When he returned, the room was settled and the attorney was reading from a folder bearing the NFP clinic's logo.

"When did this arrive?" Nicolosi asked, directing his question to Maggie.

"Two hours ago," she replied.

The attorney looked at the letter in his left hand. "Tell me again. What happened when this . . . Tamika Johnson arrived on your doorstep?"

Maggie recounted the strange details of the teenager's sudden arrival at the clinic some five weeks earlier. Nicolosi listened intently. "Did she specifically ask for the abortion pill?" he inquired.

"Yes," Maggie replied with a vigorous nod.

"And you said . . . what exactly?"

"That we didn't carry the abortion pill, and that we wouldn't give it to her even if we were forced to carry it because it would cause the death of her child. We couldn't, and wouldn't, have any part in the death of an innocent child."

"And her response was, what?"

"She left," Maggie replied.

A heavy silence fell upon the room. "What does this mean, Paul?" John Sweeney asked, breaking in.

"A lawsuit has been filed against the St. Gianna NFP Clinic in the Eastern District Court here in Philadelphia, by Tamika Johnson," he replied. "It asserts her rights were unconstitutionally abridged. We have thirty days to respond."

"What are our options, Paul?" Jim Gillespie asked.

"Whoa, wait a minute," John Sweeney interrupted. "*What* rights?" he demanded of the attorney.

"She has the right to a safe and quite legal termination of her unwanted pregnancy," Nicolosi responded coolly.

"From a private *Catholic* clinic!?"

"Sure, why not?" the attorney replied. "She walked into this clinic with a federal healthcare insurance card. This clinic honors that card and seeks reimbursement from the same government that provides that coverage. On what basis do you deny her access to a fundamental, dare I say, constitutional *liberty* to reproductive rights?"

The priest was very nearly apoplectic. "Because we have a constitutional right to provide services in accord with our mission and charter, and because the state of Pennsylvania has certified those rights," he said testily. "And our Confession of Faith, which we have a constitutional right to practice, does *not* regard abortion as a 'reproductive right' and, therefore, we do not, and will not, provide it, ever, as part of our services to women and their families." John Sweeney did not much care for the common attorney practice of detaching themselves from their client's interests and offering instead a juridically balanced view of conflicting rights.

"Well . . . this ah . . . Ms. Johnson has decided to test that proposition Father," Nicolosi answered with a full measure of directness. "And, guess what? In this country, she has that right."

This right did not sit well with this group. Jim Gillespie squirmed. "So, I ask again, what are our options?"

Nicolosi shrugged. "We don't have options, Jim," he replied patiently. "The battle must be joined."

A protracted silence greeted the sound of an uncertain trumpet. Paul Nicolosi knew well the trouble that had just been laid at his feet. He was not a constitutional lawyer. Nor was his one-man firm a match for the legion of attorneys and the limitless resources of the organization, Proper Parenthood, which was now crouched behind the skirt of Tamika Johnson. With respect to Ms. Johnson, he could only be assured of two things: 1) she was not pregnant; and 2) she had been paid for her performance.

"How do we defend ourselves, Paul?" John Sweeney asked quietly.

The lawyer startled the others by leaping to his feet and pacing briskly about the room. "We start by figuring out how they are going to come at us," he said, all but walking in circles. "It shouldn't be too hard."

The others sat transfixed as Paul Nicolosi began to outline the legal case against the St. Gianna NFP Clinic in Narbrook,

Pennsylvania. "They'll build their case on substantive due process and what they regard as settled law. We'll defend on natural law principles and their fundamental incompatibility with substantive due process, as it has evolved over the last fifty years."

Paul Nicolosi was a small, intense man, with fine features and a tidy flecked mustache and goatee. He had been a successful litigator for a large center city law firm and fast tracked for partnership early in his career. He had, however, refused one case too many—a case involving a lawsuit against Women's Right, a local abortion provider that opened a woman who was not actually "with child," closed her up again, told her the "procedure" was successful, and presented her with a nine hundred dollar invoice for their troubles.

The woman, thinking she had aborted her own child, apparently suffered what the pro-life community labeled "post abortion syndrome," and took her own life three weeks later. Paul Nicolosi wanted no part of that defense, and as a consequence, his firm wanted no part of him as a partner. He left to open his own firm when he saw peers he had outperformed leapfrogging him into the firm's partnership structure.

His resignation forced a radical change in his standard of living. He sold his center city condo, his BMW 540, and took an apartment in Narbrook. He converted a second bedroom into an office, and began chasing small cases that would never have found their way downtown, much less onto his desk. He caught and killed, and ate what he caught and killed, and survived. Then he caught a break. He met Jim and Maggie Gillespie at a parish dinner party. He heard her husband regale the diners with his wife's heroics at Regina Hospital, and the price she had paid for having the temerity to challenge the contraceptive and in vitro fertilization policies of her superiors, an order of religious women. He offered to help her collect what he called a measure of "economic justice" from those same superiors. She and her husband agreed on the spot to a contingency arrangement, and were quite astonished to learn several months later that their low profile, high wattage attorney had delivered a quick, quiet, seven figure settlement.

"Bought me five years," he told friends, relieved. It also permitted him to be a bit more selective in taking on clients. To his great surprise he discovered he actually liked practicing law, and actually preferred practicing it alone. He was forced to concede, however, that there were times when it put him and his clients at a distinct disadvantage.

"What does *that* mean?" Jim Gillespie asked a bit impatiently.

Nicolosi momentarily stopped pacing. He immediately realized he had been talking to himself. "The due process clause in the U.S. Constitution guarantees fair process under law for all citizens. The natural law principles posit that human law is legitimate only to the extent that it derives from natural law, and is manifestly in the enlightened self-interest of *both* the individual *and* the state. Its first precept is: 'good is to be done; evil is to be avoided.'"

"Which means, what exactly?" Jim Gillespie pursued, pointedly.

Nicolosi immediately understood he had to back and fill. "As a principle of jurisprudence, due process has been in and out of vogue several times over the past one hundred years. The reason: Our Constitution appears to be silent in certain areas of modern life. At the beginning of the last century, the long shadow of the Industrial Revolution cast a spirit of judicial restraint over due process adjudication. The intended, and quite practical, consequence of that restraint was to allow state legislatures to sort through these non-economic issues with the consent of the governed.

"But things changed dramatically with the advent of the Cultural Revolution in the sixties. After the introduction of the birth control pill in 1960, the Warren Court suddenly found a prevailing 'right to privacy' in both the ninth and fourteenth amendments, and rendered decisions that changed the very fabric of our society."

"You're referring to *Roe v. Wade?*" John Sweeney asked.

Nicolosi nodded. "Yes, Father. But that decision was set up by a couple of landmark High Court decisions that took place in the sixties. *Griswold v. Connecticut* established the right of married couples to use contraceptives. A few years later, *Eisenstadt v. Baird* extended this right to *un*married couples under the Equal Protection Clause."

He paused and shrugged. "It was basically just about establishing the right to fornicate without government approval."

Jim Gillespie laughed. John Sweeney did not.

"The juridical consequence of this was quite substantive. The country lost a sense of balance between the new and suddenly inviolable rights of the individual, and the traditional focus on the long term good of the community," Nicolosi continued. "In this sense, *Roe v. Wade* merely affirmed what the High Court now viewed as settled law."

John Sweeney confessed to confusion. "Then what was *Kennedy v. Proper Parenthood of Pennsylvania* about, Paul?"

The small lawyer made a throat slitting gesture with his right hand. "A lot of people think *Casey* led to legislated restrictions on abortion, and it has in certain states. But, far more ruinously, it established that a woman's right to terminate the life of the child in her womb was a *'liberty interest'* found in the fourteenth amendment itself. This effectively both elevated and expanded the concept of women's reproductive rights. In that ruling, the majority of the Court sent a message to the 'strict constructionists' among us: 'liberty' trumps 'privacy' . . . so let's see you reactionaries dig your way out of this one." He paused and added, "This was the knock-out blow to those of us who wanted to see that so called 'right' systematically dismantled."

An uneasy silence descended upon the room. Maggie jumped to her feet. "Coffee, anyone?"

John Sweeney nodded and extended his cup.

"I'm confused too," Jim Gillespie confessed, right hand above his head. "How do we defend on a natural law platform in an age that denies its existence?"

"Simple," Nicolosi smiled. "We borrow its principals without citing their source."

Jim Gillespie glanced at John Sweeney and threw up his hands in resignation. "And how would we do *that*, Paul?" the pastor asked.

"The substantive cases of the past sixty years have established the notion that the highest good is personal freedom," Nicolosi replied patiently. "The Court now asserts that one of the Constitution's primary intentions was to advance citizen freedoms, and that every generation has both the right and the responsibility to invoke its principles in search of ever greater freedoms. This is simply an error of profound magnitude. Clearly, it has served to eradicate the indispensible juridical tension between the rights of the individual and the rights of society—what John Stuart Mill famously referred to as 'one very simple principle.'"

Maggie Gillespie returned with a fresh pot of coffee and refilled all proffered cups, including her own husband's. "Now don't ruin your afternoon nap, Jim," she teased.

Jim Gillespie reddened, and replied, "I want to stay awake in case you join me."

Maggie blushed, delighting her husband, turned to her attorney, and said: "What did I miss?"

"We were just foraging, Maggie," Nicolosi replied. "Just a quick excursion through the current judicial jungle. You didn't miss anything."

John Sweeney cleared his throat. "Uh . . . Paul. You were starting, I think, to tell us how we might defend the clinic against this lawsuit."

Nicolosi nodded his head vigorously, glanced at Maggie, and started pacing about the office again. Head down, hands in his pockets, he bobbed and weaved as though ducking imaginary incoming projectiles. "Yes, yes, . . . the defense. Well, the disaster of *Casey* provides a seam. The Court, quite ludicrously I might add, wrote in the majority: 'at the heart of liberty is the right to define one's own concept of existence . . . of meaning . . . of the mystery of human life.' Now this of course is quite unsustainable. It's quite possible that, absent a dramatic reversal, legislation bearing any moral imprint may never again pass constitutional muster."

Paul Nicolosi stopped pacing and took the measure of the

room. "The pin ball wizards have tilted the machine in an attempt to end the game. But, what they don't know," he said behind an enigmatic smile "is that they have handed us the trigger mechanism for just such dramatic reversal."

Maggie Gillespie looked at her husband who frowned. Nicolosi noted the interaction. "Maggie, we are going to talk to the Court in language they understand. We will translate natural law principles into the language of substantive due process. In an empirical age, we will speak in empirical terms. We will assiduously document the true costs of shadowy 'penumbras and emanations.' We will put the voice of an aggrieved people before them, and illustrate the unsustainable burdens of unseen generations." He paused, and began to pace again. Abruptly, he stopped, and looked at John Sweeney. "We will show them a prototypical American community that can no longer bear the 'all in cost' of the personal anarchy they have loosed upon a people."

John Sweeney nodded slowly. "Paul," he asked with a measure of deliberation, "what natural law principles are we going to invoke?"

"That law is a work of *reason*, Father," Nicolosi replied quickly. "That self-preservation is more than an instinct. It is valued by man as a good. Indeed, society itself is the proof. Man organizes and systemizes to preserve self. This 'inclination' to *preserve* self is no less animating than man's drive to *perpetuate* self through procreation. The Court is in error when it *dis*enfranchises the one to *en*franchise the other. We will build our case on the basic human instinct for self-preservation. We will submit that this instinct is in fundamental harmony with all other organic elements of nature."

"Meaning . . . our community cannot afford the cost of Tamika Johnson's abortion?" John Sweeney interjected, to pierce the fog that always accompanied their attorney's theoretical discourses.

Paul Nicolosi smiled. He was only a high school student when his mother first told him she couldn't understand a word he said to her. In many respects, it had only served to heighten the satisfaction he drew from making his living from words he fashioned into arguments that persuaded judges and juries. "Meaning, our community cannot afford the cost of *not* being able to preserve itself in the face of existential threats," he replied emphatically. "Father, make no mistake," he said with pronounced seriousness, "we will frame our defense in existential terms."

"We will *prove* that when we abort another community's children, we abort our community's future?" Maggie asked, eyes wide with excitement.

The attorney laughed and held his fists above his head in triumph. "Yessss!" he hissed.

Jim Gillespie stood and reached for the coffee, pointedly glancing at his wife as he did so. "How do you expect this to play out, Paul?" he asked.

We'll lose in District Court," Nicolosi replied quickly. He looked Maggie Gillespie in the eyes and added: "And we may well lose on appeal in the Third Circuit Court." He shifted his weight, directed his gaze at John Sweeney, and said, "But we will be prepared to take our defense all the way to the Supreme Court. Then," he shrugged "who knows?"

Maggie Gillespie, as was her wont, broached the subject of the elephant in the room. "Paul, we couldn't possibly afford this."

"Not to worry," he replied. "We'll chase some deep pockets and let Father Sweeney have a go at their consciences."

John Sweeney laughed. He immediately thought of Michael Burns.

"What do we do, Paul, while this case is working its way through the courts?" Maggie asked.

"Exactly what you've been doing," he replied. "Keep helping married couples give life to their covenants and communities."

"Will they attempt to shut us down?" Jim asked.

"They have no legal basis upon which to do so," he answered carefully. What wasn't said formed a dark cloud and draped the room in gloom.

In the ensuing silence a bluebird landed on the window sill and peered inside. It glanced at the life forms in the room, moved its beak up and down rapidly as if motorized, then flew away.

Paul Nicolosi pointed to the bird and said, "At least he agrees."

John Sweeney smiled, held a forefinger in the air, and added, "Such is the attraction of nature to truth."

A gentle laughter relieved the tension in the office. Jim Gillespie stood, looked at Nicolosi, and said with a wry smile, "Did that constitute a billable hour?"

Paul Nicolosi laughed, and shook his head in feigned offense. He walked over to Maggie Gillespie and hugged her. "I can't promise anything, Maggie," he said softly.

"I know, Paul," she replied quietly. "We will simply give it to the Lord, and trust."

Paul Nicolosi hugged his pastor and started to leave. John Sweeney interrupted his departure. "Let's put this demonic attack where it belongs, in our divine Lord's hands." He bowed his head while the others clasped hands in a small circle. He led a short prayer of deliverance, followed by a Hail Mary to petition the intercession of the devil's most formidable adversary.

Solemnly, they filed out of the office one by one.

16

Abdul Ghafoor Khan misted up at the mere thought of his grandfather. Kahn the elder, for whom he was named, was murdered by Hindu mobs, while he was attempting to smuggle his family out of India and into Pakistan within hours of the ruinous partitioning of British India in 1947.

His own father, Abdul Qadeer Kahn, who had escaped into the mountains on foot in the burka of an older sister, spoke darkly about a solemn cortege of trains stuffed with Muslim corpses arriving at the station in Bhopal in the blackness of night. One of those trains bore the body of A.G.'s grandmother, Zulekha. It was an indignity whose pain never fully abated, leaving both son and grandson with an insatiable thirst for revenge.

A.Q. improbably found his revenge in a research laboratory in Amsterdam. There, quite literally under the noses of the International Atomic Energy Agency (IAEA), he created the blueprint for an Islamic bomb with which he intended to incinerate India. It was what he ultimately did with that blueprint, however, that tipped the perception of power between a dying Christian civilization and a resurgent Islam.

He sold it. A.Q. Kahn sold his nuclear secrets to Iran, Libya, and Syria, which in turn "leased" the technology to Al Qaeda, Hamas, and Hezbollah. The world's scientific community universally lamented this development as the darkened dawn of a second nuclear age.

The IAEA estimated there were currently more than fifty nations that either possessed a nuclear bomb or possessed the technical capability to develop one. No one seemed to know how many different tribal groups within some of these same countries also possessed this capability. Muslim resistance to the cultural hegemony of the West, extended largely through its music, cinema, and predatory trade, served to unite fractious kingdoms that regarded it as an existential threat to national sovereignty. It was the West, and the West alone, that now bore the locus of Islamic wrath. And no country in the West wore the bulls-eye quite so fashionably as did the United States of America.

A.G. Kahn felt more kinship with the grandfather he didn't know than the father he did. Though he admired his father's achievement and reveled in introductions to fellow insurrectionists as the son of the father of the Islamic bomb, it was his grandfather's aborted mad dash to freedom that animated his daily existence. In his mind, no one symbolized his people's plight as a denigrated and oppressed caste in quite the way his grandfather's narrative did. He reasoned that it was the imperious British Empire who had murdered him by throwing reason to the wind as it bastardized his country, then stood idly by as the Hindu majority raped, plundered, and pillaged the Muslim minority attempting to flee its borders.

His father had insisted he be educated in the West, and despite his protestations he was put on a plane to America after his high school graduation and met at the airport by an aunt who lived in west Detroit. Over the next six years, he earned an undergraduate degree in chemical engineering from Michigan

State University and developed his father's genetic endowment for networking at a neighborhood mosque on weekends. A good if plodding student, he applied for a seat in a doctoral program at MIT but his application was rejected—due, he believed, to reasons of ethnicity. He migrated east in stages, working as a house painter for almost two years in the Pittsburg suburbs, then as a rug merchant in Newark for over four years, before finally taking a job as a New York cab driver two weeks before his thirtieth birthday.

He initially became active in the Omar House community in 2010, when he was drawn to the firestorm of international controversy surrounding its proposed construction site. He met and was immediately befriended by its charismatic Imam, Feisal Abdul Omar. Over the years they grew extremely close, and indeed A.G. Kahn now viewed Imam Omar as a surrogate father in whom he confided, from whom he extracted favors, and with whom he spent holidays in a discrete Upper East Side townhouse.

This last development had caused tension with his paternal father, who was not at all pleased with his son's life trajectory. The plan had been for A.G. to secure his pedigree with a western education and return home to a life of *noblesse oblige* in his beleaguered country. A.Q. Kahn's singular fear was that his son would escape his sister's short leash, and find his way into an inner city mosque, where he would be seduced by the bile and toxin of disenfranchised urban blacks in search of an identity. Senior Kahn did not want to learn of his son's senseless and untimely end from an Al Jazeera broadcast.

The heat of a Lahore summer in high monsoon season was a shock even to acculturated western visitors. In July, temperatures typically reached 110 to 115 degrees Fahrenheit. A.Q. Kahn slept fitfully on the evening of July 6, so bedeviled was he by a dream of his only son lost at sea. Anxious and irritable, he arrived in his office in the Un-droone Shehr. He turned the lights on and immediately went into the small kitchen off the conference room, where he made a pot of coffee. He checked his watch. It was 6:14 a.m., which meant it was 9:14 p.m. in New York. His son was working, just starting his twelve-hour shift in a Manhattan cab. A.Q. Kahn reached into his pocket and withdrew his Blackberry. He flipped it open and thumbed his way through his contact list. At his son's name and number, he hit send.

The phone rang eight times without answer. At the sound of the tone he began to leave an urgent message, but was interrupted by his son. "Sorry, Father. It is dark and I could not see it was you," A.G. said.

The father's heart leapt at the sound of his voice. "A.G., you are alright?" he rasped with an urgency that embarrassed them both.

"I am fine, Father. I tell you always, you mustn't worry about me."

"And I say to you, my son, what I always say to you: in matters of blood, paternity precludes disinterest." He laughed and added, "Besides, it is dangerous in New York City at night and I do not know who is in the cab with you."

"Father, I am alone. Surely, you are not calling to see if I am with a woman?"

The father blushed in the faint yellow light of an Asian dawn. He did not want to admit he was calling to confirm his son was still alive *and* was not with a woman. "I know you are too wise to do anything so unwise," he replied evenly.

There was a brief silence. Greatly relieved that his son was not in danger, the elder Kahn did not know where to take the conversation. He did not want to ignite his son's stony wrath by asking about his work or his friends. Nor did he want to precipitate a premature end to the conversation by probing how he was spending his free time. He knew, or thought he knew, and it alarmed him.

"I do not know how you do every day what you do," he said a bit cautiously. "And I most certainly do not know how you are able to do what you do *when* you do it," he added, making reference to the shift work.

His son laughed and said, "Father, I still do not know how *you* do, and continue to do, what you do these many years."

The father seized the opening. "I am motivated by love for our people," he said with a hushed urgency.

The son immediately fell silent. This was the father he loved and admired, and longed to see again when he was a man in his own right. He was not now that man. At thirty-four, he had yet to do anything of consequence. Indeed, he readily conceded, his current life trajectory did not suggest he would ever be a man of consequence. But that would change. He had determined when he arrived in capitalism's Mecca, that upon his return to Islamabad he would be widely acknowledged as a man worthy of his surname.

"That is a love for which our people have long been worthy, Father," he replied in a tone that caught his father momentarily off guard. "Here in the West we are regarded as pestilence. This must change."

There was something in his son's voice that tripped alarms. "My son, assure your father in his old age that you are not prepared to endanger yourself."

"Father, I give you that assurance," he replied quickly. "I have no intention of endangering myself," or any other Muslim, he wanted to add, but did not.

Something akin to a wellspring of relief flooded into the elder man's mind and heart. He immediately felt light headed and looked for a chair to sit in. He moved to his desk, pulled the chair back with his free hand, and sat down in it. All the fatigue and irritation and anxiety began slowly ebbing from his aging body. For an instant, he felt young again.

"My son, you know that I love you," he said in a halting voice that he hoped was somehow filtered by the continents that separated them. "The day you return home will be the happiest day of my life."

A.G. Kahn was not prepared to hear this from his father, as he turned the corner at 86th and Third Avenue trolling for a fare. Large wet tears began running down his cheeks, falling softly onto his black shirt. In the summer heat, he assured himself, no fare would know where his perspiration ended and his tears began. He looked at the phone and fought off the urge to empty his heart. The realization that only one of them understood there would be no more conversations between them loosed a burning sensation deep within him. Its poignancy frightened him.

"That will be the happiest day of my life, too," he replied with difficulty. "You must know that I also love you very much, Father." He paused briefly before yielding to an urge he was simply unable to deny. "And I esteem you for the love of Islam I have inherited from you," his voice hardened reflexively, "and the hatred for our enemies."

A world away, the father stiffened. "Yes," he replied carefully, "there is much to hate in the decadent West. But they are imploding. I have concluded that we do not have to do anything. What they have will soon be ours without struggle."

This did not sit well with the son. "Jihad is necessary, Father," he said forcibly, his face mere inches from his cell phone. "Our people need to be roused. We must summon them to battle. The infidel threatens our existence and must be defeated. This is clear in the Koran."

A.Q. Kahn sighed wearily. He would turn eighty in September. The years did not so much mellow him as they bestowed a patience he did not possess in his middle years, when life was mission and mission was life. "My son, listen to your father," he began deliberately. "The Koran says many things; some of those things are quite contradictory. But it is clear about one thing: the victory is ours." He paused and fought back tears. "I may not live to see it, but *you* must!"

"Father, I will live to see it. And I would die that *you* would live to see it."

"Don't say that!" A.Q. Kahn thundered. "Your death is my death! You will not die. You must not die! Promise me you will not give your life for a cause we have already won."

A.G. Kahn grasped intuitively that the moment presented a threshold. His manhood lay just on the other side. He could see it and taste it and, now, he could finally reach it. "Father, do you know the significance of 7/11?"

Momentarily puzzled, the father confessed he did not.

"It is the year that our people conquered Christian Spain," he said in a hollowed out monotone. "Cordoba."

The father struggled mightily to plot and connect coordinates. "I don't know what you are saying!" he said, suddenly panicked. "Speak plainly."

"Father, what I am saying to you is this: I am my father's son." And with that, A.G. Kahn ended the last conversation he would ever have with his father.

On the other side of the world, a father panicked. He fumbled with the small portable instrument in his hand. He hit redial and clicked "send" once, twice, and a third time to no avail. He looked at his watch. It was 6:27. He quickly estimated a two-hour drive to Islamabad, an eight-hour flight to London, and another eight-hour flight to New York, with an estimated down time of roughly six hours in between drives and flights. He could not hope to see his son within the next twenty-four hours. He was instantly filled with a cold dread. His son, he understood, would not be alive in twenty-four hours.

Some eleven hours later A.G. Kahn pulled into the parking garage for Park 51. It had been a good night. He collected $343 in fares and tips from twenty-six otherwise anonymous souls, who would shortly be transported on a somewhat longer journey. The city was still full from its annual celebration of the country's independence one week earlier. The village, the Bowery, Battery Park, indeed the entirety of Lower Manhattan was clogged with rush hour traffic. Midtown was worse. It had taken him nearly forty minutes to drive from the Upper East Side to the southern tip of the Island. This made A.G. Kahn very happy. Clearly, Allah was taking phone calls.

He parked the cab, removed his briefcase, and walked to the elevator. He entered and pushed the button marked *L*. He arrived and stepped out into semidarkness. He felt immediate relief. There would be no conferences in the five hundred-seat auditorium on this eleventh day of July. Nor would there be any swimming lessons, basketball games, book store sales, dance performances, yoga classes, culinary seminars, or food court patrons. The Cordoba House was empty and would remain empty.

A.G. Kahn crossed the wide marble floor, leather soles clacking noisily, and opened the door to the basement. He descended a flight of stairs, unlocked a door to a small, windowless room, and entered. A rectangular table dominated the room. On it lay blueprints, inverter parts, cascades of slender cylinders, U-235 isotopes, and a micro centrifuge. There was a small cot in the corner. On it was an assortment of books and letters and food wrappers from take-out delicatessens and Indonesian restaurants. He took a long look at his home for the past two years. He decided he would not miss it.

He sat at the table and cleared away some of the debris. Then he opened his briefcase and removed a piece of stationary and a pen. He wrote a brief letter to Imam Omar. He got up, went to his bed, knelt, and removed a bag from under it. He removed the bills from the bag, unfolded them, and stuffed them into a large Fed Ex envelope. He removed the bills from last evening's take from his briefcase, unfolded them, and placed them in the envelope. He inserted the letter, then sealed the envelope, and addressed it. He laid it on the table.

A.G. Kahn then walked to the cot and rolled back the drab green bedspread. He delicately lifted the heavily stained pillow and set it aside. He reached down and removed a thin compact device from the cot, and held it to his breast and prayed. The device resembled a small laptop computer. It was nine inches long, twelve inches wide, and not more than two inches high. It was a one-kiloton nuclear bomb. It contained the destructive equivalency of the bomb dropped on Hiroshima. He kissed it, and carried it in both hands to the table. He laid it gently on the surface and opened his briefcase. He set the bomb inside the briefcase with great care, and set the timer for fifteen minutes.

He closed the briefcase and draped its black strap over his right shoulder. He picked up the Fed Ex envelope with his left hand and headed for the door.

He ascended the flight of stairs to the lobby, retraced his steps to the elevator and entered. He inserted a key in a small panel directly above the floor panels. The ride to the thirteenth floor was swift. The door opened suddenly, and deposited him into the private and quite palatial suite of Imam Omar. He crossed the floor and entered the cleric's private bathroom. He pushed a small, thin button on the side of the mirror and waited for a marble panel to open below the vanity. It opened within seconds, and he reached in and removed a small safe. He entered the combination, unlocked the door, inserted the Fed Ex envelope, closed the door, and scrambled the combination. He closed the marble panel below the vanity, exited the bathroom, returned to the elevator, and hit the button for the garage.

In moments he was exiting the garage, squinting into a scorching sun, and joining eight million other Manhattan commuters on the sidewalks of New York. Conscious of time, he walked briskly, head down. He covered the two blocks and roughly one hundred eighty meters to the Memorial Tower in four minutes. He saw a policeman standing by the entrance to the small park at the base of the Tower.

He approached him and asked, "Sir, are you Christian?"

The policeman smiled and said, "Sometimes."

"Do you believe you will see Jesus when you die?"

The policeman turned and shifted his weight. He was a large middle-aged man with a barrel chest. He studied the portly Muslim with the unshaven face and dark eyes before replying: "I hope to," he said. Then he paused and asked: "And you?"

"I am assured of seeing Allah this very day," A.G. Kahn declared, his eyes alight with a strange admixture of conviction and apprehension.

In that instant there was an astounding explosion. It was followed by the brief appearance of a white light of unimaginable intensity. Then, a momentary hush in which all sound and motion seemed to cease. Suddenly a tornado of fire materialized and swept north vaporizing the lower half of Manhattan's buildings and citizenry. In a seeming instant, the world's most vibrant city was transformed into a radioactive urban desert.

Some two hundred miles to the north, high in the Adirondack Mountains, Feisal Abdul Omar felt a tremor in the great room of his ten thousand–square-foot cabin with an underground bunker. He checked his watch. It was precisely 9:11 a.m. on 7/11.

He immediately turned toward the east and knelt on a small thick Persian rug. Slowly, he bowed his head to the ground until his forehead was resting heavily on the rug. In this position he began to rock back and forth gently, chanting in a fervent cadence: "Allahu Akbar."

One hour later, Feisal Abdul Omar was still chanting.

17

America was plunged into despair overnight. Even the cataclysm in California did not produce the totality of effect that the strike at America's nerve center by her enemies did. The country immediately fell into a state of paralysis.

Rumors abounded. The South had seceded. Civil war had broken out. Mexicans had reclaimed the Southwest. Anarchists commanded the streets of most large American cities. The dollar was no longer traded abroad. Urban America was migrating to Midwestern farms. Farmers were shooting squatters.

Father John Sweeney lay prostrate before the Blessed Sacrament. The rug upon which he laid was hand crafted in Pakistan. It was midday. Already, many of his flock had arrived at the front door of the rectory in search of solace. He had seen them coming, and slipped out the back over the second story transway into the church. He no longer knew what to say. He, too, was in need of hope.

Many of his parishioners had lost loved ones in Manhattan. Few Americans knew that thousands of Philadelphians commuted by Metro Liner to New York every day. They went, they told their friends, because New York was where America kept her money. Now, for most of them, there was no New York, no money, and no life.

"Mother, what is it that must be said to the people of God?" he cried aloud. "Mother, what is it that *can* be said to the people of God?" He lay in the silence awaiting an answer. None was forthcoming. He groaned in the Spirit. He heard voices outside the church. Someone was leading the Rosary. He thought it sounded like Theresa Delgado Halverson. The voices grew fainter. He imagined his people were processing toward the small grotto on the far side of the rectory.

He felt awash in guilt. He had abandoned his people when they needed him most. He felt a stirring, stood, blessed himself, and quickly left the church. A blast furnace of ungodly July heat assaulted him. He fought off the temptation to go back inside. He saw the procession and guessed there were already sixty people moving slowly around the grotto and its garden. He noted they were saying the Luminous Mysteries. They were praying for light.

He joined the rear of the procession, beads in hand. Word quickly rippled through the crowd that he was among them. He was greeted in solemn progression by small hand waves and tight lipped nods of acknowledgement.

He immediately felt peace. He was where he should be. He was in prayer with his people. When the Luminous Mysteries ended, Grace Seltzer began the Joyful Mysteries. The others offered their responses without hesitation. He understood. No one wanted to leave. No one wanted to stop praying. Prayer was the only answer to tragedy. It was only and always in prayer, and prayer alone, that resolve was reborn.

Patrick Burns led the Glorious Mysteries. There was a slight, somewhat awkward hesitation after their completion. Then Maggie Gillespie began a recitation of the Sorrowful Mysteries. John Sweeney immediately heard a marked difference in tone. In that moment he felt the strangest sensation, that the Church Triumphant, the Church Militant, and the Church Suffering were united in a way he had never before experienced during the course of his life.

It began to rain. The drops at first were small and intermittent, but soon they began falling like water balloons imploding upon impact.

No one left. No one stopped praying. No one even appeared to take notice. A peace seemed to descend from somewhere far above. Their number swelled. John Sweeney estimated there were now over one hundred souls in procession, heads bowed, voices lifted, beads moving. He drew strength from their resolve. He was blessed with an insight into the divine Intention for the intricate inner workings of the Mystical Body of Christ. *Truly, the Church beats in union with the Divine Heart. The clergy are the arteries; the laity the ventricles. When those are clogged, the body shuts down.*

In this moment he understood the Church needed a major bypass. He wondered if that was the meaning of San Francisco and New York. Would fear yield a love made pure? Would man's vision be restored? Would catastrophe of an undreamt magnitude bridge the end of the current age and the age to come?

The Rosary ended and with it the rain. The sun sent shards of light through thick dark clouds. The people stood, restless, not knowing what to do. John Sweeney immediately thought of Christ, who so pitied the people who had flocked to Him one long hot afternoon that he gathered them, told them to sit, and dispatched His apostles to feed them.

"Follow me," John Sweeney ordered, motioning the crowd. He headed to the church, flung open its doors, turned on its lights, and preceded into the sacristy to vest for Mass. The people filed in after him, sober and reflective. They huddled together in the middle of the pews on either side of the main aisle, like people afraid to lose physical contact with one another. He calmly dispatched his assistant, Fr. Bill Fregosi, to tell Carmella to prepare wine, bread, and pasta for one hundred.

He walked from the sacristy to the altar to begin Mass singing his favorite hymn, Immaculate Mary, in full voice. His parishioners marveled at the sight and sound of him. His belief was contagious. They turned to him and, subconsciously, began making withdrawals on the very deposits of faith they themselves had stored in his heart in the grotto.

He celebrated Mass with singular fervor, and chose not to offer a reflection on the apocalyptic Gospel reading. At the Consecration, he lifted the Host and held it aloft for what seemed like an eternity. He did the same with the Chalice that held the Precious Blood. Suddenly conscious of a hushed stillness among the assembled, he noted that the reverential lifting up of the Son of Man did indeed draw all men.

At the conclusion of Mass he commenced Exposition. As he catapulted the incense about the altar, he saw that it appeared to congeal, rise, then hover like a cloud above the monstrance that held the actual Body and Blood of the Son of Man. This provoked an audible murmuring from his parishioners. Beneath the cloud, at the foot of the altar, he knelt on a thick floor pad and led the Divine Praises. At the conclusion they rose as one and sang the final hymn of praise at a decibel level that threatened to lift the roof, if not the cloud. The pure release of energy was palpable. Reverently, he removed the Host from the monstrance and placed it in the tabernacle. He turned, faced his people, motioned toward the cloud that had yet to totally dissipate, and remarked, "Tonight, I no longer have a defense against those of you who claim I have my head in the clouds." He departed the altar to raucously therapeutic laughter.

Minutes later he was standing among them in his short sleeved black shirt and black slacks. They were gathered in the backyard of the rectory, which was equal parts driveway and lawn. Carmella and Bill had set up tables and chairs, and adorned them with paper plates, plastic cups, and utensils. John motioned to Jim Gillespie to get a few of the men to bring the wine up from the cellar, and to several of the women to help Carmella set up a small serving station for the pasta.

Slowly, a bit tentatively, the St. Martha's parishioners began moving toward the tables and chairs. What happened next surprised both John Sweeney and Bill Fregosi. The men and women began rearranging the tables so they were in a semi-circle. The arc of tables created a space, an amphitheater of sorts, for John Sweeney to stand before them and address them. He immediately understood. Long after the wine and pasta were consumed, his people would still hunger and thirst.

He waved for the people to take their seats. When they were settled, he led them in a brief prayer and took his place among them. He immediately noticed their mood had changed. There was no laughter to be certain, but nor was there a funereal sense of doom. The men and women at table were solicitous of one another. John observed some couples who hadn't spoken in years sitting together and talking as though family. He saw his curate mingling with several young men and women. He was listening and nodding, but saying very little. Over dinner, John was aware that his assistant's quiet gentle manner drew a widening circle of chairs to his table. *He is a jewel, a pure gift to your Church, Lord. Please send us more like him while there is still time.*

Halfway through dinner the wine ran out. When it was called to his attention, Fr. Sweeney stood and said: "My mother told me not to do anything until she gives me the word." He shrugged and sat down to an explosion of laughter. Gradually the laughter and the conversation and the sounds of people at table began to fade. In the silence he could hear a chorus of cicadas begin their evening serenade from high among the oak trees that ringed the grotto. He suddenly realized that all eyes were on him. He bowed and prayed. Then he stood and walked to the patch of open grass they had reserved for him. He looked at the ground and cleared his throat. He looked up, smiled, and said, "I understand there are some among you who believe the cover charge includes entertainment. I'm here to tell you, *I'm not it.*"

The laughter that enveloped him relaxed him. His heart stopped pounding and his pulse slowed. He looked at his people with great affection and recalled something his former mentor and model, John Paul II, once said, "There is no truth without love and no love without truth; one without the other is deception."

He vowed there would be no deception on this night. "Be not afraid," he began with a small smile. "Our hope is in Jesus Christ. And He never disappoints those who place their trust in Him."

He scanned the faces before him, paused to peer into eyes young and old, and take their measure. He saw a fragile veneer of hope; beyond the veneer he saw fear. He understood. He was looking into a mirror. "Just as our divine Lord had to undergo a baptism of fire, so too must His Church," he continued. "And *we* are His Church.

He paused and continued. "This baptism has begun. It is a baptism of fire. It must, *it will*, be completed. It is a work of Divine Mercy." He sensed rapt attention. "We are on the cusp of the New Springtime. A new age, a new era of peace, is all but upon us. We must hold out until the end." He paused again and lifted his voice. "We must help each other hold out until the end." He smiled and stretched out his arms in supplication. "Will *you* help *me*?"

He heard a woman begin to cry. He saw strong men bow their heads and stare at the ground. "Yes, Father," came a voice from the center of the arc of tables. "We will help you hold out until the end." It was Maggie Gillespie's voice, and it melted his heart. His own voice caught in his throat. He did not trust himself to continue. "As long as the wine doesn't run out," added Jim Gillespie, initiating a small tsunami of laughter.

John nodded as though he was anything but surprised that such a condition would originate in the mind of Dr. James Gillespie. "A time is coming," he replied soberly, "when the wine *will* run out." He fought the urge to veer off onto an avenue of false hope. "Here in the United States there will be no more Mass. No sacred Body, no sacred Blood." He looked at them with great resolve. "My brothers and sisters in Christ, we must prepare ourselves, for that day is fast approaching."

A peel of thunder could be heard off in the distance. The air was suddenly cooler. Night was beginning to fall. Several men put their arms around their wives shoulders. "We have been born into this time and place for a reason," he continued. "We are a Eucharistic community. We have been formed for sacrifice in the here and now by our Lord Himself." He moved closer to them. He was now standing not so much before them as among them. "Our martyrdom is to be a seedbed for the New Springtime."

"Oh my God," an older woman cried aloud. It seemed to startle and unnerve a number of others. John immediately held his hand up to restore calm. "For many of you the color of that martyrdom will be white. You will be denied *what* you need because you will be unwilling to deny *He whom you need*." He lifted a forefinger close to his head. "But for others among us, the color of our martyrdom will be blood red."

An eerie silence fell upon the gathering. John Sweeney felt rather than saw he did not need to elaborate.

"This is our destiny," he said with a shrug of his broad shoulders. "We can't wish it away. We can't even pray it away." He paused and scanned the crowd. "We can only pray ourselves *through* it."

He paused again to see if he had been less than clear. It was quickly apparent he had been all too clear. Most eyes were now peering intently at the ground. "Father," Tony Basilio shouted, giving voice to what was in the hearts of all, "when will all this happen?"

John smiled. "Tony, our dear Lord was quite clear on this point. He said 'no one knew the day or the hour.' He indicated that bit of business was reserved for His heavenly Father."

"Father, why is this happening now?" asked Theresa Delgado Halverson.

"The restrainer appears to have been lifted," he replied enigmatically.

"Father," Gloria Gaudini asked, "what did we do to lift this . . . this restrainer?"

Father John Sweeney opened his heart and emptied it on the back lawn and driveway behind St. Martha's rectory. "We ran out of oxygen," he replied evenly. "Cultures are living organisms. They must breathe too."

His knees ached and he grew momentarily angry with himself for not having replaced them when he had the opportunity several years ago. He reached for an empty chair, placed it on the spot where he stood, and sat in it. He began to teach them. "Grace is the life of the Trinity. It is the continuous love of Father for Son and Son for Father, eternally begetting a Spirit of holiness that Himself is a Divine Person. This life of divine Love, won for man on the Friday we call Good, is offered to man in the form of sanctifying grace. In every age, through the action of the Holy Spirit, this grace that sanctifies man flows through the Mystical Body of Christ and out into the world. It oxygenates the air we share, permitting a measure of harmony between Creator and creature. This harmony is essential for man to understand his eternal destiny and to order his life accordingly. This is what Pope Pius XII meant when he said, in the middle of the last century, that it is a great mystery that the salvation of the many depends upon the holiness of the few."

He shifted in his seat. "In our age, this grace has been obstructed by clogged arteries and ventricles in the very heart of the Mystical Body itself. Tragically, it has never reached the people for whom it was intended. It never found its way into the hearts of our brothers and sisters throughout the world who share this moment in time with us. Their hearts remained hardened because our hearts remained closed. In closing our hearts to the Gospel of Life and Love, we deprived civilization of the oxygen it needed to survive."

He sensed confusion. He attempted to back and fill. "I have said many times that we do not understand in this age the intimate and inextricable relationship between the physical and mystical realities. In denying sin, we deny mercy. We see this most plainly in the unconscionable disregard for the Eucharist. We do not accept that when we eat and drink unworthily from the cup of salvation, we eat and drink *condemnation* upon ourselves."

"Father, what is the meaning of this?" interrupted Terry Delgado Halverson. "What are you saying here?"

John Sweeney nodded slowly. It was a question he welcomed. "When I was in school, the good priests and sisters taught us that to *knowingly* receive the Body and Blood of Christ in Holy Communion while in the state of mortal sin was a *sacrilege.*" He straightened in his chair. "And, in my opinion they were right. It is not simply a matter of profaning the sacred." He paused and thundered, "It is profaning the greatest gift God has ever given man—the very Body and Blood, Soul and Divinity of his Eternal Son. That is a sacrilege!" He paused to back himself down. "In this generation, she teaches that we *must* be in the state of grace to receive Holy Communion. She tells us that to *knowingly* receive Holy Communion in the state of mortal sin is to receive *unworthily,* and *that* such an *un*worthy reception of the source and summit of our faith brings *condemnation* down upon the men and women who do so. And in our generation, their numbers are legion."

A hush settled upon the crowd. "Father, America lost New York . . . and San Francisco . . . because of unworthy Holy Communions!?" The question came from Patrick Burns, whose lean and rugged face gave evidence of great struggle.

"No," John Sweeney replied abruptly. "I am saying something different." He paused, and scanned the crowd. "Christ called his followers to *leaven* societies. To be their *salt.* He came, He said, to ignite a fire upon the earth. To bring *division.*" He shrugged. "We chose in our generation not to take Him seriously on this point. As a consequence, the tension that must exist between the spirit of the age and the spirit of his followers died out on our watch."

He paused to let the debris from this neutron bomb settle. "It died because *we,* who call ourselves Christians, killed it. We killed it by deciding this summons to holiness, to *division,* to the creation and maintenance of this necessary tension was simply too much work. It was far more painless to simply allow ourselves to be absorbed into the culture." He raised his arms shoulder level, palms out, and added, "And by the way, it is precisely this acquiescence that has ignited a resurgent Islam."

He lowered his arms and shook his head. "It was our *culture* that convinced us this bread and wine was not *truly* the Body and Blood of our Redeemer. It was our *culture,* a culture we allowed to pervade the very sanctuaries of our churches, that convinced us we could eat and drink *unworthily,* without *truly* eating and drinking condemnation upon ourselves."

He stood and punctuated the air with his forefinger. "And in this, we were wrong. Tragically, perhaps irreversibly, but never *irredeemably* wrong."

He lifted his hands and motioned them to stand. They stood in immediate response. "Let us place ourselves in the Ark of the New Covenant and ask for her protection in this moment of true peril."

He bowed his head and waited for his people to do likewise. "Oh Immaculate Mother, we offer ourselves and all that we have and are . . . to you. Do with us what you will. Use us in any way that you choose. We are totally yours, and we claim no rights for ourselves. Let us help you gather your children, and guide them into the safety and security of your Immaculate Heart, in preparation for the days of darkness that are to come upon the whole world. Grant us this grace that sanctifies, because we are weak and fallen flesh. Give us a zeal for your Son's Church and His people. And, Mother, when He summons us home, please be at our side to intercede for us, because our sins are many and our failings are without end."

Father John Sweeney lifted his head and said, "Amen." He smiled and instructed them, "Go now to your homes. Love one another. Pray for one another. And let us die as we have lived—in union with the Two Hearts who alone sustain humankind."

Slowly the crowd began to disperse. One by one they came to him, hugged and kissed him, and told him they loved him.

Maggie Gillespie arrived last. "I love you, Father John Sweeney," she said with tears in her eyes.

"I love you, too, Maggie Kealey Gillespie," he replied in a halting voice. "I always have and I always will."

She hugged him quickly and left.

Seeing the wine was indeed gone and the food had been put away, he turned and motioned to Carmella and Bill to leave the cleanup until tomorrow.

He entered the rectory and went to his room. There, he knelt down by his bed, and cried.

18
———

L ike most things characteristic of Michael Burns, his excitement knew no bounds.

On an unseasonably warm Saturday morning in September, he gathered his guests for a tour of Hallowed Hollow,
his twelve hundred-acre dairy and grain farm on the banks of the
Chesapeake in Cecil County, Maryland.

His guests included his entire family, his pastor and assistant
pastor, and his closest friends, the Gillespies and Delgados. They
stood on the back veranda of the Main House and gawked at the
breathtaking sight of endless green rolling to endless blue. The
Main House was five thousand square feet of single story glass
and cedar, with a Spanish tile roof adorned with solar panels. A
large and surprisingly quiet generator cooled the inside, which was
handsomely finished in early American décor.

There was a large kidney shaped pool surrounded by an inlaid
marble terrace just off the veranda, but it was covered. Michael Burns
explained that the decimation of the nation's electrical grid forced
choices. The cooling of the home was of the highest priority, given

Carole's migraine headaches. The property line extended some two hundred feet into the water. Michael pointed toward the water, and a one hundred fifty-foot dock with a thirty-six-foot sport fishing boat and an eighteen-foot outboard tied up in slips. He and his sons had already caught and prepared dinner earlier on this morning—striped bass and Maryland blue crabs. This did not elicit much enthusiasm from his guests.

He led them around to the front of the Main House and pointed to the Georgian peach trees that graced the long driveway on either side. "Had thirty-six of them shipped up from somewhere below Savannah, red clay country," he said with obvious pride. "Ain't they something?"

No response from his guests.

His left arm swept the construction off to the left of the Main House. "We're building ten houses in all," he said, eyes dancing with delight. "Six for the Burns'—one each for the three girls and their families and one each for the boys, because some day they, too, will have families. Won't you boys?"

No response.

"And, one for our priests, one for the Gillespies, one for the Delgados, and one for weary travelers who will need a safe harbor in the great storm," he continued, oblivious to the incredulity of his guests.

It appeared that three of the smaller homes were complete, at least on the outside. Three others had been started. And the foundations for the remaining three had been staked out with wooden markers and large gray cinder blocks. "We'll have all this finished within six months, won't we, Patrick?" he promised.

The son bowed his head and did not reply.

"How many men are helping you, Patrick?" John Sweeney asked, to relieve some of the pressure. "Pretty much me and Michael," he replied nodding toward his brother, a former policeman.

"Must be slow going without a crew, huh?" the pastor said, attempting to elicit a measure of sympathy from someone, anyone.

Neither son responded.

"What's going on, Michael?" John Sweeney asked, turning to Michael. "Can't you find skilled artisans?"

Michael Burns reddened. He did not want his victory tour sidetracked by a debate about illegal aliens. "Skilled, yes. Legal, no," he replied tersely.

John Sweeney nodded. "I understand, Michael," he said softly. "But, it seems to me God has decided that since our generation has forfeited the covenant of our ancestors, the meek in our hemisphere will now inherit this earth." He paused, and looked at his friend, and penitent, with great affection. He knew his blind spots. He also knew his heart. "They're here, Michael. More are coming. All I'm suggesting is that you may want to make sure you welcome them. The time may come when your grandchildren will turn to *them* for work."

Michael nodded, deflated. He did not envision a lecture from his pastor at the start of this tour. He refused to give the matter any consideration. "Okay, now, I want you all to follow me," he said, pointing to a lineup of electric golf carts, two rows of six carts each, that looked very much like a tableau from an Opening Day at a country club. He jumped into the first cart with Carole, only to jump out and excitedly wave his arms to hurry his guests. Fran Delgado was moving slowly on the arm of her daughter, and mumbling. Michael rushed back to help seat her. "Joe always said you were certifiable, Michael," she said without humor.

This stung him. He recoiled reflexively. "Mom, Dad *loved* Mr. Burns," her daughter Terry interjected with an affirming nod of her head toward Michael.

"Maybe he did," the mother grumbled. "But he *did* say he was nuts."

Michael turned, headed back to his cart, and climbed in. Carole immediately grabbed his forearm and remonstrated: "Back it down a bit, honey. You're overwhelming our guests."

He nodded in understanding. He couldn't help himself. He knew she knew. She loved him anyway. Always had, always will.

Thank you, Lord. I am indeed a man unfairly blessed. He waved his left arm in a signaling motion, and the other carts leapt in response. Three of his daughters and their husbands followed, two of them holding a pair of small children in their laps. A third followed with her husband and an infant cradled in her arms. His sons followed off his right flank. The two priests, Maggie and Jim Gillespie, and the Delgados, mother and daughter, brought up the rear.

Michael followed a well-worn dirt path through several acres of woods and came to a clearing. He jumped out and motioned the others to follow him on foot. Slowly, reluctantly, they did. About sixty yards deeper into the woods, they came to a much smaller clearing. Large stakes with portions of white sheets fastened to them signaled the advent of construction. A cathedral of large white Birch trees provided welcome relief from the heat. "What's this," Jim Gillespie inquired "the cemetery?"

Fran Delgado howled. If Michael Burns was offended, he gave no indication. "This," he said proudly "is to be the site of our chapel." He looked at Father John Sweeney for approbation.

"Wonderful idea, Michael," he affirmed. "But, why so far into the woods?"

"So no one will find it, Father," he replied quickly. "Remember how you said they will hunt us down and try to take the Mass away from us. Well, let'em try to find us in here!"

"Hell, *we* won't find us in here," cracked Jim Gillespie.

"And," Michael smiled, "if they ever do find us, we'll be ready for 'em. Won't we boys?" Patrick stood silent and regal. Michael nodded to his namesake, Patrick's twin, who walked over to a pile of brush and cleared it away with his hands and feet. A camouflaged tarp appeared. He stooped, lifted a corner of the tarp, and threw it back to reveal a ditch about twelve feet long, six feet wide, and four feet deep. He jumped into the ditch. Inside the ditch was a large silver metal drum that had been turned on its side. He removed the top and placed it on the ground above the ditch and looked at his father.

Maggie Gillespie let out a whoop, then began laughing. Jim Gillespie took the Lord's name in vain. John Sweeney audibly expelled all air in his lungs. There, staring them in the face was a cache of guns and rifles—AK 47's, Balishnicoffs, Glocks—any drug lord would envy.

"My God, I rest my case," Fran Delgado said, her astonishment piercing the uneasy silence.

"Hope we don't need 'em," Michael smiled. "But you never know." He turned cheerfully, and signaled the group with a wave of his right hand to follow him back to the golf carts. As they began walking, John Sweeney caught up to Carole Burns and asked, "Was Michael ever a Boy Scout?"

"For two months," she replied.

"What happened?"

"First camping trip, he led an *un*armed insurrection and they threw him out. His parents had to drive up into the Pocono Mountains in a thunderstorm to pick him up." Carole Burns smiled. "His mother said his father implored her all the way up to leave him there."

John Sweeney laughed.

Michael Burns was back in his cart, leading his guests out of the clearing and back to the compound. They arrived at the center of the large circular driveway in front of the Main House and Maggie Gillespie exclaimed: "Oh, Michael, that was a wonderful tour. Thank you so much for sharing all of this with us."

Michael shot her a withering glance and replied, "Maggie, that wasn't officially part of the tour. And none of you ever saw what you just saw, agreed?"

All heads nodded compliantly.

"Now," he resumed, eyes wide in pure excitement, "*now* . . . we start the tour." With his body now half in, half out of the golf cart, he motioned with his left arm and yelled over his shoulder, "Follow me!"

His guests followed.

Michael led the caravan across acres of freshly harvested corn fields in the direction of a cluster of buildings on the horizon, which included a large dairy barn, several smaller sheds, and three thirty-foot grain silos. The sheer enormity of the farm was breathtaking. Everywhere his guests turned there was land as far as the naked eye could see. The only border appeared to be the brackish waters of the great Chesapeake Bay, America's largest estuary to the east.

They arrived at the front of the barn and were greeted by the kind of distinctive smell only a dairy farm can provide. "Well, what do you think?" Carole Burns laughed when all the carts were settled, apprehensively, in a circle around their cart. "Would any of you prefer to live . . . closer to nature?"

"I've spent a lot of time around your husband," Jim Gillespie shouted in reply. "I'm not really noticing a difference."

Michael Burns' three daughters found this hilarious. Their husbands and Michael's sons did not sufficiently trust the moment to abandon themselves to laughter.

Michael dismounted, as though getting off a horse. The sheer pretense of it drew laughter from his sons. "Four hundred head of cattle," he drawled. He stooped, picked up a stray piece of straw from the ground, wiped it off and stuck it between his teeth. Only a ten gallon-hat was missing. "We got bulls, heifers, calves, pretty much everything you could want."

"*Want!*?" Jim Gillespie exclaimed, incredulously with a handkerchief over his nose. "*Want!*?"

Michael was nonplussed. "*This* is the future for those children," he said with conviction, as he nodded toward the grandchildren on their mother's laps. "They will have to work. They may not want to be dairy farmers. But they *will* learn how to be. And the lessons they learn here," he said pointing to the barn, "and there," he added, pointing in the direction of the corn fields, "will serve them well the rest of their lives."

John Sweeney saw the vision and understood it. "It is indeed grand, Michael," he said gently. "Now, can you show us the inside of the barn?"

"I'm staying out here," declared Fran Delgado. "I've smelled about enough of this."

The others disembarked warily and followed Michael, treading lightly, eyes down in search of cow dung. He did not proceed into the barn, however. Instead, he led them around back to one of three large cattle pens. He draped himself over the fence and picked up the narrative. "That there is Schmidt," he said, pointing to a large black bull that was humping a heifer in heat in plain sight. "He's just doing what Heinrich is getting ready to do to us." The reference to the global financier of the Life Science Revolution eluded all but John Sweeney, who laughed despite himself.

Had there been even a hint of a breeze, the mini-tutorial about the nature of breeding and the value of manure would have still placed exorbitant demands on the attention spans of Michael Burns' guests. Absent it, it was pure torture.

"Dad, can we go back? I think I'm getting sick?" the voice belonged to his daughter Kate. The others immediately sensed hope. "Sure, honey." Michael replied. "The sun is very hot, and it *is* high noon, and . . ."

"And we're standing in cow dung watching barnyard animals do things in plain sight that would get any of us arrested," chirped Jim Gillespie. "I mean how much fun can one group of parish seniors be allowed to have in a single morning?"

Carole Burns doubled up in laughter. Maggie Gillespie turned her head and laughed in the direction of the barn. Even Patrick Burns ducked his head and smiled.

"Okay," Michael said with resolve. "Enough of that stuff. Hey, let's take a quick look inside the barn, shall we?"

He led them in a silent forlorn procession around to the front of the barn, and they entered on wooden planks to minimize the damage to sneakers and ankles. The milking operation was in process. Michael introduced the group to his foreman, Mick Howe, who smiled but said nothing. Four other young men scurried about clamping silver stainless steel claws on the cows' teats, once they were herded into the barn from the pens in groups of eight and settled into the individual milking stations.

This activity emboldened Michael Burns. He walked up to Mick Howe and wordlessly signaled his intention to clamp the claw on one of the larger cows. Howe resisted with a polite smile. Michael *in*sisted with a firm smile. Howe stepped away. Michael grabbed the iron claw in his right hand and reached for the animal's teats with his left. It may have been the unfamiliarity of the touch, or perhaps the tightness of the grip, or perhaps the cow had just been rocked and rolled by Heinrich Schmidt, but whatever the reason, the animal lifted his right hind leg and kicked Michael Burns right in the chest. The force of the blow knocked him backwards onto his rump. The momentum of his fall caused him to tumble backward, his head landing in a freshly deposited pile of steaming manure. The sight, sound, and smell of it were simply too much for the others, who hooted in pleasure.

Humiliated and furious, Michael struggled to his feet and staggered toward the animal. He stooped and, inches away, stared into its right pupil as though to make certain there would forever be an association between what the animal was seeing and what it would remember of what happened next. Then he drew himself to his full height and quickly turned the left side of his body toward the animal. In the same motion he opened and closed the right side of his body with astonishing suddenness. The motion was punctuated by a fearfully heavy right hand punch that landed with such torque on the animal's right side that the sound alone seemed to spook the other animals, who immediately began trying to unhinge themselves from the claws and flee the barn for the safety of the pens.

The victim tottered momentarily and tipped, landing heavily on its left side. This brought a howl of outrage from Mick Howe, who climbed through the milking station to attend the fallen animal. He was immediately followed by his four colleagues. Together, they squatted on their haunches and lifted the animal back onto its feet and examined its eyes. The men looked at Michael Burns in disbelief.

Michael bowed his head and shifted his feet. He had spent weeks planning this tour and none of his plans included a fight with one of his animals. Self-consciously he wiped the back of his head only to discover it was caked with cow dung. He flung the dung at his opponent and declared a bit petulantly, "Yeah, well, he started it."

"He!?" Mick Howe echoed loudly with a look of disdain.

The gradual realization that he had just assaulted a *female* animal in front of family and guests filled Michael Burns with revulsion and self-loathing. He turned away from the others and reflexively crossed his arms over his stomach in silence.

Slowly, his guests filed out of the barn. They climbed into their carts in silence. There they sat waiting patiently for their host to arrive and lead them back to the compound. When he arrived several minutes later, freshly doused from head to toe by a garden hose, he climbed in his cart next to his wife, who involuntarily inched so far to her right she was half out of the cart. As they sped away, the others followed in hasty disorder lest they find themselves prisoners of the pens.

Over an early dinner of striped bass and Maryland blue crabs, Michael Burns was discretely advised by several of his guests that he needn't rush through the construction of the remaining homes.

19

Grace Seltzer never saw the other car.

It was early afternoon in late autumn. She was taking her twelve-year-old daughter, Margaret Ann, to see the family physician at her father-in-law's insistence. The girl was suffering from a high fever and heavy cough, and Jim Gillespie feared it could morph into bronchial pneumonia. She was headed east on Montgomery Avenue, when a large white SUV driven by a middle-aged Main Line woman ran what was once a light, before the electrical grid went down, and was now a stop sign at Old Lancaster Road, and t-boned her mother's Acura.

The shock of the collision induced trauma. In its immediate aftermath Grace was rendered numb and disoriented. Her head had made impact with some hard surface, she knew not what, despite the protection of both a seat belt and an air cushion. She looked up in confusion and saw the woman in the other car approaching in a state of panic, her arms flailing and her mouth wide open screaming something incomprehensible.

Grace was unable to lower the car window on the driver side. The woman pressed her face against the window and continued to shout. Grace heard her say: "I had the right of way. I had the right of way." She started to wave the woman off, when she suddenly remembered that she had a daughter in the front seat beside her. She turned and felt an exceedingly sharp pain in her abdomen. Her maternal instincts demanded she ignore the pain and locate her daughter.

The Acura took the impact of the collision on its passenger side. The car now presented the appearance of a broken accordion. Grace at first couldn't locate her daughter among the wreckage. She panicked. Then, between the door and seat, she saw a foot. It was covered in blood. She screamed. An elderly gentleman approached on foot, and stuck his head into the opening where the passenger door had been only minutes earlier.

"Are you alright, ma'am?" he inquired with civility and concern.

"It's my daughter," Grace rasped. "I think she is hurt badly and I can't get to her."

"I called 911, ma'am. The police and the ambulance should be here very shortly," the gentleman said, as he extended his hand through the wreckage. Grace clutched it. The old man began to pray aloud. She didn't recognize the prayer, but she immediately felt peace. She thought perhaps it was a prayer from the Old Testament. The man's eyes radiated a timeless kindness, and in his voice she could hear an ageless summons to the heavens.

In minutes, she heard the faint sound of a police siren. Then, she heard the sound of several other sirens. The cacophony grew louder as the cars carrying local law enforcement officers neared the site of the accident. Suddenly, they were there. They approached her car at relatively high speeds, which frightened her, and surrounded it aggressively before they came to a stop.

One by one, car doors opened. Grace thought she counted four police cars and six policemen. An ambulance appeared, and one of the policemen waved its driver up to the right side of her car. He ordered him to turn the vehicle around and back it up slowly, so its back door was now facing the point of the impact.

The back door to the ambulance opened and two men in white uniforms climbed out. They emerged with a giant pair of scissors connected to a thick yellow cable, plugged into a socket in the rear of the vehicle. In seconds the men were using the instrument to hack their way into the plastic, iron, and steel of the damaged vehicle to remove the stricken child. It took nearly twenty minutes just to cut through the wreckage, remove the passenger side door and dashboard, as well as a portion of the rear door.

When Grace saw the body, she screamed in horror. Her daughter lay bleeding and unconscious on what was left of the passenger seat. She gave every appearance of being dead. Grace passed out. She was lifted out of the car by two policemen, who put her in the back of the ambulance on a narrow cot. One of the men dressed in white immediately attached an IV to her left arm.

Four policemen gently lifted twelve-year-old Margaret Anne Seltzer from what was left of her grandmother's car, and into the rear of the ambulance. They placed her on a cot next to her mother. Both attendants immediately scurried to check vital signs and begin the process of hooking her to a phalanx of machines. This took a good fifteen minutes.

One of the policemen was dispatched to calm the driver of the other vehicle, and get information about the accident from eye witnesses.

The mother stirred; the child did not. The burly young ambulance driver rushed to Grace and steadied her, gently guiding her head back down onto a small flat pillow. He placed a large paw on her abdomen and spoke soothingly into her ear. He told her what was happening around her and what would happen when she and her daughter arrived at Lankenau Hospital in about ten minutes.

It was all too much for Grace, who slipped back into unconsciousness.

When both patients were safely secured to cots and machines, and both attendants were strapped onto narrow built-in seats on either side of the two cots, the ambulance driver slammed the back door shut and climbed into the front seat behind the wheel. He checked the rear view mirrors on each side of the vehicle, hit the button on the dashboard to sound the alarm, and sped away.

Approximately seven minutes later the ambulance arrived at the emergency entrance to the hospital. It was greeted by a cluster of doctors and nurses waiting to attend its passengers. "This is Jim Gillespie's stepdaughter and granddaughter," one of the doctors said to the others, as the back door opened from the inside. "Call him and tell him what we've got here," he instructed an intern, a young woman of Asian descent. She nodded wordlessly and departed quickly.

The ambulance attendants carefully lifted Margaret Anne's cot and placed it on one of two steel gurneys just off the curb. Two large orderlies immediately commandeered the gurney, hurried it through the open double doors, past admissions, past the triage center, and into an open patient enclosure on the far side of the large and busy room. They centered and settled the gurney and immediately drew the curtain. They proceeded to quickly hook the patient up to a battery of monitors.

Grace Seltzer was wheeled into the emergency room about two minutes later, and placed in a patient enclosure on the opposite side of the room. It was clear the attending staff did not want the mother overhearing anything that might be said about the condition of her daughter. They needn't have worried. As they were about to discover, the child's mother was unconscious.

An internist, Dr. Albert Montero, who headed up a team of doctors, which included a neurologist and a cardiologist, drew the curtain, and motioned the others to enter Margaret Anne Seltzer's enclosure. They did so in silence. Inside, they stared at the battery of monitors that pulsed critical information on the young girl's vital signs. After several minutes, the neurologist stared at the internist, shook his head, opened the curtain, and left quietly. The others followed.

They crossed the room like a swarm of lethargic bees in late September and entered Grace's enclosure. The internist took one look at the monitors and ordered a young male resident to immediately intubate the patient. The neurologist held the mother's pulse and stared at the monitor for almost a full minute. Gently, he placed her hand by her side. He looked at the internist and nodded. Then he drew the curtain and left.

One by one the others followed, filing out and into a small windowless conference room just off the main floor of the ER. They took seats at the table, in silence. The internist turned to the neurologist and said, "What do we have, Doctor?"

"The mother will make it; the daughter will not," Dr. Phil Cavanaugh replied evenly.

A heavy silence filled the small room. Several of the physicians began to fidget in their seats. "Who will send the diagnosis to the National Board for Patient Treatment?" Josh Kimberton, the cardiologist, inquired. "And who will notify the Gillespies?"

No one volunteered for either duty.

A middle-aged nurse ducked her head into the conference room and announced the arrival of the Gillespies.

"My God, they got here fast," Dr. Al Montero exclaimed to no one in particular. He was the hospital's head of internal medicine. The silence that greeted his observation merely confirmed what they all understood. Notification was his responsibility.

He rose to meet the Gillespies, his feet moving slowly. On the way he looked in on the child once again, hoping for . . . *what?*

As he approached the reception area he saw Jim and Maggie Gillespie bowed in prayer. Each had rosaries in hand. His feet triggered the opening of the double doors and the sound lifted the Gillespies heads in anticipation. He shuffled through the doors and immediately encountered their hopeful stares. He struggled to avoid averting his eyes.

Jim rose quickly to greet him. "Al, how are they?" he asked so anxiously that Al Montero thought he gave every appearance of a man who was borrowing oxygen from depleted reserves.

Maggie Gillespie was on her husband's arm in an instant. "They're both okay, aren't they, Al?" she asked in near panic.

Al Montero pointed to a small vacant room in a corner of the reception area. He motioned for the Gillespies to lead the way. When the three were inside, he closed the door and asked them to sit. "I'm afraid I have bad news for you," he said, looking directly at Jim Gillespie, careful to avoid Maggie's eyes.

Maggie Gillespie screamed so loudly that both men felt the thin plywood walls in the room shake. Jim immediately wrapped her in his arms and held tightly. He turned to Montero and asked, "How bad, Al?"

Montero shifted his feet under the table. His hands began to tremble. "The child won't make it, Jim. She's all but brain dead," he replied softly. "The mother will be okay," he quickly added. "She's been intubated and sent to the intensive care unit. She'll probably be released in a few days with a bad headache and a few cracked ribs." He eyed the mother, and lowered his voice: "She'll heal, at least physically."

Maggie Gillespie began to wail uncontrollably. Her body writhed in pure agony. Her husband grew alarmed. He asked the other physician to call for a sedative immediately, which he did. "All but?" he asked Montero when he had reseated himself.

"Jim," Montero replied defensively, "her brain is completely clotted. She's suffering from massive internal bleeding. The pressure on her inner cranium is beyond excessive. There is an astonishing amount of swelling everywhere." He paused, and shrugged. "Jim," he said quietly, "I've seen a lot of head trauma. I've never seen anything that approaches this. At this moment, the child is a virtual vegetable."

The sedative arrived. Maggie Gillespie refused it. She began to wail anew. It was a pain that could only have found voice through the heart of a mother.

Jim Gillespie was torn between wanting to comfort his wife and needing to vacate the small room, which had begun to take on the feel of a holding cell. He stood and motioned Montero outside. Montero nodded. He got up, opened the door, and waved Gillespie through it. Outside, he shut the door and turned to face the inevitable. "I know what you're going to ask me to do, Jim," he said with a tight smile.

"Then go do it," Gillespie replied without warmth.

"Won't do any good."

"You don't know that. We're talking here about a young child of enormous promise who has her whole life ahead of her."

"They won't care, Jim," Montero replied. "I've been through this countless times."

Jim Gillespie felt a flash of anger. Uncharacteristically, he did not feel a need to control it. "I don't give a damn!" he yelled at very near the top of his lungs. Montero felt rather than saw all eyes in the reception room turn toward him. "You tell those sons of bitches I will take every damn one of them before the National Physician Review Board! We're talking about a twelve-year-old child!" he thundered.

Albert Montero was a powerfully built man in his mid-fifties. He understood something of what his former colleague was going through. His own brother had lost a child in a traffic accident several years ago. Montero continued to be haunted by nightmares of helplessness. He intended to give Jim Gillespie wide latitude, as long as there were no sudden lurches in his direction.

"I'll upload the diagnosis to the National Board for Patient Treatment and ask for a treatment protocol, Jim," he said quietly. "We'll get a decision within five minutes. You go take care of Maggie."

Al Montero left to input mission impossible. He knew the Board Chairman personally. He also knew that would not make one whit of difference. These decisions, he had been told, were birthed in algorithms. The men who designed them were no doubt creating new ones in their spare time; the bureaucrats who applied them to the "hard cases" were no doubt hanging out in chat rooms.

Jim Gillespie guided his wife out of the small waiting room and toward a bank of elevators just off the entrance to the emergency room. They entered and Jim pushed the button for the second floor. The elevator grunted, and lifted off with all the energy of a geriatric patient. When it stopped and the door finally opened, Jim burst through it and led Maggie down the hall to the intensive care unit. As he approached the nurse's station he made eye contact with a somewhat overweight woman who appeared to be in her early fifties. "Seltzer?" he asked as he continued to move his feet.

"Room 226," she answered in a monotone.

Jim nodded and picked up the pace. He arrived at the room to discover the door wide open, and Grace unattended. He squeezed his wife protectively, and led her into the room and onto a chair by her daughter's bed. Maggie immediately clutched her daughter's hand and began to speak to her. The daughter did not respond, and indeed gave no indication of having heard anything her mother said to her. Her head was slumped too far to the right and it seemed to restrict her breathing, which was being forced through ventilator tubes. Jim leaned over the bed, lifted her head gently, and set it more squarely against her pillow. The heart monitor instantly beeped its approval. Grace's eyes fluttered briefly.

Maggie began to cry. Jim pulled a chair over and sat down next to her. "Honey, let's give it to the Lord, right now," he said gently.

"Why?" she cried aloud, head lifted to the heavens. "Why ?" Her eyes signaled she was adrift, lost somewhere in a heaving sea.

A wave of helplessness crashed over him. He saw himself splattered against a jetty, alone, dazed and bleeding. He had no answer. No answer for a woman who had known only suffering for as long as he had known her.

He pulled the beads from his pocket and began to pray to himself. He was two decades into the Sorrowful Mysteries when he heard a knock at the door. He turned and saw Albert Montero. Jim immediately stuffed his rosary beads in his pocket and walked over to greet him. Montero motioned him outside and down the hall to an unoccupied patient room. He entered and waited until Jim was inside the room before he shut the heavy door.

He looked at Jim and simply shook his head.

Jim Gillespie's entire body sagged under the weight of a single unheard syllable. He felt a shortness of breath and his temples began to pound. He walked over to a patient bed and sat down. Montero did not follow.

"Did they offer any reason?" he asked after he had settled himself.

Montero shrugged. "Cost–Benefit Ratio" he replied without emotion. "Cost of keeping the child alive divided by number of years of benefit. It takes all the subjectivity out of these difficult choices, Jim."

Gillespie straightened. "How about we ignore the bastards and just do the right thing, Al, he said defiantly.

"No chance," Montero cut him off. "It would cost me one hundred thousand dollars. The second time, I'd lose my license." He softened his tone. "Look Jim, I love you and Maggie. I really do. But I can't place my career in jeopardy."

"Can I talk to Lankenau's Board Chairman?" Jim asked, with a sense of futility.

Montero was nothing if not a patient man. "Jim, please. The hospital itself would be on the line. The wording of our government contract is purposely vague, but our attorneys have advised us we could be shut down if we violate the federally mandated statute for rationed services."

"These are our children, Al," Jim Gillespie pleaded. "They are not entries on some actuarial table."

Montero took exception to this. "At 18 percent of GDP, maybe," he snapped, making reference to the percentage of the country's gross domestic product consumed by health care costs. "At 20 percent, absolutely not. At 24 percent, which is where we are today, there is simply no way to rationalize 'Hail Mary' treatment for a young girl who will consume far too many of our services and yield far too little by way of contribution in the out years. Particularly, if she decides she's going to have children."

"So, we're going to deny this child food and water . . . and just let her die . . . because we can't afford to give her a chance to live?" Gillespie asked coldly.

Montero reached for the door and opened it. He started to leave, turned to say something, thought better of it, and left.

Jim Gillespie stood and walked to the window. He watched a young family climb out of an SUV and make their way to the entrance of the ER.

He immediately said a prayer for them.

20

H anley Siliezar looked at his watch and signaled the others it was time to begin.

His breakfast guests at the Sofitel Villa Borghese in Rome rose from the table as one, and followed him into a large living room, which lay at the center of the penthouse suite. The room was fashionably small, but large enough for a small group of men, and one woman, with large geopolitical portfolios. The décor was neoclassical, featured coordinated fabrics, brocade curtains, and antique-style furnishings. The penthouse suite was named after the family who had owned the Villa's former stables, the Ludovisi Boncampagnis.

Siliezar took his seat in a high-backed wing chair that he positioned against the large, ornately draped and curtained double window, so that he might not be fully visible to the others, and then only with difficulty. The Roman day had dawned crisp and clear.

His guests dropped into the cluster of formal sofas and classically upholstered chairs. They included Nicholas Kubosvak, who ran the IMF, Dag Schoenbrun, who presided at the World Court,

Kimbe Motumbo, who headed up the United Nations, Geoff Benton, who was the chairman of the world's largest conglomerate, Vennitti Inc., Musa Bin Alamin of the Saudi Royal family, Lu Xiaoping of the Chinese government, and Halle Simpson, the forty-sixth president of the United States of America, whom Siliezar regarded as insufferable.

Missing was one Vladimir Piranchenko, who was so disturbed by the prospect of Simpson's presence that he notified Siliezar he would not attend the ad hoc soiree of the Global Governance Council. Rather than contest the indefensible, Siliezar had simply assured the Russian oligarch that the woman would be treated as the vassal she was. Piranchenko took the opportunity to remind Siliezar of their written agreement, which stipulated that the president of the United States was now, officially, *his* vassal.

"Vladimir sends his best to all of you," Siliezar intoned, to open an informal discussion of a formal agenda. The others nodded wordlessly. Kubosvak and Schoenbrun stole glances at Halle Simpson to see if she understood the signal that had just set the tone and boundaries for her petition. It was not at all clear to either of them that she had.

"Okay," Siliezar resumed smoothly, turning to Simpson: "What news do you bring us from the land of the free?"

Halle Simpson was simply too focused on her talking points to take note of the irony in Hanley Siliezar's invitation. She looked at him with cloying deference, and replied, "We are a people in panic. It is not at all clear that the union of states will hold."

Siliezar's eyebrows arched reflexively. "Really?" he answered, inviting details.

"We need your help," she said in reply, now looking from one to the other of the men with whom she was seated. "We are facing anarchy."

The other men did their level best to disguise the deep joy her lament induced in the depths of their hearts.

"Tell us of this, this anarchy," Siliezar said expansively.

"We have stationed troops along the northern borders of our Southern states. They are threatening to secede because I did not take aggressive action against the terrorists who destroyed New York."

The other men nodded on cue in feigned sympathy.

"The Southwest is facing war with Mexico, which is hell bent on reclaiming what they contend we stole from them in the nineteenth century, for God's sake," she extended her palms up in exasperation. Again, heads nodded, eyes cast in tacit support.

"Our infrastructure has been destroyed. The earthquake decimated our technology center and the bomb decimated our capital center. We've lost two generations of our best and brightest innovators and financiers." She folded her hands on her lap, looked at Siliezar, and said simply. "We will not recover. It is simply too much. We have lost hope."

The silence that greeted this summation of the American plight was one of an indifference that could not accurately be described as callous in nature. Despite their disregard for the pain of what had until quite recently been the world's sole remaining superpower, the men in the room understood the United States of America still had an important role to play in the consolidation of global governance.

"Tell us about your currency," Siliezar said, to bring the conversation back into focus.

Simpson shrugged, and looked at Kubosvak. "We are in a free fall," she replied in a voice that bordered on desperation. "Nobody knows from one day to the next the value of what they carry in their own pockets."

She shifted uneasily in her seat. "Our poor are under siege," she continued. "It is becoming increasingly difficult to get food to people in large cities. Our trucks and trains are attacked. Our police will not shoot the pirates who have created a black market around staples, because they regard them as neighbors." Her eyes fluttered, signaling anxiety, and her skin reddened, perhaps in embarrassment. "We suspect many of them are involved in this black market."

"What about your soldiers? asked Motumbo.

"We need them on our borders," she replied defensively. "Besides, our generals tell me their troops regard inner city duty as more dangerous than their tours in the Islamic nations."

Silence.

"What about the rural areas?" Siliezar probed. "What's going on out there?"

Halle Simpson stared vacantly. It was immediately apparent she did not know. "I'd say . . . well . . . what we are hearing . . . is that our farmers have created a barter system. They have formed collectives for their products and citizen patrols to protect their property. From what I understand, they forcibly evict squatters and shoot thieves. The inner city folk won't go near those farms."

"Are the farms automated?" Siliezar inquired.

Simpson seemed surprised by the question, and shrugged her shoulders. "I don't know."

Geoff Benton cleared his throat. "Uh . . . most are not," he interjected discretely, not wishing to cause further embarrassment to his head of state. "Some have rigged up primitive electrical stations that provide some power, but most have decided it is simply too risky. They do not want government inspectors invading their properties, assessing fines, and threatening foreclosure." He scanned the small room, and added: "These are law abiding citizens. They're quite content to live or perish on what they can extract from the land. They just want to be left alone."

"Well, we'd all like that, wouldn't we?" Simpson interjected. "But in a modern democracy we must acknowledge we have a shared responsibility for the general welfare."

Her comments were so pointed and devoid of tolerance, that Siliezar eagerly welcomed them. "But of course, Madam President," he said with a thinly veiled hint of patronization. "And that is the difficult, thankless job of leaders."

Simpson, feeling affirmed, nodded agreement.

"How much cash do you have on hand?" Kubosvak inquired.

Simpson's aging body went rigid. "About $6.2 trillion, enough to get us through fall," she replied, staring past him.

"Then what?" Siliezar asked.

"Then, we close down the government," she replied "and head for our underground bunkers."

She was staring at them now, daring them to challenge her apocalyptic vision.

None did.

"So, how much are you looking for?" Kubosvak asked.

"$24.8 trillion," she replied evenly. "That would get us through the next two years."

She did not have to point out there would be a presidential election before the end of those two years.

"How much of that is for federal and state government payroll?" Kubosvak probed.

"Maybe 20 percent," Simpson replied defensively.

Kubosvak stared at Siliezar.

"Well, let's see what we can do to help here," Siliezar said. "We can't have the United States of America in anarchy, now can we?" He glanced at the others and settled his gaze on Geoff Benton, who struggled to maintain his equanimity.

Hanley Siliezar turned to Nicholas Kubosvak and Lu Xiaoping and said, "Let's ask the World Bank to authorize the Chinese to print 16.2 trillion in Chinese hard currency over the next two years, and release it in monthly tranches," Siliezar proposed to Kubosvak. "Make it clear that it is to be in Yuan denominations, and air shipped to the United States at a time, and a destination, of Ms. Simpson's choosing. Explain that I will warrant that it will not be used in any way that will inflate their own currency."

He turned to Simpson: "And, let's challenge Madam President to do something about that federal payroll."

"But I can't!" Simpson started to protest.

Siliezar quickly cut her off with a wave of his hand. "You do what you can, Madam President." He narrowed his eyes, and leaned forward. "Now, in exchange for this . . . consideration, we will require some collaboration from our friends in the United States." His magnetic blue eyes honed in on Halle Simpson's small dark coals. "First, we will need the U.S. government to allow our officials to monitor your Energy Department's performance, and take appropriate steps to ensure it is in full compliance with United Nations' protocol. Second, your docket of Supreme Court first amendment decisions will be reviewed by Schoenbrun and his people before they are announced. Third, you are to enact, and begin adopting, effective legislation for the Heinrich Schmidt Constitution that the American people passed in a referendum two years ago. And," he paused briefly, "effective immediately upon your return, all school curriculums are to include the Universal Creed and use its syllabus to promote harmony among the various peoples of the United States."

Siliezar paused to assess his supplicant's response. There was nothing to assess. Halle Simpson was shell shocked into total silence.

"This is nothing more than we are requiring of other . . ." Motumbo started to explain before Siliezar waved him off.

Simpson needed water. She stood, walked to a beverage cart next to a small fireplace, removed a canister of bottled water, and returned to her seat. She removed the cap and took several quick sips. "May I ask a few questions, Hanley?" she petitioned, nostrils flaring.

"But of course," he replied graciously.

"Why now? Why the Schmidt Constitution now?"

"Why not now?" he replied imperiously.

She bristled. "We can't afford it. Weren't you listening to me!?"

Siliezar had a habit of growing quiet and remote in the face of insolence. This, he now did in the presence of all.

Dag Schoenbrun tried to intervene. "Why is it a matter of affordability?"

She looked at him incredulous. "I am not believing this conversation," she said in a thin high-pitched voice. "You were all involved in this!" she threw frozen daggers around the room with her eyes.

The president of the World Court glanced nervously at Hanley Siliezar, and said softly, "Madame President, please, just humor us. Why is the issue one of money?"

"Because the new U.S. Constitution declares and enumerates universal rights!" she snapped. "A right to free education and healthcare," she glared. "It promises good jobs with equal pay and affordable housing for all citizens!" She paused and sputtered. "I just told you the government of the United States of America will run out of money this fall! We're broke. We can't afford any of that crap now!" She stood and threw her arms in the air. "Why, in God's name, would you be pressing me on that damned thing . . . now!?"

Siliezar held a hand up to signal enough.

Halle Simpson sat down, convinced she had dodged a bullet. She lightened her features and directed her attention to Siliezar, "Okay, tell me about this Creed," she said evenly.

"Ah . . . yes," Siliezar replied with a smile. "Clearly, with all the problems you are having, problems I must confess that are not unique to the United States, we must do something to promote harmony among the peoples. If we do not, we will simply destroy one another. And that," he said with dark intentionality, "cannot be permitted to happen right now. We are simply too close now to a New Age of Man."

Halle Simpson stared blankly.

Kimbe Motumbo made another attempt to ameliorate the tension. This one his superior permitted. "Madame President, the new Creed is quite simple. It simply confirms what all men know in their hearts. That there is a God and that He is in everyone and everything. We call this the 'Divine Consciousness Principle.' It pervades the universe, and every member of the human family can tap into it to reach his or her full potential."

Simpson nodded slowly.

This served to greatly encourage Motumbo. "This is precisely how man will take his last great evolutionary leap into the New Age. We will no longer be divided by ethnicity or nationalism. The Universal Creed will bind up our wounds and unite our hearts." He had worked himself into a form of tribal animation that somewhat frightened his subject. "We will be one family. Living, working, worshipping as one," he concluded triumphantly.

"Do you have a copy of it with you?" she asked pointedly.

Motumbo blinked. "No, not with me." He paused awkwardly, and said, "But I can recite it for you."

This greatly surprised the president of the United States, and made her feel uneasy without her precisely knowing why. She nonetheless invited him to do so with a quick nod.

The secretary general of the United Nations stood and cleared his throat, in part to hide his embarrassment, and recited in the earnest manner of a schoolboy.

"It is self-evident that the universe is filled with a Divine Consciousness that is the property and possession of all men. Therefore, no nation or religion is free to deny, suppress, or appropriate it. Indeed, all men are encouraged to access the limitless power of Divine Consciousness to improve their station in life."

Motumbo glanced at Siliezar and sat down.

Halle Simpson had no difficulty with this part of what she was hearing. She understood that it was her generation's culture wars that had ruinously divided her people and brought the union of states to the very precipice of dissolution. She thought, incorrectly it would turn out, that there might be a win in this Creed for both sides. "Tell me about this syllabus," she said to Motumbo.

Motumbo's eyes danced, and his voice attained a lyrical quality unique to the African continent. "We are almost finished," he exclaimed. "It is level specific through high school. Within the next several years we will have addendums for the universities."

Simpson nodded. "How will you, we, mainstream it for our adult population?"

Motumbo quickly glanced at Siliezar, who signaled he would advance the conversation. "Madame President," he began with marked deliberation, "that will not be a problem." He looked at Benton, who nodded diffidently. "Vennitti Inc. will introduce the Key this spring. It is a microchip that will store personal records and permit its bearers to receive health care, to trade and transact, and to travel and worship."

Halle Simpson's eyes widened. She had been advised the advent of such a chip was several years away. "How, what?" she started and stopped, confused.

Siliezar held up his right arm patiently. He paused for several moments; then continued: "It's an 'opt in' program, Madame President," he said with a tight smile notable for its lack of warmth. "Nobody will be forced to accept one."

Slowly, Halle Simpson began to understand what she was hearing. "Is this chip actually inserted . . . *in* . . . the body?" she asked.

"There are two applications," Siliezar replied quickly by way of clarification. "And, yes, for women it is a matter of self-insertion."

Simpson nodded. "What about the men?"

Siliezar glanced at Benton and nodded.

"Our physician networks will be accountable for . . . the application . . . for men," Benton interjected. "It will take less than thirty seconds in a doctor's office." He smiled, and clenched and unclenched his right hand. "Just a quick staple."

Simpson winced.

Benton paused, until he had her full attention. "For women, the application is a vaginal ring, again distributed, but not inserted, by physicians." He was troubled by a cloud that had formed in her eyes. "Madame President, women will insert the ring themselves in the privacy of their own homes." He smiled. "In other words, an invasive procedure for men; a non-invasive procedure for women."

"Why a vaginal ring?" Simpson asked, her face a mask of confusion.

Benton looked at Siliezar, who decided to finish up. "Breed-ing," the South American said pointedly. "There's far too much of it right now." He smiled. "We simply can no longer afford it." His eyes narrowed, and he added darkly, "We need to get some things in place before we resume repopulating the earth. It must be done in a more rational and cost justified way."

Halle Simpson decided to let that pass. "What about people who do *not* 'opt in'? What happens to them?"

Siliezar's eyes narrowed and his tone changed. "Then, that is their choice."

The president of the United States suddenly felt cold. She thought briefly about going to her room for a sweater but dismissed the notion, fearing the men in the room would regard it as a sign of weakness. "How is this Creed a part of the program?"

"The technology will permit us to monitor the behavior of its bearers," Siliezar replied with a hint of malice. "We will know when they are gathered in assembly, whether public or private." He paused and added, "As history has well documented, no good has ever come from man's conflicting creeds. It is time to put an end to them all and greatly simplify, and universalize, belief."

Halle Simpson had heard enough. She had petitioned Hanley Siliezar directly for a hearing for her country. She would leave with an apple in hand that had a worm in it. She stood to leave. Siliezar waved her down. "There is one final matter, Madame President," he suggested with good cheer.

The president of the United States sat as ordered.

"Your nuclear arsenal and your Navy will now be subject to United Nations oversight," he said matter-of-factly, with a nod to Kimbe Motumbo. "And lest you think I am discriminating in some way, the Secretary General will affirm I am insisting that this be required of *all* nations, including Asian nations," he said with a nod to Xiaoping, who nodded immediately. He paused, and looked to the others. Heads nodded in near perfect unison. "Mankind can no longer take the chance that one nation could end civilization," he added with an air of self-righteousness.

Halle Simpson was shocked: "I cannot agree to this, and I won't," she said in defiance. "We are a sovereign nation. We will *not* be told how we are to defend ourselves."

There was no reaction to her declaration. The men sat as though she had not spoken, or if she had, as though they had not heard.

"Well, we would ask you to give this very reasonable request some consideration, rather than simply reject it out of hand," Hanley Siliezar said quietly. "We know you intend no insult to this body."

The president of the United States probed the eyes of the man she now understood to be her adversary. What she saw in his eyes frightened her. This was a man, she realized, who was not governed in any sense by legal or creedal restraint. He was a man clearly possessed of ferocious ambition and force of will. This, she concluded, was not a man she could do business with.

"You have my answer, Mr. Chairman," she said as she stood. "And you can keep your money. The United States is perfectly capable of printing its own."

Halle Simpson lifted her chin and took her leave.

When the door closed behind her, Hanley Siliezar looked at the others and smiled.

21

J ohn Sweeney heard a knock on the front door of the rectory. He checked his watch. It was almost 5:00 p.m. He heard Carmella in the kitchen and realized she probably hadn't heard the knock. Not wishing to disturb her, he got up from his desk and went to the door. When he opened it he found Dick and Ann Marie Amoroso sharing the worn welcome mat and wearing thin, forced smiles.

"Dick and Ann Marie, God love you both!" he said in welcome. "Please come in."

The Amorosos entered tentatively. They stood awkwardly in the hallway as if awaiting instructions.

"Please, please come in," John said, motioning with his hands and shoulders toward the front room, which served as a formal receiving room.

The Amorosos did as bidden and found seats on a somewhat tattered couch positioned at a right angle to the room's only window. John took the wing chair directly opposite them. "So, tell me," he said as he settled, "how are you both?" He chose not to add that his question was occasioned by his not having seen the Amorosos in church for at least three weeks.

"Anne Marie's been a bit under the weather, Father," Dick Amoroso answered defensively. He looked at his wife, who cast her eyes to the floor. "And, truth be told, I'm not feeling so well myself," he added.

This immediately triggered alarm bells. The Amorosos were in their early eighties, and had been married parishioners of St. Martha's for sixty years. They had raised two children, who lived on the west coast, one in Oregon, the other in California. Dick Amoroso had worked in the accounting department for Conrail for fifty years before retiring at age seventy-two. His annual pension was said to be 50 percent of his best five years of salary, and included full medical benefits. John knew Conrail had been restructured several years ago, but had not followed the outcome much less its impact on parishioners like the Amorosos.

"Are you seeing a doctor?" he asked with evident concern.

"Oh, we saw our doctor, both of us," Dick replied.

John waited for further explanation and realized, slowly, none would be forthcoming. "And?" he asked.

"Anne Marie has lung problems and I have kidney problems," he replied with a smile. "If we were horses, they'd shoot us."

"But you're *not* horses, Dick," John replied pointedly. "Who's your doctor?"

"Bill Steele," he replied.

"Has he prescribed medication?"

"He has," Dick Amoroso nodded.

"Are you taking it?"

The husband and wife exchanged nervous glances but neither said anything.

"Dick, are you and Anne Marie taking the medications Dr. Steele has prescribed for you?" John asked again, patiently.

Anne Marie Amoroso shook her head.

"Why!?" John implored.

"Can't afford them," Dick blurted.

John was dumbfounded. "Why . . . how . . . what's going on?" he stammered. "I don't understand. Why can't you afford your co-pay?"

"We lost our insurance. We no longer have a co-pay," Dick replied.

"When did you lose your insurance?" John asked, incredulous.

"When Conrail was restructured three years ago."

John felt a surge of guilt. He'd lost touch with a portion of his flock. "What about Medicare, Dick?" he asked softly.

"Cutbacks," he replied tersely.

"What do you mean?"

"We both need surgery. I need a replacement. Dr. Steele told us our prescriptions will only slow the deterioration. The National Board for Patient Treatment has rejected his requests." Dick Amoroso shrugged. "We're pretty much on our own."

"Doesn't Medicare cover your medications?" John asked. He was now sitting forward, back rigid, on the edge of his chair.

"They cover one third, Father," Dick replied. "And that one third amounts to about two thousand dollars a month." He looked at the priest to see if he understood. "That means we have to come up with the other four thousand dollars," he added.

John Sweeney was struggling to find a seam to permit his entry into the problem. "Well, how can I help you, Dick?" he asked gently.

The Amorosos held hands, and let their eyes fall to the ground.

John thought he finally understood. "Dick, would you permit me to share some of the personal funds I have set aside for just this purpose?" he asked discretely.

Anne Marie Amoroso shook her head vigorously. "We're not asking for money, Father," she said emphatically. "We're asking for food."

John Sweeney fell back in his chair. His mind scampered to connect new dots.

"Father, we're eating through our retirement funds," Dick rushed to explain. "Conrail converted our annuity into a lump sum. This damn inflation thing," he paused in embarrassment, "is making it tougher and tougher to pay our taxes and utilities *and* buy medicine, *and* buy food."

John understood.

"I don't have much food, Dick," he said apologetically. "What little I have is yours."

An awkward, heavy silence descended, and settled within and among them.

It was broken by Anne Marie Amoroso. "What about Michael Burns, Father?" she asked, eyes hooded and voice muted.

John Sweeney nodded slowly as he tried to get his mind around what was actually being sought. *Does she mean food from Michael and Carole Burns' cupboard? Does she know something I don't know? Have the Burns' stored canned goods in a cellar? And if they have, how do I approach Michael and ask him to share it with one couple in the parish without asking him to do so with others, perhaps many others?*

"Well, I'd be happy to ask him, Anne Marie," he replied without enthusiasm. "Of course I don't know what he's got over there."

Another silence. This one was broken by Dick Amoroso. "Father, we're talking about his farm on the Chesapeake," he said directly.

John Sweeney felt a thunderbolt strike somewhere in the dark neural regions of his brain. In an instant he intuited, more than apprehended, an action of the Holy Spirit. He thought of the biblical figure of Joseph bound and thrust into captivity. He thought of Michael Burns dead ended in his professional careers as Adman and Publisher. He saw God using both men to feed His people in their hour of need. "That is a truly inspired idea," he said with palpable excitement, looking from one Amoroso to another. "I'm sure we can figure out a way to do this on a scale that will help a lot of other parishioners who may be in a similar situation," he added.

The Amorosos smiled.

"I was down there not too long ago," John continued. "He's

got a lot going. He really does." He stopped himself. *God, I hope he doesn't kill himself before God can find a use for him.*

"We're very grateful, Father," Dick Amoroso said, head bowed.

"Dick, Anne Marie, please stay for dinner," John implored.

The elderly couple helped each other to their feet. "No thank you, Father," Dick replied, standing but stooped. "But we *will* be happy to get your blessing."

John jumped to his feet. He laid the palm of his hands on their foreheads. He bowed his own head and closed his eyes. He began to pray, "Heavenly Father, I commend this holy and loving couple to your merciful care. They have been faithful to your Son for the whole of their lives. Thank you for being so good to them. Thank you for giving each of them the treasure that is each other. Thank you for letting this parish family share a portion of their lives and earthly pilgrimages. Please bless them, Abba, and protect them from any and all harm. Allow those of us who can help them, at this moment in their lives, to please do so in a spirit of intimate cooperation with your Holy Spirit."

He paused and concluded, "Father, we ask this as we ask all things, in your Son's Holy Name through the intercession of His Immaculate Mother."

When he opened his eyes, the Amorosos were crying.

"Father, when you were praying over us I felt heat coming through your hand," Anne Marie said, her voice quivering.

John looked at Dick. He saw no such acknowledgment in his eyes. He turned to Anne Marie and said, "Tell Bill Steele I said you have a fever and he's to give you a *free* antibiotic to knock it back."

The Amorosos laughed the effortless laugh of the grateful, and slowly made their way to the front door. Dick held the door for his wife and turned to face his pastor. He tapped John's forearm twice, smiled and left.

John shut the door, and immediately went to the window in the drawing room to make sure the couple made it safely to their car. He picked them up as they were turning down Narbrook

Avenue, and suddenly realized they had no car. The Amorosos were walking home in the cold, dark, and, soon, the wetness of late autumn.

His heart plunged. He did not know if they were walking home because they had been forced to sell their car or because they could no longer afford to put gas in it.

22

Michael Burns Jr. stood transfixed.

A young willowy blonde rose to her feet, and cradled a lap full of tomatoes in her print cotton dress, with remarkable dexterity. As she lifted her eyes, they met the eyes of an admirer a mere twenty yards from her. She smiled as one accustomed to the gaze of men, and turned to look for her basket.

The young man's feet started moving, following the quickened beat of his heart. He reached the basket before she did. He stooped, picked it up, and held it for her. She smiled again, nodded, and emptied the tomatoes in her dress into the empty basket.

"What's your name?" he asked.

"Rebecca."

"Rebecca what?"

"Rebecca Wlodarczyk."

The young man frowned. He thought he knew all the young women in Narbrook. "Did you come down with the others?" he asked, surveying a dozen or so other women, all of whom were kneeling in various sections of the huge vegetable garden at Hallowed Hollow.

"No," she replied shaking her head. "I came down with my Father."

"Where is your father?" he asked.

"Out in the corn fields," she answered.

"Do you have a mother?"

"No," the young woman answered quietly, eyes averted.

Michael Burns Jr. was not his father's son. He spoke seldom, and when he did, it was with temperance and prudence. "What time will you be leaving to go back?" he inquired.

She shrugged her slender shoulders. "I do not know," she replied, squinting into the early afternoon sun. "This is our first day here."

He smiled and said, "You will find out my father is a slave driver."

"I have heard this," she answered, with the hint of a smile paying at the corners of her mouth. "Are you like your father?"

He found her beguiling. She wore her hair up, which accentuated her lovely neck and sapphire eyes. Her face was handsome, if not beautiful, and suggestive of great resolve. When she spoke, something in him stirred. "No," he replied. "My father is a great man."

She searched his eyes without giving voice to her thoughts.

"The ladies usually leave around 2:00 p.m.," he said. "My dad wants the produce and vegetables in the cellar of the parish rectory by 4:00 p.m., so the seniors can pick them up before dinner."

She nodded. "What about the other things he sends?" she asked. "When do those go to the rectory?"

"The dairy products go up at 10:00 a.m., so they are in the big refrigeration unit in the rectory garage by noon every day. The meat I bring up once a week, usually on Saturday afternoons."

"Do you make all the dairy trips yourself?" she asked.

He shook his head. "No, we rotate them."

"Why?"

"My dad does not want to draw attention to the deliveries," he replied. "He thinks it will cause Father Sweeney problems."

"What kind of problems?" she asked.

He shrugged. "I don't know," he replied.

She thought he did know.

"Anyway, you'll be leaving with the women, not the men," he offered. "I have to make a run with some bacon and ham from our hog nursery. You can ride up with me if you want."

"When are you leaving?"

"In about an hour."

"Will it be okay?"

He laughed, and its purity gave her a small window into his soul. She decided instantly she liked what she saw. "I think I can get clearance," he said, eyes alert and alive. "I'm going to need some help storing the stuff anyway."

"Will the others mind?"

He smiled again. "I'll take care of it," he said. "Meet me in front of the compound in one hour." He placed the basket at her feet, turned, and headed for the barn off in the distance.

Hallowed Hollow was functioning like a well-oiled machine in the spring of its second year of operation under new ownership. The oats were sown, the corn was planted, the new hens, hogs, cows, and steers were in their nurseries and pens producing eggs and milk before their transformation into chicken, bacon, ham, and beef.

Summer was the time to cut hay, mostly alfalfa, to keep the cows and steers fed. It was also the time to make sure the cow manure was properly spread over the corn fields to ensure a good harvest in the fall. Michael Burns Sr. took a proprietary interest in this task, claiming his years in the advertising industry had uniquely prepared him for such work.

Fall meant harvest. A good harvest meant food for the winter and spring. A bad harvest meant trouble for man and beast.

Winter was a time for raising and repairing fences, buying and fixing tractors and other farm machinery, painting barns, mending roofs, and maintaining roads and lanes.

And always, there was the milking of cows. Twice a day. At 4:00 a.m. and 4:00 p.m. 365 days a year. It was a difficult, monotonous, odiferous job. By universal consensus, Michael Burns Sr. no longer attempted to milk cows.

Michael Burns Sr. now had twenty-two men and fourteen women from St. Martha's working on the farm. The men handled planting and harvesting, milking and feeding, butchering and slaughtering, repair and maintenance.

The women planted, cultivated, and harvested the vegetable garden. They planted tomatoes, cucumbers, pickles, green beans, potatoes, cantaloupe, and watermelon. They made ice cream and coleslaw and apple cider and pies.

The Burns women, Carole and her three married daughters, did the cleaning, cooking, and the management of the food inventory in the cellar of the Main House, and in the two clapboard sheds for the parishioners of St. Martha's. The sons, Patrick and Michael Jr., managed the operation for their father. Patrick was responsible for what went into, and came out of, the ground, pens, and nurseries. Michael Jr. was responsible for packing, storing, and distributing the yield to his own family and to Fr. John Sweeney for distribution to the needy among the parish family of St. Martha's, two hours to the north.

It was a few minutes after 2:00 p.m. when Michael Burns Jr. wheeled his pickup into the large circular portion of the driveway, which hubbed the compound's ten houses. Rebecca Wlodarczyk, with a small, dark vinyl bag slung over her right shoulder, stood waiting in front of the Main House. Michael brought the truck to a stop, leaned across the divider, and opened the passenger side front door. She used his extended hand to step up and into the truck. As soon as she was settled, he accelerated in search of lost minutes.

It was the better part of a mile from the Main House to the road. They rode in silence. Michael Jr. felt a deep peace in her presence. He was moved to say so but was unable to find its expression.

She, too, felt an immediate comfort, previously unknown in the presence of men her age. In her native country, she thought to herself, a hand would have already found a preliminary target.

"Tell me about yourself," he said, when they were on the main road heading north.

Americans are direct, she reminded herself. *Do not take offense.* "You first," she replied quickly.

She has something to hide, he immediately concluded. "Not much to tell," he shrugged. "Grew up in Philly; went to prep school and a university in Philly; worked as a cop in Philly." He laughed. "Now I'm a farmer in Maryland."

She laughed too. "Okay," she said in a measured tone. "I grew up in Poland; went to school in Poland; went to a university in Connecticut; worked as a consultant in New York; and now, I too, am a farmer in Maryland."

"Where in Connecticut?" he asked.

"New Haven," she replied matter-of-factly.

"Yale?"

"Yes."

He immediately felt intimidated. Yet there was something in her manner that suggested he should not feel intimidated. "What kind of work did you do in New York?" he asked.

"I was a consultant," she replied.

"What company?" he probed.

"McKinsey."

A thoroughbred, he deduced. "How did you get out in time?"

Her pause announced an awkward silence. "My mother left my father," she disclosed quietly several moments later. "So I left my mother."

Don't go there, he advised himself. "What kind of work did your dad do?" he asked a bit more brightly.

"He was a professor at Columbia University," she replied.

"What brought him to Philadelphia?"

"The chairmanship of the Economics Department at Penn."

He mused on the significance of apparent randomness. "Saved your life," he said, attempting and failing to project an emotional distance.

She did not respond.

"How long was he at Penn?"

"Three years."

He knew he need go no further. Universities were among those hardest hit when America lost her technology and finance centers and, consequently, her energy infrastructure. The new global cap and trade agreement required even the most robustly endowed universities to ration energy, and this greatly limited competition for lucrative research grants, which now went almost exclusively to the Life Sciences Departments. Whole departments in other disciplines were either dismantled or consolidated. He suspected Rebecca Wlodarczyk's father was a victim of that bloodbath.

"I know of at least two doctors, one lawyer, and one former CEO working on the farm right now," he offered as a measure of sympathy.

She did not respond. He wondered how many other wounds he would open over the next hour and a half. She fell into a silence that lasted until they hit Route 476 North, roughly half an hour from Narbrook. Abruptly, she turned to him and said, "Do you have a girlfriend?"

The question caught him off guard. "No," he replied. He wanted to add that he hadn't had a girlfriend since he broke off a relationship with a young lady from New York over ten years ago. But he did not trust himself to think about that woman and what may have befallen her much less speak of her.

"Do you like farm work?" she probed.

"I like work," he replied.

"Did you like police work?"

"I did," he answered.

"Do wish you were still a cop?"

"No," he said flatly. "It's no longer law enforcement. It's basically a hell tour, civil war duty." He paused and turned and added, "I don't much like the idea of shooting citizens."

"What do you do in your free time?" she asked, changing the subject.

"I go to bars to pick up women," he replied with mock sincerity.

She immediately detected a telltale change in tone. "Tell me what bars so I'll know where to go," she said.

He laughed, and the laughter freed him from the deep anxieties he almost always felt in the presence of people he did not know well. Suddenly, with an impulsivity that was well out of character, he reached for her hand.

She felt more than saw it coming, and opened her left palm to receive it. His strong, thick hand grasped and enveloped hers, and she instantly felt a sensation of joy. She squeezed his hand, clasped it in both of her hands, and rested it in her lap.

He felt a peace previously unknown. Suddenly, he did not want this trip to end. He did not want to stop the truck to unload its contents in the rectory garage, turn and say goodbye to her, and then get back in the truck and drive home, alone.

Neither spoke until he turned into the rectory driveway just off Narbrook Avenue some twenty minutes later. "Will you need help?" she asked.

"Are you offering?" he replied with a smile.

"Yes," she said, eyes wide and earnest.

Michael Burns Jr. pulled around back and parked the back of the truck in front of the garage, which was closed as it generally was during daylight hours. John Sweeney heard the truck and came rushing out the backdoor of the rectory. "Finally," he needled, "a little bacon and ham for my Eggs Benedict in the morning."

"Father, you know Rebecca?" Michael said, nodding in her direction as she climbed down from the cabin and came around to where they were standing.

"I do indeed," he replied graciously. "I told her father we wouldn't register him unless she was part of the package." He extended his hand, and she took it on the tips of long, elegant fingers. "How did your first day go?" he asked.

"Sixty-four bushels of tomatoes," she said triumphantly.

John Sweeney nodded. "That will be very good news to our families," he said softly. He turned to Michael. "And you, young man, what do you bring us today?"

Michael turned, went to the back of the truck, and released the handle to its tail end. It fell noisily. He hopped up, removed several layers of green tarps, yanked the large built-in freezer open, and pointed to its contents. "We've got over fourteen hundred pounds of bacon and ham," he replied with pride.

John Sweeney whistled, went around to the back of the truck, and hoisted himself up with some difficulty onto the flat portion of its rear. He approached the freezer and beheld manna from heaven—hundreds of carefully wrapped and labeled five and ten pound packages of farm fresh bacon and ham.

He immediately bowed his head and prayed. "Heavenly Father, we give you praise and thanks. You are too good to us. Truly it is only goodness and kindness that follow us all the days of our lives. Our dependence on you is our only rightful claim to your mercy. We ask your continued blessings on the Burns family for the work and the food they provide for your people. And we ask you to look not upon our sins and failings, but the gratitude you have placed in our hearts for the bounty you have so graciously shared with us this day." He opened his eyes, lifted his hands and arms, and shouted, "Amen."

Michael jumped down from the truck and walked to the garage and opened both doors. He headed to the four commercial sized freezers the Burns family had installed, and opened the doors to each. He re-emerged from the garage and asked Rebecca to man the station on the back of the truck. He asked John Sweeney to stand between Rebecca and him. He smiled and blew an imaginary whistle to start the assembly line.

In twenty-five minutes they were finished. John Sweeney, breathing audibly, mopped his brow and said, "It's hotter than I thought. How about some iced tea?"

"Sounds good, Father," Michael replied.

Rebecca nodded her assent.

"Meet you on the front porch," John Sweeney said.

Several minutes later he emerged through the front screen door with a brown wooden tray. On the tray were a large pitcher of iced tea and three glasses filled with ice cubes. He poured two of the glasses nearly full and handed them to his guests. He poured one for himself and sat down. "This is truly a day of the Lord," he proclaimed, as he lifted his glass over his head. Michael and Rebecca paused, looked at each other, and proceeded to lift their glasses a bit awkwardly. In response, John Sweeney wasted no time draining his.

They sat and talked until sundown. Then the families began to arrive. They arrived, as scheduled, in clusters of three or four families at a time, with the older children straggling behind, not wanting to be seen with their parents, or seen standing in line at what had become a parish food distribution center.

Michael was astonished at the sheer number of families who came in search of food. He was more astonished at the identity of some of them. The word on the street was that U.S. unemployment had reached nearly 30 percent within the last month, though the government steadfastly refused to publish any figures. America was broke. Her families were hungry. Her resolve was being tested as never before in her two hundred fifty year history.

He decided to stay and help parcel out the food. He was impressed with Father Sweeney's inventory management system, which was run by a three-man team of former accountants. Each item was numbered and tracked by date and family. John Sweeney received a written report at the end of the night, which he carefully reviewed and filed in a vault in the attic.

It was almost 9:00 p.m. when the last of the families left, carrying brown burlap sacks and green hefty bags filled with four days of provision. Michael saw Rebecca standing near the grotto, head bowed. The moon cast an ethereal light on her head and shoulders. He studied her from a distance, viscerally attracted to her beauty and nobility. He approached quietly. As he drew near he saw that she was crying. He reached for her face, cupped it, turned it gently, and lifted it toward his. "Why are you sad?" he asked softly.

"I am not sad," she replied unselfconsciously. "I am afraid."

"Why are you afraid?" he asked, moving his face within inches of hers.

She blinked back tears and replied, "Because I have never been this happy, and I am afraid it is not real."

He kissed her. She moaned softly. He felt her body collapse into his. He kissed her again, and again. He pulled back. He waited until she opened her eyes. "Do you believe I am real?" he asked.

She nodded.

"If you believe what you *see* is real, then you can believe what you *feel* is real," he said gently.

She buried her head in his chest and cried.

He walked her to his truck, helped her make her way up and in, and drove her to her home over the bridge in South Narbrook. In minutes they arrived. Michael waited for an invitation that was not forthcoming. She let herself out of the truck, smiled at him, and started for her door.

Michael Burns Jr. waited until she was safely insider her home. Then, he turned his truck around and headed home.

23

Bill Draper walked into the courtroom like a man who was late for a train. Indeed, he had been a man in a hurry his entire life.

He grew up in the shadow of the Philadelphia Main line. He understood early in life that its wealth and prestige was not something to which he was likely to gain access. Fatherless at twelve, he was forced to drop out of high school to work as a porter to help support his mother and eight younger brothers and sisters.

He met a young female passenger one night on the run from Washington to Boston. He encountered her again three nights later on the return trip. He proposed in the café car somewhere between Newark and Trenton. Ten months later he was back in school, at night. This time as a husband and father.

The GED earned him a promotion. He landed a job as a gas station attendant. He worked six days a week and went to school four nights a week. He earned an undergraduate degree in sociology at Temple University in five years. It cost him his first marriage.

A university professor, who had befriended him, arranged for a job as a legal aid for a center city law firm with a number of large government contracts. The good professor also helped him gain admission to the Temple University Law School. He needed only four years, at night, to finish. He graduated 16th in a class of 327.

He remarried and settled into a comfortable middle class neighborhood on the southern divide of the Main Line. He was named Montgomery County's first African American common pleas judge at forty-seven. Eleven years later, he was appointed to the bench at the Third District Court for the Eastern District of Pennsylvania.

His second wife was killed in a car accident one year to the day after giving birth to their only child, a son. A divorced sister moved in with him to help raise the child.

During his years on the bench, Bill Draper had earned a reputation as an impartial arbiter with little tolerance for breaches of courtroom etiquette. His case load and his docket moved like his old trains, predictably and efficiently.

Maggie Gillespie studied him carefully from her seat next to her husband at the defense counsel table. She knew him in passing in another life. A mutual friend had suggested she approach him for counsel when her first husband left her and ran off with his legal secretary. She found him approachable, but ultimately chose not to act on his counsel. She now wondered if he knew, or cared.

He took his seat on the riser behind the bench and banged the gavel. He waited impatiently while the assembled, having risen at his entrance, again took possession of their seats. He was a small, wiry man with speckled grey above and below his weathered face. Maggie thought she saw the painful cost of dreams fulfilled in his doleful, reddened eyes.

Bill Draper cleared his throat. "Good morning members of the jury. Welcome to the Federal District Court for the Eastern District of Pennsylvania. I am Judge William Draper, and this is courtroom number six. I want to thank each of you for your presence here this morning, and for your acceptance of your civic duty to your fellow citizens of the Commonwealth of Pennsylvania.

He paused momentarily. "Ladies and gentlemen of the jury, *you* will decide the facts in Tamika Johnson and the U.S. Department of Health and Human Services v. Dr. James and Margaret Gillespie and the St. Gianna Molla Natural Family Planning Clinic in Narbrook, Pennsylvania."

He paused, and offered a thin smile. "And I will decide the legal issues."

He briefly glanced at his notes. "This case involves the Substantive Due Process clause of the U.S. Constitution, which guarantees fair process under law for all citizens. The Plaintiffs will argue Ms. Johnson was wrongfully denied due process when she went to the Clinic on April 1 for mifepristone—'the abortion pill.' She was told the clinic neither carried nor dispensed the pill for, essentially, religious reasons.

"The Plaintiffs will lodge their claim on the *'essential service'* clause in the federal government's insurance contract with the Gillespies, and will assert that in denying the Plaintiffs this service, the clinic has also denied the Plaintiffs' *Liberty Interest,* as defined by the Supreme Court in *Kennedy* v. *Proper Parenthood of Pennsylvania.*"

He paused, glanced toward the plaintiff's table, and continued. "The Defendants will argue that they received no notification from either the federal government that the dispensation of mifepristone was an *'essential service'* subject to the Due Process clause, and that in pursuing the Plaintiffs' right to define her own 'mystery of life' through access to abortion services as decided in *Kennedy,* the Gillespie's and the Narbrook community is being wrongfully denied the application of that same right, to the long term detriment of their community."

He paused again, and consulted his notes. "The legal issue here involves competing *Liberty Interests.* Does the Plaintiff's right to the provision of abortion services from a federally licensed and funded clinic, impinge on said clinic's freedom to define its own concept of existence, and the right of the community in which it operates to exist?"

Bill Draper paused, and looked sternly over his glasses at the twelve men and women impaneled. "Now, I am instructing you *not* to talk to anyone about this case until it is over, including each other, outside the jury room." He scanned the faces in the jury box. "Am I clear?" he added.

In immediate response, twelve heads nodded silently in unison.

He turned to the Plaintiff's bench and nodded. "Is the Plaintiff ready to make its opening statement?"

Heather Watkins smiled engagingly as she rose from the Plaintiff's table, and said: "Yes, your honor." Bill Draper nodded in response. She was a tall, elegant black woman in her middle thirties. Both her parents were attorneys, and had adorned her keen intelligence and natural grace with an Ivy League pedigree—Yale undergraduate, Harvard Law School. At twenty-eight, she was named president of Proper Parenthood of Pennsylvania amid much media attention. She had been recruited by the U.S. Attorney's office three years later after doubling PP's annual development fund.

She gathered herself and walked to a spot approximately ten feet from the center of the jury box. She slowly scanned the faces. They represented a rough cross section of the Eastern District's seven-county demography—six jurors over forty-five, five of whom were men. Of the four minorities, three were women. Heather Watkins carried no notes in her classically trained hands. She began in a soft, clear, mellifluous voice. "Tamika Johnson is everywoman." She paused to intuit acceptance or rejection of that foundational claim. She sensed acceptance, with reservations. "I ask you who are women," she smiled at a male juror, "and you who are married to women," larger smile, "what woman have you ever known, that at some point in her life was not entirely vulnerable to forces beyond her control?"

Several heads nodded. Heather Watkins' cadence kicked up a notch. "Defenseless. Powerless. Voiceless." She moved her feet, and approached a middle-aged minority woman in the first row of the jury box. "Tamika Johnson was sexually abused when she was six. She was raped for the first time at twelve. She was forced into prostitution by one of her mother's boyfriends at fourteen. She had her first abortion at fifteen. Her second at sixteen. Both decisions were made *for* her. By men who used her body to feed a drug addiction."

She started walking slowly back and forth in front of the jury. Her eyes darted between her fellow Plaintiff and the women in the jury. "Tamika Johnson has been beaten and disfigured. She has been traumatized and emotionally scarred for life."

She stopped abruptly. "She has learned her body is not her own. She has learned it exists for men who control it for their own interests. Ladies and gentlemen of the jury, it was *this* hellish reality that drove her out of the West Philadelphia home she shares with her mother, her mother's two boyfriends, and her twelve brothers and sisters, and onto the street."

Watkins' carefully elevated the decibel level. "Once again, young Tamika Johnson found herself pregnant. Once again, she was in trouble. Once again, she faced a life threatening beating. But this time, she vowed, it would be different. This time, she would find a safe, private, *legal* solution to her problems."

She paused, and pointed to her fellow Plaintiff. "This is what drove Tamika Johnson to the door of the Gianna Molla Clinic in Narbrook six months ago on April 1. She simply wanted a safe, painless way out of her nightmare, nothing more, nothing less, than what the U.S. government regards as an *essential service* in its contract with its service providers, like the Gianna Molla Clinic." She paused, and added, "Given Ms. Johnson's history, I'd say it's not too difficult to see why she and the U.S. government believe what she sought, and what she was denied, was, indeed, essential."

Heather Watkins turned and strolled in the direction of the Defendant's table. She stopped several feet from the table. "But what did she find?" Brief, dramatic pause. "She found *more rejection*! And I submit to you, in at least one way, the rejection she experienced at the Gianna Molla Clinic was *even more painful* to Tamika Johnson. She was told she was *wrong* for wanting the abortion pill. She was *wrong* to want to abort the fetus forced on her by a man she didn't know and would never see again. She was *wrong* to come to a clinic like Gianna Molla, and ask people like Jim and Margaret Gillespie for a pill, a pill, to end her nightmare!"

Heather Watkins paused to allow her disdain for the Defendants to settle in the courtroom. "Never mind that this solution, this end to her latest nightmare, this blessed pill, is a legal right by virtue of her U.S. citizenship. Never mind that the Gianna Molla Clinic signed a contract with a U.S. government chartered and subsidized insurance carrier that they would provide essential services to U.S. citizens. Never mind that Gianna Molla has collected over two million dollars in patient reimbursement funds from that same U.S. government over the past ten years."

She paused and pointed to the Defendants. "Tamika Johnson went to the Gianna Molla Clinic for a life preserver. What she got instead was a lecture. She went to the clinic believing she had a constitutionally protected right, a *Liberty Interest* as defined by the highest court in the land, to a private abortion of an unwanted fetus that was imposed upon her. What she got instead was the unwanted Christian religious belief of the clinic's founders imposed upon her."

She strolled purposefully toward the jury, stopped at the railing, and said, "By what right do the Defendants deny the Plaintiff a constitutionally protected liberty, and continue collecting money from the U.S. government? By what right do they continue collecting our tax dollars, and continue imposing the restrictive tenets of Catholic doctrine? By what right do they challenge settled law regarding privacy rights, and expect this Plaintiff, and this court, to look the other way?"

She turned to walk back to the Plaintiff's table, stopped abruptly, turned to the jury, and said with a trace of mock dudgeon, "I am fully confident that you will make it clear to the Defendants, at the end of this trial, that they have no such right." She turned, walked back to her table, and sat down. As she did so, she patted the left knee of her co-plaintiff, who leaned her head upon her attorney's shoulder in response.

The courtroom was near perfectly still. William Draper gave the U.S. Attorney a long, indecipherable stare. He turned to Paul Nicolosi, who was seated at the table with Jim and Maggie Gillespie, and said, "Does the defense counsel wish to make an opening statement?"

Nicolosi nodded and replied, "Yes, your honor." He stood and walked quickly to the jury box. He held a yellow legal pad in his left hand. He glanced at it briefly, set it on the rail in front of him, and began, "Ladies and gentlemen, first of all let me thank you for your participation in this trial." He paused, and added, "I thank you for two reasons. First, you are truly the jury the defendants hoped to draw—attentive, reasoned, and honest. Secondly, as you will quickly discover, this trial in a very real sense involves *your interests,* in precisely the same way it involves the interests of Jim and Maggie Gillespie, and all others who share their dilemma, which is to say every man, woman, and *particularly child,* in America."

He paused to allow the jury to absorb that declaration. "You will come to see that after fifty years of juridical innovation, the balance between the right of an individual and the right of a society has irreversibly tipped toward the individual to the detriment of society. You will see that there is *no* language in the clinic's contract with the U.S. government's preferred insurance provider that refers to abortion as an *essential service,* absolutely none. You will see that the legal basis for the Plaintiff's complaint, the so-called right to define 'one's own concept of existence, of meaning, of the mystery of life' found in Kennedy is not a one way street. It cannot be applied to one individual even as it is being denied to two individuals," he paused and pointed to the Gillespie's.

"But it is not merely the claims we will make on behalf of the Defendants, but the *facts* . . . *the stubborn, irrefutable, empirical facts* . . . which underlie those claims, that will allow you to see, beyond a shadow of a doubt, that if the Plaintiff's argument is to prevail, our communities will not."

He started to pace quickly along the railing, which separated him from the first row of the jury. "In summary, you will be asked to address a very simple, fundamental question: "Does the right of an individual extend all the way up to *and through* the clearly foreseeable end of a cohesive society as the Framers understood it?" He walked back and forth, shaking his head. "In other words, does the *Liberty Interest* the High Court found for the individual in Kennedy, extend to the systematic loss of the 'blessings of liberty' for all, *including that individual?*" He stopped abruptly, scanned the eyes of the jurors quickly, and said, "In plain language, you will be asked to decide if an individual can be permitted to destroy the very society upon which he or she depends for the very services, *essential*, to his or her survival?"

He quickly reached for his legal pad on the jury railing, turned, and walked back to the defense table. There he paused, looked at the jury, and concluded: "I dare say, when all the evidence in this case has been presented, *none of us will dare say* that the U.S. Constitution guarantees this right to any individual, even Tamika Johnson."

Paul Nicolosi sat down. Maggie Gillespie leaned over and hugged him. He turned away in non-verbal rebuke.

Bill Draper missed none of the interactions in his courtroom, including those among jurors and spectators. He waited for several long minutes before looking in the direction of Heather Watkins, and said, "Would the Plaintiffs like to present their first witness?"

The Assistant U.S. Attorney rose quickly and assisted Tamika Johnson to her feet. She walked with her to the witness stand, and stood several steps away as she was sworn in. When the witness was settled in, Heather Watkins, again working without notes, initiated the questioning: "Would the witness please state her name for the record?"

"Tamika Johnson."

"Would the witness state her age?"

"Seventeen."

Ms. Watkins' tone softened. "Tamika, could you please tell the court what happened on April 1 of this year?"

"I went to the clinic to get me that abortion pill," she replied, in what appeared to be a rehearsed monotone. "But that lady there," she pointed to Maggie Gillespie, "she say she didn't have those pills. Then she told me that even if she did have those pills, she wouldn't give me one, because it was wrong to take it, because it would kill the baby."

"And how did this make you feel, Tamika?"

"I dunno," the witness responded, warily searching her attorney's eyes for some cue she may have missed.

The U.S. Attorney was nothing if not a patient woman. "Did you have any concerns about returning to your neighborhood, still pregnant?"

"Objection! Leading your honor," Paul Nicolosi claimed, loudly, as he half rose to his feet.

"Sustained," Bill Draper replied, casting a sharp glance in the U.S. Attorney's direction.

"Yes, your honor," Heather Watkins acknowledged with a ready smile. "Let me rephrase the question." She turned back to the witness and said, "Tamika, what did you think when you heard Mrs. Gillespie say she wasn't going to give you the abortion pill?"

The girl shrugged. "I dunno. I was . . . like . . . why not? Why I can't get me one? I'll bet you be givin' 'em to the white girls," she eyed her attorney for some indication of approval, but received a different kind of signal that she did not understand.

Heather Watkins decided to go in a different direction. "Tamika, tell us about your home life?"

"What you mean home life?"

"I mean, can you describe for the jury what life is like for you at home?"

"I told y'all, I ain't got a home."

"Well, what was life like when you *did* have a home?"

"Bad."

"How bad?"

"Real bad."

"Tamika, what kind of things happened when you lived at home?"

The girl slunk down in her seat. "Lots of bad stuff. People be drinkin' and yellin' and doin' drugs and doin' sex and beatin' on each other."

"Did that happen to you too?"

"Yeah."

"Tamika, how many abortions have you had?"

The girl shrugged. "I dunno."

"More than three?"

"I guess."

Heather Watkins stiffened: "Tamika, how much money are you given for a . . . transaction with a man?"

"Twenty dollar."

"How many . . . uh . . . how often do you do those . . . that sort of thing in one day?"

"I dunno."

"Do you always get paid? Do you get twenty dollars each time you provide this service for a man?"

"No," the girl replied emphatically. "Lots of times they be givin me nothin'."

"What happens when you ask for the money?"

She shrugged. "Some guys just beat me till I don't aks again."

"Tamika, do your John's give you birth control pills?"

"Sometime they do but most of the time they don't."

"Do you take them when they do give them to you?"

The girl probed her attorney's eyes for the correct answer. She did not find the answer she was looking for. "No, they don't work anyway. So I just buy my own rubbers." She frowned. "But they don't really work either."

Caught off guard, the U.S. Attorney asked, "Tamika, do you think the fact that the Johns don't give you birth control pills regularly, so you can't take them regularly, might have something to do with the pills not working?"

The girl shrugged in indifference. "I guess."

"Tamika, final question, what happened when you went back to the street after leaving the Gianna Molla Clinic without the abortion pill?"

The girl sat up straight and replied on cue, "I got beat for being pregnant. It was a real bad beating," she said, as she glanced nervously at the jury and then back to her attorney.

Heather Watkins looked at Bill Draper and said, "No further questions your honor."

Draper turned to Paul Nicolosi and said, "Would the counsel for the defense like to question the witness?"

"Yes, your honor," Nicolosi replied, jumping quickly to his feet. He closed the distance between the defense table and the witness stand in small hurried steps, not unlike a cocker spaniel on a linoleum kitchen floor.

"Ms. Johnson, how many brothers and sisters do you have?"

"Objection your honor!" Heather Watkins claimed from her seat. "Relevance?"

The Judge looked at Nicolosi, who quickly interjected: "Your honor, if it pleases the court, the Plaintiff's attorney provided a number of biographical details about Ms. Johnson in her opening statement. I think it is only fair to test the veracity of some of them on behalf of the jury."

Bill Draper nodded, looked at the U.S. Attorney, and said tersely: "Overruled." He then turned to Tamika Johnson and said, "The witness will answer the question."

The witness was clearly confused. "What question?"

Paul Nicolosi repeated the question.

"I dunno," the girl replied. "I don't know who my daddy is."

Nicolosi glanced at the jury, and pursued, "How many surgical abortions have you had, Ms. Johnson?"

The girl glanced at her attorney before answering. "I think one or two."

Nicolosi glanced at the jury, and continued. "How many times have you been beaten because you got pregnant?"

The girl glanced at her attorney and shrugged. "I dunno."

"A lot or a little?"

"A little . . . I guess."

Nicolosi quickly resettled his feet, and lowered the boom: "Ms. Johnson, how did you get to the Gianna Molla Clinic on April 1?"

The girl pointed to a middle-aged Caucasian woman in the first row of spectators, and replied: "She took me."

"Do you know the name of the woman who provided transportation, Ms. Johnson?"

"Objection, your honor!" Heather Watkins fairly howled in protest. "Relevance?"

Draper looked at Nicolosi and asked, "Where are you going with this, counselor?"

"Judge, I am simply testing the veracity of the Plaintiff's facts in the case," he replied hastily.

"I'll let you go a little bit further down this road counselor, but you better get where you're going quickly," Draper replied. "The witness will answer the question," he added, as he stole a furtive glance at the U.S. Attorney who was clearly unhappy.

"I don't know her name," the girl replied in a low monotone, sensing trouble.

"Is she employed by Proper Parenthood?"

"Your honor!" Watkins screamed.

"Sustained," Draper said, behind a withering stare aimed at the back of Paul Nicolosi's pupils.

"Ms. Johnson, how much were you paid to go to the Gianna Molla Clinic on April 1?"

Instant bedlam. The shouts from a small cluster of spectators actually drowned out the high decibel cries issuing forth from the U.S. Attorney. Judge William Draper was very nearly apoplectic. He banged his gavel furiously once, twice, three times. "Order! Order! Order," he bellowed. He glared at Nicolosi who quickly interjected: "I withdraw the question your honor, and I only have one final question for the witness."

"Make it quick, counselor," the Judge replied. "You have already exhausted my patience."

Nicolosi nodded. He looked at the jury to assess the impact from the scrum. He couldn't read it. He turned to the witness and said, "Ms. Johnson, were you actually pregnant when you entered the clinic on the morning of April 1?"

It was not clear if the witness's shrug was observable to members of the jury in the commotion that followed. Nicolosi's eyes were trained on them, and he feared the subtle turn of the witness's shoulders may have been too nuanced to be detected from across the courtroom. His heart began to beat at a precipitously higher rate. He turned his attention back to the Judge, who once again was banging his gavel. When the noise died down, the Judge glared at Nicolosi and the U.S. Attorney and said: "I want to see you both in my chambers. Now!"

Bill Draper looked at the jury and declared, "This court is in recess. You are to go to the jury room and you are not to talk to each other about this case, or anything that transpired this morning. Is that clear?"

Eyes wide, the twelve jurors nodded in silent submission. The bailiff appeared and led the jury, single file, out of the courtroom, down a narrow hallway, and into the jury room.

The trial of the St. Gianna Molla Natural Family Planning Clinic had begun.

24

Judge William Draper re-entered a notably subdued court-room with the courtly air of an Ethiopian prince.

He sat quickly, looked at the Plaintiff table, nodded and said, "You may call your next witness."

Heather Watkins stood erect and enunciated carefully, "Your Honor, the U.S. Government calls Dr. Jim Gillespie to the stand."

Jim Gillespie looked at his wife in surprise, stood, and walked to the witness stand and was quickly sworn in.

"Dr. Gillespie, were you at the Gianna Molla Clinic on the morning of April 1 of this year?"

"No, I decided to get a co-rectal examination instead." Jim Gillespie looked at the jury and added, "Wish I had known about this trial." The men laughed; the women did not.

The U.S. Attorney looked nervously at the Judge before deciding to plow ahead. "Do you know how many women have passed through the clinic since you opened nearly ten years ago?"

"'Passed' as in gas or 'passed' as in death?"

Ms. Watkins frowned. "Patrons of the clinic's services?"

"I'd say about half."

She ignored his evasion. "What are the clinic's annual gross receipts?"

"Not enough."

The U.S. Attorney had had enough. "No further questions, Your Honor."

The Judge looked at Paul Nicolosi, and said, "Does Defense Counsel want to cross?"

Nicolosi smiled and replied, "Wouldn't dare, Your Honor." A small spasm of nervous laughter erupted from the jurors and spectators. It fell as quickly as it rose.

"Next Witness?" Bill Draper said, nodding to Heather Watkins.

Heather Watkins, who had not moved from her spot near the witness stand, turned to the Judge and said, "The U.S. Government calls Margaret Ann Gillespie to the stand."

Maggie wasted no time getting to the stand and getting sworn in. When she was settled, she looked at her husband and smiled.

"Mrs. Gillespie, were *you* at the Gianna Molla Clinic in Narbrook, Pennsylvania on the morning of April 1?"

"Yes."

"Did you have any interaction with the Plaintiff?"

"Yes."

"Could you describe it for the Court?"

Maggie looked at Tamika Johnson with a mother's love. "I'd be happy to," she replied, as she folded her hands on her lap. "Tamika told us she was pregnant and asked us if we carried the abortion pill. I said we didn't carry it and would never even consider carrying it."

"Did you tell her why you didn't carry mifepristone?"

Maggie nodded. "I did. I told her she was carrying the miracle of precious new life in her womb, and that this pill would kill that tiny treasure. I also told her the clinic existed, primarily, to help couples conceive and carry just such new life to term."

The U.S. Attorney quickly glanced at the jury. "Mrs. Gillespie, how did Tamika react to what you told her?"

"She seemed interested at first. Then, I don't know . . ." Maggie's voice trailed off.

"Mrs. Gillespie, I know you believe what you told Tamika to be true, that the fetus is a child, but my question is this: Isn't this what you Catholics are taught by your priests and nuns in your schools and parishes?"

Maggie Gillespie took visible exception to this charge. "The scientific evidence that what you call a fetus is in fact a human being is irrefutable, Ms. Watkins. Catholic priests and nuns only teach in our schools and parishes what we Catholics are taught in our homes by our parents. As we grow and learn, we are happy to discover that this wondrous truth is affirmed in our hearts through the great gift of Natural Law."

The U.S. Attorney took visible exception to this claim. She was, however, sufficiently disciplined to resist challenging it. She looked instead at the jury to ensure they had heard the zealot clearly. It appeared they had.

"No further questions, Your Honor," she advised the Judge.

Bill Draper nodded toward Paul Nicolosi. "Does Defense Counsel have any questions for the witness?"

"Just one, Your Honor," Nicolosi replied, already on his feet and moving toward the witness stand.

"Mrs. Gillespie," he began while in full motion. "Did you offer Ms. Johnson an alternative to this abortion pill?"

Maggie looked at Tamika Johnson, whose impassive face gave no hint that she was even interested in, much less following, the proceedings. "Yes," she replied.

"And could you share that alternative plan with the Court?"

Maggie resettled herself in her seat and said, "I told Tamika that I would personally introduce her to a woman who runs a home in Darby for homeless expectant mothers." A woman juror was heard to moan in apparent sympathy. The courtroom fell silent in contemplation of the signal.

"Anything else?" Nicolosi prodded.

Maggie shrugged. "I told her we would arrange for a good

family to adopt her child if she didn't think she was in a position to raise the child after giving birth."

Nicolosi allowed that response to settle for several long moments before he concluded, "No further questions, Your Honor."

Maggie dismounted to a barely perceptible nod from Nicolosi. She glanced at the jury. Two women were crying.

Bill Draper looked at Heather Watkins. "Does the Plaintiff wish to call its next witness?"

"Yes, Your Honor. The U.S. Government calls Mr. Joseph Flauck."

A tall, reed thin man with rimless spectacles stood, and approached the witness stand to be sworn in. When he was seated, the U.S. Attorney approached the stand and commenced the questioning. "Would the witness give his full name?"

"Joseph Francis Flauck."

"Mr. Flauck, would you tell the court what you do for a living?"

"I am the executive director of the non-profit division of the Internal Revenue Service."

There was an audible gasp in the courtroom, though it was not clear whether it originated among the jury or the spectators.

"Mr. Flauck, have you ever done an audit on the Gianna Molla Clinic in Narbrook, Pennsylvania?"

"No, I have not."

The U.S. Attorney pointedly bounced her gaze from the Judge to the jury, to the defendants, to signal fair play. "Have you taken a look at the clinic's filings over the past several years?"

"Yes, I have."

"Any irregularities?"

"Objection Your Honor!" Paul Nicolosi bellowed. "This is an invasion of privacy, and it does not bear on the issues being contested before this court!"

"I am going to permit it," Judge Draper said carefully. "The witness may answer the question."

"No," Joe Flauck replied shaking his head. "Everything looks to be in order."

A small squall of laughter greeted the witness's response.

Heather Watkins turned toward the jury, lifted her jaw, and said, "Mr. Flauck, how much money has the U.S. Government paid the Gillespies, and the Gianna Molla Clinic, over the past ten years, just in reimbursement fees for the services they provide the clinic's patrons?"

"$2,186,437.48."

The U.S. Attorney paused to allow that disclosure to settle in and about the courtroom. It induced at least one modest but nonetheless audible gasp from a spectator. "No further questions, Your Honor," she said a bit too theatrically.

Bill Draper looked at Paul Nicolosi, but before he could release his question the Defense Counsel was waving his arms in an international signal of surrender. "I wouldn't dare cross examine the IRS, Your Honor," Nicolosi said to howls of laughter from the jury and the spectators. Even Heather Watkins smiled, though Tamika Johnson did not.

"Any other witnesses for the Plaintiff?" Bill Draper asked, when the laughter had died down and out.

"Yes, one more, Your Honor," the U.S. Attorney replied. "The U.S. Government calls Judith von Hedrick to the stand."

A slightly overweight middle-aged woman with a butch cut stood and approached the witness stand. She was sworn in and immediately proceeded to stare down Maggie Gillespie.

"Would the witness state her name and occupation for the court?" Heather Watkins prompted.

"My name is Judith Ashley von Hedrick, and I am the deputy director for Health and Human Services."

"Ms. von Hedrick, are you familiar with the federal government's standard health insurance contract with non-profit providers, like the Gianna Molla Clinic in Narbrook, Pennsylvania?"

"I am."

"Does that contract require that federally regulated health

care providers, like the Gianna Molla Clinic, make *essential services* available to U.S. citizens in full accordance with the U.S. Constitution's guarantee of Substantive Due Process?"

At the Defense table Jim Gillespie glanced at Tamika Johnson and scripted an imaginary shout out: "Yeah baby! That's what I'm talkin' 'bout!"

"Yes," she replied tersely. She looked at Maggie Gillespie and added, "It most certainly does."

"And does the U.S. Department of Health and Human Services regard the right to an abortion as an *essential service* for a woman like Tamika Johnson?"

"Objection!" Nicolosi exclaimed. "Your Honor, that's a question for the jury to answer."

Bill Draper frowned. "Overruled! Ms. von Hedrick represents an organization with standing in this court and is party to the contract in dispute. Seems to me she ought to be able to provide the court with her organization's understanding of their own contract, Counselor."

Nicolosi's shoulders sagged.

"The witness will answer the question," the Judge ordered.

"I should say so!" von Hedrick rasped, her eyes fixed on the women in the jury.

"Would you tell us why HHS regards abortion as an essential service?"

Von Hedrick's eyes widened. She stared at Maggie Gillespie, and said, "Life threatening conditions, psychological harm, family impairment, child anomalies, career derailment, and the stigma of unwed motherhood, to name a few." She paused, looked at the jury, and added, "I'm sure I don't have to remind anyone in this courtroom that this is precisely why the Supreme Court declared abortion to be a fundamental constitutional right in Roe v. Wade."

Heather Watkins let her witness's response settle for a long moment, before she continued. "Can you think of a single reason why the Gianna Molla Clinic in Narbrook, Pennsylvania would be justified in denying Ms. Johnson her constitutional right to mifepristone?"

"Objection Your Honor!" Nicolosi shouted in frustration.

"Overruled!" Bill Draper said at a matching decibel level. "The witness may answer the question."

"No, I cannot," von Hedrick replied, staring through each Gillespie in turn.

"No further questions, Your Honor," Heather Watkins said to Bill Draper, who turned to Paul Nicolosi and said, "Does the defense have any questions for the witness?"

"No Your Honor," Nicolosi replied from his seat. "I find Ms. von Hedrick even more frightening than the gentleman from the IRS."

Scattered and spontaneous laughter assured the attorney that he had just scored more points for his defendants with a throw-away line than he would have won with a cross examination.

Bill Draper was not smiling. He nodded to the witness that she could stand down, and turned to Paul Nicolosi and said, "Does the Defense have any witnesses it would like to call to the stand?"

"Yes, Your Honor," Nicolosi replied, reaching for his legal pad on the table in front of him. "The Defense would like to call Mr. Raymond Pizzaro to the stand."

A smallish, middle-aged man in an elegantly tailored Armani suit rose, approached the stand, and was sworn in.

"Mr. Pizzaro, would you please state your full name and occupation for the court," Nicolosi prodded.

"Mr. Raymond Anthony Pizzaro. I am the chairman of the Federal Reserve Board here in Philadelphia."

The courtroom immediately grew still. Nicolosi allowed the silence to set his trajectory. "Mr. Pizzaro, would you please tell the court how much debt the United States is presently carrying?"

Ray Pizzaro affected the air of a sage, and tugged at his monogrammed cuffs before answering. Nicolosi accepted the local coloring as a necessary quid pro quo for what he prayed would be seismic testimony. "We are now just below twenty-one trillion dollars."

"And what is the current value our annual Gross Domestic Product, our GDP?"

"We're down now to around fourteen trillion."

"Can you explain for the court what this means in practical terms?"

Ray Pizzaro shrugged. "Sure. It means for every dollar of goods we Americans annually produce, we have borrowed a dollar and a half to maintain our comfortable, secure lifestyles."

Paul Nicolosi was not certain the jurors had grasped the full significance of that disclosure. "Mr. Pizzaro, would you tell the court what it means when a nation is twenty-one trillion dollars in debt?"

Ray Pizzaro had been bullied unmercifully as an undersized child in his Catholic grade school playground in South Philadelphia. It was a matter of no small pride that a number of his former tormentors were employees of his potato chip company, which had its offices and manufacturing plant on the site of the former Navy Yard in Southwest Philadelphia. His rise to power and influence was well chronicled in the local media, and his stature as a civic leader was further enhanced by his many philanthropic endeavors on behalf of city's underclass. His wardrobe, his bearing, even the slight affectation in dialect, gave notice to all that he had arrived. "It means we are broke," he said with dramatic purpose. "Not going broke," he added. "But *actually* broke."

"And what does that mean to those of us in this courtroom?"

Ray Pizzaro looked at the jury and thrust his jaw in the air to signal the imminence of Gospel truth. "It means we can no longer afford our schools, our police departments, our hospitals. We can no longer afford to maintain our roads and highways and bridges. It means our banks can no longer lend us money to buy homes and start businesses. It means the actual value of the homes we live in are worth pennies on the dollar. It means our pension funds and IRAs are essentially worthless."

"Break that down for us a bit if you would, Mr. Pizzaro. How much federal and state debt is each of us in this courtroom carrying at this very moment?"

"A little over three hundred fifty thousand dollars," Pizzaro replied quickly.

"And just who will inherit our debt?"

"Our children and grandchildren."

"How will our children and grandchildren pay down our debt?" Nicolosi probed, eyes on the jury.

"They can't, and won't."

"How can you be certain?"

"Because they are about to be hit with an absolute wipeout tsunami within the next five to ten years."

"What kind of tsunami, Mr. Pizzaro?"

"A debt tsunami."

"Could you explain?"

Ray Pizzaro was having fun. He loved being an authority, the answer man, the 'go-to' guy in his company, in his community, and now in this courtroom. "Because the federal government is basically just printing money now," he said with affected grimness. "We have a situation where we don't know what a U.S. dollar is worth from one day to the next." He paused, and looked at the jurors, several of whom nodded in agreement. "But on top of that we have an *additional* one hundred trillion dollars in IOUs coming due. Those are the Social Security, Medicare, Medicaid promises the U.S. Government has made *to us*, by us, I mean, us adults, on behalf of our children and grandchildren." He shuddered involuntarily. "There is simply no way these obligations can be met."

"Why not?"

"Not enough children and grandchildren." Ray Pizzaro paused, and looked at the jury. "Not near enough children and grandchildren." He looked at the spectators in the courtroom and added, "Two generations ago we had five taxpayers for every retiree. In this generation to come, those numbers will be reversed."

There was an audible murmuring in the courtroom that drew a stern, voiceless rebuke from Judge William Draper.

Paul Nicolosi felt momentum. "And what happens when a government can't meet its obligation to its citizens?"

Ray Pizzaro shrugged. "It falls," he replied matter-of-factly.

"And what would that mean, again to those of us in this courtroom?"

"Anarchy," he replied quickly "Blood in the streets." He paused and added, "And, as I say, no police to stop it. We will no longer be able to afford to pay them."

Paul Nicolosi looked at Bill Draper, and said, "No further questions, Your Honor."

Draper looked at Heather Watkins, who shook her head. He turned back to Nicolosi and said, "Do you have any more witnesses?"

"Yes, Your Honor," he chirped. "The Defense calls Paula Condino."

A striking, dark haired, doe-eyed beauty in her early forties rose and made her way to the witness stand, where she was promptly sworn in.

"Ms. Condino, could you please state your full name and occupation for the court," Nicolosi requested.

"I am Pauline Francesca Condino, and I am the executive director of the U.S. Census Bureau."

"And for those of us who are not familiar with what the Bureau does, would you please tell us about its activities and functions?"

"Yes, of course," she replied, flashing a disarming smile. She looked at the jury and said, "Basically, we keep track of the U.S. population, its composition, its trends, its socio-economic dimensions."

"Socio-economic dimensions, what does that mean?" Nicolosi probed, eyes on the jurors.

Ms. Condino nodded in anticipation. "We are constantly examining the data for public policy implications and planning purposes."

"What would be an example of a significant public policy issue embedded in the Census data?"

The witness lost her smile. She looked at her hands, which were folded in her lap, and said, "Uh, replacement levels."

"And what does that mean, replacement levels?" Nicolosi asked, inching closer to the stand.

"A nation's replacement level is the average number of children per couple that is required to maintain and perpetuate a population."

"And, what is that number?"

"2.1 children per couple."

"And what is the current average number of children born to each U.S. couple?"

"I.4."

"And what is the significance of that?"

"It means we are not replacing ourselves."

"Yes, I know," Nicolosi said patiently. "What I'm asking is what happens when a population does not replace itself?"

The witness squirmed. "Historically, it leads to massive and unmanageable immigration levels, cultural diffusion and confusion, loss of identity and sovereignty."

"Is that what the United States of America is experiencing now?"

"Objection! Speculative," shouted Heather Watkins.

"Over-ruled," replied Judge William Draper calmly. He nodded at the witness to continue.

Paula Condino was now clearly uncomfortable. "Yes," she replied tentatively.

"Can you give the court some specifics, some way to look at the data that would help us understand the full significance of what you are saying?"

Paula Condino blinked. "Uh, yes. The 18–44's were under-represented in the last generation by about 22 percent. They're under-represented in this generation by 46 percent."

"By 18–44's, do you mean men and women of child bearing age?"

"Yes."

"And by under-represented, do you mean less than the previous generation?"

"Yes."

Paul Nicolosi looked at the jurors. "Does that mean we haven't produced enough children?"

"Yes, I suppose that's one way of putting it," Condino replied.

"Is there another, perhaps better, way of putting it?" Nicolosi asked, careful to scrub any condescension out of his tone.

The witness squirmed uncomfortably. "Well, I don't suppose so," she replied, eyes cast to the floor.

"No further questions, Your Honor."

Bill Draper looked at Heather Watkins who, again, signaled she had no desire to cross examine the Defense's witness. Draper looked at Nicolosi and asked, "Any other witnesses, Counselor?"

"Just one, Your Honor," Nicolosi replied eagerly. "The Defense calls Erik Halloway," he said, nodding to a formidable young man in his mid-thirties, sitting in the back of the courtroom with his right leg crossed over his left knee. He rose slowly and walked with a discernibly athletic gait to the witness stand to be sworn in.

"Would the witness state his full name and occupation for the court," Nicolosi said quickly.

"My name is Erik Nicholas Halloway, and I am the owner of Halloway Real Estate in Narbrook."

Paul Nicolosi started to pace. "So, Erik, how's the real estate market?"

The young man grimaced, and replied, "Not good."

"And what exactly does 'not good' mean, Erik?"

The young man squirmed. "Well, my dad said he's never seen it this bad," he replied, with a nod to an older man occupying a chair next to the one he had just vacated.

"What seems to be the problem?"

Erik Halloway laughed. "Where to start!?"

"Start anywhere you want," Nicolosi replied expansively, eyes on the jurors.

"Well, *demand,* I don't even think we can use that word anymore. I mean there just isn't any demand, so prices keep plummeting."

"So what are the people who need to sell their homes doing?"

"Nothing." Halloway looked at his father and said, "I mean there's nothing they can do."

"So there are not enough buyers for people who want to sell their homes."

"Not even close," the witness replied emphatically.

"So what will happen to the sellers of those homes?"

Erik Halloway shifted uneasily in his chair. "With the cost of everything rising so fast now, and the value of the dollar plummeting even faster, a lot of people can't afford to stay in their homes," he replied quietly.

"Where are they going?"

"Some are going to live with children. Some, I don't know, I really don't know where the others end up."

"How many homes are there in Narbrook?"

"618."

"How many are up for sale?"

"273."

"How many legitimate buyers do you see out there for those 273 homes?" Nicolosi probed.

Erik Halloway shrugged. "Well, *legitimate* used to mean people who could get a mortgage, but banks aren't lending anymore, so," he shrugged his massive shoulders, "I don't know what to tell you." He paused, and added, "Not more than a small handful, that's for sure."

Paul Nicolosi eyed the jurors, and asked one final question. "Three generations of Halloways have lived and sold real estate in Narbrook for over one hundred years. How would you characterize the town today?"

The youngest Halloway's eyes fell to the ground, and his reply was brief and muted: "It's a ghost town," he said softly. "We used to have twenty-six merchants in town. There are only eight left, and they tell me they'd get out too if they could."

"Where are Narbrook residents doing their shopping?"

A frown creased Erik Halloway's classic features. "I don't really know. Most of them are old and depend on their children to bring them the things they need." He paused, looked at his father, and added, "Some of them don't have children close by. Dad and I try to help the ones we can."

Paul Nicolosi looked at Bill Draper and said, "No further questions, Your Honor."

The Judge turned to Heather Watkins and asked, "Any questions for the witness?"

The Assistant U.S. Attorney for the Eastern District shook her head. She had no interest in being a foil for the Defense.

"Very well," Bill Draper said, eyes darting from one counsel to the other. "Are you each prepared to make your closing statement?"

Both attorneys nodded. Paul Nicolosi appeared to nod a bit more eagerly.

Heather Watkins rose a bit uncertainly, and walked slowly toward the jury. She held a yellow legal pad in her hand. On the pad were hand written notes. She consulted the notes briefly, then stood erect, scanned the faces of the jurors, and began, "Ladies and gentlemen of the jury. We have just witnessed the Defendants' attempt to divert your attention from the singular issue in this case." She paused and scanned the eyes of her audience. "And that is this. Do James and Margaret Gillespie, and the Gianna Molla Clinic they own and operate, have the right to accept our federal tax dollars on the one hand, and deny an *essential service* to Tamika Johnson on the other, simply because *they* maintain that the provision of this service is *not compatible* with *their* private religious beliefs?"

She began to move her feet in slow measured steps in front of the jury. "We did not hear the counsel for the Defendants contest this point, did we?" She stopped abruptly. "And why not!? Because, he knows he can't! It is simply incontestable. Like a rose, a law is a law is a law. And though in a free society some of us may not *like* a particular law, we are nonetheless obligated to *obey* it." She paused, and looked at Paul Nicolosi. "Because if we citizens do not obey our nation's laws, instead picking and choosing those we like and therefore will obey, and those we don't like and therefore won't obey, we know what will happen." She paused and stabbed the air with a forefinger. "We will end up with the very anarchy the Defense Counsel tried to frighten us into believing is imminent!"

She shifted her weight. "Ladies and gentlemen, Tamika Johnson is trapped in a hellish existence. She has no power, no voice, and no hope. The men who control her body control her life. These men demand that she continue to generate cash to feed their addictions. The minute her body is shut down by an unwanted pregnancy, her very life is in danger. You have heard her describe what this is like. You have taken the full measure of her desperation. You have felt her fear."

She moved closer to the jury. "The U.S. Constitution speaks to these holes in society's safety net. It is called Due Process. It means simply that every one of us, *including Tamika Johnson*, has an equal standing before the law. None of us can be denied our rights."

She leaned both hands on the railing. "You have heard the U.S. Government say very clearly that the contract it has with the Gillespie's and the Gianna Molla Clinic *mandates* the provision of *essential services*. You have heard the U.S. Government say this morning that the abortion pill *is an essential service*. And you have heard this morning *precisely why* the abortion pill is an essential service for a woman like Tamika Johnson."

Heather Watkins pulled back and stood erect. "The highest court in all the land termed this essential service a *Liberty Interest*. In saying this, the Supreme Court is telling us that Tamika Johnson's right to an abortion is at the very heart of what it means to be free in America."

The U.S. Attorney paused, summoned a requisite emphasis, and concluded: "Ladies and gentlemen. In reality, Tamika Johnson may not be free *outside* this courtroom. But," she raised a forefinger above her head, "she can . . . and she *must* . . . be set free *inside* this courtroom." She turned, walked back to the Plaintiff's table, and sat down.

The courtroom was eerily still. Judge William Draper turned to Paul Nicolosi, and nodded. He stood and walked briskly to the jury box, stopping abruptly several feet in front of it. He silently scanned the eyes of the jurors, bobbed his head reflexively, and began, "Ladies and gentlemen of the jury, first let me thank you for your careful attention to what is really at stake in this case." He smiled. "I was watching you closely. And I saw that you understood what was being said in this courtroom this morning. I saw that you understood we have finally arrived at a new threshold in America."

He paused and began to pace, never taking his eyes off the jury. "Ladies and gentlemen, it is clear, is it not? We can *finally* put a price tag on radical autonomy. We can *finally* put a price tag on the canard that is unbridled Substantive Due Process, to *excuse* wanton excess . . . to *excuse* a refusal to accept personal responsibility . . . to *excuse* a refusal to acknowledge what each of us in our heart knows . . . has always known," he stopped and thundered: "*That the indefensible is unsustainable!*"

He resumed his pacing. "My mother, God rest her soul, used to say, 'Sin is expensive.'"

He smiled. "And what in the name of God is grand theft from our children and grandchildren, if not *sin*?"

The courtroom grew still. "My friends, radical autonomy, this notion that a society can grant every individual unlimited and unfettered freedoms to the clear detriment of all others, is absurd! And, as we have learned today, this absurdity has a cost! And that cost is the very foundation, the very bricks and mortar, of society itself.

"My friends, in declaring the murder of a child in the womb a *Liberty Interest,* in categorizing it contractually as an *essential service* mandated under law, we have put the barrel of a gun in our own mouths and pulled the trigger.

"We have shot and killed ourselves!" Paul Nicolosi's voice rose in pitch and decibel. "We no longer have enough children and grandchildren to survive as a free and sovereign nation. All that remains is the final loosening of the bonds that have bound us for two hundred fifty years before we descend into the unspeakable."

He paused and changed his inflection. "And still, *still*, our government, a government supposedly of, by, and for the people, presses its case for more!" He half yelled: "More!!!" He shook his head. "You have heard this morning that the little town of Narbrook is a ghost town. Most of its residents simply can't afford to live there anymore, and, even worse, they can't even find enough young people to buy their homes!"

He paused, and grimaced. "These men and women are Americans too. These men and women have rights too. They have a right to live in a community of their choosing. They have a right to know the value of their currency. They have a right to a secure future to the degree that they have worked a lifetime to provide for that secure future.

"But these rights have been effectively denied them! Make no mistake. In the name of *Liberty Interests* for people like Tamika Johnson, in the name of *essential services* that include abortion that are nothing less than government mandates forced upon people like Jim and Maggie Gillespie, these Americans have been abandoned by the very government their tax dollars have long subsidized. They have been refused protection from ruinous government decisions, which have decimated the value of their currency and eviscerated the sustainability of their community."

He paused and looked at the male jurors. "Who will speak for them? Who will speak for our fathers and mothers? Who will speak for our sons and daughters, who have stopped bobbing on a sea of debt that was not of their creation, and are now beginning to sink below the surface of our society?"

Paul Nicolosi strode to the jury box, and leaned his upper body over the railing. "My friends, let us be clear! The real issue in this case is this: Must our communities continue to be denied the oxygen supply of new life by their own government!? Can the U.S. Government continue to mandate the killing of the very children our communities need to survive? Can the U.S. Department of Health and Human Services demand that our children and grandchildren be denied the very help, and hope, they so desperately need to sustain the American Experiment?"

He pulled back from the railing slowly, and deliberately. "Ladies and gentlemen of the jury, if you believe Jim and Maggie Gillespie represent not only *their* generation and our *next* generation, but also generations of Americans yet unborn, who will want what we once had, the right to build a future worthy of American citizens, you must render a clear verdict on their behalf."

He summoned a final rhetorical push. "My friends, you must render a verdict that is a powerful, unmistakable, full-bodied roar, originating in the very marrow of your beings. A verdict that proclaims from the rooftops of this courthouse that we Americans have finally reached our limit with the idea of every man, woman, and child having the right to define their own mystery of life at our expense!" He turned and started back to the Defense table only to stop, turn, and declare with vehemence, "Because, my friends, our society can simply no longer afford it!"

A loud murmur arose from the spectators, forcing Judge William Draper to bang his gavel twice. He fashioned a stern look of rebuke across all sections of the gallery. He looked at Heather Watkins and Paul Nicolosi, and nodded in silent respect.

Then he turned to the jury and said, "Okay, you may now begin your deliberations."

The bailiff appeared quite suddenly, seemingly from nowhere, and led the jurors in a single file to the jury room, where they would spend the better part of the next two weeks in historic debate, disputation, and decision.

25

Halle Simpson was incredulous.

"What do you mean we lost Laredo?" the president of the United States asked Winston Strobe, director of Homeland Security.

"Reports indicate the town is . . . uh, currently under the control of Mexican insurgents," he replied.

"Send the U.S. Army down there immediately, and give orders they are to take no prisoners!" she shouted, red with rage. Her failure to nuke Pakistan in retaliation for the suitcase bomb that obliterated lower Manhattan had cost her thirty-six points in the Gallup Poll. The loss of an American town on her watch, she understood, would prove even more devastating. It would mean no second term.

"They're on their way Madame President," he replied quickly. "But there is a problem."

"And what is the problem, Winston?" she asked with obvious irritation.

"Our people on the ground say the insurgents have effectively bought off many of our National Guardsmen, and there is speculation that when the shooting starts, the Guardsmen will be fighting with the enemy and, unfortunately, they'll be much better armed than our own forces."

Halle Simpson looked at the ceiling and exhaled audibly. She was surrounded by key advisers in a small, windowless conference room just off the Oval Office. It was an unseasonably warm spring afternoon, and the air conditioning was not working due to continuing problems with the electrical grid. Winston Strobe sat next to her. Graham Forrester, secretary of the Treasury, sat opposite her saying nothing. Derek Kaminski, secretary of Defense, sat next to Forrester, also tightlipped. Secretary of State, Heidi Schmidt, sat on one end of the table, and Sarah Wong, director of Health and Human Services, sat on the other. It pained the two women greatly to see their friend's administration unraveling at an accelerating pace.

The emergency meeting had been called to discuss Hanley Siliezar's proposal to provide the United States with the equivalency of almost twenty-five trillion U.S. dollars in Chinese-backed currency, in exchange for what in effect was U.S. sovereignty. The timing of a border skirmish with Mexico was not altogether helpful.

Halle Simpson stood, walked to a stationary coffee cart in the corner of the office, and poured herself a cup of Jamaican brewed caffeine in an attempt to rouse her synapses. "Why is all this happening at once?" she asked petulantly.

There was no answer.

"Maybe we should just hand the keys over to Siliezar," she suggested as she probed the eyes of her advisors. "I mean, what are our options?"

"We are the United States of America," Derek Kaminski retorted with far more rhetorical vehemence than required. "We are a sovereign nation, and we will not abrogate our constitutional form of government in response to a bribe from an architect of some global governance scheme." This declaration was met with silence. The others understood their colleague was simply rehearsing for what he hoped would be a subsequent press conference.

"How serious is the situation on the ground, Madame President?" Heidi Schmidt asked her friend and occasional lover.

"It is quite serious," Simpson replied. "I'm told most of the people in Laredo are sympathetic to the insurgents. They do not believe the U.S. government has the will to evict them and regain control of the town. Their leaders are talking to the other side and trying to cut the best deal possible in the event we do not prevail."

"We *will* prevail!" Kaminski interrupted.

The president of the United States simply looked at him and said nothing.

"Well, we really don't have a choice do we Mr. Secretary?" Winston Strobe said coolly. "Our border towns would fall like dominos. Then they would come after our cities." He looked at the others and said, "Think Corpus Christi, El Paso, Tucson." He stared at Kaminski and added, darkly, "And don't think for a minute they don't want Albuquerque, San Diego, and Los Angeles."

Halle Simpson had heard enough. "Back to the matter at hand," she barked. "We won't even *have* an army to defend our border cities if we don't get hard cash into the U.S. Treasury, fast."

Graham Forrester stirred. "Tell us again, Madame President, what Mr. Siliezar is proposing?"

Simpson distrusted Forrester. She had been effectively coerced into retaining his services by the prior administration, and she regarded him as a Siliezar plant. She knew Siliezar would know the details of whatever agreement was reached in this office well before the U.S. Congress.

"He . . . they . . . are asking for . . . ah . . . several things," she began guardedly. "They want to monitor the Department of Energy's records of carbon credit transactions with U.S. corporations. They want to review the Supreme Court's decisions on first amendment issues before they are announced. They want us to enact the Schmidt Constitution immediately, and introduce something they call a Universal Creed into our schools and universities to promote religious harmony; and . . ." her eyes darted nervously from one cabinet official to the other, "and, in pursuit of global peace, they are requesting joint oversight of our nuclear arsenal and our Navy."

"Outrageous!" Kaminski shouted.

Apparently none of the others agreed. Their silence spoke with greater force than the defense secretary's bellicosity.

"In exchange for how much cash?" Forrester inquired discretely.

"Who the hell cares how much, Graham!?" Kaminski remonstrated. "The United States of America is not for sale!"

"Perhaps," Forrester replied, his eyes locked on the eyes of the president.

Halle Simpson turned to her secretary of the Treasury and asked, "What are our options, Graham?"

"Two, and neither very good," Forrester replied quickly. "One, we can print more money, which will only cause even greater chaos in world markets and in our local super markets. Two, we can take a machete and cut the cost of federal government in half, trigger another round of deflation, and take unemployment from 23 percent to 34 percent."

Silence.

Halle Simpson leveled her gaze at Derek Kaminski, and asked, "Which of those options do you prefer, Mr. Secretary?"

Kaminski did not reply.

Simpson looked at Forrester and said, "Tell me the actual dollar value of an equivalency of sixteen trillion in Chinese hard currency?"

Forrester shrugged. "Depends on what day you ask me," he replied, with a wry smile that only served to increase the president's level of aggravation.

"I'm asking you today!" she said at an elevated decibel level.

Forrester winced and replied, "The conversion rate for the Yuan is . . ." he checked his watch " . . . 1.50:1 as of twenty-two minutes ago."

"Dollars to Yuan?" Heidi Schmidt asked on behalf of her president.

Forrester hesitated, as if he had been asked whether China had its own currency. "Yes, of course. $1.52 cents for each Yuan."

"What's the significance of that conversion in our . . . uh . . . current economic climate?" Simpson asked.

Forrester nodded. "Well about twenty-four trillion in U.S. dollars for starters," he smiled. He noted that his president was not smiling. "More to the point," he quickly added, "the Yuan is undervalued; the dollar is overvalued. The Yuan is carefully controlled; the dollar is carelessly manipulated. The Yuan inflates at less than 1 percent a year; the dollar is currently inflating at roughly 20 percent a year." He paused and added, "If you order another round of quantitative easing, that number would probably approach 25 percent."

The president scanned the room. "What do we do?" she asked plainly.

"We take the deal." The voice belonged to tiny Sarah Wong, and it surprised even Halle Simpson.

"Sarah," the president responded tenderly. Wong was an intimate and a protégé. "I just don't know how we'd ever get it past Congress."

Heidi Schmidt observed the interplay and simmered.

"Oh, I don't think that will be a problem," Graham Forrester suggested, a small smile playing at the corners of his mouth.

"Oh?" The president retorted, eyebrows arched.

"I think the U.S. Congress will find a way to spin the equivalent of a roughly twenty-five-trillion-dollar gift from China," Forrester said matter-of-factly. "And I think 60 percent of Americans will support it when it is presented to them in the right way."

"And what would be the right way to present such treason?" Kaminski challenged.

Forrester shrugged. "Oh, I don't know. Something along the lines that the Chinese government has too much invested in the U.S. government to let it fail. And," he paused, "this one-time gift will help us avoid austere measures and, at the same time, bend the curve on inflation, which of course happens to be in the interests of the Chinese government."

"I'm referring to the *concessions* required of the United States, Graham," the defense secretary replied impatiently.

"I don't see a problem," Forrester said, eyes darting around the room in search of a connection. "I really don't." He paused. "I mean, who has to know who this administration has permitted to monitor our corporate energy transactions, and an insignificant portion of our Supreme Court rulings?" He re-directed his gaze to the president and summarily answered his own question: "No one."

The secretary of the Treasury turned back to Kaminski and added, "And I believe Madam President will have no difficulty persuading the American people that the time has at long last come to end the ruinously divisive cultural wars, and unite our people around a common creed." He looked at the others and added, "I just don't think Americans care right now. They have a lot of other things on their minds."

Around the table, heads nodded.

"What about our nukes and our navy?" Kaminski petitioned theatrically.

"The common good," Forrester replied with a shrug. "Civilizational stability." He let his eyes scan the room. "We will explain that the *United States* has made this offer. We have done so to set an example for other nuclear powers." He paused and extended his arms in a gesture of magnanimity: "And we will hint that if the other countries do not follow suit, we will withdraw our offer."

"And when Iran and Saudi Arabia and Syria and Pakistan and North Korea *all* refuse, what will we *actually* do?" Kaminski challenged.

Forrester smiled. "Nothing."

Silence. No clarifications were required.

Winston Strobe gently intruded. "We could also sweeten the deal for the Senate and the House," he offered.

Halle Simpson turned abruptly to the thin, thoughtful man sitting immediately to her left and asked, "How?"

"We could tell them that some of this hard currency from China will be earmarked to their pet re-election projects," he replied. "And we'll make it clear this applies to men and women on *both* sides of the aisle."

All eyes turned to the president. "Okay," she said after several moments of preliminary thought. "Once again, this group has given me more things to lose sleep over," she said with a forced smile. "Now how about you all get back to the people's business."

The others stood to file out. She kept her eyes on Graham Forrester, who was the last to leave and was chatting with Derek Kaminski on the way out. She would wait until the morning to call Hanley Siliezar. She would give her Treasury secretary time to place the first call. Then she would find a clever way to discredit him as a reliable source on cabinet discussions.

Halle Simpson stood, relieved. Her worst problem was suddenly manageable. It was time to turn to the little border skirmish with her neighbor to the South.

26

Teresa Delgado Halverson entered the confessional, and with some hesitation took a seat opposite her pastor.

"How is Mom?" John Sweeney asked as soon as she was settled.

"Not good, Father."

John nodded sympathetically. "What can we do for her?"

"Bring my father back from the dead," she suggested with a forlorn smile.

John looked at his watch. "Can you give me an hour?"

Terry Halverson's laugh echoed beyond the tight confines of the confessional.

This did not concern her pastor. The church was empty. It was a little before 5:00 p.m. on a Saturday afternoon in early summer. The afternoon had already featured two sun showers, which served to cool the baked lawns and asphalt streets of the little town of Narbrook, encouraging its residents to venture out in search of life.

John smiled at his young penitent and began with the sign of the cross: "Let us begin, Terry, in the name of the Father and of the Son of the Holy Spirit." He completed the prayers of initiation for the penitential rite, and nodded in gentle invitation.

Terry Delgado clasped her hands and leaned forward. "Bless me, Father, for I have sinned. It's been one month since my last confession." She cast her eyes at her pastor's feet and said, "Father, I . . . uh . . . I think I did something wrong."

John stiffened. He had introduced her to Patrick Burns several months ago. He feared the worst, which, he told himself, was more a comment on him than his penitent.

"Not to worry. You've come to the right place to find out."

She looked into his eyes with a sudden boldness that startled him, and said: "Father, I 'Ringed' myself, as we women are saying."

He winced. He had no wish to probe this matter. For him the Sacrament of Reconciliation was never about a sin hunt. It was an opportunity for a penitent to reconcile with his or her Savior.

"I don't know if 'Ringing' yourself is a sin in and of itself, Terry," he replied with caution. "I tend to think it would be a matter of intention."

"What does that mean, Father?"

"It means, I think it would only be sinful if you were married and closing yourself off to new life, or in an adulterous relationship with a man and trying to avoid conception."

"Well, that's not the case, Father," she said with forced conviction.

"Which?" he asked with a smile.

"Either," she replied quickly without a smile.

"Okay," he nodded with a deferential smile. "We're not talking about sin, Terry. But may I ask you a question?"

"Yes, Father."

"What was your intention in . . . uh . . . doing this . . . thing with the Ring?" John Sweeney was clearly uncomfortable. "It just doesn't seem like something you would do."

"I did it for my Mom," she replied, tears welling up in her eyes.

"Why!?" he said struggling to mask his incomprehension.

"Her medications, Father," she replied in a halting voice. "They say we women won't be able to shop anymore without the Ring." She searched his eyes in hope of approbation. "Father, the thumb pads at store checkout counters will be able to detect whether women have been ringed."

John was dumbstruck. "Are you saying your mother's doctor won't be able to call in prescriptions for her heart and liver ailments, and have them filled at the local pharmacy, unless *she* has one of those Rings?"

"No, Father," she smiled. "Not Mom! She's too old." Her face clouded over. "It's the caregiver they care about. They want to make sure *I am* Ringed."

John Sweeney shuddered. "Well, why wouldn't the devil try to nullify J.R. Tolkien?"

"Father?" the woman asked, her face a portrait in confusion.

"Satan has determined that *he* will be 'Lord of the Rings' during the final countdown."

The confusion flushed from her face. "Father, what am I to do?" she asked.

John hesitated. "Once you are Ringed, then what? What do they want?"

Terry Halverson shrugged. "I don't know."

"Where are you getting this information, Terry?"

"From the retailers, Father," she replied, clearly surprised she was telling him things of which he was unaware. "They've been giving us red slips with our receipts for the past two weeks."

"What do the slips say?"

"They say as of July 4th, all purchases must be accompanied by a thumbprint. They say the thumbprint will detect whether the men have Keys and the women have Rings."

"And for those who don't?"

"No transactions, Father," she replied, with a measure of incredulity at his ignorance. "Hasn't Carmella told you about any of this?"

"No, Terry. All our food comes from the farm," he replied defensively.

"What about your medications?"

"Dr. Steele makes sure Carmella and I have what we need."

She looked at the priest with undisguised envy. "You live a privileged life, Father," she said. "I don't know what's going to happen to me and Mom after Independence Day."

John felt a flash of panic. "Terry, if I could arrange to get you and your mom what you need—meds from Dr. Steele and food from the Burns' farm, would you consider removing that Ring?"

"Father, in a heartbeat."

John nodded and said, "Okay, anything else to confess?"

"Just one thing, Father."

"At least once every week, I have this overwhelming desire to kill my mother," she disclosed with a mischievous smile. "I ask God to please forgive my impatience with her."

Father John Sweeney smiled. "Terry, you're a Godsend to your mother. I'm going to give you absolution, and for your penance, please say a Rosary, if you would, for the Church of Philadelphia." He paused, and added, "Please beg the Immaculate to intercede for us. We are the Church of Revelation Three. We have been called to fidelity in just such difficult moments as these."

He leaned forward and said gently, "Terry, you may now make your act of contrition."

The woman closed her eyes and recited the short penitential prayer with fervor. John studied her face. It possessed the purity and innocence of an angel. *How vulnerable she is, how vulnerable we all are now. Please 'O Immaculate Mother, please thoroughly bathe us in grace that we may hold out to the end.*

Terry Delgado Halverson concluded her prayer while her pastor conferred absolution. She rose quickly, bowed slightly but

courteously, and said, "Thank you, Father. Mom and I love you."
She turned and let herself out of the confessional.

John sat alone in the dark of the small box. He began to pray.
In his prayer he felt a stirring of the Spirit. Suddenly he understood
what he was being called to do.

He also knew there were no guarantees he would succeed.

27

The black Acura was 17 years old and had 106,000 miles on it, and as John Sweeney often needled his beloved housekeeper of 34 years, he would sooner part with her than it.

He drove through the stone portico entrance to the cardinal's mansion, about fifteen miles west of the city and less than five miles from his rectory, and parked in an unreserved spot opposite the front door. The mansion was an anachronism. Built nearly one hundred years earlier by Philadelphia's largely Irish and Italian tradesmen to signal *they* had arrived, it consumed nearly ten acres of highly coveted real estate at the front door to the city's fabled Main Line, where many of their great grandchildren now lived in comfortable apostasy.

The most persistent bidder was the cardinal's next door neighbor—the ever expanding, ever more heretical, Loyola University—whose ravenous appetite for land had already consumed large portions of the Jewish enclave to the east and west.

Cardinal McManus privately told close friends he'd rather give the mansion and the land upon which it sat to the poor than sell it to the Jesuits of Loyola. Giving the property to the poor was precisely what a growing number of Catholics thought should be done with the property. They thought its manifest luxury was a corrupting influence on their prelates, not to mention a public embarrassment in an age of acute political correctness.

John pulled his keys out of the ignition, eased himself out of the car, and promptly locked its doors. He, too, did not trust the Jesuits. He crossed the driveway, rang the front door bell, and waited patiently. A matronly nun eventually answered it with a smile and small nod of acknowledgment. "Father Sweeney," she said. "Good morning. His Eminence is expecting you. Please come in."

John flashed a high wattage smile, stepped up and in, happy to escape a light rain that had begun to fall. "Sister Kathleen, is my friend treating you well?" he inquired.

"But of course," she answered quickly, lest something untoward seep from her subconscious. "His Eminence is a most gracious man."

"That he is, sister," John replied. "Of course it is not difficult to be gracious when you are surrounded with sanctity."

The nun allowed her light blue eyes to fall to earth in practiced humility. It reminded John of Oscar Wilde's insight that modesty was always the best vanity. This he reminded himself was a condition with which he himself was not unfamiliar.

"John!" Joe McManus bellowed from the other side of a large, formal sitting room. He was moving quickly, equal parts black and crimson, to close the distance with his oldest, dearest friend and former seminary classmate.

John stepped into a gentle hug and returned it with a demonstrably tighter squeeze of the smaller man's slender shoulders. "Joe, Sister Kathleen was just asking me if I would help her get a small raise," he said with mock seriousness.

"Father!" the nun exclaimed, mouth and eyes wide with horror.

The cardinal turned to the ashen nun and said: "Sister, I do wish you would reserve these business matters for our private conversations."

John thought the woman's breathing may have momentarily stopped, so rigidly still was she in response to this mortal embarrassment. It was only the cardinal's exaggerated wink that appeared to restart the oxygen system laboring somewhere above her ample midriff. She exhaled most of the tension and laughed the anxious laugh of the pardoned. "Sister," John said in apology, "now you see why the seminary rector would not let us room together."

The cardinal looked at his housekeeper with the hint of a smile and said, "And Sister Kathleen, now you also understand why I must have sufficient advance notice of Fr. Sweeney's visits." The dutiful nun was happy to take her leave, excused or unexcused.

Cardinal Joe McManus led his classmate into a small parlor off the sitting room. He motioned his friend to a small couch next to the fireplace. When John Sweeney was seated, he unceremoniously dropped into a matching couch opposite him. The two men looked at each other, measuring the impact of the years and the tensions of ministry. Each thought himself slightly less tread worn.

"How's your health, John?" the cardinal inquired.

"Just these blasted knees, Joe," John replied with a half smile. "Other than that, I'd run it back."

"You would?"

John nodded. "I would."

McManus paused to let this settle. He knew his friend to be happy in his ministry, but a redo? It was simply unthinkable at a time when an encroaching darkness had cast the last generation of an age in an ominous pale twilight. "You are a saintly man, John," he said, shaking his head in an awkward mixture of admiration and incredulity.

"I am nothing of the sort," John replied softly. "And you above all know that."

"What is it you finally understand about the Divine Proclamation?" McManus asked in pursuit of the elusive mysteries of salvation.

John Sweeney hesitated. He did not want his friend to think he had come to lecture him. "I have finally learned *trust*," he replied with circumspection.

"Ah, yes," McManus affirmed with a nod. "It does indeed take a lifetime." In silent assent they permitted a brief tranquility to fill the space between them. The cardinal's smile chased its shadow. "And, of course," he said "I am a bit younger than you."

John laughed. "In his wisdom, however, His Holiness has declared you a prince of the Church." He shrugged. "Me, he has kept hidden away lest I open my mouth and ignite a schism."

McManus winced inadvertently and nodded. That single word had become the elephant in every room he entered where there were serious men and women preoccupied with first things. "So, tell me, John," he said in pursuit of a direction for the conversation. "What are you hearing out there?"

John thought his friend was asking him for a referendum on his stewardship. "Long live the Prince!" he replied with forced vigor.

The cardinal had no wish to embarrass his friend. "And," he followed gently "what do they ask of the Church?"

John felt himself stiffen, he hoped without detection. "A clear trumpet signal, Joe," he replied, face masked of intent.

McManus nodded patiently. He knew what was coming. He knew it when his housekeeper told him earlier in the week that Fr. Sweeney was on the phone. He knew it when he heard his voice and agreed to see him. And he knew it the instant he looked into his friend's eyes from across the large sitting room off the mansion's center hallway. "And what sound might that trumpet make, John?" he asked with a disarming smile.

"I think it might take the form of a pastoral letter, Joe," John replied, eyes locked on his friend's.

"On?"

"The Key and the Ring."

McManus blinked. He cast his eyes in search of relief and stopped momentarily on an enlarged Caravaggio print hanging on an opposite wall. It captured the moment Paul was thrown from his horse. It did not provide the relief for which he was searching. "And what would it say, John?" he inquired, patience slightly strained.

"That each is a diabolical ploy to imprison the people of God," John replied quickly. "That each represents a renunciation of the Gospel. That each *non serviam* brings us that much closer to a total eclipse of the light."

The cardinal nodded. "All true," he replied.

John was not surprised by the ensuing silence. He expected resistance. Indeed, he had prepared himself for it. "May I perhaps draft something for your review?" he suggested. His friend's visceral response signaled he had crossed a line friends are careful not to even approach. "Or maybe just send along a few notes from my own pastoral experience?" he added quickly in a vain attempt to recover.

The cardinal quickly bound his wound in deference to their many better moments. "John, tell me about those notes," he said quietly.

John felt a stab of pain. He had transgressed humility and charity. In his hubris, he had vindicated wisdom, which had greatly enlarged the ministry of one while diminishing the other. "My people are afraid. They hear my voice, but it is but one voice among many. They are confused and, Joe, they are scattering."

"What are they telling you?"

It was John's intention to be circumspect. "There are women who fear they must purchase this contraceptive 'Ring,' or else they will be denied access to pharmaceutical compounds for themselves and their ailing parents," he replied, eyes again intent on reading those of his friend.

Joe McManus appeared to shudder ever so slightly. "What do you say to them, John?" he asked quietly.

"I tell them I understand, Joe," he replied. "I tell them, more importantly, Christ understands. Then I ask them if they would remove the Ring if I could find a way to get them the medications they need."

"And what do they say?"

John leaned forward slightly and enunciated clearly, "Joe, as one of them said, 'Father, in a heartbeat.'"

The cardinal's head dropped to his chest. His eyes darted from his lap to the ground and back. He looked up abruptly and said, "But John, what do I ask your brother priests to do who are not as resourceful as you?"

"You tell them you will help them do what Pius XII did during the Holocaust. You will help them organize a black market to defend and sustain life. Instead of transporting Jews, we will transport medicines and other necessities."

"Do you have any idea how patently impractical that is, John?" he asked, making no attempt to hide his irritation.

"I do," John replied evenly.

The cardinal fell silent for a moment. Then he raised his hands, palms out. "It would be shut down in a fortnight and I would be arrested and imprisoned," he replied with conviction. "Please tell me how that would advance the Church's mission?"

"It would change everything, Joe," he replied quietly. "Everything."

The cardinal squirmed and looked past John to a distant horizon. "I don't know how to begin to do such things," he said anxiously. "I would be severely criticized by my brother bishops. Many of my priests would have nothing to do with me. The Vatican would be forced to remove me. I would end my episcopal ministry in disgrace."

"Perhaps," John replied matter-of-factly. "Perhaps not." He leaned forward and fired a dart into his friend's heart: "In any event, you would save your own soul, Joe. And I dare say your heroic witness would help many, many other souls to stand up for the Gospel and save theirs."

Joe McManus struggled to his feet. He looked at his watch. "John," he said in a tone suddenly official. "I will give this matter careful thought." He extended his hand. John rose on uncertain knees and took his friend's outstretched hand. "Thank you, Joe," he replied, "but if I may . . . instead of careful thought . . . perhaps you might give it careful prayer."

The cardinal winced and removed his hand. "I will indeed, John," he said through a tight smile.

They stood in awkward silence. John turned to leave but stopped suddenly, and said, "Joe, you do know of course those Keys and Rings will follow our people into church. In time, the authorities will shut us all down. Then we will only have the domestic church of our faithful families. And these will be scattered among the wolves." He paused and added ominously, "No institutional Church here in America, Joe." He shifted his weight. "No shepherds. No pastors. No Eucharist."

He watched his friend recoil in fear and confusion.

He turned and left.

It would be the last time Joe McManus and John Sweeney would ever see each other.

28

———

Even in his early seventies Michael Burns Sr. was a seminal force of nature. His volcanic temper, mythical strength, and Zeus-like will seemed at times to bend the earth's trajectory.

In his advertising career it was often said he did not hear the word "no." In his publishing career it was often said he did not hear the word "don't." And in his third career, as that of a gentleman farmer, it was being said he did not hear the word "can't."

In a little over two years he had cleverly annexed three adjoining farms by persuading their owners that the government was planning to confiscate private farms and use them as holding cells for enemies of the state. Indeed there was a measure of truth in this. He bought the farms and leased them back to their former owners, effectively doubling the total acreage under his care to 2,365 acres.

He was now listed among the owners of the ten largest family farms in the state of Maryland. This did not please him. The man occupying the number one spot, Bobby Robertson, owned over forty-eight hundred acres. Worse, there was only one seven hundred-acre farm between the reach of their properties, and both men were now bidding on it. Robertson was a tenth-generation farmer whose family had received an initial land grant courtesy of King George. He did not think much of the upstart adman-publisher from the north. For his part, the owner of Hallowed Hollow could not bring himself to even so much as talk to a man whose family had accepted land from a King, who had declared war on his country.

Michael Burns Sr. now employed seventeen men and women full time and another thirty-two part time during harvest season. It was estimated that the yield from their labor fed several hundred people in Narbrook daily. Over the winter, Carole Burns and her three married daughters had organized a small collective of seamstresses to begin making clothes for Father John Sweeney's parishioners. And, periodically, Michael Burns would disappear from his land for several weeks at a time to forage Triangle Park in North Carolina for potential partners in a black market operation for antibiotics and other essential medications. Thus far, a deal had proven elusive. The problem was not supply. There were a small handful of men willing to divert portions of shipments headed north and west. The problem was distribution. No one Michael talked to wanted to be arrested, indicted, and imprisoned for the federal crime of transporting contraband across state lines.

Michael knew better than to tell his sons about his predicament. He also knew he couldn't ask any of the other men to wear the risk of imprisonment. Almost all had families, and those who didn't were almost universally sole providers for elderly parents.

The problem for Michael was identity. The Michael Burns he had grown to accept with reservations did not say no to someone in need. When his pastor asked a second time about a source for essential medicines for his parishioners, the request became a charge that had impaled itself within the deep recesses of his heart.

So Michael Burns made a vow and, as he always did when he made a vow, he asked the Mother of his Savior to grant him the fortitude to honor it. Then he carefully compartmentalized it and awaited further instructions in the form of a familiar stirring of his spirit. He knew from long experience his wait would be short.

He emerged from the Main House, on a glorious summer afternoon, a man very much at peace with himself and the new world he had created for his family and friends. From his large flagstone terrace, which surrounded an oversized pool, he beheld a sight that brought tears to his eyes. The rolling land that lay beneath his feet and extended a good hundred yards to the placid blue waters of the Chesapeake Bay was overrun with humanity. There were, he guessed, roughly one hundred sixty to one hundred seventy families—easily five hundred to six hundred souls—celebrating the two hundred fiftieth anniversary of America's birth. The familiar swatches of Old Glory's colors adorned the backs and bottoms of nearly all.

Michael scanned the crowd for familiar shapes and forms. There were twelve tents offering hand carved gifts and homemade foods. There was a mini-Hallowed Hollows' Pops Orchestra of fourteen pieces playing standards from the early Americana song book in a hollow near the Main House. There were serving stations every fifty yards offering the midsummer classics. His chest swelled momentarily that all the food being served was produced on his farm and all the stations manned by members of his family.

Beyond all of this were at least thirty families happily encamped on a two hundred-yard slender stretch of pristine beach, which abruptly interrupted the outstretched arm of green's mad dash to blue. Young fathers splashed about in shallow waters with toddlers, who fell repeatedly on the soft sandy bottom before deciding it was simply easier to remain sitting. The slightly older children were riding Shetland ponies, accompanied by young adults in a three-acre paddock cordoned off by a thirty-six-inch fence that a handful of teenagers insisted on leaping over in order to unsettle the little ones. Early teens were riding dirt bikes and four wheelers in the woods behind the paddock. Michael heard them rather than saw them, which was his preference. Older teens were riding Jet Skis in the open bay, and churning up the water in an attempt to knock the toddlers in the shallows down again and again. From the sound of it, he sensed they were keeping score.

Michael Burns Sr. was never troubled by the vestiges of concupiscence. In his mind, he was a living, breathing, stumbling embodiment of man's fallen nature. He marveled that his sons Patrick and Michael Jr. seemed able to hide the scars of the universal wound within the fold of a laudable self-mastery and a singular selflessness. He nonetheless found it inexplicable that these men, now in their early forties, were still unmarried.

Perhaps that is why his heart began to sing a song it did not know when he caught sight of his sons escorting a cluster of young passengers to the pier in the family's twenty-six-foot Chris Craft. In the boat with them, in fact snuggled up but not scandalously so next to them, were two women. He could not make out who they were from his veranda, and determined that this surprising tableau merited closer inspection.

As he made his way toward the twelve foot-high stone bar-beque pit midway between the veranda and the beach, he studied the movement in and about the boat carefully. He counted six passengers who disembarked. The two women were not among them. Five passengers were now waiting patiently on the dock for instructions to board. The instructions came in the form of an outstretched arm for the first passenger in line, a small girl that he thought might be somewhere between eight and ten years old. The arm belonged not to one of his sons but to one of the two women. As he strained to see who she was, he tripped and almost fell into a small group of senior citizens assembled in an arc of lawn chairs facing the water. He caught himself in time and nimbly danced away in an attempt to pass it off as mere revelry. They shouted after him, and he bowed his head in a practiced self-deprecating manner, waving and silently mouthing 'I love you,' as he kept his feet moving toward the pier.

He passed the barbeque pit, grabbed a hamburger from an outstretched arm, and finished it in four carnivorous bites. He stopped at the water's edge and waived to the families dotting the shoreline. He allowed his gaze to slowly, unobtrusively he hoped, scan the horizon before settling on the boat and its boarding passengers. His eyes met those of his son, Patrick, who seemed, he thought, to squirm a bit uncomfortably. He waved a bit too vigorously, and silently chastised himself for signaling the keenness of his interest in such an inept manner. The young lady next to Patrick waved back. He recognized her as the eldest daughter of his once and forever friend, Joe Delgado. He could not recall her name.

His eyes roamed the boat in search of its stern, and settled on his son, Michael Jr., who appeared transfixed by the woman on his elbow. They were gazing at each other but neither was talking. Michael Sr. recognized the woman as the daughter of one of his farm hands from St. Martha's. He knew the man to have been a former Ivy League professor. His daughter, it was plain to see, was stunningly attractive. He could not recall her father's name, and he had never been introduced to her, though he thought he recognized her as one of the women who worked the large gardens across from the Main House.

Michael did not want to appear to be doing what he was doing, so he turned and headed back to the barbeque pit, where he made small talk with a number of his farm hands and their families. He also nonchalantly seized the opportunity to down two more hamburgers and nearly a quart of homemade coleslaw. This small heist sent him in search of a cold Heineken or two.

The beer tent was manned by a son-in-law, Doug Harrison. He saw his father-in-law enter and immediately turned, reached into a large bucket filled with ice and beer, grabbed two cold Heinekens by the neck, popped the tops and thrust them across the counter. "Hey, Pop," he said with an elaborate grin. "Mom catch up with you yet?"

"No," he replied, his mind more focused on what was now in his hands. "And don't tell her you saw me in here," he deadpanned, to some light laughter and heckling from the loosely assembled.

He put one bottle to his lips and used the other to part the tent in departure. The sun was high, the sky even higher. It was seasonally warm without being excessively humid. As he resurveyed the panorama of activity, he felt a tug on his sleeve. He turned and beheld the love of his life. "Michael, why aren't you wearing a hat?" Carole Burns asked with a frown on her face. "You know how susceptible you are to skin cancer."

"I'm more susceptible to the heat I feel when I'm around you my love," he replied behind a disarming smile.

Reflexively she removed her cap and set it on his head, a protective measure that bore eloquent testimony to nearly a half century of covenantal fidelity. "Did you see your sons?" she asked, unable to disguise her excitement.

"I did," he replied matter-of-factly, returning the hat to her head. "I also saw two women who were trying to steal their virginity."

She had long ago perfected the art of ignoring his impertinence. Some questioned if she even heard it anymore. "I am just so happy," she gushed. "This is the answer to my prayers. I just know it is."

"How do you know?" he asked, his own heart suddenly floating in hope.

"Because of the women," she replied. "They are so good, like our boys."

"Who are they?"

"The one with Patrick is Terry Delgado Halverson; the other is Rebecca Wlodarczyk."

"Did Terry get her annulment?"

"Yes."

"Isn't she older than Patrick?"

"Three and a half years."

"Are her two sons out of the house?"

"One is. He's working in Chicago. The other lives with Terry and her mom in Narbrook, and works on our sheep farm."

Michael squinted into the mid-afternoon sun. "What do we know about the other one?"

"Why must you always insist on conducting an FBI investigation?" she replied, a measure of joy sapped. "Don't you trust our sons?"

He felt a stab of pain and recognized it as hers. It never ceased to surprise him that the union of two hearts, which took the better part of a lifetime to actualize, brought with it parallel joy and suffering. He put his right arm around her and hugged her. She understood the gesture as his signature mea culpa and changed her tone in response. "Rebecca is Stan's daughter," she said softly. "The mother left some years back. It's just the two of them. She's good people, Michael."

He nodded in silent assent. He wondered if she had ever been married but chose not to ask.

They began walking back toward the Main House. "I've begged God for years to let me live long enough to see my sons married," she said as she leaned heavily on his arm to navigate the incline. "Michael, there is not a doubt in my mind that God has finally seen fit to answer my prayer."

This surprised him. She had never spoken of the absolute primacy of this petition. He understood of course. He harbored the same intention. It had simply remained unspoken. "Well," he replied, "how do you suppose I could be of help to the boys?"

"By leaving them alone!" she exclaimed in mock horror.

"Really?" he said with feigned seriousness. "You don't think I should arrange to have the girls propose?"

She howled like a banshee. The sound of sheer desperation in it delighted him. He led her up the steps and onto the veranda. He guided her around the pool toward two comfortable lounge chairs under a red, white, and blue awning, and eased her down into one of them. Her increasing fragility was a thorn he bore day and night in his heart. "Can I get you an iced tea, or maybe some lemonade?"

"No, dear," she replied contentedly.

He thought he should move about the crowd below if only to disturb their tranquility. He disliked disappointing people. The sight of his wife breathing audibly from the slight climb, however, compelled him onto the other lounge chair. He kicked off his sandals, stretched his legs to settle himself, and reached for her hand. She extended it, thin and light, in appreciation. He held it tightly as if to ward off the further encroachment of age. "I love you, Carole," he said softly.

"I love you, too, Michael," she replied somewhat breathlessly.

In less than twenty minutes she was asleep, snoring ever so lightly. Michael Burns rose quietly, stooped to kiss her softly on the forehead, and descended the gently rolling hill to join his guests.

29

The sun lifted a golden eyebrow over the Chesapeake Bay at 5:19 a.m. on the morning after America's last grand hurrah.

Several minutes later Michael Burns Sr. quietly slipped out of the Main House, made his way down the rolling incline to the pier, and his thirty-eight-foot sport fishing vessel. As he approached the pier he saw the twin outlines of his sons. One was hauling tackle onboard and the other was beginning to loosen the lines binding the boat to the pilings.

He walked onto the pier and delighted in the sights and sounds of the gulls and osprey hovering above them. He called out to his sons, who returned his greeting with grunts. The sunrise fishing expedition had been his idea. Sleep, not striped bass, was their preferred catch of the day.

He boarded the boat, thermal coffee cup in one hand, morning prayer cards in the other. He stuck the prayers between his teeth and climbed the stainless steel ladder to the flying bridge, where he placed the coffee thermos in a holder next to the captain's chair.

He sat, bowed his head, blessed himself and prayed, occasionally consulting prayer cards to St. Francis of Assisi and St. Maximilian Kolbe for intercession. He took great comfort in the knowledge that the driven, militant Kolbe could be elevated to the pantheon of the heroic in the order founded by a man who conversed with animals.

With a nod below, he fired up the engines. He paused to take a sip of hot coffee and enjoy the muffled roar of turbines churning water several feet below its surface. The last line had been cut and the boat was adrift. The tide was out and the current was all but still. He shifted into reverse and eased out of the slip. Once he cleared the pier, he nosed the bow west and slowly began the twelve mile run up the Sassafras to the open bay.

The soft morning breeze hugged his unshaven face, and for a brief moment all seemed right with the world in a time when all seemed wrong with the world. He gently nudged the RPM's to 2100 and checked below to spot his sons. They were seated in matching white captain's chairs in the stern. Dark sunglasses covered their eyes, and their heads were back in position for catnapping. Looking at the still horizon he saw no reason to disturb them.

About twenty minutes later he cleared the mouth of the Sassafras and veered south toward Rock Hall. He spotted a huge tanker just north of Annapolis heading his way in the middle of the channel. It was over three hundred feet long and twelve stories high. He calculated its draw to be about fifteen feet. He glanced at his depth finder and noted he was now in nineteen feet of water at dead low tide. The tanker would be given wide berth.

About thirty minutes later, roughly a mile from Rock Hall, he cut the engines. He glanced below and saw Patrick rise to drop anchor. In moments they were all sitting with one hundred pound lines in the water, rocking back and forth in their own wake.

"Pretty good shindig, yesterday, huh?" Michael said to neither in particular.

Mumbled replies. *Long morning*, he decided. To keep them off balance, he determined he would say nothing further unless and until one of them chose to say something.

An hour later they had hauled six stripers out of the brackish waters, including a forty-five pounder, had packed them carefully in ice, and had spoken nary a word.

Michael decided to reverse course. "Fellas, listen up," he said abruptly. His sons turned in surprise, poles dangling with fresh bait over the water. "Couple things I need to say."

Patrick smiled and replied, "Whatever it is, Pop, we forgive you."

Michael laughed despite himself. He hit the mute button on several alternative quips, determined to set a mood of seriousness. "We are heading into turbulent waters," he began tentatively, trusting the nautical metaphor would focus their attention. "The country is in deep trouble. The Church is in worse trouble. If you're going to . . . do anything . . . now's the time."

His sons looked at each other with equal parts disinterest and confusion, and let their rods fall and their spools run.

Michael rebooted. "I'm referring to . . . uh . . . any plans you have to start a family," he said with a nervous glance at each.

Michael Jr. shrugged his shoulders and said, "Not to worry, Dad. That's not something we do."

"*What* isn't something you do?"

"Plan," Patrick replied, laughing.

Michael Sr. was nothing if not relentless. He veered in an unexpected direction and tried again: "Boys, I really don't think we're going to have priests around much longer," he said, as if tossing a knife into a block of wood.

The remark found flesh. With awakened interest, Michael Jr. said, "What's going to happen to them, Dad?"

"They will be arrested and imprisoned," he replied evenly. "Some may even be killed."

"Why?" Patrick asked.

"Because they will resist the muzzle," Michael Sr. replied.

"What's going down, Dad?" Michael Jr. asked with evident concern.

"The U.S. government is going to start tracking Keys and Rings, and the people wearing them into our churches and synagogues and mosques. My sources tell me they will mandate full and immediate compliance. They will introduce something they are calling the Universal Creed. It will become a Pledge that must be recited before and after every Mass and every service. The places that comply will stay open, and those that don't comply will be quietly shut down.

"I'm also told that most of our Catholic bishops will wave a white flag quickly. They will do as ordered." He paused, looked at them pointedly, and added, "Their capitulation will transform what has been a de facto schism over the past three generations into an actual schism. Most of our priests will follow them."

"What about the priests who won't?" Patrick asked.

"They'll go underground."

"What does that mean?" Patrick followed.

"They'll disappear for a brief time and reappear where they can offer the sacraments to people who, like them, are willing to die for the Faith. And like their priests, many of these people *will* die if they are caught celebrating a Mass."

This disclosure arrested the attention of his sons, and focused their quiet reflection. "Father John will be one of those priests, won't he?" Michael Jr. said above a chorus of squawking sea gulls.

Michael Sr. nodded quickly in assent. "Yes, I'm certain that he will."

"How about Fr. Bill?" Patrick asked.

"I would think so."

"Why is the government doing this now?" Patrick followed.

Michael Sr. narrowed his eyes and replied, "They cut a bad deal with some bad men who have decided now is the time to move to consolidate their power and influence."

"Why now?" Michael Jr. asked.

Michael Sr. looked at his sons. His heart ached for them, and the world they had inherited from what he regarded as the country's most despicable generation—his own. "Because America is at its weakest point since the Revolution we celebrated yesterday. The collapse of the economic order has given way to the collapse of the social order, which is now giving way to the collapse of our political order."

"But who is stronger than the U.S.?" Patrick asked, incredulous.

"The people who control the money we now depend on," he replied matter-of-factly.

"Who are they and what do they want?" Michael Jr. asked.

"Oh, there are probably only a few thousand of them scattered around the developed world," Michael Sr. answered. "There is, however, a hierarchical structure. A governing council of twelve men has cornered the world's supply of gold and other precious metals. They oversee the major global institutions—the United Nations, the International Monetary Fund, the World Bank, the World Court, all the major NGOs." Michael paused and reflected, before adding, "And what do they want? They want the levers of global power in their hands."

There was a brief silence and then Patrick asked, "But why?"

"They are convinced they have maneuvered man to the very doorstep of the utopian ideal, and they believe it is now their principal charge to stand sentry and make sure we Neanderthals don't screw it up."

Neither son understood the full implications of what they were hearing. "What is a utopian ideal?" Michael Jr. asked.

"Oh, to live to be hundreds of years old, to be smarter than main frame computers, to be able to create life in pretty much whatever form you want," Michael Sr. replied. "A world free from want, war, and waste." He paused and smiled. "Nothing major."

The sons nodded, eyes wide in apprehension. "What does this have to do with our priests?" Patrick asked.

"Everything," Michael Sr. answered quickly. "When a flock of sheep is endangered, they reflexively look to the shepherd. If our shepherds scatter, so too will we."

"When is this going to happen? Michael Jr. asked eyes wide with alarm.

His father looked at his son directly and replied, "I'm told this . . . Council . . . has ordered the Pledge be introduced after Labor Day. It's short, maybe three lines long and apparently reads like some New Age prayer, which I'm sure it is.

"To ensure compliance it will also be printed on the back of all drivers' licenses in the new year, and all licenses will now have to be renewed annually." He paused and added ominously, "Our signatures will be required and regarded as a pledge."

He watched his sons absorb what he had told them. He knew them well enough to know they would resist the usurpation of their freedom with their very lives. He now intended to steer the conversation in pursuit of his original aim. "Fellas, your mother and I will never sign any such document, and we know Fr. John and I believe Fr. Bill would never sign and allow these people or their representatives here in the United States to shut them down." He allowed this to settle, then added with a smile, "None of us are going to accept those Keys and Rings either. We're far too old for that nonsense."

His sons laughed. He watched Patrick connecting dots. "Dad, why are you telling us all this?"

Michael Sr. smiled. He prided himself on his transparency, and was forever offended when people correctly read his ulterior motives. "Well," he replied, ducking his head somewhat defensively, "I figured you might want to get those wedding Masses scheduled while we still have priests."

There was a pause for the briefest instant, perhaps a reflection of disbelief. Then Michael Burns' sons began to hoot and holler and heckle him unmercifully.

Not content with this, they then did something they had never dared to do in their entire lives. They picked their father up out of his captain's chair, carried him over to the port side of the boat, and dropped him unceremoniously into the Chesapeake Bay.

30

Grace Seltzer no longer wanted to live. Every minute of every day was torture. She felt the pain of her lost daughter with every labored breath she took. She could not look at her four other children and not see death. She could not look at her husband and not feel guilt. She could not look at children anywhere and not feel her divine Lord's reproach.

Her prayer life died in the same emergency room where her daughter was pronounced brain dead and removed from her life sustaining ventilator nearly one year earlier. Her faith was as dry and desiccated as the desert floor in late summer. She had only one wish left for her life in this world—that it would end quickly.

On a cloudless, crisp autumn morning she let herself into the Gianna Molla Clinic in Narbrook. It was a few minutes after 8:00 a.m. She turned the lights on in the hallway, in the kitchen and, finally, in her own office. She dropped her coat and attaché on her chair, and glanced quickly at her schedule for the day. She was relieved to see her morning calendar was light.

It had been six months since she had returned to work with her husband and her mother's encouragement. But work had not proven the welcome distraction they had promised, much less the quiet satisfaction for which she longed. Working with women who believed they were incapable of having children, and experiencing their joy when they conceived and delivered new life, only brought a succession of fresh pain.

Her step father-in-law, Jim Gillespie, told her she was in deep depression. He then made her smile for the first time in months by pointing out that most people who worked with him suffered from a similar affliction.

She started down the hallway to the kitchen to make coffee, but heard the buzzing of the front door bell and hastily retreated. She opened the door to find her pastor, Father John Sweeney. "Brought some Starbucks," he said, holding up two twelve-ounce cups with lids still emitting thin streams of steam. "A couple of Café Grandes with whipped cream."

Her heart leapt. His smile, his pure goodness, and his small act of kindness retrieved something she thought had been lost deep within her. "Father John, so good to see you. Please come in," she said behind a smile.

He entered and followed her into her office. He set both coffees down on her desk, immediately walked over to the windows, pulled the drapes and opened the curtains. Suddenly the room was bathed in light. He returned and took a seat opposite Grace's desk. He reached for one of the coffees, removed the lid, and sipped slowly, never taking his eyes off the woman now seated behind her desk.

"So, tell me," he said, motioning softly with his coffee. "How are you doing?"

"I'm okay, Father," she replied with a forced half smile.

"That good, huh?"

She smiled again and said, "Of course, I've been known to exaggerate."

The priest nodded in understanding. He removed the lid from her coffee and handed it to her. She took it in both hands and said, "Thank you, Father. You are so very kind."

"Sometimes," he replied with a grin.

A brief silence ensued, interrupted only by a small coughing spell that Grace attempted to minimize, without success.

"You okay?" John Sweeney inquired with a measure of concern.

Grace nodded. "Must have picked something up from one of the kids," she replied with a self-conscious shake of her head.

John Sweeney had learned late in life it was altogether better to be direct when the occasion called for directness. "Grace, we've missed you at church."

Her eyes fell, and for a long while she said nothing. Then she raised her eyes and said, "Father, I am still struggling. I'm sorry."

"How is Scott?" he asked, to divert her attention away from herself.

"Fine," she replied, puzzled.

"I do see *him* and the children," he ventured a bit more pointedly than he intended. "He seems a bit lost to me," he added to cushion the impact.

"Well, I suppose he *is* a bit lost, Father. We all are," she replied looking past him.

"How can I help?"

His offer caught her off guard. She had not the slightest idea how to respond. She merely stared blankly without making eye contact.

"How about I arrange for someone to take the children, and you and Scott get away for a long weekend?"

She was nearly overwhelmed. "Oh Father."

He dismissed her gushing gratitude with a wave of his hand. "Not at all," he said. "Fr. Bill needs the opportunity to see how the other half lives."

She laughed, and the sound of it reverberated throughout the office and the hallway beyond. "I couldn't do that to that poor man," she replied before the echo of her laughter had faded.

John Sweeney pivoted. "Grace, I'm extremely worried."

She stiffened. "Why, Father?"

"Every week we are losing more and more people."

"Are you talking about Mass attendance?"

"Yes," he replied tersely.

She felt acutely self-conscious. She did not know where this conversation was going but her antennae signaled danger. "Why, Father, I really don't know," she said a bit lamely.

"More and more women are opting out," he said with concern. "And with them we are losing more and more families."

She thought perhaps her best defense might be a good offense. "Father, what do you think is going on?"

He leveled his gaze and said, "I think we are being 'Ringed' by the enemy."

She felt her cheeks warm. She did not know what to do to cover them. "What do you mean, Father?"

He looked at her with great affection. "I think the enemy has frightened our women into believing they can only be saved by the Ring."

She was momentarily speechless. "What makes you think that?"

"Your eyes, your cheeks, your voice," he replied directly.

She was unable to contain an audible gasp, which seeped into the space between them and immediately filled it. She did not trust herself to speak, so acute was her embarrassment.

"How did you know, Father?" she finally asked, eyes imploring his.

"I didn't," he replied.

She felt a flash of anger but it passed with the swiftness of a sun shower. "I'm so ashamed."

He leaned forward and said soothingly, "Don't be. I've lost count of the number of times I've felt shame."

She began to cry, softly at first, then loudly in wrenching sobs, interrupted only by coughing spasms that frightened him. He stood and walked out of the office and into the kitchen. He opened the refrigerator, poured a glass of ice water, walked back and handed it to her wordlessly. He returned to his seat, and sat with his hands in his lap watching her compose herself.

"Father," she said haltingly "I don't want to lose any more children."

"I understand," he replied gently.

"If I don't use the Ring, they will deny me medications for the other children," she said with a half sob.

"I understand."

"And if I use the Ring and come to church, they will track it and demand I remove it."

"I understand."

"And if I use the Ring, have relations with Scott, and we conceive, I will abort the living child. And if I go to Mass, I won't be able to go to Holy Communion without committing another, even graver mortal sin."

"I understand."

"Oh, Father! What am I to do? My life is a living hell." She began to cry uncontrollably.

He sat in equal discomfort. He now understood what had happened to the remnant of his flock. There was no longer a way to justify two priests in a parish where Sunday Mass attendance was now less than fifty souls, nearly all of whom were elderly. What angered him was the realization that his people had allowed themselves to be "Keyed" and "Ringed" for hospital care and medications, while still helping themselves to food and clothing from the farm.

"Well, when all else fails, there's always the arms of our divine Lord," he said gently.

She felt a sudden shaft of peace penetrate her heart, and settle amidst the unspeakable pain of loss and shame. She closed her eyes for a moment and felt a warmth rise from somewhere within her.

She opened them to see her pastor's head bowed in prayer. She sat transfixed in utter amazement at the power of his intercession.

Presently, he lifted his head and opened his eyes. He looked at her, smiled, and said: "Grace, what a prompting of the Holy Spirit your mother received when she named you."

She smiled awkwardly.

He looked at her in a way no one ever had. She felt as if he was peering into the depths of her soul. "Would you like me to hear your confession?" he asked softly.

She was startled by the invitation and fumbled the reply. He was nonplussed. He picked up his chair, positioned it adjacent to hers, and seated himself in silent anticipation. Slowly, quietly, she turned to him, blessed herself, and began to confess her sins. When she finished she felt a dead weight lift from around her neck and shoulders. She felt lighter, freer, happier than she had in months, many months.

He watched the transformation from several feet away. He opened his mouth to speak but heard nothing in his heart, and closed it again. Her eyes slowly filled with tears that began leaking onto her cheeks and blouse. She sniffled and wiped her eyes and cheeks with both open palms. She rummaged through her hand bag, pulled out a small box of tissues, and cleared her sinuses.

He stood and awaited her. She stood momentarily and reached out to hug him. He permitted it but did not return it. "Would you like me to come to your house this evening and say Mass?"

"Yes, Father, I would, we would like that very much."

"Maybe we could say a family Rosary to start?"

She smiled and nodded eagerly: "Yes, Father."

He turned and started to take his leave. Immediately, she called after him. "Father, please let me walk you to the door."

He slowed to allow her to join him. As they neared the front door they heard sounds that surprised and puzzled them both. In stride, John Sweeney reached to open the door and Grace rushed through it and stooped, then knelt on the flat stone door step in utter amazement. Below her feet lay a tiny black infant girl bundled in a large, tattered football jersey. She was crying.

Grace quickly lifted the baby to her breast, began to rock the child, and speak to her in soft, soothing tones, which did nothing to allay the child's hunger. The jersey was wet, Grace assumed from the child. She quickly lifted the child out of the jersey and allowed the jersey to fall to the ground. She noticed a small white piece of paper fall to the stone door step.

John Sweeney reached for it first, picked it up, realized it was a note of sorts, and immediately began to read it. When he finished he silently handed the note to Grace. She took it, and with difficulty read the barely legible hand writing.

The note read, "I heard ya'all lost a child, so I thought I'd share one of mine."

It was unsigned.

For John Sweeney and Grace Seltzer, no signature was required.

31

The bailiff cried: "All rise."

All rose.

A full half minute later District Judge William Draper strode purposefully to his seat behind the bench in court-room number six in the Federal Courthouse in Philadelphia and sat down. He nodded in perfunctory acknowledgement to U.S. Attorney Heather Watkins and Defense Attorney Paul Nicolosi. He glanced briefly at the jury and smiled narrowly. Then his eyes settled on its elected foreman, a beefy middle-aged man with a tattoo peeking out of a stiff white collar, and inquired, "Has the jury reached a verdict?"

Maggie Gillespie sat at the Defense counsel table with her right hand in Jim Gillespie's left hand. She noted with surprise that the palm of his hand was quite moist. She suddenly felt faint. The room began to spin. She wanted to lie down but did not dare. She clutched her husband's left arm to steady herself.

"We have Your Honor," the foreman responded, while

looking straight ahead in the manner of a man who had spent a meaningful portion of his life in the military.

Judge Draper nodded and said, "With regard to the first question before the jury, did the jury find that mifepristone—the abortion pill—was an *essential service* that the defendants were obligated to provide the Plaintiff?"

Maggie Gillespie immediately withdrew her eyes from the foreman and cast about for a tranquil place to hide them. Not finding one she closed them and began to pray. Her heart was pounding, her head throbbing. She could feel Jim's pulse racing in what was now her own sweaty palm. The foreman's delay in answering, she was to say later, was nothing short of cruel, though her husband would be quick to point out the delay was only momentary.

"Your Honor, the answer is no."

All of a sudden the room stopped spinning. She became aware of an animated murmur in the gallery, equal parts delight and disappointment. Maggie thought perhaps she had only dreamt what she heard, but her palm was being squeezed so tightly that she was immediately confused. At that moment, her husband turned and hugged her so tightly she experienced momentary difficulty breathing. She glanced over her husband's shoulder at Paul Nicolosi, who stood straight and still, emotions carefully cloaked.

"Very well," Judge William Draper replied, clearly surprised. He glanced quickly at the U.S. Attorney, then back to the jury and said, "The verdict, of course, renders the second question before the jury moot—whether the Gillespies and the Gianna Molla Clinic breached a federal contract when they denied the Plaintiff access to mifepristone."

He turned, scanned the courtroom for clouds, and not seeing any turned back toward the jury and said, "I thank you men and women."

"Your Honor!" Heather Watkins interrupted, loudly.

Bill Draper turned to her in slight agitation. "Yes, Counselor?" he replied tersely.

"Your Honor, will the court please poll the jury?"

The Judge nodded quickly in response, "Yes, of course," he answered. He turned to the jury, fixed his eyes on the foreman and said, "Juror number one, did you find mifepristone to be an *essential service* that the Defendants were obligated to provide to the Plaintiff?"

Maggie glanced quickly at the foreman and, for a moment, thought he might salute and shout a "yes sir!" or "no sir!" that would clear the courtroom.

He surprised her. He clenched and unclenched his jaw, and said, simply: "No, I did not."

Jim leaned over and whispered too loudly into her ear, "It'll be a shutout. Whaddya wanna bet?"

He was wrong.

Indeed ten jurors found the abortion pill to be something less than an *essential service*, among them two black female jurors. But there were two other black female jurors who found otherwise. When the last of them had responded to the polling, the U.S. Attorney stood immediately and said, "Your Honor, I'd like to advise the court the Plaintiffs will appeal the verdict to the Third Circuit Court of Appeals."

Maggie turned quickly to Paul Nicolosi, who was not registering surprise. She glanced at Judge William Draper who was also registering no surprise. The two men exchanged glances she couldn't quite read.

The Judge looked at Heather Watkins and said, "The court has so noted, Counselor."

He then turned to the jury and thanked them for their service and adjourned.

Paul Nicolosi turned to Jim and Maggie and said, "Let's celebrate this one. We may not be celebrating the next one."

Jim Gillespie laughed delightedly and replied, "Yes, yes!" He paused and added, "Hey, shall we ask Heather and Tamika, and the two holdouts, to join us?"

Nicolosi glanced anxiously at the U.S. Attorney. It appeared she may have overheard. He coughed loudly and nervously, as if to suggest perhaps *he* hadn't heard his client correctly. He grabbed Maggie by the arm and led her out of the courtroom.

Outside the federal courthouse, in an area cordoned off from the vagrants and miscreants, who had all but taken over the city, the Gillespies welcomed supporters with hugs and, in Maggie's case, tears. When the crowd of about forty had safely dispersed with the aid of police, Nicolosi hailed a cab and directed the Russian driver to Old City. It was late morning, and what remained of the city's once considerable lunch crowd was still shuffling paper inside its tall buildings.

The cabbie pulled up in front of an Irish pub just off Dock Street, whose owner had once been a popular media executive in town. He was a particular favorite of Jim Gillespie, and greeted him with a celebratory bear hug as soon as he crossed the threshold. "Gillespie!" he shouted en route, "How much did that verdict cost you?"

It did not surprise Dr. James Gillespie one whit that Jim Delaney, one of the city's most assiduously networked proprietors, was in possession of a verdict in a federal trial within minutes of its announcement. In fact, it would not have surprised him to discover Delaney knew the verdict *before* it was announced.

"My lips are sealed, Boyo," Gillespie replied coyly. "But I *will* tell you what it's going to cost *you!*" He waved his arm to cover his wife and attorney and said, "One lunch and two beverage buffets."

Delaney laughed and nodded as he said, "I'll feed Maggie. I'll even buy you and your lawyer the first drink. After that you're on your own."

He introduced himself to Paul Nicolosi and led the party of three to a table in the back overlooking Penn's Landing. He quickly took a drink order and departed.

Jim Gillespie surveyed the room, looked at his watch and said, "This place used to be filled, even at this hour. You had to arrive a half hour early to get a table." He paused and mused aloud, "I wonder how he's doing it?"

"Same way we all are," Paul Nicolosi replied. "Fingernails on the ledge."

A college age waitress arrived with a thin stemmed glass half filled with Merlot and two draughts of Guinness. Maggie lifted her glass carefully, held it across the table, and said, "Here's to a wonderful man . . . and a truly remarkable lawyer."

Paul Nicolosi blushed.

"Hear, hear," Jim Gillespie boomed before downing half his pint.

"Paul, you were . . . *are* . . . magnificent!" Maggie smiled after several sips. "Your closing argument had at least four members of the jury crying."

"And at least four others texting their brokers," Jim Gillespie deadpanned.

The attorney laughed. He took a modest draw on his draught, looked at his clients, and said soberly, "We'll lose on appeal."

Jim and Maggie Gillespie blinked. "But Paul," she said quietly "you told us only about 15 percent of all appeals are overturned."

He looked at her clear eyed and nodded, "Yes, and we'll be among that 15 percent."

Silence.

A waitress came to take a luncheon order. She collected three requests for various cold salads and departed.

"But why?" Jim Gillespie asked directly when the waitress was out of range.

The small attorney wrapped his hands around his draught and appeared reluctant to engage. Neither Gillespie pressed him, content to give him space. This, he appreciated. In fact, it was for this reason alone that he shared the run of his mind with them despite knowing it would dampen their spirits, and that their spirits were the very backbone of his case. "Because," he began slowly, "the Court of Appeals is an even more closely integrated branch of the government than the District Court. They will uphold the U.S. Government's definition of the abortion pill being an *essential service*. And they will regard our denial of this *essential service* as a breach of contract, pure and simple, completely unencumbered from any and all other considerations. They will reason that if the U.S. government can't look to its co-equal branch to enforce its contracts, then . . ." he shrugged the rest of his thought into the space between them.

"Then, what?" Jim Gillespie demanded.

"Then . . . anarchy," Nicolosi replied pointedly.

Maggie Gillespie leaned forward and said softly, "But Paul, can't they see that's precisely what we have now?"

Nicolosi shook his head. "No, what we have now is . . . civil unrest . . . on its way to anarchy."

Jim Gillespie laughed and said, "So, just when *does* civil unrest become anarchy?"

Paul Nicolosi stared at him and said, "When our judges can't find caddies."

Maggie Gillespie smiled. "I'm more optimistic than you are, Paul. I think we're going to win again. Their appeal will be denied."

"There will be no jury next time, Maggie," he said quietly.

"So," she stared at him defiantly, "we'll just convince the Judge again, like we did this time."

Paul paused. He did not want to aid and abet illusion. "We didn't convince Bill Draper of anything, Maggie."

This silenced the Gillespies again.

The food arrived. Nobody touched it.

"Paul," Maggie said plaintively, "can't we just pray and trust that our Lord will prevail in this matter? I mean, it must be close to His heart."

He looked at her with great affection. He found her among the most remarkable women he had ever known. "He will prevail, Maggie," he said simply. "He doesn't need any help from an Appellate Court Judge."

Less than thirty minutes later, Jim and Maggie Gillespie left the Irish pub in Old City with their attorney. They took a taxi to the federal courthouse parking garage where they parted. The

Gillespies took an elevator to the third level below the ground. There, after a frantic search lasting almost twenty minutes, they finally found their car. They entered, ignited the engine, and headed for the garage exit.

The ride home was quiet.

Seven months later, the Third Circuit Court of Appeals Judge Leonard Kempner, in an opinion adopted by the court, overturned the verdict in Tamika Johnson et al vs. Dr. James and Margaret Anne Gillespie et al.

32

The meeting had an agenda. Its code name was Operation Vise. There was no pun intended.

It also had an address. The address was 10 Place de la Concorde in District 8 at the foot of the Champs-Elysées. It belonged to the Saudi owner of the de Crillon, the world's oldest luxury hotel.

It was an unseasonably mild evening in late autumn. The penthouse suite occupied by Hanley Siliezar possessed a marble terrace overlooking the Eiffel Tower, the Seine, and the Louvre. Dinner, a gastronomic triumph catered by L'Obe—a five-star French restaurant located just off the hotel lobby—was coming to an unhurried conclusion. Tuxedoed waiters busied themselves clearing Persian flatware and Waterford crystal, delivering Louis XV decanters of cognac, and offering a discrete selection of Cuban contraband in elegant chinaware to the small dinner party.

The City of Light lay glittering above the heads and below the feet of the men assembled. Hanley Siliezar embraced the metaphor with characteristic élan. He held a decanter in one hand and waved

a cigar ever so grandly in the other. "My friends . . . we have chosen well," he said behind an expansive smile. "We have come to
the one city in the world that both embodies and symbolizes our
mission to bring a transcendent new light to humanity." He paused
and surveyed the exquisite jewel of a moon-lit Parisian evening.
"Certainly, our work has not been without its difficulties," he
smiled "but we have persevered and we are now on the threshold
of fulfilling the mission we set for ourselves some time ago."

He stood to aid the members of the Global Governance
Council to focus their attention on him. He walked to the balcony, peered intently into the illumined tranquility, turned and
said, "From the beginning we understood there would be three
forces that would rise to impede our progress—the United States
of America, the Roman Catholic Church, and a potentially chaotic
mass of fearful and ignorant humanity."

He strolled the width of the penthouse terrace and back,
examining the faces of the men before him. They included Nicholas Kubosvak, managing director of the IMF, Kimbe Motumbo,
secretary general of the UN, Dag Schoenbrun, chairman of the
World Court, Geoffrey Benton, chief executive officer of Vennitti Inc., Vladimir Piranchenko, chief executive officer of Western
integration, Hu Enlai, chief executive officer of Eastern integration,
appointed by Lu Xiaoping on behalf of the Chinese government,
Musa Bin Alamin of the Saudi Royal family, Graham Forrester,
secretary of the U.S. Treasury, and David Moskowitz, managing
director of the renowned Ben Gurion Labs in Israel. Missing were
the world's two richest men and its most influential free masons,
industrial tycoon Pablo Gutiérrez of Mexico and renowned American investor, William Warren, who were obsessive in pursuit of
ever elusive anonymity.

Despite a succession of fits and starts, they were now Hanley
Siliezar's men. They had come to realize that only he could offer,
and deliver, the one thing their money and achievements could
not purchase—a hand on the lever of global power as mankind
transitioned from one age to another. These were men who in their

formative years knew the inextinguishable pain of being considered outsiders. Hanley Siliezar had made them insiders.

He stood now as a sovereign in their midst. "We have brought low the first of those forces, although in fairness we must credit the Americans themselves. They, and a certain Pakistani, did much of the heavy lifting for us," he said with a dark grin. "Now we must move decisively to capture what is left of the Roman Catholic Church," he continued, eyes darting from one man to the next. "Make no mistake: it is our ancient enemy. It alone throughout the ages has perpetuated the myth that there is a God whom man must serve." He paused and thundered, "It exists to rationalize death. Nothing more. We must rid the earth of this scourge!"

He walked to the balcony, turned, and rested his back on the Italian marble railing. "My friends, it is only the dissolution of the Catholic Church that will direct a fearful, ignorant humanity to us for assistance and guidance." He paused and lowered his voice until it was barely audible above the traffic on the Champs Elysées twelve stories below. "We have her in a vise. The moment has arrived for a final, fatal turn of the wrench."

Hanley Siliezar walked to his seat and sat down. He picked up the decanter, sniffed, and then tasted the cognac in the manner of an effete. The others watched in silence. Presently, he turned to Vladimir Piranchenko and said, "Vlady, tell us where the integration of the Western block stands."

The tall Russian smiled. He made no attempt to stand. His report would be delivered from his seat, which some said was the sole source of his thought anyway. "All is good," he grinned. "I have five things to say to you: *First*, the U.S. government is very happy we have provided hard currency for their administration to continue. Americans have embraced the Yuan, inflation has slowed, but there is a thriving black market in many cities. The central government now accepts that we must remove all barriers to trade and movement of peoples among the countries of the consolidated Americas. The national governments have effectively become regional governments. Revenues are being shared in proportion to output and population." He frowned. "Not all have accepted this, but we have relaxed the pressure on the Americans by telling them there is no reason to make this known to their people . . . yet," he smiled cagily. "The Americans, as we all understand, have been slowly suffocated by their own penchant for self-indulgence, and they do not wish to hear bad news, ever!" This drew muffled laughter.

"*Second*, the Carbon Credit Bank in Switzerland has begun redistribution of revenues among energy consumers and energy producers throughout the consolidated Americas in accordance with the UN energy quotas policy. The heads of regional governments in central and south America are very pleased with this," he said a bit too triumphantly for the others, who had never quite conquered their fear that this man represented Hanley Siliezar's sole mistake. They universally regarded him as a product of a quasi-patriotic Bolshevik socialism that had pillaged its own land, plundered its own treasury, and raped and murdered its own people. He was the worst of humanity—a man with blood on his hands who did not realize it.

"*Third*, the new U.S. Constitution that was voted on in a national referendum several years ago has now been enacted, and is being exported throughout the regions of the north and south." He paused and added, darkly, "but there is much opposition to this in the streets and town halls of America's southern and western states." Then, in a pique of frustration he half shouted, "There is the threat of civil unrest because this administration refuses to explain to the people that this new constitution is necessary for the introduction of the Universal Creed." He stood and shook his fists well above their heads, a frightening spectacle. "I tell this woman . . . Halle Simpson, 'How can you mandate a Universal Creed unless you explain why the new constitution cannot promise free speech.' But she does not understand!" He paused and added, "I do not believe this woman is a true globalist."

"Perhaps she does understand." The voice belonged to Hanley Siliezar, and what he said caused heads to nod. "Where are we with the introduction of the Creed?" he asked a bit too impatiently for Russian sensibilities.

Piranchenko appeared to ignore him. "*Fourth,*" he said deliberately, turning a portion of his back to Siliezar and in the direction of the others clustered about the terrace. "The Creed has been introduced into the schools, at least all the public schools," he declared pointedly. "Some schools have resisted." He spat on the ground next to his feet. "We will penetrate the two-year colleges next fall and the four-year universities the year after."

He then turned back to Siliezar and said, "And *finally*, the U.S. president and the secretary general of the United Nations," he nodded toward Motumbo, "have developed a confidential joint protocol for shared oversight of the American nuclear arsenal that is to take effect in the new year." He paused and added, "But this is not to be made public until after the next election."

Siliezar asked, "What about the U.S. Navy?"

"The president of the United States says that is off the table for now," Piranchenko replied testily.

This appeared to anger Siliezar. He turned to Kubosvak and said, "Slow down the payment transfers." Then he turned to the others and said, "We'll soon see what is on Madame President's table and what is not." Heads nodded in silent assent.

Slightly embarrassed, Piranchenko glanced around the terrace, walked to his seat, and sat down. It was clear he did not wish to answer questions, and so there were none directed his way. Hanley Siliezar allowed a few moments of silence to permit the tension on the terrace to evaporate within the currents of the soft Parisian evening. Then he looked at Geoff Benton and nodded. Benton stood and walked to the head of the table. He pulled several index cards from inside his coat pocket and laid them on the end of the table in front of him.

He nodded to Hanley Siliezar, fixed his gaze on the men in front of him and said, "The best current estimates from our therapeutic division suggest that 57 percent of working men in America have opted to have the Key inserted by their own physicians; and

64 percent of working women have inserted the Ring themselves." He paused to let those staggering numbers settle. "We believe we will achieve 80 percent compliance for each group within twelve months."

"And the rest,?" Siliezar asked.

Benton shrugged and replied, "We project them to be the hard-core religionists who will be told by their priests, ministers, and rabbis not to accept what we have been calling," he smiled, "simply person-alized medical record-storage devices and retail transaction enablers."

Siliezar nodded thoughtfully but said nothing.

Benton continued, "The touchpad devices have been installed in over 50 percent of all American retail establishments, beginning with the large chains. We expect that number to hit 70 percent within twelve months."

"And the rest?" Siliezar asked again.

Again Geoffrey Benton shrugged. "I have been told by a senior member of the president's cabinet, they will be shut down, quietly, as homeland security risks."

Siliezar smiled. The Key and the Ring were, in his mind, tasers that would permit the Global Governance Council, which was to say Hanley Siliezar, to control entire populations that were otherwise beyond their control.

Benton continued, "Importantly, these devices, each of which utilizes billions of nanobots, are permitting us to track the where-abouts of their owners . . . even, and especially, into their places of worship." This disclosure, he noted, was greeted with an elevated level of attention.

"Too bad we can't hear what their preachers are saying," laughed Piranchenko.

"Why? We're about to put them out of business," Siliezar said to more general laughter.

Benton waited for quiet and continued, "The U.S. government is reporting that currently about 55 percent of American motorists are carrying valid drivers' licenses, signed with the Creed on the back. They claim by this time next year this will be universal."

"Do you believe them?" Siliezar asked.

"No," Benton replied. "But we believe *effective universality* is the target. We see that to be in the 80 percent range, and we believe the U.S. government will get there eventually."

"Why?" Siliezar probed.

"Traffic violators who are stopped with invalid licenses will be imprisoned," Benton replied matter-of-factly.

"Anything else?" Siliezar asked summarily.

"Yes," Benton replied. "The U.S. government is reporting that 78 percent of all current retail and commercial transactions are being recorded through our enabling technology."

Siliezar turned to Piranchenko and remarked, "You've got your work cut out for you, my friend."

Piranchenko blinked.

"We will expect those numbers to be exceeded in *all* regions of the Americas within two years," Siliezar clarified.

"No problem," Piranchenko bluffed.

Siliezar turned to David Moskowitz and nodded. The thin, frizzy haired, bespectacled bolt of energy sprang from his seat and all but bounded to the front of the group. "We are close!" he exclaimed breathlessly to viral laughter. This customary opening for his oral progress reports had become something of a standing joke since he had been given a seat on the Council several years ago. Hanley Siliezar, to the shared anxiety of most, had proven himself unable to grasp the humor.

The managing director of the Ben Gurion Laboratories well understood that the eight hundred pound gorilla in every steering committee meeting he entered, like this one, was the ten pound new man he was expected to produce by 2030. "Homo Evolutis," as what remained of the coordinated media referred to him. "Man 2.0" as scientists and other evolutionists called him. This prodigious achievement was to be the final, decisive step in evolution, and the final nail in the coffin of the myth of creation.

"We are tracking schedule," he assured the assembled, again to raucous laughter. For it was a well-known fact the BGL, as the Labs were known within the Global Governance Council, was perpetually behind in its milestones and deliverables. Moskowitz glanced nervously at Siliezar and said, "We have succeeded in mapping all the neural regions of the brain, and we have . . . preliminarily . . . and I stress preliminarily . . . fused the principle operational forces of human intelligence with other packages of software . . . in lay terms, artificial intelligence."

Silence greeted this disclosure, and David Moskowitz sensed it may have something to do with his credibility. "We are now prepared to implant highly refined software in a small beta sample," he said somewhat defensively. "And we expect there will be some . . . uh . . . iterative refinement . . . required before we begin uploading on a limited rollout basis."

"Tell us about the sample," Kimbe Motumbo asked apprehensively.

Moskowitz glanced nervously at Siliezar and awaited a signal. None was forthcoming. He waded in. "One dozen Hutus from Rwanda," he replied forthrightly. "Six men, six women. All young, healthy, and illiterate."

Motumbo turned to Siliezar and stared through him. "You have denied me plausible deniability. You have created a problem for me."

Siliezar did not reply.

In an attempt to regain momentum, David Moskowitz nodded toward Geoffrey Benton and said, "With the aid of Vennitti's diagnostic division we will be testing for skill formation, pattern recognition, and logical analysis." He removed his black horn rimmed glasses and added, "We are expecting the non-biological portion of the brains that are uploaded will create infinitely greater capabilities and capacities in our subjects. We believe these people will experience a radically transformed humanity . . . immediately."

"What do we do with them after this work is completed?" asked Motumbo.

Moskowitz looked again to Siliezar. It was readily apparent to all there was no operating blueprint. "We send them back to their country and put them in government jobs," Siliezar replied to spontaneous laughter. Geoffrey Benton studied Siliezar intently. He did not think the chairman of the Global Governance Council was joking.

Siliezar looked at Benton and said, "Who is coordinating the integration of the new hardware and this new software?"

Benton nodded in understanding while the others stared in incomprehension. "We've created a new division whose specific mission is to schedule, install, record, and track all joint and organ replacements . . . and uploaded neural implants."

"You are assuring me, then, we will keep accurate digital records of *who* has received *what* . . . and *when* . . . and correlate these data points with anticipated gains in productivity?" Siliezar challenged.

"Yes, yes," Benton replied patiently. "Vennitti Inc. will assume responsibility for all *initial* record keeping, and then it will be transferred to the regional governments once they are settled." He nodded to Motumbo for confirmation. Motumbo glanced nervously about the terrace before replying, "I will report out on our progress in this area."

Hanley Siliezar turned back to David Moskowitz and signaled him to resume, which he did immediately. "Phase Two will be the limited rollout. And, as Hanley implied, the men and women Motumbo identifies for regional government positions around the globe will be the next beneficiaries of this technology."

Siliezar was not one to defer opportunities to clarify. "Kimbe, tell us *now* about your plans for these men and women."

Motumbo swallowed hard, and it was apparent to the others that somewhere in his organization there was a struggle involving the screening process. "We have approved and distributed specifications for candidates to all the heads of our regional governments throughout the world," he began cautiously. "Essentially we are looking for potentially progressive thinking, generally uneducated, relatively poor men and women of diversity to fill what we regard as five core ministries in regional government—budget, commerce,

Life Sciences, propaganda, and, of course, governance. We expect to have one recommended team and two backups for all one hundred fifty key regional governments by spring."

"Process?" Siliezar probed.

Motumbo stumbled momentarily. "Uh, we send the regional governors the candidates we have screened and selected. They choose the individuals they want, we . . . uh . . . schedule them with David's people . . . then . . . uh . . . they're sent to Israel where they are screened again, then prepped, and . . . uh . . . then David's people proceed with the uploading of the new software."

Siliezar nodded, satisfied. He turned to Moskowitz and said, "Okay, tell us about your progress with Homo Evolutis 3.0."

David Moskowitz beamed. "The Hybrid!" The others sat up abruptly and leaned forward. Even the sounds from the glittering Champs Elysées seemed suddenly muted at the prospect of an important disclosure. "We have learned from our failures. Over the past six years we have tried over one hundred times to integrate alpha animal kingdom cellular tissue with human DNA and current state-of-the-art non-biological intelligence. We have experienced nearly every conceivable difficulty—the lack of adaptability of human molecular structure, the inability to implant various animal tissues and have them take, a myriad of code inconsistencies in preferred artificial data packages." He paused, and shook his head. "But, each time, we have learned something of value." He smiled and lifted his head. "We are so very close."

"How close, David?" asked Siliezar with more than a hint of impatience.

David Moskowitz held up two fingers.

"Two years!?" Geoff Benton exclaimed.

Moskowitz nodded amidst a low murmur among the assembled.

"Do we have a new target date?" Siliezar asked with interest.

"We do," David Moskowitz replied. "January 1, 2030."

"Well, well, this is cause for celebration," Nicholas Kubosvak said with enthusiasm.

Siliezar waved him off. "Let's hold off the celebration until we actually meet this man." The others turned to Moskowitz, who nodded in glum assent and took his seat.

Hanley Siliezar turned to Hu Enlai and said, "Hu, you've been very quiet. What do you have to share with us?"

The pudgy Chinese official was reportedly able to trace his lineage back to the Ming dynasty. He was an enigma to the others. He observed all but said little. He was recommended by Lu Xiaoping, appointed by the Chinese premiere, and was said to have his ear on a wide portfolio of issues. He stood at his seat, licked his lips twice, and said, "First, all the regional governments in the east have been integrated and are currently hubbed around Beijing. These include the island nations we have absorbed with your gracious assistance . . . and of course America's demise. I speak of the governments of Japan and Taiwan," he smiled triumphantly. "These also include Russia and its satellite Ukraine, unified Korea, all the Islamic Asian nations, India, whose government has been merged with Indonesia, and Australia, whose government has been merged with New Zealand."

Heads nodded. No questions were asked.

"Secondly, all regional governments have been officially advised by Beijing that a one-child policy will be in effect for all countries in the Asian block for one full generation, that is to say for at least the next twenty years," Enlai continued. This raised eyebrows. Enlai sensed a challenge and chose to pre-empt it. "In the Far East we are well familiar with the benefits of a one-child policy. It permitted our country to create a demographic phenomenon of twenty million more young men than women in one generation. The other nations have seen the economic and military advantages of such a policy." He smiled coyly. "We do not expect serious resistance."

Siliezar turned to Piranchenko and said, "This is what you will be asked to do in time." He looked at the others and added, "The West is not ready for this policy at the present time. That is precisely why we are pursuing other avenues there."

The others immediately turned to the Russian, whose facial expression suggested he wished he were elsewhere.

"Where are we with the Key and the Ring?" Siliezar challenged Enlai.

"All members of the producer classes in the Asian countries are in compliance," Enlai replied with a polite bow intended to highlight both a deference and performance that was in sharp contrast to his rival in the West. "We are experiencing some level of resistance in the rural parts of India and Australia, which is to be expected."

"Local currencies?" Siliezar probed.

"Outside of China . . . raging inflation," Enlai replied quickly to laughter from the others. He took his seat with a satisfied smile.

Siliezar nodded, turned to Kubosvak, and asked, "Okay. So tell us. Where are we on the new currency?"

Kubosvak nodded and replied, "Our people now control over 80 percent of the world's gold and other precious metal reserves. We expect to bump that over 90 percent within the next six to nine months. At that level, the regional governments will now be totally dependent on us for economic stability. We will announce the new currency on April 1 of next year."

Siliezar smiled. "How will we monitor conversion?"

"We've notified all twelve core regional governments that they will have six months to convert from their local currencies," Kubosvak replied. "Then we send our spot inspection teams in to sample local markets. If the government hasn't hit their conversion milestones, there will be penalties."

"Such as?"

"They will receive one warning. The second milestone missed will put them on a global 'no trade' list. Then we officially notify Dag's body and copy the regional president."

"Response?"

Nicholas Kubosvak glanced at Enlai and smiled thinly. "We are mud wrestling with the Chinese and the Americans."

Siliezar frowned. "Yes, well, if we must play hardball with them, then we must. I am growing weary of their constant whining for concessions. Their currencies will not remain protected in the midst of such obstinacy." He turned to Schoenbrun and said, "Where do we stand on control of internet communications and transactions?"

"It is essentially within our control," he said without equivocation. "The regionals have taken over the social networks and are in control of all the transaction routes. Each user's ID number has been digitally recorded and stored with the regional intelligence agencies. All that is left is a global consolidation."

"What is being done with the social networks?" Siliezar probed.

Kubosvak smiled. "Users are being encouraged to maintain the currency of their own life narrative so the regional governments can consider them for unspecified positions in either the public or private spheres." He paused and laughed. "And our target segments, those who are productively engaged in regulated private industry, are doing just that!"

"And what are *we* doing with all that information?" Siliezar challenged.

Schoenbrun smiled and said, "We have begun the consolidation. We are feeding it to the beast in Zurich!"

The others convulsed.

Siliezar nodded in contentment. He called for a waiter standing on the other side of the glass inside the suite's sitting room. He emerged to replenish decanters and departed. He turned to Musa Bin Alamin, bowed ever so slightly, and asked the question on everyone's mind, "Are you keeping the Sunnis and Shiites from each others' throats?"

Bin Alamin, quite pleased with any form of obeisance, bowed himself and smiled. "We are indeed."

"How is it you are so certain my esteemed friend?" Siliezar's skepticism somewhat disarmed by a bemused smile.

Bin Alamin smiled at the others, and ran both thumbs over both forefingers in the international symbol for graft.

"Can we be equally sure there will be no more attacks on the West?"

"Yes."

"And no missiles of any type launched at Israel."

"Absolutely not."

"And no baiting of Israel into launching their weapons as an excuse for a massive retaliation?"

"Would never occur to us," Bin Alamin replied to an outburst of laughter.

Hanley Siliezar himself laughed, lit another cigar, and stood. He puffed away for several moments before slowly making his way to the front. When he arrived, he stood and stared out into the gentle evening in further reflection. Then he turned abruptly and said, "Operation Vise is incomplete." He began to walk across the terrace and back, slowly, puffing, and waving his cigar. "Our final tightening of the screw must commence in eight weeks, on Christmas Day." There was a gasp from Dag Schoenbrun who immediately understood the implications.

Siliezar took note of the response and its source, and continued, "We will prepare a letter for the regional presidents to distribute to all pastors, rabbis, and imams forty-eight hours in advance. I will draft the letter myself," he declared proudly. "It is to be read on Christmas day in all Christian churches and no later than January 1 in all synagogues and mosques." He paused dramatically and continued, "The letter will advise that all denominational services are to be discontinued indefinitely in the interests of social stability. It will point to civil unrest in their own country and in countries throughout the world, and make it clear we can no longer divide ourselves along religious or ethnic lines. They will be told we are a people who share a common and transcendent destiny." He paused theatrically and added, "It will conclude by outlining our vision for this new age of man, the unique benefits to those who embrace it, and the consequences for those who do not."

Hanley Siliezar planted his feet where he stopped, and inclined his ear for a response that never quite arrived. This seemed to displease him. "You are silent. Why?" he asked the assembled.

Dag Schoenbrun alone had the temerity to challenge him. "You will drive them underground," he said starkly.

"That's the point," Siliezar snapped.

The others stiffened. They saw impending complications from this over-reach. "And when we drive them underground, then what?" Piranchenko inquired.

"We arrest them and send them to the rural detention centers we have set up," Siliezar responded coldly.

"It is likely there will be more people in those centers than outside," interjected Kubosvak.

"I don't care!" Siliezar thundered.

The others shifted uneasily in their seats. They simply could not account for their leader's antipathy for organized religion, particularly the Catholic Church, and his urge to destroy it. To each of them it was merely a harmless remnant of another age, and simply allowing it to die of natural causes at the beginning of a new age of man was the wiser course of action.

Siliezar sensed he was losing his men, but he had no interest in assuaging their fears. "Listen to me," he said with quiet passion, "this Catholic Church stands sentinel over a long age of darkness, which it insists on extending simply to preserve itself. It carries no brief for man, any man, in any age. It cares only for itself and its doctrines that it uses to beat men down in every generation."

He moved closer to them, inclined slightly from the waist and said, "As I have long told you, we will not possess the hearts of men until we rid those same hearts of this grand deception and refill them with the truth of new scientific possibilities, which will transform their existence."

"We are so close to achieving our goals, Hanley. Why risk triggering massive resistance on a global scale?" The question came from an unlikely source, Hu Enlai, who sat stone-faced awaiting an explanation.

Hanley Siliezar did not blink. He simply stared back at his chief operative among Eastern nations and said with chilling effect, "Mark my words. If we fail to bury this all but comatose institution . . . *now* . . . it will rise again and consume us, and put an end to all our dreams."

It was left for Graham Forrester to venture into the uneasy silence that followed. "Hanley," he said softly, "you have won. Your ancient nemesis is as good as dead. You have divided her and conquered her. Only the United States, about 15 of her 245 bishops and, we're reliably told, about 2,300 of her 31,000 priests sided with Rome on the Universal Creed, and abandoned their chanceries and pulpits." He paused, looked at the other members of the Council, and added, "The others are now ours. They read the Creed at the beginning and end of every service. They carry it in their wallets. Why shut them down?"

Hanley Siliezar's face turned a dark shade of purple. But before he could erupt, the Saudi sheik stood and implored, "Do not do this! It will be regarded as an extreme provocation by our people." He narrowed his eyes and lowered his voice. "They will assume it is a ploy of the infidel in the West to further humiliate and subjugate them. I warn you, they will not accept this. If you shut down our mosques and madrassahs, I will no longer be able to guarantee the West protection from their ire."

Hanley Siliezar stood. The Sheik sat. The others stirred uncomfortably. "My friends," he said in a voice devoid of emotion, "either you are with me or you are not." He paused, slowly looked from one to the other, and added, "And this is for each of you to decide."

He turned, crossed the terrace, and re-entered his suite.

The others avoided looking at each other. No one moved for several long moments. Slowly, one by one, the men of the Global Governance Council stood and followed Hanley Siliezar back into the suite.

33

John Sweeney stared incredulously at the form at the foot of his bed. He could not tell at first if it was human. The head looked to be that of an animal. The shoulders and upper torso appeared to be those of a man.

There was no sound and no movement.

"Who are you?" he heard himself say in a tremulous voice.

There was no response. He wanted to get out of bed to confront the bestial form, but when he attempted to do so he discovered he could not move.

Suddenly it opened its mouth to speak. The sound that issued forth from its mouth was so guttural and so menacing that he knew instantly who stood before him. "Do you now see you have been given over to my control?" Sweeney heard the words clearly and saw the outline of a malicious smile.

He opened his mouth to speak but no sounds came from of his mouth.

The beast roared and extended his head well over the foot of his bed, and stopped within three feet of his face. He could smell the stench of its breath and recoiled in horror. This evoked a suffocating laughter that immediately seemed to fill the entire room.

"What do you want!?" he yelled at the top of his lungs.

"You have nothing to give me!" the beast roared in response. "I have in one generation consumed everything past generations held dear."

"That is a lie!" John replied contemptuously. "You will be resisted to the death by many even in the final moments of this age."

The beast laughed. This time the sound was not unlike the sound of fingernails on a blackboard. "I have come for you, priest. And I shall have you!"

John was filled with terror. He sat up and quickly prayed a Hail Mary, but the beast did not vanish. Instead he seemed to grow larger though John thought perhaps it was because he could now see more of him from his somewhat elevated position.

"Tomorrow, on your midwinter festival, you will read my letter to your congregation," the beast said with obvious delight. "A letter I dictated to my own herald." He paused and smiled fiendishly and said, "Know that I will regard it as your unconditional surrender."

"I will not read it!" John thundered.

"You *will* read it!" the beast bellowed in reply, outraged by the priest's impudence. "Then you will be delivered into my hands."

"I am not yours, and the one whom I serve would never permit me to be delivered into your hands," John shouted, more in hope than certainty.

"*You* don't even believe that," the beast replied at a sharply reduced decibel level that sent chills racing up and down John's spine. "You know what a miserable failure your ministry has been. You know you are not worthy of the very salvation you preach. You know you will spend eternity with me!"

John fell silent. He opened his mouth to speak but no words came out. A cold paralyzing dread filled him head to toe.

Seeing this, the beast laughed again. In response the temperature in the room seemed to fall ten degrees. "My moment has arrived and I shall not be denied it," he declared. "Your Church long ago surrendered to deception and comfort. Our mating ritual is over."

John thought perhaps he might be dreaming. He decided to strike. "You are Moloch. Blood is your ritual. Your lies have turned ovums into ovens in our time. You midwifed the birth of a pill that ushered in a reign of terror in the womb that has rendered mankind all but childless. But because the preponderance of that blood sacrifice is not sufficiently public, it does not sate you. So there must be more. Always, for you, there must be more."

"Now you seek nullification of the Creator's essence. He creates in love from his very substance. You destroy in hate from your very absence. From the beginning in Genesis you stalked the family from the tall grass. It is only in our time that you have dared to slither into the open—into our living rooms, our bedrooms, our medicine cabinets . . . and now into our hospitals and clinics and laboratories.

"In your perversity you have convinced man he is entitled to create the next generation of men in his own image and likeness. And so he does. But you have overreached, and in your overweening pride you have unwittingly set off an alarm. You have released the cries of billions of lost souls in our time whose blood you have consumed. The cries of these souls have reached the throne of God and demanded an intervention from His vanguard. And in His great mercy, your Creator has granted their wish. You have been delivered into the hands of your original tormentors. They have prepared the bonds with which you will be clothed in the age to come. An age of triumph, a new springtime of life and love, which you will not be permitted to see from the everlasting fires of the netherworld."

The beast leaned back and bellowed fire in John's direction. The blast seemed to stop inches from his face, which only served to further enrage him. "Your God is a liar!" he charged. "From the beginning, this was to be my realm. I am its prince. He reneged. In every age He has interfered. But in every age we have prevailed, just as we will prevail at the close of this age."

He stood erect and thrust out his chest, which appeared to John to be that of a horse. "And the age to come will be mine!" he bellowed. "Not His!" he roared. "Mine!" As he said this his nostrils flared and something like a milky smoke filled the room before it settled and began to fall as a light mist.

John felt its moisture and tried vainly to prevent it from clinging to him. He rubbed his wrists and forearms vigorously as if trying to remove their very skin. "I will not read your letter!" he shouted. "And I will continue to say Mass even if they shut us down. You will not stop us! And if we die, we will die for the hope within us, and you will have seen the last of us, for where we go you will never be permitted to go." He paused and bellowed, "For you there will never, ever, be a return to light."

There was a chilling pause that John did not understand. Then, abruptly, the beast began laughing. John recognized the sound as something akin to an uneven mixture of jackal and hyena. Slowly it began to advance. It placed one giant foot on the end of his bed, rocked back and forth quickly, then launched itself toward him—its mouth contorted in uncontrollable rage.

This so thoroughly frightened John that he immediately took to his covers to hide. His heart, pulse, and temples were beating so wildly he could hear them. He thought one of them would surely explode and he would die of a stroke or aneurism.

It was in that moment that Father John Sweeney awakened. He looked at the digital clock on his nightstand. It was 5:00 a.m.

In precisely twelve hours he would say Christmas Mass for the last time.

34

Terry Delgado turned to her mother for affirmation. She stood hands on hips in a vintage antique white-lace wedding dress awaiting a hug, a smile, a nod, anything. It was the dress Fran Delgado wore fifty years ago, almost to the day, when her father walked her down the aisle of St. Martha's Church in Narbrook, and linked her arm to the arm of a young accountant who worked for a large pharmaceutical company.

The memories tripped wires somewhere deep within Fran Delgado's neural regions. She opened her mouth to speak but the words lodged in her throat. Her heart began to burn. She clutched her breast and sat down on the end of the bed in her daughter's bedroom. Terry rushed to her mother's side just as the damn burst. Fran Delgado convulsed in the singular sadness that is loss. Her daughter understood. "He *is* here, Mom," she said softly.

The knock on the front door of their colonial rancher in the Hallowed Hollow compound startled them in its abruptness. "Golf carts leave for the chapel from the Main House in fifteen minutes!" a disembodied voice announced with ruthless detachment.

The Delgado women stared at each other for what seemed like an eternity, and then burst out laughing. "Tell me this isn't a forced marriage," the mother cried, mascara leaking on cue. "My Lord, these people think they're roping steers!"

Minutes later they were squinting into a brilliant midmorning sun on the first day of May. It was about fifty yards from their home to the Main House, and Terry encouraged her mother to negotiate it with her arm in arm. Coming in the opposite direction was a distinguished gentleman, with a bride on his arm. As they drew closer, Terry recognized Rebecca, and her father, Stanislaw Wlodarczyk. Rebecca appeared stunningly regal in a Carolina Herrera gown that had once been worn by Carole Burns. Her long blonde hair was swept up in a magnificent chignon. As they closed the distance between them, Terry observed her unstudied innocence, and declared, "Rebecca, you are simply stunning!"

The younger bride broke free of her father's arm and threw herself on Terry's neck and shoulders. "Oh Terry, isn't it just a perfect day!" she cried. "Why is God so good to us?"

Standing next to her daughter, Fran Delgado half snorted in reply, "Get hold of yourself, honey. Remember, you're still marrying the seed of Michael Burns."

Stanislaw Wlodarczyk stepped forward and introduced himself to Fran Delgado. He lifted her hand, bowed from the waist, and kissed it gently, causing her heart to flutter and her cheeks to redden slightly. She immediately calculated that he was younger but convinced herself he was not out of range.

The invasive sound of two tricked-up golf carts arrested their attention. They sped up the Belgian block entrance to the Main House, wheeled precariously and arrived within inches of half the bridal party, stopping abruptly. Each cart was adorned with elaborate floral displays and bows and ribbons. Out stepped two handsome young men whom Terry recognized as field hands from Narbrook. They wore ill-fitting charcoal gray worsted suits with starched white collars and dark ties. The taller of the two extended his hand to Terry and introduced himself as Ted Wilcox. The other young man introduced himself to Rebecca Wlodarczyk as simply Eduardo. The men immediately escorted the brides into the rear seats of the respective carts. They quickly returned and attended Terry's mother and Rebecca's father, as they made their way into the other side of the carts' rear seats. Then, without so much as a word, they climbed into the front seats and sped off.

The distance from the Main House to the chapel in the woods was perhaps six hundred yards. As she passed beyond the twelve-story grain silos, through fields of eight-foot corn stalks, and around the two bucolic lily ponds, Terry Delgado reflected on the circuitous path her life had taken and the unlikely circumstances of her marriage to Patrick Burns. When her first husband walked out on her in London nearly sixteen years ago, leaving her with two young children, she packed her heart in ice and vowed she'd never trust it to another man again. But one night a priest knocked on the door of her parent's home in Penn Valley, and everything changed. It was Father John Sweeney who opened her heart to the mercy of God. It was John Sweeney who had encouraged her to seek an annulment. It was John Sweeney who introduced her to Grace Seltzer, who had welcomed her to the Gianna Molla Clinic where she had worked for the past ten years. And it was John Sweeney who had introduced her to Patrick Burns, several years younger but many years wiser than she.

She had never known joy like she knew in his presence. His strength of mind and body and soul reminded her of her own father, whose murder twelve years prior in a New York apartment remained unsolved. This time love was not in a hurry, and carefully dug its roots into the vary marrow of her being. When it finally stirred within her heart and began to kindle, it slowly ignited an inextinguishable fire in her breast.

It was Patrick Burns' idea, she loved telling friends, to have her eldest son, Joseph Jr., who was now twenty-two, walk her down the aisle of Our Lady of the Bay chapel on this glorious Saturday morning. And it would be this enduring gift of a son from her first marriage who would give her over to the purifying love of an enduring second marriage.

She scanned the horizon and saw the converted sheep barn off in the distance. A second floor had been hastily constructed this past winter and early spring, and it now housed ten extended families. She let her gaze wander south to the two converted hog barns that now hosted an additional twenty families. She calculated that when the compound's ten homes were factored in, nearly two hundred fifty souls now called the two thousand-plus acre farm, known also as Hallowed Hollow or Hollowed Halo, "home." Miraculously, though the dislocation had been bitter to many, there was sufficient food and clothing for all. Only medicine for the aged and infirmed was presently lacking, and the community had been told Michael Burns himself now regarded this as his top priority.

Terry glanced momentarily at the flying chariot off her right side and marveled at the sheer radiance of Rebecca Wlodarczyk. They would now be next-door neighbors in the compound and would share responsibility for storing and distributing food from the ten-acre gardens. Terry had lost contact with her own two sisters several years ago. Both were married with young families. One lived in San Francisco, the other in New York. She presumed each to be dead, though her mother was not at all prepared to make such a concession. Rebecca Wlodarczyk, she determined, would take the place of the younger sisters she had lost.

As they approached the woods they heard music. It was the festive sound of a marshal band. The chapel itself was roughly seventy-five yards into the woods in the center of a clearing that was perhaps half an acre in circumference. It had been expanded twice since its construction fifteen years ago. It now housed nearly two hundred people in two sets of ten long pews constructed from redwood from the Brazilian rain forest. The sanctuary was hand carved out of Carrara marble, which Michael Burns had shipped in from Italy. The tabernacle was caste in gold, said to be from what had been the middle kingdom in China, and adorned in diamonds from the DeBeers mines in South Africa.

The golf carts slowed as they came to the clearing. Terry Delgado was the first to behold the wondrous sight of over two hundred men, women, and children holding long corn stalks and waving them like palm branches. They formed an arch from the entrance of the clearing to the entrance of the chapel. They were singing, though she couldn't make out precisely what they were singing.

She began to cry. She glanced quickly at Rebecca and saw that she was crying too, eyes wide in astonishment and tears moisturizing her smooth pale skin. Terry suddenly felt her mother hug her tightly and the warm wetness of her mother's tears on her neck. As they drew closer they were able to hear the singing more clearly. The children and their parents were singing the Ave Maria.

The carts stopped just under the entrance to the arch they had formed. Terry and her mother were the first to disembark. The applause was spontaneous and raucous. Rebecca climbed out of the second cart with assistance from her father. Another wave of sound rose and fell. The band started playing a John Phillips Sousa march, and out of the crowd Joe Delgado Jr. emerged and reached for his mother's arm. Terry looked at him and burst into tears. He was dressed in the black tuxedo his father had worn to walk her down the aisle in London. She never remembered him being as handsome, nor as happy.

They made their way through the arch and were stopped along the way by old friends and neighbors who reached for her hand or sleeve, or in one case, her train. She hugged and kissed every cheek offered and worried that her own make up was unsettled in the process. As they neared the entrance to the chapel she saw Michael and Carole Burns. Carole Burns was arrestingly beautiful in a light green cantilevered strapless gown. Terry was taken aback. Her magnetic smile and deep blue eyes made her look twenty years younger. Michael Burns, in an immaculate white linen tuxedo accented with a pink carnation, was smiling too, in the manner of a man who had fulfilled a promise.

Terry felt herself being tugged to her right. She was immediately aware of Maggie Gillespie's arms around her neck. "Oh

Terry, you are ravishing," she said, hot tears running down her cheeks. "Oh . . . your father . . . your father!" Dr. Jim Gillespie was standing behind her with a large, infectious grin. When Maggie withdrew, unable to say anything more, he leaned in and said in a stage whisper, "What Mrs. Gillespie is trying to say is that your father would have absolutely loved the idea of tying a massive one on at Michael Burns' expense!"

Terry's heart took flight. Her laughter was instant and pure, and loosed the bonds of a half lifetime of pain in the affairs of the heart. She heard a voice within coaxing her, *"You are experiencing near perfect joy. Give thanks immediately."* She closed her eyes momentarily in submissive compliance. When she opened them she was entering the chapel. She was whisked to the side and escorted into a small, nearly all-glass observance room for parents with small children. She and her mother behind her were soon joined by Rebecca and Stanislaw Wlodarczyk, each of whom was smiling and breathing heavily. "Did you ever see anything like that?" cried Rebecca to no one in particular. Terry rushed to hug her. She held her at something close to arm's length, looked into her eyes and said, "You were so right, Rebecca. God is too good to us! What have we ever done to deserve all this . . . *and Patrick and Michael Burns*!?"

Fran Delgado sat down flushed with excitement. Stanislaw Wlodarczyk sat down beside her. She looked at him and said, "What time do you suppose Old Burnsie will open the bar?"

The gentleman smiled and replied in stiff formal English, "Whenever this bar is opened, I will be the first man in line to get for you what you desire."

A round young man with heavily calloused hands in what was clearly a borrowed suit entered the small room and wordlessly extended an arm in Fran Delgado's direction. She grabbed it with both hands and struggled to her feet. Once she was steady, the two of them departed for her seat. Stanislaw Wlodarczyk followed quietly, head bowed.

The organist played a lovely orchestral arrangement from Bach as the people entered the chapel and filled its pews. It took a good fifteen minutes for the chapel to completely settle. When it did, Father John Sweeney emerged from the sacristy with two young altar boys and Father Bill Fregosi processing ahead of him. Eight young men in black tuxedos and eight young women in pink satin gowns rose from the first pews on either side of the aisle and took their places at the foot of the altar.

Suddenly a furious crescendo of sound commenced in the loft. The little chapel shook with the familiar sound of "Gather Us In." Two brides immediately appeared in the back of the church. They were escorted by men in black tuxedoes. Terry Simpson signaled Rebecca to precede her down the aisle. She and her father began with his setting a snail's pace to allow his daughter to bask in the pure joy of a people who longed for a reason to share joy. Terry and her son followed.

The walk within "Gather Us In" seemed to take a lifetime. Terry smiled and waved to the luminous faces that had been a constant in the videography of her life. Nearly every soul she encountered on her journey to the altar reminded her of some part of her blessedly innocent life as a child and young adult in Narbrook. This filled her with an otherworldly peace not of her acquaintance. Suddenly the faces began to dissolve and she saw herself enveloped in a brilliant white light. She heard an interior voice say with quiet urgency, *"This is indeed the day the Lord has made! Let us give thanks and praise."* And so she did.

As Rebecca arrived at the altar, Michael Burns Jr. appeared from the wings. He was dressed in a whiter than white tuxedo dramatically set off by a wine red rose. He was smiling. Stanislaw Wlodarczyk grinned at the sight of him, lifted his daughter's hand to his, and clasped the two hands together so tightly that Michael Jr. had to fight off a reflexive urge to counter with a left hook—once the source of his rather considerable notoriety. Instead he smiled and led his bride to two kneelers on the right side of the altar, where he waved to Father John Sweeney. He assisted Rebecca with her gown and only then knelt beside her.

Standing at the entrance to the sanctuary, Joe Delgado Jr. welcomed Patrick Burns, dressed in a mirror image of his twin brother, who emerged from the wings with a wide grin. Joe Delgado Jr. eagerly joined his mother's hand in the groom's and gave him a chest hug. He leaned in and whispered, "Please take good care of my mom." Patrick smiled, looked at the young man's iridescent mother and said, "I will, Joe. I promise." Terry stood on her toes to kiss her tall and handsome son, and to tell him she loved him. Observing this and overhearing a portion of it, the congregation murmured their delight.

Hand in hand, she and Patrick made their way to the two kneelers on the left side of the altar. They smiled at Father John Sweeney, who was standing on the top step of the altar and who winked at them behind a broad smile. They looked across the altar, waved to Michael Jr. and Rebecca, and knelt down. Unfortunately Patrick Burns knelt on a portion of his bride's train, which did not go unobserved by those assembled. It was their gentle laughter that alerted him that he had to rise and reset himself, which drew an all too knowing smile from the woman who was only moments away from becoming the new Mrs. Patrick Burns.

Father John Sweeney looked at the congregation and drew a deep breath. Then he crossed the first two fingers in each hand in an international symbol of hope and raised them high over his head. The assembly let out a roar that purged whatever remaining tension may have entered the chapel with a people who had been buffeted about from an unrelenting series of calamities over the past ten years. The laughter rolled in a wave from the congregation to the top step of the altar and enveloped their beloved pastor before receding gently.

John Sweeney smiled at them with deep affection and began the holy rite with a slow, reverent sign of the cross, and said, "In the name of the Father and of the Son and of the Holy Spirit." They responded, "Amen." He continued, "My brothers and sisters in Christ, the purest form of love—the selfless and boundaryless covenantal union of a man and a woman—brings us together on this very first day in this most special month of our Immaculate Mother." He smiled, ducked his head and said, "Uh . . . check that. Make it the selfless and boundaryless love of two men and two women." The congregation laughed spiritedly. As the laughter began to ebb, Dr. Jim Gillespie cried out, "Leave it to Burns, Father. If it's worth doing, it's worth *over*doing!" This drew another outburst.

Father Sweeney let the laughter rise and fall. Then, when the little chapel was again settled, he bowed his head and initiated the penitential rite. He followed it with the opening prayer in which he gave thanks to God for the generosity of Michael and Carole Burns, and asked His continued blessing on that family, on the families of all the assembled, and in particular on the two brides and two grooms who, as he characterized it, "modeled St. Paul's description of pure Christian love in their young lives as perfectly as humanly possible."

The congregation sat noisily as Rebecca's father rose to approach the pulpit for the first reading. In a somewhat thick but largely accessible Polish accent, he read what St. Paul had to say about the nature of love that can fairly be called Christian. Maggie Gillespie followed Stanislaw Wlodarczyk to the pulpit to lead the congregation in the responsorial psalm. She was resplendent in a pale lavender satin gown, her hair swept artfully up to reveal the ageless beauty of her face. Grace Seltzer followed her mother and read from the first chapter of St. Peter on the power and dictates of mutual love. When she finished, she descended the pulpit carefully, smiled at her pastor, and made her way to her seat. Immediately all eyes turned to Father John Sweeney. He rose, walked deliberately to the pulpit, climbed two steps on stiff and painful knees, and read the Gospel from John, chapter 15, on the Vine and the branches. At its completion he held the lectionary aloft and said, "The Gospel of the Lord!" On cue, slightly over two hundred men, women, and children fell into their seats with a clatter. Roughly forty others stood across the back or up in the loft behind the organist and the small choir.

John Sweeney bowed his head in silent prayer and asked the Immaculate to nudge him out of the way so her Spouse, the Third Person of the Blessed Trinity, would have free reign over the next ten minutes. He waited for a familiar stirring in his heart, and when it came, he opened his eyes and began, "What a joy filled moment in time this is!" Several among the congregation seemed to sense what was coming and laughed. "I mean . . . look at the celestial combination of exquisite beauty and extraordinary virtue it took to finally get the Burns brothers to the altar!" Loud spontaneous laughter erupted.

He waited for it to settle, then looked at the brothers seated to the left and right of him and said, "You both know of course, you're the luckiest men alive." The brothers smiled sheepishly. "Somehow, and I truly do not know how, you managed to find women to rival your incomparable mother." The congregation broke out in sustained applause. Carole Burns bowed her head in embarrassment. Michael Burns Sr. managed to apprehend one of his wife's arms and lifted it high above her head despite heavy resistance, which served to intensify the applause as indeed was his intention. "And . . ." John Sweeney added while nodding toward the two women, "I dare say Teresa and Rebecca, you two will have a much easier time of it than she did." Raucous laughter filled the chapel quickly breaking into more applause.

The congregation fell silent. John Sweeney ducked his head slightly and said, "Jesus tells us today that he is the Vine, and we are the branches. He says, 'Whoever remains in me and I in him will bear much fruit.' Today we celebrate the sprouting of two new and soon to be wondrously fruitful branches on the mystical vine that is, still, St. Martha's Parish in Narbrook." He paused to let the full significance of that statement settle.

"Yes, our own Church in America betrayed our beloved little church. And, yes, now our own government has closed it." He grimaced. "And, yes, we who were nourished for generations there have been dispersed to all parts of the country, and beyond. And, yes, they have effectively robbed us of our property and possessions through the mark of the beast—their Keys and Rings—which we have refused." He paused and thundered, "But, as all can plainly see, they have not been permitted to strip us from the Vine who *unites* us, the Vine who *nurtures* us, the Vine who *sustains* us."

He paused and shifted his weight to ease the pain in his knees. "It is the Vinemaster who has replanted a remnant of our community here in a hollow that is truly hallowed. It is hallowed because *He* is here. It is hallowed because *He* has graciously willed it so. He tells us today that He is the living and eternal Word of the Vinedresser. A Vinedresser, He reminds us, who is always about the work of pruning branches so that each and every branch will bear more fruit.

"My brothers and sisters . . . we are the beneficiaries of a Grand Pruning! Indeed, *we are still being pruned*. And what a glorious fruit this pruning has borne!" He paused and leaned in to the mic, "There is holiness in the hollow. I see it in your eyes, hear it in your voices, observe it in your countless acts of love for one another." He paused and bellowed, "This is a community of love! And because we have put Christ first, because we have chosen to remain in Him, He has given us every good thing—safe and secure lodging, bountiful harvests, and loving care for our aged and infirmed."

He felt himself begin to well up, and bowed his head toward the pulpit in embarrassment. "Jesus reminds us on this glorious day of spring that if we continue to remain in Him, and if His words continue to remain in our hearts . . . we can ask anything of Him and it will be done for us." He turned to the two couples and said, "Therefore, I ask this in Jesus' Holy Name for you—that your joy may always be rooted in Him who has joined you at this altar today, and who wishes to be an invited Collaborator in your covenantal union. I ask that He may never cease to prune your united hearts that you will know and love Him . . . and each other . . . more with each passing day."

He let his eyes canvas the assembly. He suddenly felt a dark premonition. He shook himself to rid his mind of it but was unable to do so. He opened his mouth to speak and no words issued forth. He panicked. He bowed his head, prayed to the Immaculate, felt a faint stirring, raised his head, and said in a loud, clear voice, "Our divine Lord calls us to love one another as He has loved us. He tells us that there is no greater love than for a man to lay down his life for another." He suddenly felt tears on his cheeks. The warmth of them surprised him. "I say this to all of you today. I love this Jesus with my whole mind and heart and soul. And I love each of you *far more* than I love myself. And please know this . . ." He felt a hush fall upon an assembly he could no longer see clearly. "I would gladly lay down my life for any one of you."

He turned and grabbed the railing to ease himself down the two steps, wiping his eyes and cheeks with the sleeve of his other arm. He walked slowly, heavily to the center of the altar, climbed one step, turned and beckoned the two couples. They rose and made their way slowly to him. The groomsmen and bridesmaids filed out of their pews and filled in behind them, creating a second arc before the altar table that was now two steps above and behind John Sweeney. He noted the particular anxiousness of the two brides and sought to allay it. "Please do not be apprehensive," he whispered. "I'll lead you step by step just as I did in the rehearsal."

Terry Delgado blinked. "But Father, this *is* our rehearsal!"

The congregation did not hear this byplay and therefore was startled by the sudden outbreak of laughter coming from the altar. Father John Sweeney shrugged and smiled without embarrassment. This, too, elicited laughter. "Okay, we're going to start down this road together," he said, nodding to each couple. "Then we're going to separate and go one on one. That way, we'll all be certain both couples are actually officially married!" This only prompted more laughter from the groomsmen and bridesmaids.

John lifted his chin and his decibel level, and said to the congregation, "My brothers and sisters, please take note. Patrick and Teresa, Michael and Rebecca, are the actual ministers of this Sacrament of Holy Matrimony." He paused. "Father Bill and I are from corporate and we're just here to help." This produced a small tsunami of laughter.

He looked at each couple and said, "You have come here freely to give yourself without reservation to each other in marriage?" The two couples nodded and answered, "Yes."

"Will you love and honor each other as man and wife for the rest of your lives?" The couples replied in the affirmative.

"Will you accept children lovingly and bring them up according to the law of Christ and His Church?" The couples nodded vigorously, answering yes.

John smiled, paused, and continued, "Patrick and Teresa, Michael and Rebecca, since it is your intent to enter into marriage, please join your right hands, face one another, and declare your consent before God and His Church." The two couples did as bidden. John moved to Patrick and led him in his vow before God and man, "I, Patrick, take you, Teresa, to be my wife. I promise to be true to you in good times and in bad, in sickness and in health. I will love and honor you all the days of my life."

John Sweeney turned to Teresa Delgado and led her through the same vow.

Then he beckoned Michael Burns Jr. and Rebecca Wlodarczyk and led them in their consent.

When he had finished he looked at the two couples and said, "You have declared your consent before the Church. May the Lord in His goodness strengthen your consent and fill you each with His blessings." Then he wagged his finger and added with measured emphasis, "What God has joined together, men must not divide."

Father John Sweeney then signaled for the rings. One of Grace Seltzer's children, a son of preschool age, arrived bearing a small pillow with four small, navy blue, velvet boxes lying upon it. He climbed the step and handed the pillow to Father Fregosi, who bowed to him, elaborately, and took possession of the pillow. The little fellow mimicked the elaborate gesture, and promptly fell down the step and onto his side. Patrick Burns reached down with one strong hand, clasped both his coat and shirt collar from behind, lifted him clean off the floor and set him upright.

John Sweeney lifted his eyes to heaven and prayed, "May the Lord himself bless these rings which you give to each other as a sign of your love and fidelity." He then reached for the first of the rings that Bill Fregosi had extracted from its small box, handed it to Patrick Burns, who immediately placed it on the fourth finger of Teresa Burns' left hand, and said, "Teresa, please take this ring as a sign of my love and fidelity in the name of the Father, of the Son, and of the Holy Spirit."

Teresa Delgado in turn took a ring from Father Bill Fregosi and slipped it on the fourth finger of her husband's left hand, smiled, and repeated the pledge. The couple then stepped aside as the ritual was repeated for Michael Burns Jr. and Rebecca Wlodarczyk.

When it was completed, John Sweeney looked at Patrick and Teresa, smiled and said, "I now pronounce you husband and wife." A small roar erupted from the back of the chapel and quickly made its way to the altar, where it elicited embarrassed smiles and an awkward kiss from the groom and his bride.

John let it settle, and then he turned to Michael and Rebecca, smiled and said, "And lest we start a riot, I now pronounce *you* husband and wife." Another roar, greater than the first, was drawn from the congregation, and in its midst Michael Burns Jr. enveloped his beautiful wife in an expansive hug and kissed her passionately. This occasioned a second outburst that drew another wag of the finger and shake of the head in mock dudgeon from their pastor. He understood his people had precious little to celebrate in their lives. He also knew how deeply they loved the Burns family and their sons. But he now needed to settle them down for the Prayer of the Faithful and the Offertory.

As the groomsmen and bridesmaids returned to their pews and the two married couples to their kneelers, John Sweeney climbed the two remaining steps to the altar table and half circled it so he was facing his congregation. After reciting the Prayers of the Faithful, he paused and held up his arms, hands extended, in the universal symbol of a call to deep prayer. He lifted his eyes to heaven and prayed, "You are indeed Holy, O Lord, the fount of all holiness." He lowered his eyes, joined his hands, extended them over the bread and wine on the table in front of him, and continued, "Make holy these gifts we pray, by sending down your Holy Spirit upon them." He joined his hands, made the sign of the cross over the bread and the chalice, and added, "that they may become for us the Body and Blood of our Lord, Jesus Christ."

He bowed deeply from the waist and held the large host in his hands. The upper part of his body was now extended over the altar and his entire body tingled with excitement. He instantly recalled Mother Theresa of Calcutta's admonition to him one day in Harlem. "Pray every Mass like it's your last Mass, Father John." He had tried to do so but had not always succeeded. On this day, he vowed, he would do as the little Saint had directed. He continued, "At the time he was betrayed, and entered willingly into his Passion, he took bread, and giving thanks, broke it, and gave it to his disciples, saying: 'Take this, all of you, and eat of it: for this is my Body which will be given up for you.'" He raised the host high and held it aloft for all to see. As he beheld what was now the very flesh of his Lord and Savior, he received a strange prompting of the Holy Spirit to make a perfect act of contrition. This he did, eyes shut tight. When he completed it, he placed the Host lovingly on the altar with both hands and genuflected before it in humble submission.

Then he reached for the chalice and prayed, "In a similiar way, when supper was ended he took the chalice and, once more giving thanks, he gave to his disciples, saying: 'Take this, all of you, and drink from it: for this is the chalice of my Blood, the Blood of the new and eternal covenant, which will be poured out . . .'"

Suddenly there was a commotion in the back of the chapel. Uniformed men began pouring through the back door, rifles raised. They raced to positions across the back and of the chapel, stopped and pointed their rifles toward the altar, awaiting further instruction. There were twelve of them. Their uniforms were dark blue with red trim. Their helmets were white. The men were quickly recognized by the men in the congregation as a local platoon from America's widely feared Homeland Security Force. The shock of what was transpiring in their midst overwhelmed the entire assembly into a silence born of disbelief.

One of the twelve stepped forward and lowered his rifle to his side. His eyes scanned the assembly. He appeared nervous. He looked toward the altar and shouted, "Father John Sweeney, you have had your warning!" A loud murmur from the congregation rose quickly. The leader of the platoon took the butt of his rifle and pounded it into the marble floor repeatedly, occasioning a swift and thorough silence in the chapel.

All eyes turned to the altar. What they saw terrified them. Father John Sweeney was either oblivious to what was transpiring or he was irrationally defiant. Many years later, his own people would never reach agreement on precisely which it was. Slowly and with singular concentration he lifted the chalice over his head and held it there seemingly transfixed.

From the back of the church came a command. "Priest . . . you are to stop now!" The next sound heard in the chapel of Our Lady of the Bay was the chilling sound of eleven rifles cocking.

Maggie Gillespie shrieked, and could be seen attempting to rise and run to her pastor's defense, but she was instantly and roughly pulled back into the pew by her wide eyed husband. Michael Burns Sr. stood and began to run up the aisle. His sons rose at the sight of his vulnerability. Just then, came the single solitary command that forever impaled itself in the consciousness of all who were to live through what happened next. "Fire!" yelled the platoon leader.

Bullets from eleven AK 47s fired into and around the body of a priest in the midst of the Consecration. The assembly ducked in sheer fright in their pews. The Burns brothers dove over the falling bodies of their brides, all four hitting the ground at the same time. Michael Burns Sr. reached the bottom step of the altar before he was hit in the right shoulder and fell head first into the top step, knocking himself unconscious. The barrage continued for an impossibly long time. Over two hundred shell casings would be

found in the hours after the assault. The body of the priest was rid-
dled with an extraordinary volume of bullets, which sent it twisting
and turning like a weather vane on the roof of a barn. As he fell,
the chalice fell from his hands and hit the floor, its contents spilling
out onto the cold marble. On the ground, the priest reached for
the lost Blood of his Savior with his fingers and tried to drink it.
He tasted its bitter herb and fell onto his back.

The platoon of assassins turned and fled. Patrick Burns stood
and shouted to the men in the congregation, "The shed." The men
raced behind the chapel and watched Michael Burns Jr. rip the
hinges off the munitions shed. There were over forty men. Those
that could, perhaps twenty, grabbed a Balishnicoff and pursued the
platoon on foot. The others grabbed Glocks and followed.

Maggie Gillespie reached Father John Sweeney first. She
knelt, cradled his head in her hands, kissed his forehead and hugged
him to her chest, and wailed in utter desperation as she had done
only one other time in her life. She looked at her hands and arms
and dress. They were covered in blood. She watched in horror as
a torrent of blood began to cover the altar, seeping into the spilled
contents of the chalice. She suddenly realized it was no longer possible to tell where the Blood of Christ began and the blood of His
alter Christus ended.

She bent down, removed a tuft of hair from his eyes, kissed his
forehead and said, "I love you, Father." He stared up at her blankly,
and she feared he was already dead. Then, abruptly, he opened his
mouth and said in a hoarse whisper, "He lives!"

She blinked and cried out at the top of her lungs: "Father,
Father, please don't leave us!" She raised her eyes to heaven and
screeched, "Lord, please! Not Father John! Not Father John! Please
Lord."

A crowd of nearly two hundred souls now ringed the dying
priest on the altar.

Most of them did not see Father John Sweeney take his final
breath.

35

The funeral of Father John Sweeney was life passing through death and not quite re-emerging intact for the men and women of Hallowed Hollow.

It began the following morning at 10:00 a.m. with Father Bill Fregosi breaking down before the closed casket at the sign of the cross and ended with him sitting in his chair on the altar unable to rise to complete the rite.

John Sweeney was buried in a simple hardwood casket that Michael Burns had purchased for himself, so certain was he that he would be the first to slip the veil. Eight pall bearers, among them his sons, hoisted the casket up three steps and placed it under the altar table, which yielded less than an inch of clearance. Here it was to remain through the epic events that soon brought a swift and cataclysmic end to an age.

One by one the faithful approached their fallen pastor, and laid blessed items and treasured artifacts by the side of his casket. Over two hundred forty men, women, and children made their way up the white Carrara marble steps, many falling to their knees in grief. The altar soon resembled a shrine, and indeed there was open speculation that the body of the man in the casket would one day be discovered incorrupt.

Maggie Gillespie's eulogy changed the air inside the little chapel by the bay. She claimed to say only what virtually any of the others could have said. She recalled the major inflection points in her life, and how her pastor had helped her navigate through and around them by placing her trust in the person of Jesus Christ. She spoke of his resolute accompaniment in the life of her family and the difference it had made in the lives of her children and grandchildren. She talked about John Sweeney's own dark night of the soul, about his fears of inadequacy, and how he had faced each struggle alone, at night, on his stomach, in front of the tabernacle, rosary in hand. When she finished, a strange stillness seemed to descend from the heavens that penetrated, settled, and filled the hearts of John Sweeney's former parishioners with a joy that surpassed their own understanding.

The reception that followed lasted until almost 8:00 p.m. It had a distinctly Irish character. Michael Burns Jr. became the center of attention late in the day with respect to rumors about what he had done to the man who had given the order to fire upon John Sweeney in the midst of the Consecration. But Michael Burns Jr., nothing if not circumspect, refused to address the questions directed to him. He sat quietly on the gentle rolling hill leading to the bay behind the Main House with his wife at his side nursing a Guinness. His brother sat next to him attempting to console a bride who was simply inconsolable. John Sweeney had opened a door to new life in Teresa Burns. Now his death seemed to close that door and bring an end to that life. At one point Patrick Burns put an arm around his wife, kissed her, and said, "The gift we are to each other is his legacy to us." She grabbed his arm and buried her head into his chest.

About forty-five minutes later, Michael Burns Sr., his wound cauterized and wrapped carefully in white linen under a bulky spring windbreaker, was behind the wheel of a forty-foot truck. His sons sat beside him in the cab. Behind the front seat was a trunk, and in it were eight rifles and fourteen hand guns. They were headed north on 301 to Elkton, where they would pick up Route 95 South through southern Maryland and Virginia. Their destination: The Kangaroo Express, a truck stop in Cary, North Carolina, about forty minutes south of Durham and twenty minutes west of Raleigh. Estimated time of arrival was 4:15 a.m.

In Cary, Michael Burns Sr. would meet Bill Lavery for the first time, the middleman in a contraband transaction involving no less than six major pharmaceutical houses headquartered in Triangle Park. Part of the deal involved barter. In the back of the truck were no less than one hundred squealing hogs from the Hallowed Hollow nursery. For Bill Lavery, the hogs were a "sweetener." He intended to sell them at a black market auction the following morning in Charlestown, South Carolina and pocket the proceeds.

Michael Burns Sr. had readily agreed to the barter exchange, believing the animals would provide a cover on their trip south in the event the truck was stopped by Homeland Security forces patrolling the major highways. The Burns men had decided they would take the major highways down and risk being stopped by Homeland Security with hogs in the truck, and then take back roads home and risk being stopped by vigilantes with nearly a million dollars' worth of pharmaceuticals in the truck.

They hit Baltimore around 9:40. Michael Burns was startled and thought perhaps a curfew was in effect. The darkened city had been transformed into an enlarged detention center with cyclone fences encircling endless encampments of tents. From the truck they could see small figures running about at play, and larger figures sitting on suitcases in front of the tents drinking from large dark bottles and laughing.

An hour and a half later they took the 495 spur around D.C. looking to pick up Route 95 South below Alexandria, but they missed the cutoff and ended up in Annandale about twenty minutes to the west. There they ran into a vigilante patrol who forced them at gun point to pull over and get out of the truck.

A huge man with a hunting rifle resting on his shoulders saun-
tered toward them and said, "Where y'all from?"

"Cecil County," Michael Burns Sr. replied.

"What's your business in Annandale?"

"We ain't got no business in Annandale," Michael replied.

At this a smaller man laughed, nodded in the direction of
the back of the truck and the squealing hogs, and said, "Y'all hog
farmers?"

Michael knew immediately he was talking to the man who
gave the orders. "Yes sir. Hogs, dairy, sheep, grain, vegetables.
Pretty much anything and everything we can to keep us goin'."

The small man nodded in understanding. "How 'bout givin'
us a looksee?" he commanded.

Michael nodded to Patrick, who went to the back of the
truck, picked the lock, and shoved the door that was on a roll bar
up into the ceiling of the truck. About a dozen Annandale men
who had followed, rifles in hand, now stood staring through a green
wire mesh fence into the faces of one hundred squealing hogs. "My
God, shut that damn door," the behemoth shouted. "How y'all
stand that smell?"

"That's a question you right ought to put to our wives,"
Michael Sr. replied.

The smaller man laughed and said, "S'posin' you right about
that." He looked at Michael with a twinkle in his eye. "How 'bout
sharing a few of those little fellers with us?"

Michael looked at his sons who were clearly not happy at the
prospect of being robbed. The father, however, preferred being
robbed to being shot. "Well, I'll tell you what," he said in an
affected draw intended for the amusement of his sons. "I'm s'posin'
we could part with a few of those little guys in exchange for some
help gettin' back on the highway."

Ten minutes and six hogs later they were heading south in
search of Route 95.

They passed through Ashland about midnight. It, too, was
pitch black. There were groups of vagrants wandering about the

intersections of the town carrying their possessions in green plastic bags. There was an air of lawlessness, and it surprised Michael Burns Sr. that Homeland Security had so clearly abandoned the field of play just twenty-five minutes outside of Richmond. He slowed the truck to avoid hitting several men who were stumbling about in the middle of the road. Just then Michael heard a loud thump. Something, or someone, had hit the side of the truck. Though he had no intention of stopping the truck to determine which it had been, he slowed to a crawl to avoid hitting anyone. The sounds outside grew louder and awakened his sons who had been catnapping. Upon seeing the truck was now all but surrounded, Patrick uttered an expletive and Michael Jr. quickly reached behind the front seat and lifted the lid of the trunk where the weapons were stored. His father just as quickly grabbed the lid and slammed it shut, nearly severing his son's fingers.

Several dozen vagrants stood in front of the truck bringing it to a reluctant stop. They raced to the driver's side and began rocking it violently. It was manifestly clear they intended to tip it in order to rob and kill its occupants. Michael Burns Sr. bowed his head, said a prayer, then put his foot on the accelerator and floored it. He immediately struck two men knocking one of them into the air and onto the hood of truck, from which he slid to the ground. The other man was propelled like an airborne bowling ball, felling two men who were standing behind him. A dozen of the others began chasing the truck—running alongside it, thumping it with iron bars and wooden bats, and shouting obscenities at the figures in the cabin. One of them managed to crack the passenger side window, but it didn't shatter. When the mob was safely in the rearview mirror several minutes later, Michael Jr. turned to his father and asked, "When do we get to use our guns?"

The father grimaced and replied, "When our lives are in danger."

They took the 295 spur around Richmond. From several miles away they could see a long caravan of U.S. military trucks coming into the darkened city from Route 64 to the west. "Probably provisions," the father remarked.

"Why are all these cities dark?" Michael Jr. asked.

"The government did a half-assed job of patching up the grid after the disasters in San Francisco and New York," the father replied. "Makes you wonder how serious they were."

They drove in silence until Patrick looked at the gas gauge and said, "We need gas, Pop." The father looked and saw he had less than a quarter tank left. He nodded glumly. He had miscalculated. He thought, more hoped actually, they would make it to the truck stop in Cary without having to refill. It was clear, he now realized, he hadn't factored in the additional two ton weight of one hundred hogs.

They decided to pick up Route 85 below Petersburg, which offered a straight shot to Durham. The decision almost cost them their lives. In South Hill, just north of the Carolina border, they stopped for gas. As they pulled into the small station, the father took note of a white van parked on the far side of the lot. There were two uniformed men sitting in the front seat. The van's lights were off. Michael immediately thought about pulling out and back onto the road, but realized that maneuver would only draw greater suspicion and, possibly, entail a chase which he knew would not end well.

He stopped the truck at the self-serve pump and his sons jumped out to pump and pay. Within seconds, the front doors of the van opened, two barrel-chested men appeared, and began walking toward the truck. Michael saw they were in the custom tailored navy blue uniforms with red trim of America's universally loathed Homeland Security Force. They approached the cabin and signaled for him to lower his window, which he promptly did. "Good evening, men," he said with a cheerful smile.

"Papers," one of the men ordered.

Michael felt a sharp pain in the pit of his stomach. He reached into his glove box for his driver's license, owner's card, and insurance card, knowing none had been signed and none were current. He grabbed them without looking and handed them over in a cold sweat. The man took the papers and headed back to the van.

The other man headed around to the pump to check on his sons. Michael quickly climbed out of the truck. The Homeland Security official ambled up to the pump, looked at the truck's license plate, and said to his sons, "Hey, where you Yankees from?"

"We ain't Yankees," Michael Jr. answered with a hint of menace.

The official smiled and said, "Well, what you boys from Maryland doin' down here near the Ca'lina border?"

"Hog auction," Patrick answered moving quickly to head off trouble.

"Where?" the official probed with suspicion.

Patrick looked at his father who shook his head imperceptibly. "Dunno exactly. Supposed to meet a guy in Durham."

The official lunged quickly, grabbed Patrick's wrist, and held it with both hands while he inspected it closely. "Boy, I ain't seeing no Key," he bellowed. "You ain't one of them papists, is you?"

The next sound heard was the sound of a bat hitting wood, only it wasn't a bat and what was struck wasn't wood. Michael Burns Sr. felled the official with a single ferocious punch to the temple. The man dropped like a sack and hit the pavement head first. There he lay, unconscious, in an expanding pool of blood. The father immediately knelt and felt for the man's pulse. He looked up at his wide-eyed sons and shook his head without remorse. "Get the guns, boys," he said.

As they raced for the cabin they saw the other official approaching, papers in hand. At the sight of his prey escaping, he pulled his gun and began to yell. "Halt! Halt! Do *not* get in that truck. I repeat, do *not* get in that truck!" To punctuate his order he fired once above the hood of the truck, almost hitting Patrick. Michael Sr. jumped into the truck, reached into the trunk, and grabbed the first weapon his right hand touched. In rapid succession he felt a stinging sensation in his left arm and another in his left shoulder. He cocked the Glock, pointed at the official who was now less than twenty yards away, and fired. The shot hit the man between the eyes barely leaving a trace. He dropped like a deer in his tracks, gun still in his hand. In a panic, Michael fired up the engine and lurched out of the station and back onto the main road only to stun his sons by turning around almost immediately and heading back into the station. He pulled up to the pump that was lying on the ground. He got out of the truck, put the pump back into its holster, reached into his pocket for several large denominations of essentially worthless American currency, and wedged them between the pump and its holster. He climbed back into the truck, turned to his sons and said, "Stealing is a sin."

When they were safely out of town, Patrick looked at his father and said, "Tell me again, why are we doing this?"

His father did not so much as turn to his son in response. "Because I made a promise," he replied softly, eyes fixed on the road ahead.

They encountered only a few other vehicles on the highway headed in either direction for the next ten miles. None carried uniformed security officers. Michael, however, was under no illusions. He understood the truck had been tagged and would be pursued eventually. He was now anxious to get off Route 85 and onto a back road that would take them directly into Durham. As he was driving, he slipped his windbreaker over his head and used it as a tourniquet for the shoulder wound. He was certain the wound in his arm was merely a flesh wound. In a small clearing just over the North Carolina border, below Henderson, he decided to pull over and take a look at both wounds. Patrick jumped out of the truck, came to the driver's side, and climbed up the step. He unwrapped his father's makeshift tourniquet and peered into his shoulder. "You got a bullet in there, Pop," he said grimly. "We're gonna have to find someone to take a look at that."

"Like hell we will," the father replied through gritted teeth. "Get back in the truck. We gotta make Cary while it's still dark. Lavery said he's taking off first sign of light . . . whether we're loaded up . . . or even there."

They rolled into an all but empty Durham a little after 4:00 a.m., and looked for signs for Route 40 South toward Fayetteville.

Michael Jr., shocked at the desolation of what he knew to be a once thriving city, asked his father what had happened to its residents.

"Probably fled to the mountains," his father replied matter-of-factly, without taking his eyes off the road.

"Which mountains?" the son inquired.

"Blue Ridge," the father replied, nodding to his right, "about an hour west."

At precisely 4:20 they saw the outline of what looked to be a truck stop. As they drew closer they saw a darkened sign that read, *Kangaroo Express*. They maneuvered the truck gently over a median strip and pulled into a large rest stop with a small convenience store in the middle of it, about one hundred yards from the road. The store, which was lit by large wax candles set within the frames of its four windows, appeared to be empty, and indeed so too was the lot save for two large sixteen wheelers that appeared to have been abandoned, and an old brown UPS truck that looked to be about forty feet in length in between the trailers.

Michael pulled the truck up next to the c-store and blinked its lights on and off in search of signs of life in the other vehicles. One blinked back. It was the UPS truck. Out stepped a tall, thin, slightly stooped man with horned rimmed glasses dressed in a dark sport coat, light colored turtleneck, and blue jeans. Michael had imagined a younger man and immediately wondered if Lavery had sent a surrogate.

He jumped out of the cab and quickly closed the distance between them. He extended his hand and said, "Bill . . .? Michael Burns."

The man took the hand and shook it. "No, sir. Name's Ames. Hank Ames, and I work with Bill."

"Where's Bill?" Michael asked making no attempt to hide his disappointment.

"Other business," the other man replied.

Michael could see he was extremely nervous and smelled trouble. He nodded and said, "Well, how about you tell Bill Lavery that me and the boys were countin' on seein' him. Will you do that for us?"

The man thought perhaps his associate had just been threatened. His hands started to shake. "How about we get ourselves squared away . . . and be on our way . . ." he suggested, nodding toward Michael's truck.

Michael looked at the man for a long moment as though he was uploading his countenance into cerebral storage. "Okay," he replied. "We'll pull over to you."

"No!" the man half shouted in panic. "We'll both pull around back, out of view from the road."

Michael smiled and nodded. "Works for me."

The man double-timed it to his truck. He turned the ignition over, pulled out quickly, and gunned it to the far side of the lot behind the little store. A dense pine forest bordered the property in the rear. Michael climbed back into the truck and followed without a word to his sons. His stomach was churning.

He stopped next to the other truck and sat waiting for Hank Ames to disembark. "That Bill Lavery?" Michael Jr. asked after several minutes of silence.

"Nope," his father replied.

"He the guy we're looking for?" Patrick asked.

"Yep," his father replied.

The boys looked at each other. They knew from long experience that when their father got quiet, bad things usually happened.

Eventually, Hank Ames got out of the truck and stood with his arms wide in apparent exasperation that he had to disembark first. It was just a little too much attitude for Michael Burns Sr., who had never quite mastered the art of suffering disappointments gracefully. It had been a long and painful night. He was tired and hungry, and his limited reservoir of patience had been exhausted. He felt a slight tug in his heart urging him to pray. He ignored it.

He climbed out of the truck and slammed the door with a fury that seemed to cause the cabin to vibrate, and walked over to where Ames was standing. He was now in a familiar place, on a precipice. "Give me the keys to your truck," he said with barely suppressed distemper, eyes staring through the other man's pupils.

"What!?" Hank Ames exclaimed. "Are you out of your mind?"

Michael took a step toward him and said calmly, "I'm not going to ask again."

Ames heard a door to the other truck open, watched as two powerfully built young men leapt to the ground in succession, and started walking in his direction. He began to urinate, unfortunately with his pants still on.

"Open up," Michael ordered. The man half waddled to the far side of the truck, unlocked the door, slid it back, and stood off to the side. Michael turned to his sons and said, "Count the lots. There should be sixty-four." He walked back to his truck and picked the lock. With difficulty he lifted the door and slid it up into the ceiling. He took a step back reflexively, repulsed by the smell. He turned to Hank Ames and waved him over. When he arrived, still shaking, Michael Burns Sr. said to him, "Look, there are ninety-four hogs in there. I owe Lavery one hundred. I'm going to give you cash for the difference. If he still wants the other six, I'll have them sent down." The man nodded and let his head fall to his chest in embarrassment.

Patrick Burns jumped down from the old UPS truck, saw his father with the other man and yelled, "Pop, there's only thirty-two." Michael Burns Sr. started shaking with rage. He lunged for the other man, put his hands around his neck, and started to squeeze. Patrick, seeing what was about to unfold, ran to his father and tackled him. Michael Jr. arrived seconds later and leapt onto both men in an attempt to further subdue his father.

To Hank Ames shock and dismay, Michael Burns Sr. managed to throw off both his sons, and leapt to his feet to continue the attack. Just as he reached for Hank Ames' neck a second time, however, his sons took him down again. This time they each pinned a shoulder that had been shot in the past forty hours. Michael Burns

Sr. immediately howled in pain, letting loose a torrent of invective. Within moments he stopped struggling.

Patrick jumped up and quickly confronted a frozen Hank Ames, "Where's the rest of the shipment?"

Hank Ames tried to speak but could not. It was clear at least to Patrick Burns that the quivering man in front of him was no longer a source of any useful information. He walked around the cabin of their truck and opened the locker. He removed a large green plastic bag and dumped its contents on the ground. There were packets of Chinese Yuans in denominations of one hundred, fifty, and twenty. He knelt on the ground and separated the packets with astonishing alacrity. He went back to the truck for another green bag, and returned to retrieve roughly half of what was on the ground. When he was finished he lifted the bag, shook it, folded it in half, and returned to the truck where he wedged it into the bottom of the weapons trunk.

He returned to Hank Ames, pointed to the packets lying on the ground and said, "Rest is yours. Tell Lavery we better not catch him in Maryland."

Neither father nor brother saw or heard Michael Jr. slip around to the back of their truck. When they heard the door being shoved violently up into the ceiling they immediately understood, and knew it was too late. The next sound was that of ninety-four squealing hogs leaping to the ground and beginning a mad dash to freedom. The father saw them scurrying across the lot toward the open road, and thought of the passage in Mark about the swine of Gerasene, filled with unclean spirits, plunging to their death in the sea. He turned to his son who was smiling at him in anticipation of approval. The sight of his son seeking approval for a misdeed was more than the father could bear. He went to the truck and returned with about a dozen packets of cash, handed it to Hank Ames and said, "Give this to Bill. Tell him we're Christians. We don't steal." Hank Ames blinked in disbelief.

Then he turned to his sons and motioned them into the UPS truck. He turned back to Ames and handed him the keys to his truck. He lifted one of his arms, wincing as he did so, placed it on Ames' left shoulder and said quietly, "Hank, trust me. This switch will work out better for both of us." Then he turned and walked to the UPS truck. He saw that Patrick was behind the wheel. He motioned him to move out. Patrick refused saying, "Let us take you home, Pop. You're all dinged up."

"Not yet, son," he said as he mounted the step to the driver's seat. Reluctantly, his son moved out and parked himself on a small stool behind the two seats in the front. Michael Sr. turned the engine over and checked the gas gauge and cursed. "Boys, we gotta fill up," he said angrily. He drove the truck around to the front of the store and pulled up to a pump. Michael Jr. leapt out to fill the tank. His father reached into his pocket, pulled out several Yuan, and handed it to Patrick to leave in the pump. Patrick climbed out of the truck and handed the currency to his brother, who was now crestfallen at having embarrassed his father.

The boys climbed back in and Michael Jr. looked at his father and said forlornly, "Sorry, Pop."

Every part of Michael Burns Sr.'s body now ached. His shoulders throbbed. His right hand, he thought, may well be fractured. But none of it compared with the pain in his heart at this moment. He loved all his children savagely. But his sons were his miracle gift from God. That one of them would think their father capable of defrauding another man was pain beyond all telling. "It's okay, Michael," he replied softly. "You know that I love you?" he added, choking on the words. In the darkness, the son nodded through his own tears.

They pulled out of the Kangaroo Express truck stop just as the dawn's first light cracked the peak of the mountain range to the west. Michael Sr. thought this a good omen, and he turned to his sons and said, "Guess they're gonna have to rename this place, Hogs Express." His sons merely grunted.

He headed south on Route 40 in search of Route 440, which he intended to take east to Route 64 north. The trip down had taken a little over seven and a half hours, an hour and a half longer than he anticipated. He had planned for the return home, which involved back roads, to be accomplished in eight hours. He looked at his watch. It was 5:25 a.m., and the pain in his left shoulder and right hand were getting worse.

Patrick turned to his father and said, "Think they'll rat us out on the truck?"

The father shook his head and said, soberly, "No. We got more on them than they got on us."

They picked up 64 above Zebulon. Michael glanced over at his sons. They were wide awake. "Well," he said with resignation, "we came down to pick up a two-year supply of pills for our families. We're going back with only one. We'll just have to trust it'll be enough." His sons nodded in silence. Michael stared straight ahead at the road and said, "Fellas, I should have led a Rosary for a safe trip on the way down. How about helping me make up for it on the way back?" Patrick and Michael Burns Jr. astonished their father by quietly reaching into their pockets and pulling out black rosaries. He led them through the Joyful Mysteries in thanksgiving for the Blessed Mother's intercession, realized and anticipated.

They soon hit Route 4 above Rocky Mount, and were making good time. Michael Sr. was beginning to think all the adventure on this sojourn would prove to be on the front end. In this, he would be proven wrong.

Daylight permitted them to see for the first time the desolation of rural southern towns. Traffic lights were down, street signs had been pulled from the ground, store fronts were blown out. Here and there a small knot of people, generally older people, could be seen huddling by the side of the road, hoping someone would stop and pick them up and take them . . . anywhere.

"My God, I had no idea things were this bad," Patrick remarked as another empty village filled the rearview mirror.

"Yes, yes," his father replied theatrically, more with bitterness than sarcasm, ". . . all of this . . . brought to you by your Beloved Boomers."

They turned onto Route 36 above Petersburg in Prince George County, Virginia. About fifteen minutes north they arrived in Hopewell. A local militia was out in force. A lookout must have tipped them off, because they rode into a blockade of a dozen or so pickup trucks strewn across the little hamlet's main road. Their owners stood behind them with rifles fixed on their truck. Michael Sr.'s first thought was to ram the empty cars and keep going. "Boys, get the rifles," he said between gritted teeth.

"Uh, Dad," Michael Jr. said, "we left them in the other truck."

Michael felt panic. He looked at his sons and said, "If we don't make it through this, I want you to know how much I loved you."

Patrick's chest expanded and the muscles in the side of his face contorted. He looked at his father and said with conviction, "We *will* make it through this."

Michael Sr. came to a stop about twenty yards from the pickup trucks. Patrick quickly jumped out and approached the townsmen. He calmly engaged the leader, an athletic looking young man in what appeared to be worn army fatigues. After several minutes, Michael Sr. saw the man's head began to nod, and he followed Patrick to the driver's side window.

Patrick motioned his father to lower the window, which he did. The man stuck his head in the window and peered at Michael's shoulder wounds. He looked at Michael and smiled. "Heard you killed two of them Homeland Security bastards," he said with a hint of wonder. "One of 'em with your bare hands!" Then he smirked and added, "Not bad, old man."

Michael Sr. flew into a rage at the insult and began cursing. In a fit of fury, he opened the door, jumped out, and started for the man. Patrick intervened. He herded his father off to the side, admonishing him calmly but forcefully. The militia began to hoot and holler in utter amusement. Michael Jr. started toward them only to be grabbed from behind by his brother.

The leader looked at his men, shook his head, and said loud enough for all to hear: "Fellas, let's jess clear the damn road. These bad boys is jess plain crazy." He laughed and added, "Hell, they's as likely to kill their own damn selves as one of us."

Patrick helped his father back into the truck and gave his brother a sharp look of rebuke. This time Michael Jr. ended up on the small stool behind the two front seats. The cars in front of them parted and the truck moved through slowly. Michael Burns Jr., unable to restrain himself, gave the Hopewell militia the digital salute from his seat on the stool.

They found Route 301 by chance about a half hour outside of Richmond. They had all but given up hope, most road signage having been destroyed by marauders foraging for human flesh and treasure. They headed north and east, and arrived at the lower Potomac about an hour later. The two-lane bridge appeared partially washed out from the spring rains. Michael Sr. stopped the truck to let his sons get out and see if it would be possible to navigate their way to the other side without endangering the shipment. The brothers paced the bridge for a long time. Abruptly, they turned to their father and waved him on. He proceeded with a caution that was uncharacteristic in the extreme. His sons hopped into the truck as it was moving, even as its wheels were finding the grooves created by other vehicles that had crossed the bridge recently. They proceeded at a snail's pace acutely aware of the rushing waters below them and the destruction of what had once been the bridge's barriers.

The crossing was only about sixty yards, but the incline on the far side was quite steep. In acute pain, Michael Sr. momentarily lost concentration and the truck began to drift sideways toward the edge of the bridge. For a moment, the three men in the truck panicked. The father heard his sons curse and yell, and move toward him in an attempt to evade what they were certain was to be a watery end to their mission if not life.

The truck stopped with its front and rear right wheels literally straddling the edge of the bridge. Looking at the slope of the bridge it was difficult to understand why it had not already tipped. The Burns' had to decamp from the driver's side. They walked to the rear of the truck and studied their predicament. "No way, Pop," Patrick said after several moments, unable to take his eyes off the rushing torrent of uncertain depth below. "There are not enough of us to nudge it off the edge, and even if there were, there's no place for us to stand without falling into the river."

His father nodded glumly.

Michael Burns Jr. looked at his devastated father, and understood the crushing burden this would forever represent. Knowing his father, he knew he would take this humiliation to his grave. He had failed people who depended on him. He was no longer Michael Burns—the man many people looked to for assistance in times of uncertainty. In that moment the son was overwhelmed by a love in his heart and a desire to return it to its source. He turned to his father, put his hand lightly on his shoulder and said, "Dad, it's going to be alright."

His father stared at him vacantly. He was no longer present in the here and now. Michael Jr. fell to his knees and bowed his head so that it rested on the surface of the bridge. There he remained for the next ten minutes deep in prayer, while his father and brother stood helplessly transfixed in despair. Suddenly he rose and wordlessly climbed into the truck, and re-emerged with a long rope. He went to the front of the truck, dropped to his knees, slid under the front end of the truck on his back, and draped the rope over the front axle. He tied a fairly intricate nautical knot and reinforced it. Then he slid out from under the truck and tied the other end of the rope around his waist. His brother screamed in protest. His father stared numbly. He looked at both and said, "Grab my waist and pull."

The sheer lunacy of it arrested the attention of his father who began laughing. Patrick saw his father laughing, and began laughing at the sight of him laughing. They both looked at Michael Jr. and saw in his eyes absolute conviction that the three of them were going to tug the five ton truck off the edge of the bridge. They burst out laughing all over again, bringing them to their knees in the process and draining nearly all of the tension they'd been ware-housing since they began planning this trip over six months ago. Their laughter was as pure and irrepressible as the water passing swiftly under the bridge upon which they stood.

Michael Jr. took no offense. He waited for his father and brother to stop laughing. When they did, they slowly rose to their feet and looked at Michael Jr., then each other. They walked over and hugged him for his innocence and the purity of his intention. His father kissed him on the forehead and said, "God, you're a special soul. Where in hell did you come from?"

Michael looked at his brother and said, "Just grab me around the waist and pull."

Patrick wrapped his arms around his brother's waist and pulled. Nothing.

Michael Jr. looked at his father and said, "See, Dad . . . we need you."

Michael Sr.'s heart leapt into his throat. His eyes filled. He couldn't speak. He was overwhelmed at the pure goodness of a son whose trust was so great he believed the impossible was possible with God, even for a sinful man like himself. In that instant Michael Burns Sr. knew for the first time he could give an accounting for his time on earth.

He struggled to his feet. He put his arms around his two sons' waists. Together they pulled. Nothing. They tried again. Still nothing. Again and again and again they pulled and twisted and strained and shouted in their futility before finally collapsing onto the ground together, one on top of the other. And still the truck did not budge from the precipice.

As they lay on the ground, chests heaving, they heard footsteps behind them. They were unable to lift themselves, so they turned their heads in the direction of the footsteps and saw two very large men approaching. Their sheer size stunned them. With difficulty they lifted themselves into a sitting position to get a better look. As they drew near one of the men said to them, "Men . . . why do you lay in the middle of the bridge under a noonday sun?"

Looking up, Michael Jr. shielded his eyes from the sun and replied, "We have driven our truck over the edge of the bridge and cannot pull it back from the brink."

The man who had spoken to them walked over to the truck and spent several minutes studying its precarious position. Finally, he turned to them and said, "Come . . . we'll help you."

The sons jumped to their feet immediately, went to their father and, together, lifted him from the waist so as not to do further damage to his shoulders. They followed the two giants to the left side of the truck. One of the men crouched down in a lifting position near the front. The other went to the rear and crouched in a similar position. The Burns' filled in between them. The man who spoke looked at them and said, "I'm going to count to three and we're all going to lift . . . and pull . . . together. Understood?"

The Burns' nodded, incredulously. The man counted. The five men lifted more or less together. The truck did not move. Michael Burns Sr. groaned in despair. The man said, "Again." Again, they lifted. Nothing. The man smiled and said, "Perhaps we are not all thinking the right thoughts." He looked at the father and said, "I think this time, the truck will come to us."

They grunted in unison and on the count they lifted a third time. They felt the truck move but they had no idea whether the movement was sufficient. As soon as they let it down, Michael Burns Jr. raced to the other side, saw that truck had moved about a foot and a half, and yelled over its roof to the others, "It's clear!"

Patrick Burns looked at his father in astonishment and walked quickly to the other side to see for himself. He called to his father: "Dad, come see this!"

The father joined his sons. Seeing was not believing. The truck's right front and rear wheels were clear of the precipice and now actually inside a two inch high wooden rail that ran the length of the bridge on both sides. The Burns' shrieked to the heavens in pure joy. They pumped their fists in the air and hugged one another and shouted at the top of their lungs.

Then they remembered the men on the other side of the truck. "Let's go thank those fellas, boys," Michael Sr. said, now subdued. Together, they walked around to the other side of the truck. The men were gone.

Michael Burns Sr. felt chills running up and down his spine. He looked at his sons. Their mouths were open and their eyes were as wide as old silver dollars. Suddenly, he was overwhelmed by an intense warmth coursing through his body. He fell to his knees and began to sob. His sons rushed to his side and put their arms around him. They had never seen their father cry, and the sight of it reduced them to tears.

For a long time they remained in that position, the tears cleansing their hearts and souls of the pain of unworthiness. Then, slowly, they rose to their feet one by one. The father walked slowly to the truck. His sons saw him heading for the driver's side and followed him. As he opened the door, Patrick grabbed him gently in his arms and said, "We'll take it from here, Dad." His father started to protest. His son cupped the back of his head with a strong hand and pulled him to his breast and said, "A lot of us have been riding your back for a long time, Dad. It's time we began to pull our own weight."

The father's eyes filled with tears. He couldn't see. Michael Jr. took him gently by the arm, led him to the passenger side of the truck, and lifted him up and into his seat. The two doors slammed shut at about the same moment. They turned the engine over, and ever so slowly began to make their way down the rest of the incline.

When they were back on 301 heading north, Michael Burns looked at his sons and said, "The pain is gone from my shoulders." His sons smiled. "Of course," he added, "my right hand still hurts pretty good."

Two hours later they were on the Annapolis Bay Bridge, less than an hour from home.

They were singing.

36

L ife took a turn for the worse for David Moskowitz on January 1, 2030.

He missed a deadline.

Hanley Siliezar regarded work milestones as biblical. You either delivered or you perished. So at 5:00 a.m. Geneva time on the first morning of the New Year, he called the executive director of Ben Gurion Labs in Tel Aviv to fire him.

David Moskowitz was wide awake in anticipation of the call. Rather than answering the phone in his study he quickly lifted it off the receiver on the first ring and launched an offensive. He shared what he claimed to be a most recent and quite astounding development with his caller and explained its meaning in layman's terms.

To both their surprise, Hanley Siliezar granted a temporary stay of execution. He immediately phoned his pilot and told him to prepare a flight to Tel Aviv in one hour. When he landed he was greeted on the tarmac by David Moskowitz, whom he thought may have been on lithium, but who nonetheless drove him to Ben

Gurion Labs, nestled in the woods about sixteen miles southwest of the airport.

What Hanley Siliezar saw on the main floor that day took his breath away and renewed his sagging spirits. Among those assembled to greet him were one hundred Israeli scientists and engineers who had successfully undergone neural implants over the past three months. The uploaded implants, Moskowitz was quick to point out, included each individual's "mind files" to anchor new capabilities in historic memory and identity patterns. The new capabilities were imbedded in legions of nanobots, which were designed into what Moskowitz proposed would be three standard software packages. The *first* package provided an expanded capacity to store and instantly access thousands of trillions of bytes of information in patterns highly familiar to the brain; the *second* offered a gene therapy package, which permitted an individual to alter his own genetic code to identify and turn off destructive genes, while triggering an expression of genes that would delay or prevent the natural cell death associated with the aging process; and the *third* software package treated the individual to an ever expandable array of sensual experiences beginning with sexual intimacy with, as Moskowitz boasted, a male or female partner of your personal design and selection.

Siliezar blinked and even blushed slightly at this last. He was immediately fearful that this standard package, while clearly intended to erode potential resistance to neural implants among targeted men, would be misused by the weak. He foresaw this having the effect of flattening the trajectory of his creation—a transcendent new man who would announce the dawn of a new and final age of ageless men. This he told Moskowitz, who did not receive the news well. Perhaps, the executive director had suggested, this software might be optional and granted only to those men personally approved by Hanley Siliezar. This drew a smile and an inconclusive nod from the chairman of the Global Governance Council.

Moskowitz recovered quickly, and with a magnanimous sweep of his arm introduced the assembled as the vanguard of

Homo Evolutis 2.0. He boasted that the "limitless expansion" of their cognitive capabilities, and the ability to reverse the aging process and extend their lives indefinitely, would renew and revitalize them as a cohort, and permit them to make quick work of the transition to Homo Evolutis 3.0.

Hanley Siliezar smiled tightly and said, "Define 'quick.'"

David Moskowitz froze. "One year," he heard himself say.

"Very well, you may have one additional year," Siliezar replied with a chilling stare. He then plunged into the crowd to meet and assess men he regarded as mere transitional figures. He emerged visibly impressed with their alacrity, sanguinity, and determination. On the ride back to the airport he said as much to Moskowitz and told him, ominously, he was pulling for him.

David Moskowitz lost his job on January 1, 2031. He did not choose to answer his phone when it rang at 5:00 a.m. on that morning, which only served to further enrage Hanley Siliezar. Moskowitz was replaced by his top aide, Seth Abrahamson, an iconic scientist largely credited with mapping and re-engineering the final regions of the human brain—effectively integrating the genetic, nanotechnology, and robotic revolutions—the very foundations of the Life Sciences Revolution.

Abrahamson, a bachelor in his early forties with no known outside interests, had politicked for the job behind the scenes and thrust the final dagger into his boss' exposed backside by suggesting that the finalization of Homo Evolutis 3.0 was still a good two to two and half years away. Siliezar did not bother calling an emergency meeting of the Global Governance Council. He simply communicated the bitter news over a secure private satellite network and reset the milestones.

When Abrahamson called *him* at 5:00 a.m. on the morning of January 1, 2033 and told him to prepare himself for the realization of his pinnacle achievement, Hanley Siliezar's eyes had filled with tears. For several long moments he was speechless, and Seth Abrahamson thought he'd lost the connection. When he did finally speak, Hanley Siliezar's unburdened heart yielded a single word: "When?"

The answer to his question brought him to a private airport just outside Geneva, Switzerland on a brisk spring Friday morning in 2033. His pilot had the Gulf Stream G2000 purring on the tarmac, ready to go, wheels up upon his arrival, to whisk him to Tel Aviv airport in a little over three hours. He made his way slowly up the steps and was greeted by his stewardess, a young French beauty who claimed to be studying art at the Sorbonne. She escorted him to his captain's chair and immediately went to the galley to get him a canister of orange juice, a warm baguette, and, for the occasion, a flute of champagne accompanied by a petite portion of caviar.

He took his seat and strapped himself in. He nodded as the woman placed a silver serving tray bearing his breakfast on a marble credenza beside his chair. Then he closed his eyes and did something he had never done before. He permitted himself a life scan. On the cusp of his greatest achievement Hanley Siliezar thought about his childhood and the traumatic loss of his mother when he was eight. He thought about the abuse he suffered from his own father and the relentless ridicule to which he was subjected as a Jew by other students in the primary grades of the convent schools he was forced to attend. He thought about his university career and how he had been denied the number one position in his senior class at Harvard, despite finishing two hundredths of a point ahead of his rival, an Irish Catholic from Boston, and the exhilaration of all but expunging that travesty by finishing number one by over four and a half tenths of a point at the University of Chicago Graduate School of Business.

His short marriage to a Brazilian model briefly flickered in and out of his mind. He instinctively veered away from the night of her death, at his hands, in their modest apartment in Sao Paulo, and the traumatic death twenty-two years later of their only child, at the hands of a rapist in Central Park one summer evening just below his window as he lay sleeping.

Instead he retrieved the highlights of his advertising career and retraced his clever leveraging of the global reach of the Free Mason network from an outpost in Brazil into the ownership of the world's largest advertising conglomerate in New York. He reflected on his rise to global prominence as the premiere architect of the new age of man, packaged around the utopian promise of the Life Sciences Revolution. And he ruminated on his singular managerial triumph of choosing and convening a council of powerful men, through which he was to govern global affairs through the transition to this age.

Whatever happened in mankind's history from here on out, he told himself, would have to be regarded as part of *his* enduring legacy. With the advent of Homo Evolutis 3.0 on this day of days, he had prevailed over all manner of adversity in his long and distinguished life. He had risen from obscurity to govern those who governed all others. He had orchestrated man's transformation from a short brutish existence into a utopian reality that virtually no one on earth had thought possible. And, most importantly, he had at long last defeated his archenemy, the Roman Catholic Church, which now lay in schismatic ruins throughout both the developed and undeveloped world.

Hanley Siliezar was seventy-seven years old and he realized perhaps for the first time that he had never truly known happiness. On this day, however, he believed he would experience something that would approximate it. For it was on this day that he would become father to the New Man . . . and father to the new and limitless possibilities in the New Age of Man.

The G2000 touched down on a Tel Aviv International runway at precisely 11:23 a.m. on April 6, 2033. Hanley Siliezar emerged several minutes later, made his way gingerly down the steps, and into a perfunctory hug by Seth Abrahamson. It was, he noted, sunny and warm.

"Welcome to the first day of the rest of your life, Hanley Siliezar!" Abrahamson said, smiling broadly.

"Depending on how the rest of the day goes, the rest of *my* life . . . and *your* life . . . may be quite short, my friend," he replied behind a dark smile. "But the New Age of Man will know no such limitation."

He followed the executive director of Ben Gurion Labs to a black stretch Mercedes limousine and entered without nodding to the heavily-muscled, black-tuxedoed driver who held his door. Once safely ensconced, he accepted a Waterford goblet half filled with champagne from Seth Abrahamson, who extended his own glass, smiled and said quietly, "Congratulations, Hanley."

Siliezar looked away. He did not trust himself. He was, he reminded himself, still only a man, a primitive man, one fully capable of manifesting womanly emotion in a weak moment. He placed the champagne, untouched, on the granite minibar next to him, and reclined as the limo driver gently eased the car off the tarmac and onto the highway. Within minutes they were heading to Jerusalem at a cruising speed, at times, in excess of 100 miles per hour.

They entered the city less than two hours later from the southwest and navigated their way north until they entered Sachem Park in the central district and advanced to its northern perimeter. A row of office buildings stood guard over the park just south of Yehuda Halevy Avenue. Siliezar immediately observed two elderly men talking on the sidewalk and was struck by how much one of the men resembled his father. For a brief moment his thoughts drifted to what might have been had the Nazis chosen to launch their grand scheme one generation later . . . or one generation sooner.

As the limo slowed to stop, his jaw dropped, and his heart began to race. There, standing in front of the entrance to an otherwise nondescript four story glass and brick building, were an elite team of one hundred men and women who had been working around the clock for the past eighteen months on the final phase of Project "I". They stood waiting with champagne glasses in hand. At the sight of his car they lifted their glasses and began to chant his name. His eyes filled and he instinctively lowered his head. He had never, ever, known affection. Fear, yes; respect, of course; admiration, occasionally . . . begrudgingly. But never this . . . thing . . .

whatever it was . . . that he was seeing in the eyes of the men and women awaiting him.

The driver pulled to a stop in front of the entrance, about ten yards from the crowd, and leapt out of the limo to open Hanley Siliezar's door, but several of the men in the crowd reached the door first, eagerly opened it and extended their arms to assist him. He winced at the thunderous decibel level that now invaded the car, but nonetheless turned to Abrahamson, who had not moved and who was watching him intently, and said, "My public awaits."

He was escorted through the two story lobby, around the concentric rings of work stations organized by project task, and into the open conference center in the middle of the main floor. The room had a large glass table in the middle of it, and on the table was a small gray cylindrical chamber connected to two pumps, which pulsed rhythmically and appeared to be programmed from a battery of small customized work stations near the perimeter of the room. Hanley Siliezar stopped for a long moment and stared in wonder. He was gently escorted into a tight circle of twelve high backed, elegantly appointed, burgundy cushioned chairs that encircled the table. One of the chairs he noted belonged to the executive director and bore a leather bound notebook of sorts.

He was seated in a slightly elevated chair directly opposite the monstrosity. He noted he was surrounded by five concentric circles of metal folding chairs. He watched and listened as the others took their seats chattering like school children. When all were seated, stillness descended, which hung thick and close and seemed to envelope all who were assembled. Hanley thought he could hear the quickened heartbeat of several of those now seated behind him.

Seth Abrahamson entered from the rear and made his way to the center, and the table, with his chin and chest thrust up and out. He seemed surprised at the empty chairs in the inner circle. He was greeted by a low murmur that built slowly into a dull roar of approval. Siliezar scanned the crowd and was surprised to see David Moskowitz standing in the back, head bowed. Abrahamson opened his mouth to speak, but before he could do so a tall figure ducked under a makeshift arch and entered the room through a curtain from the side. It was the Russian, Vladimir Piranchenko, and it was clear he would make his own grand entrance, and do so at a moment of his choosing. Left no choice, the rest of the Global Governance Council followed more or less in pairs of twos. The employees of Ben Gurion Labs stood in welcome and applauded raucously. Siliezar was forced to stand, awkwardly, while the others took their seat, which grievously wounded him and stirred him to a quiet fury. He acknowledged each of their smiles and waves with a cold, clinical nod of his head. His curiosity was suddenly piqued by a second empty chair. He quickly realized it had been reserved for Musa Bin Alamin.

When all were seated, Abrahamson bowed to Hanley Siliezar and began, "Well, Hanley, welcome to our rehearsal." The room was quickly engulfed in laughter. Abrahamson looked at Siliezar sheepishly and said. "Believe me, it was our intention to seat you last, my esteemed friend." He glanced nervously at Piranchenko, reddened slightly, and said, "We just couldn't get things coordinated." Then he scanned the crowd and beamed and said, "But we *did* get the most important entrance right, didn't we men and women of Ben Gurion Labs?"

The din that greeted this singular question was so immediate and so energized that Hanley Siliezar felt for a moment like he was in an indoor soccer stadium in his home town of Sao Paulo. He watched as Abrahamson basked in the adulation and ultimately returned his gaze to him. "None of us knows when a new vision of man first appeared as a gleam in your eye," he said as the crowd started to quiet. "But we do know that it was *your* eye in which this gleam first appeared." This evoked loud, prolonged applause. Siliezar noted happily that the Russian was squirming uncomfortably. His eyes canvassed the others. Dag Schoenbrun, Kimbe Motumbo, Nicholas Kubosvak, Geoff Benton, Hu Enlai, Graham Forrester, Pablo Gutierrez, and Bill Warren were all staring at him as if awaiting a signal. He permitted himself, and them, a small smile.

"By my calculations," Abrahamson continued, "it has taken thirty-three years and untold billions of Yuan for this gleam in your eye to become a living, breathing, and, dare I say, life transforming reality." More applause, largely perfunctory. Sensing his windup, as planned, was too long, he paused abruptly, pointed to the tank and said, "Hanley, and esteemed members of the Global Governance Council, this is an ectogenetic chamber." He extended his hand and pointed to the pumps. "And these pumps feed oxygen and nutrients into this chamber." He then pointed dramatically to the small cluster of work stations on the perimeter of the room and said, "And those workstations perform two functions. They program the flow of oxygen and nutrients into the chamber, and they monitor the vital organs of the . . ." he paused briefly then thundered, ". . . living, breathing, new alpha humanity inside this chamber!"

The uproar was immediate and sustained. The men and women of Ben Gurion Labs were on their feet and cheering in a manner most unbecoming, Hanley Siliezar thought, for scientists and engineers. He was immediately seized by a cold panic. In his mind's eye, Hanley saw the child, the new man, being handed to him by Abrahamson. He watched as he feverishly unwrapped the child's garments as if he were some Christmas toy, and discovered to his horror that the child was stillborn.

His attention was arrested by the sound of Seth Abrahamson's sonorous voice. "Hanley, this chamber is an artificial womb. The new form of humanity inside was conceived in this Laboratory by the brilliant men and women who surround you." This tribute was greeted by an awkward silence. "They have worked themselves to exhaustion. There have been many, many failures." This was greeted by scattered, nervous laughter. "But not once did we give in to futility." He paused and continued breathlessly, "And when it became obvious that we had to create a new and totally unique algorithm to recalibrate and coordinate the expression of genes from the West African orangutan and the Spanish Appaloosa, these men and women set themselves to the task and refused to stop until the requisite tissue was able to be seamlessly integrated with a cloned human embryo of advanced human pedigree. Then, and only then, did they tackle the final and most complex challenge of all—the custom design and programmatic uploading of an intellectual software package anchored in nanotechnology that represents the ultimate fusion of biological and artificial intelligence."

Seth Abrahamson paused to catch his breath and canvas the audience in the inner circle. He saw they sat transfixed, but could not tell if they were really following him or merely captivated by his adrenalin rush. "This new man . . ." he gushed, ". . . by age twelve will have the strength of ten men, the speed of a swift animal, and the intellect of a chess champion neurologically powered by a main frame." His eyes suddenly filled with tears. "At eighteen he will be fully prepared to lead a new age of men, similarly endowed. They will conquer fear and ignorance and want. They will have the power to reverse climactic trends two centuries in the making. They will integrate humanity behind a common purpose and rule with tranquility. And they will fill the earth with an unimagined wisdom that will redound to the benefit of all and will direct its luminescence to the outer edges of our universe and beyond, which will come to know intelligence for the first time."

"Enough!" shouted Hanley Siliezar now on his feet in a purple rage. A stunned silence filled the open conference room and seemed to settle uneasily upon Seth Abrahamson, who stood with his legs crossed as though badly needing to relieve himself. Hanley Siliezar tapped his wrist watch so loudly it was the only sound that could be heard, and it reverberated throughout the room. The tapping created a hollow metallic sound that generated an instant anxiety in the minds and hearts of the others. They sat for what seemed an eternity, still as blackbirds perched on an electrical wire, their eyes alternating between Hanley Siliezar and Seth Abrahamson. The next voice they heard belonged to Hanley Siliezar. "I have waited long enough! It is now 2:55 p.m. You have five minutes to deliver that man child."

Abrahamson nodded anxiously. He pointed to two men in the second row behind Hanley Siliezar and the GGC, and motioned them to join him at the table. They rose, scrambled over the feet of others, and emerged at the end of the row where they made their way to their boss, the table, and the chamber. Abrahamson shook their hands in silence as they arrived and bid them, not so grandly, to remove the child from the artificial womb.

The men went to the chamber and removed the glass bubble that covered the cylinder. They stared into the chamber, presumably at the child, and then at one another. Their hands trembled in plain view of all who sat in the closest rows. The shorter of the two men, handsome and ruddy cheeked, and dressed in a brilliant white lab coat, inserted his hands into the chamber and lifted, anxiously motioning with his head for the other man to remove the encased plastic electrical circuitry that lay beneath the child. The other man worked quickly and began unplugging the myriad of wires that were attached to the child's brain, heart, lungs, kidneys, and sex organs. When he had finished, he put his left arm under the arms of his colleague and together they lifted the child gently from the chamber.

An eerie hush greeted this new man. Not a word was spoken. All seemed to be awaiting a sound, any sound, from the child but none was forthcoming. Gradually something resembling a panic began to build and spread among the men and women of Ben Gurion Labs and their guests that the child had in fact been stillborn.

Then, suddenly, there arose a sound. It was a sound that startled all who were present. It was the disturbing sound, not of an infant crying, but the sound of an older child laughing. The smaller of the two men, visibly relieved, quickly handed the laughing child to his superior, who wrapped him in an oversized white linen tunic and held him aloft for all to see and hear. "Men and women of Ben Gurion Labs . . . I introduce you to Icarus Redux . . . the new man who himself is the advent of the new age of man." He placed the child on the scale and pushed the measures until they were properly balanced. "Icarus is twenty-one pounds and twelve ounces of limitless promise," he declared as he lifted the child from the scale and again held him aloft to another roar of approval.

Then he walked to Hanley Siliezar with the child held above his head, and in a grand gesture deposited the child into his reluctant hands. The assembly immediately roared its approval again. Siliezar quickly unwrapped the tunic and looked into the face of the child and shivered. The new age of man had dawned in the form of a long armed, cloven hoofed child, with an enlarged head, whose face resembled a gargoyle. The infant's eyes blinked when they encountered the face of his creator. It was then the child cried for the first time.

Hanley Siliezar looked at his watch. It was precisely 3:00 p.m. April 10, 2033, he noted, when the new man drew his first breath. This was of immeasurable significance to him. By his calculation, it was precisely two thousand years to the day, hour, and minute when the Son of Man had drawn his last breath on a small hill less than fifty yards from the very spot where the men and women of Ben Gurion Labs now stood cheering.

Hanley Siliezar was momentarily unsettled by an enormous surge of pride rising from somewhere deep within him. He felt affirmed in his long held conviction that his own life held a transcendent purpose and mission, which had, at long last, been realized in this moment. He basked in the adulation that encircled him, nodding his head, and lifting the new man for all to see.

Suddenly, without warning, he fell violently ill. He turned abruptly and threw the child in his arms to Seth Abrahamson, pushed through the crowd in a frenzy and rushed outside. When he emerged from the building, he was deeply disturbed to discover he was perspiring profusely and soaking wet, and his heart was pounding wildly.

His eyes scanned the horizon. There was no discernable movement of any kind on the hills that surrounded the ancient city of Jerusalem. Indeed, it appeared to be empty. He was also surprised to discover he was not hearing sound, which made him wonder if he had suffered damage to his ears from the extensive use of electromagnetic waves inside the Laboratory.

The stillness and silence were unsettling in the extreme.

There was one other thing that caught Hanley Siliezar by surprise, and this disturbed him above all else.

As he looked to the heavens, he saw a huge billowing ball of fire approaching quickly in an otherwise darkening sky.

In a panic, he canvassed the sky for the sun but it appeared to be gone.

EPILOGUE

History was never granted an opportunity to reach consensus on the origin of man's ultimate purification in the age of apostasy.

The very last thought that entered the mind of Hanley Siliezar, as he felt for the first time the incinerating heat from the monstrous ball of fire rushing toward earth, was that Musa Bin Alamin had deceived him.

The Islamic world, he now suspected, was raining fire down upon the people of Israel. He, Hanley Siliezar, man of peace though he was, had been deceived by one of his own number. Deceived by a man he had entrusted with the purse strings for the Muslim world. A world he had worked so tirelessly to include in the Grand Project. In a travesty of justice, he told himself in a final act of consciousness, he would die the innocent victim of a lie.

It was true, of course. The Muslim world had launched its long anticipated attack on the State of Israel. They also surrounded the Jewish people on land and sea with one million men—Arabs, Russians, and Chinese—to seize and occupy whatever remained of the country after the attack. But, alerted in advance by a strange and calming interior voice, the people of the house of David rushed to the shrines they had built in the basements of their homes, fell to their collective knees, and summoned their messiah.

He did not appear. At least not in the manner summoned or anticipated. Nor, however, did the armies of the night. Some unknown force seemed to restrain them. The nuclear tipped missiles themselves inexplicably fell short.

The Muslim world also attacked the old world and the new world. They launched Russian engineered and subsidized intercontinental nuclear missiles at Paris and Washington, D.C. moments after they launched their strike on Jerusalem.

The West's vaunted technology failed. Its elaborately complex and costly missile defense systems malfunctioned due to relatively simple coding errors. Only a thin remnant of NATO's anti-ballistic weaponry made it airborne and none were able to intercept the flaming incoming wrath of Allah.

They didn't have to. The nuclear missiles failed to hit their mark. Instead they fell harmlessly into the sea, or so it was thought by a jubilant West. Within six hours, however, there were ominous warnings of a new and unanticipated disaster. The Atlantic Ocean began to rise to the East and to the West. One hundred foot waves hit the East coast of the United States and the West coast of Europe within hours of each other. They swept inland destroying coastal villages and towns and, ultimately, whole cities.

It was at that moment, however, that fire inexplicably began falling from the sky. It was not clear at first the origin of this fire. Some were of the opinion that the nuclear missiles that roiled the seas had somehow stripped the earth of its electromagnetic position relative to the two poles, and sent the earth careening toward the sun. Others believed the source was a reported comet the size of Texas that struck somewhere in the middle of the South Pacific, east of the Philippines.

A tsunami roughly twice the size of the one that crested in the Atlantic Ocean built quickly in the Pacific and headed east for the coast of California. The fallout from the comet's splash down immediately ionized the air, destroying all electrical current and triggering twelve successive sonic booms of thunder, which in turn appeared to unleash a series of cataclysmic lightning storms that painted the sky blood red.

The thunderous roar from the sky and the subsequent lightening that struck the earth seemed to set off the equivalent of a Cambrian Explosion of seismic shifts within the tectonic plates below the earth's surface. All manner of radioactive matter emerged from the bowels of the earth and spewed into the earth's atmosphere, before being alchemized as something resembling an acid rain and falling gently back to earth like a spring mist.

Hurricanes of fire fell from the sky blanketing the entire earth. They appeared to spawn tornadoes that began as dark funnels, but which built quickly into fiery bee hives that seemed to touch down with complete randomness across much of the earth's surface. This rain of terror blotted out the sun and the moon and the stars for a period of three days and three nights.

The earth, and those who survived the holocaust of fire, suddenly and without warning found themselves in the midst of an intense ethereal blackness that served to exhaust the last bit of hope in the heart of fallen man.

But not every fallen man.

There were remnants in every land under what had been the sun, and they were alerted by an action of the Holy Spirit to prepare for a "Great Chastisement" seven days prior to its commencement. This they did, as prescribed, by preparing their homes and hearts. They bolted shut windows and doors, and covered them with thick dark curtains and black masking tape. They hung crucifixes, lit blessed candles, and filled holy water fonts, which they displayed in their common areas and hallways. And, despite raging demonic temptation, they obeyed the directive to stay inside when the darkness fell.

At Hallowed Hall, the extended Burns family welcomed Father Bill Fregosi, the Gillespies, and the Seltzers, and a bewildered Fran

Delgado to the Main House. The rest of the St. Martha's remnant from Narbrook was hunkered down in the nine other homes within the compound—five families to a home. The forty or so others, mostly single young men and women, found segregated accommodations in the converted hog nursery, cow shed, and sheep house.

The men and women who entered the homes, nurseries, and sheds carried three days and nights of provision, no more, as instructed.

The animals were also carefully locked down in covered shelter with sufficient provision.

As darkness fell on the first day, Michael Burns Sr. rose in the Main House, blessed the assembled, and led a twenty-decade Rosary comprised of the Joyful, Sorrowful, Glorious, and Luminous Mysteries. When he finished he invited the pastor to hear confessions in the Great Room in the rear of the home, and announced that Holy Mass would follow immediately in the same room.

It was during confessions that a sharp and terrifying escalation in the velocity of the wind occurred. The St. Martha families had been warned that the wind would become 'a spear' bearing poisonous gasses to all corners of the earth, and a pestilence that would afflict the evil in every land.

But it was the sounds that rode on the back of the wind that frightened every man, woman, and child of Hallowed Hollow. They were the sounds of legions upon legions of demons unleashed from hell that were now preying on those who had done their bidding and somehow managed to survive the holocaust of fire. They were hideous, bone chilling, teeth rattling sounds of rage, blasphemy, and obscenity that also greatly frightened the animals.

So disturbing were these sounds at their peak that Michael Burns, taking temporary leave of his senses, posted his sons with rifles at the front and back door of the Main House and told them to shoot "any evil spirits" that managed to penetrate doors or windows. Observing this from the floor of a clothes closet in the hallway, where she was hiding, Fran Delgado was heard to shriek, "My God, don't shoot! I'll drink the Kool-Aid."

Time seemed to end. The people of Hallowed Hollow fell into a deep slumber. Two days and nights passed. On the night of the third day, Maggie Gillespie stirred, awakened by the fearful screams of a daughter she had loved unto death in another time and place. She sat up in a twin bed she was sharing with her husband, and inclined her head to his chest to ensure he was still breathing. She glanced over at the other twin bed on which her daughter Grace was sleeping with her husband Scott. All was still in the small bedroom. She arose quietly and went to the back door at the far end of the center hallway. She laid her head against the bolted door and listened. The cries had stopped. Instead there was a gentle whisper. It was the voice of her daughter, Moia, precisely as she remembered it. There on the other side of the door, speaking into the sealed crack was the muffled cry of a frightened little girl begging for her mother's help.

Maggie immediately began struggling with the door. She opened the drape and the curtain and stared at the masking tape which covered the panes of glass. She grabbed the door knob and pulled again in frustration. She tried the dead bolt but was unable to force it open. She stood back, looked at the door, and saw it had been nailed shut across its top and bottom.

She began to panic and whispered into the crack, "Moia, it's Mommy! I am here, Moia. Don't worry. I will find a way to get this door open. I love you, Moia . . . I love you. Mommy loves you." She started to cry. In a rage she began pulling again on the door knob. It would not budge. She leaned in and whispered into the sealed crack, "Moia . . . wait right here. Mommy will be right back."

She hurried into the kitchen to look for a tool—a hammer, a screw driver, a wrench, a knife—anything. She was determined to remove the hardened putty seal so that she and her daughter could at least talk to each other unimpeded. If they could just talk, she reasoned, anything was possible. She grabbed a large wax candle from the granite kitchen counter and immediately began opening drawers in a frenzy. She quickly discovered there were no tools and very little silverware. She cursed Michael Burns under her breath. In the middle of her oath she spied the dishwasher. She opened it and saw that it was full. She reached into a plastic container that was filled with silverware, and removed two knives and two forks. She returned to the backdoor and whispered to her daughter, "Moia . . . honey . . . mommy's back. I'm going to remove the seal, honey. Just stay right where you are."

She listened for a response but she heard nothing. In her fear, she savagely attacked the door. She quickly discovered the forks were better at cracking and digging out the encased putty. Within several minutes she had removed well over half of it from the upper portion of the back door. She leaned into the crack and said loudly, "Moia . . . honey . . . are you still there?"

She heard her daughter cry out, "Mommy . . . please . . . I'm frightened. Come quick. Save me. People are dying out here. The monsters are killing the women first, Mommy. Please . . . help me!"

Maggie Gillespie began shouting at the top of her lungs, "Help me! Help me! Please, God . . . help me!"

The sound of her desperation awakened her husband, who rushed from their room and ran to her side. He grabbed her around the waist and pulled her kicking and screaming away from the door. They fell to the ground interlocked in struggle. Maggie momentarily broke free. She ran back to the door and yanked on the knob in furious futility. Her husband scrambled to his feet, ran to her, grabbed her around waist, and this time pulled her, with great difficulty, out of the hallway, through the kitchen, and into the Great Room, where the commotion immediately awakened the others sleeping on the floor. With candles cupped in their hands, they looked to see what was causing the anxiety.

Maggie started coughing violently and turned a dark shade of purple. In a panic, Jim Gillespie turned her over and pounded her back. The others who were awakened rushed to her side, laid hands on her, and began praying to the Virgin for her intercession. Jim Gillespie turned and asked a wide eyed Rebecca Burns to get a hand towel and run it under the faucet. She immediately ran into the kitchen and returned to say there was no water in the faucet. This induced immediate prayer. Slowly, gradually, the coughing subsided. Jim Gillespie gently turned his wife on her back and cradled her head in his arms.

Michael Burns Sr. appeared in the doorway in a white robe. Behind him stood his wife in a matching robe. They rushed to Maggie and stared into her eyes, and saw that they were vacant. Michael's heart plunged, and he turned to his son, Patrick, who was kneeling on the floor and said, "Get Father Bill . . ."

Moments later the priest appeared and moved quickly to the side of the stricken woman. He knelt, sprinkled holy water on her head and heart, placed his hands on her head, and began to pray. "Satan, I command you in the Holy Name of Jesus Christ to leave this faithful woman and go to Him to do with you as He pleases. You have no power or control over her," he paused and looked up, "or anyone else in this home . . . or on this hallowed property." He clenched his jaw, gritted his teeth, and concluded, "Go now. Be gone. Depart ye accursed one, back into the fires of everlasting hell!"

There was no sound or movement of any kind for several minutes. Then, Jim Gillespie saw light return slowly to his wife's eyes. They flickered and she blinked several times. He bowed down and kissed her on the lips. She put her right hand on the back of his neck and pulled him to her bosom. "Oh, Jim, it was so awful."

"I know sweetheart," he said, as he lifted his head and kissed her on her forehead and both cheeks. "I know. I heard." Then he leaned in and whispered in her ear, "Maggie, that was *not* Moia. She awaits. But not here, and not now."

She started to cry again. Jim hugged her, turned to the others and said, "We have cause to rejoice!"

Father Bill Fregosi immediately broke into a verse from the Song of Songs and the others followed. When he finished he looked around the room and said, "I have something for you. I was instructed to hold it until all of this passed, but I feel led to share it with you who are here now."

He departed for his room and returned with an envelope. He made his way to the center of the Great Room, opened the envelope, quickly scanned its contents, and smiled. Jim Gillespie shouted, "It's from Father John; he wants you to take up a collection."

The laughter that erupted immediately purged the room of its fear and tension. Bill Fregosi looked at Jim Gillespie and laughed, "That's half right!" His eyes surveyed the room and settled on the fourteen children who were scattered about the floor. "It's from Father John all right, but as you will quickly see, he's not asking for anything."

He accepted a candle from Terry Burns who was seated beside her husband on the floor. He held the candle up to the letter and began to read, "My brothers and sisters in Christ . . ." Sobs arose immediately from a number of women who heard in the salutation the voice of their fallen spiritual leader. "How I miss you!" There were audible gasps, this time from men. "You, my beloved little ones, have been chosen by our divine Lord to witness a glorious New Springtime of Man. To experience the Triumph of the Two Hearts. To live through the dawn of a Millennium of Peace. How I wish I could be there to share it with you!"

Father Bill Fregosi's voice choked. He paused until the better part of the burning in his heart eased, then continued. "The purification the world just experienced was necessary. How I prayed it could be avoided . . . or lightened. In prayer I came to understand God's desire to begin again with a purified remnant, chastened a little and ever alert to the movement of His Holy Spirit. For as the Psalmist said, 'Wait a little and the wicked will be no more; look for them and they will not be there. But the poor will possess the land, will delight in great prosperity.'

"I was not given to see the form the chastisement was to take; but I was permitted to see a glimpse of the New Springtime. My brothers and sisters . . . there are no words! No words! It is beyond anything any of us could have dreamt.

"Jesus Christ has indeed made all things new. All creation is rejoicing in the moment in which you are hearing this. Heaven and earth! North and South and East and West! The mountains and valleys! The oceans and rivers!

"And *you* my dear friends were chosen to be a part of it! Your beloved Chesapeake Bay is alive with new and vibrant colors and fish of every kind. Your fields are full of the best of the earth's bounty, just ready to be plucked. Your soft green hills that roll to the water ever so gently are colored in the pastels of every living flower. The air is so clear you can see it and touch it. The water from your wells is so pure it tastes like honey. The birds of the air are so exotic you will believe you are in another part of the world. Every part of the animal kingdom is so gentle and docile, you will welcome them into your very homes.

"My beloved friends in Christ, there is a unity again within creation! Something of the Creator's original vision is infused in every particle of matter. It is something you will feel as you re-enter a very new and different world. There is nothing you have experienced that has prepared you for what you are about to experience. It is nothing less than the glory of the risen Lord who has at long last purged His creation of every form of evil!

"He is alive! He lives! And now you will live in Him, and He in you, as you never dared to dream!

"You have been chosen to rebuild creation in truth and in love, from which an authentic justice will flow like a river yielding its fruit from the trees along its banks. The long promised fruit of a true and lasting peace in the hearts of all men.

"Know this my brothers and sisters: I have begged the Lord for many years to create a space for you in His New Springtime. He has seen fit to answer my prayer. And not merely answer it, for in His great mercy He has permitted me to witness a portion of it. He has allowed me to see you as you enter the Dawn of a new light and behold Him in the fullness of His glory. I have indeed been unfairly blessed!

"Go now and take possession of what He has made an unimaginable new gift to you, and know always that I am with you."

Fr. Bill Fregosi squinted and added with hesitation, "It is signed, Father John . . . but there is a p.s. Hold on." He adjusted his reading glasses. "It reads, 'When you see the first ray of light, get down on your knees and welcome it with praise and thanks to God. Then join hands, leave your homes and sheds, and walk into the new light together with your eyes closed. When you are all outside, open your eyes on Father Bill's instructions and look to the heavens. There you will see the Object of your longing.'"

When he finished reading the letter, Father Bill Fregosi knelt and bowed his head to the ground and began to cry. A deep, all-surpassing peace seemed to descend from the very heavens and penetrate the hearts of all the souls assembled in the Great Room of the Main House. After several minutes, the priest rose to his feet and began to give praise and thanks in an Easter Alleluia song. The others broke into full throated song behind him.

Michael Burns Sr. went to the large double doors in the Great Room that led to the patio outside. He peeled back the drapes, then the curtains, then the black masking tape that covered the windows. The women shrieked and the men shouted. There was an extraordinary light suddenly streaming into the room. They immediately fell to their knees as Father John Sweeney instructed. They remained there in vocal and silent prayer for several minutes.

Then, Fr. Bill rose to his feet and beckoned the others to follow him through the doors to the back patio. They held hands and moved like a giant amoeba through the large double doors and emerged into the radiant sunlight together, eyes closed as instructed.

When they were all on the patio, Fr. Bill gave the signal to open their eyes and lift them toward the heavens.

What happened next would never adequately be recounted. Men and women and children screamed, jumped, danced, laughed, cried, hugged, sang, prayed and, finally, fell to their knees as if in a trance.

There in the heavens was the surprise Father John Sweeney had promised. It stretched across the dome of the sky like a colossus, enveloping the new dawn of humanity not unlike a giant fresco hand-stitched by angelic choirs.

It was the Lord himself.

He hung on a cross of ethereal luminescence. There was no crown of thorns on his head but from his five wounds radiated a rainbow of colors so brilliant that those who gazed upon them reflexively shielded their eyes in anticipation of pain and damage. And yet, to their great surprise, there was no pain; there was no damage. Only an inexpressible wonder that rendered its voice in muted homage.

The eyes of humanity's Savior sparkled like jewels—alternately the color of burgundy and sapphire, emerald and gold—that was beyond their capacity to absorb fully. The eyes of their Savior seemed to peer into the souls of each one of them and radiated a love that was unaccountably palpable.

"Look!" Maggie Gillespie cried. "He is smiling at us!"

The smile on the face of the living, breathing figure across the sky transformed hearts in an instant. Gone forever were the virulent pride and lust and anger and greed that were the most visible manifestations of concupiscence in the last age of man. A peace and joy beyond all telling flooded every heart, saturating and healing the deep wounds and divisions within the soul of every man.

The people leapt to their feet in an attempt to reach out and touch what seemed within their grasp.

Suddenly, a pulsing heart appeared in the sky next to the cross. The color of the heart was an incandescent red and from it luminous white rays streamed into the heart of mankind's Savior while rays of bejeweled crimson streamed to earth, like heat seeking missiles in search of humanity's aching heart.

No one needed to be told whose heart they were now contemplating. Their own hearts, filled now with the inexpressible joy of perfect love, experienced the evisceration of all mystery. They fell to their knees again as one and bowed their heads and exclaimed in unison, "O Mary conceived without sin pray for us who have recourse to thee."

As they knelt in hushed wonder at the extraordinary events unfolding in the sky, Maggie Gillespie shouted, "My Lord and my God! This is the reign of the two hearts Father John told us about!"

Upon hearing this, the others, no longer able to contain the kindling of the fire of divine Love within their own hearts, began to cry aloud and rock back and forth on their knees, arms outstretched to the sky as children imploring the embrace of a mother.

Suddenly, Carole Burns saw movement near the Main House and shouted, "Look! Here come the others!" All eyes turned to the west where their brothers and sisters in the Lord were approaching as though sleepwalking amidst a dream. From around both sides of the Main House came the families who had garrisoned themselves in the other homes within the compound.

They ran to greet each other. They hugged, laughed, cried, danced, and pointed to the sky. *En masse* they began to move slowly to the water as if drawn by a mystical presence. They walked through tulips and daffodils and poinsettia and hydrangea and fields of flowers they had never seen before. They began to dance like children, and discovered their limbs were loose, agile, free of pain and restriction. They arrived at the water and stood in reverent awe of its transformation into a rainbow of pulsing colors and leaping bass. The children stood on the pure whiteness of the small beach, and then suddenly shed their clothes and ran into the water. The older children stripped to their waist and followed. One by one, the male adults did the same. The women hiked their skirts and waded out to join their husbands and children.

Michael and Carole Burns waited until the others were in the water, then waded in up to their waist. They felt an extraordinary cleansing power in this strange new water that seemed to penetrate to the very marrow of their being. They held hands and plunged in like children. When they resurfaced they looked at each other and gasped in astonishment. They were young again. They immediately fell to their knees, embraced passionately, and rolled in the surf.

Some forty yards to their left, Jim and Maggie Gillespie were experiencing the very same transformation. They emerged from the water and beheld each other at arm's length and gaped in wonder. "My God, woman!" Jim exclaimed. "You are beyond beautiful."

Maggie Gillespie laughed, cupped his head in her hands, giggled like a schoolgirl and said, "And to think . . . I use to doubt you when you told me you once had hair."

Slowly, mostly in small groups, the people of the remnant came out of the water laughing and crying at what they had seen and experienced. As their feet hit the beach they were astonished to discover their clothes were dry. They began to cry out in utter amazement.

Then, suddenly, they heard the voice of Father Bill Fregosi who was shouting "Look! Look! Look!" They turned to find him, and saw him standing on the edge of the beach, pointing to the middle of the sloping hill that led to the Main House. There in its midst stood a pack of red wolves that had migrated south from Maine and had been terrorizing the farms along the Bay for the past year.

There were six of them, and they were laying with their heads resting on the grass, watching their fellow survivors with great interest.

At their feet lay a dozen sheep that had found the door to the shed ajar and wandered out in search of life.

They were sleeping.

Brian J. Gail is a former college and semi-pro athlete, Madison Avenue ad-man, Fortune 500 senior executive, entrepreneur, and CEO. He is currently an educator and author. Mr. Gail has served on numerous civic boards in his hometown of Philadelphia, including The World Affairs Conference, the National Adoption Center, the William Booth Society, St. Charles Borromeo Seminary, and the Regina Academies. He is a husband, father of seven, and grandfather of five. He and his wife of 40 years, Joan M. Gail, live in Villanova, Pennsylvania.

Fatherless is the first of a three volume narrative entitled *The American Tragedy in Trilogy*. It has been translated into several languages and is now selling in Europe and Australia. *Motherless* is the second volume in the series, and *Childless* is the final volume.